STATE OF TREASON
A William Constable Spy Thriller

PAUL WALKER

First published in 2019 by Sharpe Books.

CONTENTS

STATE OF TREASON

One

November 1578.

The captain stands and waits square-footed before me. He presents a formidable figure in my hallway; tall with broad shoulders and well-muscled legs. A handsome face in the half-light disappoints when the candles draw near and show the deep scarring of pox on his cheeks. I cannot refuse or delay his invitation.

'I will be with you presently, Captain. I must attend to my mother's needs before we depart.' He has an air of impatience, but nods his assent.

'Walsingham', – a name to catch in one's breath, rouse the senses and scratch the surface of forgotten or hidden misdeeds, even in those who praise our Queen and worship in the proscribed manner. At this late hour and with a company of armed men, a summons to his presence settles a deep unease on my spirits. What could Mister Secretary want of me; a scholar of no great reputation and only moderate wealth? My thoughts drift back some ten years to my only other visit to the Palace of Whitehall when I assisted Doctor Dee in his mathematical presentations to the Privy Council for the better navigation of our ships. For me, that was an unhappy experience. I was fired with youthful ambition and an eagerness to display my scholarship. My manner was lively, exuberant and naïve, resulting in eventual admonishment by some members of that Council for not treating their inquiries with sufficient respect. The Duke of Norfolk was particular in his damning of my supposed lack of civility and deference to my betters. I recall my guilty pleasure when he met his end with the axeman some five years past. That occasion with the Privy Council was also the start of my disagreements with Doctor Dee and I am thankful I have been spared another call to that place – until now.

'Mistress Hilliard.' I beckon to the shadowy figure of my housekeeper waiting by the inner doorway. 'Please have

Gregory ready my horse. We will be away within the quarter-hour.'

Captain Askham declines my offers of refreshment and seating, reinforcing his sense of urgency. I take my leave of him, lock the library and make for my mother's room meeting her maid, Rose, on the stairs. She's carrying a chamber pot in both hands with great care.

'How is she, Rose?'

'Restful now, sir. She had some pain, but took your preparation well and managed some broth. Will you wish to examine her piss, sir?' She offers me the pot.

'Not now, Rose. If mother wakes and asks for me, then please counsel her that I have important business at the Palace of Whitehall, but expect to return before daybreak.'

She gapes at my news, then shakes her head, clamps her mouth tightly and continues down the stairs and along the corridor to the privy. My training is in mathematics and astrology, but I have also taken on the mantle of a physician acquiring many patients in recent years, mostly from the Mercers Guild. My first love is the subtle mathematics of the heavenly bodies, but have set this aside in favour of the clamour for healing. A reading of the stars is undoubtedly beneficial to treatments, and I possess sufficient vanity to suppose that my ministrations will be more effective than many other physicians I know.

I open the door to Mother's chamber and see that she is sleeping. Breathing snags in her throat and her face wears a puzzled frown, which has become a fixture of this particular confinement to her bed. I am fearful that her end is near, although she is not yet fifty and has so much to offer life and those near to her – most especially me.

I meet with Captain Askham at the front door and we step out into a clear, cold evening together. We are of similar age and height, with trim, dark beards, but his width of shoulder and soldierly bearing give me a sense of softness and vulnerability at his side. The moon is full and the next few hours would present a perfect time for an examination of the heavens. I will be denied this pleasure tonight. Askham and his four soldiers mount up and their horses clatter, stamp and snort their steam as they wait impatiently for Gregory to bring out my mount. Cassius is a bay gelding of nineteen years; I have had him since I was a youth of ten and he was a yearling. He is not an imposing horse and could be considered too small now for my length of leg, but he is sturdy and faithful. I will admit to harbouring occasional temptations to replace him with a younger, more dashing animal, but such thoughts are soon overcome by feelings of guilt at my infidelity.

The jagged outline of the Palace of Whitehall shows sharply against the moonlight as we approach our destination. Its sprawl is impressive and it is said that over five thousand souls live there in service to our Queen; a contained and functioning town. We enter by a gate into an area that Askham tells me is a new addition to the Palace. We are no more than two hours from midnight, but the courtyard is alive with soldiers, women, doxies, hawkers and cart men selling hot chestnuts, mutton pies, codlings and ale. The burning beacons placed around the courtyard throw a festive aspect on the scene and this, together with the mouth-watering odours of spiced food and drink, help to raise my spirits. Before I have time to frame a question, I am informed by one of the soldiers that this is a celebration furnished by Mister Secretary Walsingham, as acknowledgement and thanks for their role in detaining a Jesuit priest and two accomplices last week. They were at the core of a plot of treason and bloody murder. I suppose I should rejoice at this success, but my imagining of the tortured fate of those three unfortunates has a depressing effect on my humor, which returns to its former state of dread and wonderment.

We turn a corner to be confronted by a strange and grisly sight. The bloody carcasses of three scalded and slit pigs are hanging on a scaffold. As we draw near my gut cramps and I close my mouth tight to stop bile in my throat rising. These are not pigs. They were men, with naked white flesh laid open by gaping slashes to their bellies. Black holes between their legs and patterns of dried blood on their thighs evidence more terrible cuts. The genitals are roughly stuffed in the mouth and tied with cord on one of the men. Soldiers mutter 'wicked

3

sodomites', 'windfuckers' and 'papist turds' before Askham turns and quiets them with a stare. The torture and brutal ending of these men will be the cause of tonight's celebrations.

The nearest cadaver sways on the rope and turns an accusing face as we pass. I should look away, but cannot. Do I know him? There is a familiarity in the face, but it is disfigured… It is… It cannot be, but the white streak in his hair by the left temple is unmistakeable. Godfrey Baskin, what have you done to deserve such a fate? We shared lodgings in Cambridge, travelled to Geneva and shared many pleasant hours together in younger times. It is some years since we last met, but to my knowledge he is no papist. I heard that he married well and had a child. Did a wife with forceful mind change him? This surely cannot be the reason I have been brought here. But, what other reason? Was my name uttered by Godfrey in his agony? I look quickly at Askham, but his view is directly ahead and his expression tells me nothing.

We leave our horses with the soldiers and Askham leads me deeper into the precincts where activity and the senses subside. We arrive at a large arched doorway where two pikemen stand guard. One of them takes my dagger from me, we climb the stairs and I am ushered into a plain anteroom where Askham bids me farewell and departs. The room has only one small window for natural light and one candle. It is dark, quiet and I am alone. I cannot rid myself of the image of poor Godfrey, no matter how I try. There is a bench and small table along one wall and a tapestry hanging opposite, but the light is too poor to make out the scene portrayed. I wonder how long I will be kept waiting. I would make a better impression if I stood foursquare in the middle of the room to receive my call to Walsingham's presence, but my time here is unlikely to be short as my status is undeserving of such courtesy. I sit on the bench resigned to a protracted and apprehensive delay.

The echoes of the midnight bell are fading when the door opens and a small weasel-faced man in black gown and skull cap approaches me with hands clasped together as in preparation for prayer. He introduces himself as Stephen Padget, scribe to Secretary Walsingham, and bids me follow him into the adjoining room. I steel myself for an introduction to the most feared man in the land. I'm surprised and almost disappointed to find myself in yet another small anteroom, although somewhat lighter and better furnished than the one I have left. Padget opens the next door, peers inside and beckons me to follow him. Finally, I enter what is clearly Walsingham's room of business in Whitehall. It is a large room with high ceilings, brightly lit and decorated to impress. The gold leaf pressed on wall carvings catches the dancing light from a large roaring fire and the walls are covered with paintings, velvet tasselled hangings, several maps and various schematics. Walsingham, for it must be him, is seated at an extravagantly large table which is strewn with papers and posted either side by two imposing silver candlesticks. The man himself sits and watches me carefully as I approach. He is a handsome man of more than forty years, with short dark hair and neat beard. He is dressed entirely in black, save for subtle white and silver trimmings around his shoulders. His gaze is steady and unflinching. I stop and bow before him with a respectful doffing of my hat.

'Mister Secretary, thank you for this honour.'

'Doctor Constable, forgive the lateness of this meeting. I regret that my affairs often spill into unsocial hours.'

I incline my head and smile to indicate that the hour is of no matter. His eyes do not leave mine and I wonder whether my expression betrays an understanding that his consultations at this hour are designed to impose a sense of fear and loosen tongues more easily. He leans back a little and says, 'I have seen you before, William Constable, in a room no more than one hundred paces from here.'

I hesitate a moment before answering. 'That would be for the mathematical exposition with Doctor Dee, I assume. I regret that my memory does not serve me well enough to recall a conversation with you at that time, Mister Secretary.'

'We did not converse. I simply observed. The presentation was well-received as I recollect. Doctor Dee made several others of a similar nature to expound his theories, but you were not in attendance for those that followed.'

His observation invites a response, but I am unsure how to frame this as I don't know whether Doctor Dee continues to enjoy the Council's favour. 'It… it was some ten years past and as I remember, Doctor Dee decided that he no longer required my assistance after our first exposition.'

Walsingham pushes back his chair and rises. He signals to Padget to leave the room. We are alone. He extends his arm and says, 'Come William, take a seat and let us be free in our exchanges. It will make this meeting easier and there are soft beds eager for our company.'

I wait for Walsingham to regain his chair before taking mine. I hope that he does not wish me to give evidence against the Doctor, for although he is no friend to me, I should not wish to feel responsible for his maltreatment.

'If I remember well,' he continues, 'your descriptions of the mathematics of navigation were better received than those of Doctor Dee. Yours were generally well-understood, while the promulgations of the Doctor were wrapped in terms which could have been devised to confuse. Perhaps Doctor Dee has a jealous nature and did not wish you to obtain preferment at his expense?'

'I am flattered that you thought well of my exposition. My memory of that event is somewhat different and I believe I upset some members of the Council with my forthright views and expressions.'

He smiles and replies, 'You were direct and you did make an impression. You should not concern yourself with such small offences which will have been long forgotten.' He pauses for a few seconds while he picks at a troublesome tooth with a short, pointed wooden stick. 'And the Doctor?'

'The Doctor has a scholarly learning and understanding of many matters in addition to mathematics. His library is extensive and the breadth and depth of his knowledge far outweighs mine.'

'You may be correct in your assessment, but the Doctor's interests and inclinations often touch the edge of what may be termed proper and spiritual.' He clears his throat and adds, 'Besides, Doctor Dee is currently in the Low Countries and unable to offer an opinion. Hence your presence here.'

'You wish for my opinion, Sir Francis?'

He ignores my question. 'You assisted Doctor Dee in the examination of an unusual gemstone once, I believe?'

'Yes, that was at the Doctor's house in the year of 'sixty-six, in the company of an Italian gentleman named Gerolamo Cardano.'

'Tell me about your examination and considerations.'

'It was a large piece of polished quartz rock, soft burgundy in colour and about the size of a man's hand. It was brought to London by Signor Cardano.'

'I understand it was thought to have magical properties?'

'It was an attractive stone, no more. Doctor Dee and Signor Cardano considered it may have some purpose as the tool of a scryer, but…'

'But what?'

I hesitate before answering trying to weigh responses which may satisfy without being too definite one way or the other. 'I have no belief in scrying. The idea that glimpses of the future may be seen in the reflections of a polished stone are fanciful to my mind.'

'It had no religious or magical connection?'

'None.'

'It is reported that Doctor Dee was entranced by the gem, so his conclusions did not accord with yours.'

'Doctor Dee and I disagreed. His approach was more… mystical in nature, whereas my considerations were practical. Our views diverged on this and other questions. I have not worked with him for more than nine years.'

'I am also a practical man; in life, politics and religion. The practicalities of worship in Her Majesty's realm requires a gentleman to be seen in church, but I am told that you attend rarely. In this aspect, you would seem to be less than practical.'

'I am a Protestant, Mister Secretary, but see no reason to parade my belief in public. I worship at St Giles in Cripplegate, but much of my communication with Christ is in private.'

He waves his hand dismissively as though all this is known to him already. The reason for my summons is no clearer than it was when Askham came to my door. 'I beg your indulgence, but would not our discourse have more profit if I understood the purpose behind my summons?' I am made too bold by the absence of any mention of Godfrey. The question is out before I have chance to consider whether my tone may offend.

'In good time. I am a careful man and this is an affair of some delicacy.' He clasps his hands together and leans forward on the table, moving a collection of papers aside. 'It is known that you are proficient in mathematics, astrology and physik. I understand that you also have a facility with languages?'

'Yes, I speak and write the languages of Latin, Greek, French, Italian and I understand some of the tongues spoken in the Low Countries, but I am no expert.'

'Do you have a familiarity with Aramaic and the Canaanite language of the Hebrews?'

'That was only a passing fancy during my studies in Louvain. A few friends and I sought to explore the language of the original gospels. It was a very short and inexact examination.'

'And a dangerous one.'

'We were younger and did not fully comprehend the sensitive nature of our enquiry. We were warned and we desisted.' I suppress my surprise at the detail of his intelligence on these small, historical matters and I am thankful to recall that Godfrey was not in my company at Louvain.

He makes a signal with his left hand and in a few short moments a man appears noiselessly with a silver tray. He pours two glasses of wine and seems to glide across the floor until he disappears behind a curtained area. I wait for Walsingham, then follow suit and take a glass. It is good wine – very good, or am I deceived by my eagerness to slake a dry mouth?

'William Constable…' He pauses as if he has mislaid his next word. 'Our acquaintance is brief and the notes from my intelligencers on you are hurried and partial… yet, I think I must trust you. I know you to be a scholar of some note and your learning appears to be complemented with balanced humors and a steady heart. For my part, I look favourably on your separation from Doctor Dee who is too fanciful in his strivings with Hermetic Philosophy and magic. Her Majesty retains a fondness for Doctor Dee and he has often been our choice to advise on certain special matters which require the utmost secrecy. As I have said, the Doctor is too distant to be of urgent service, and so I turn to you.'

My thoughts run too quickly to form any logical deductions from what is being said. What advice can I possibly offer on high affairs of state to such a man as Walsingham? I can think of no phrases to fill this heavy and confusing period of silence, so I sit and wait to hear more.

'An object has come into my possession,' he says finally. 'An unusual and perplexing object, both in itself and in the nature of its presentation.' I incline my head and he fixes me with an expression of directness before continuing. 'Our affairs in France have reached a heightened state of activity. Recently, a courier was intercepted; a man named Brouillard who we know to have strong connections to Rome. The prosecution was bloody and Brouillard suffered a mortal wound before his intentions were uncovered. The nature of his death and our part in it were disguised by setting a fire to his lodgings and the quieting of a witness.'

He pauses to let the weight and nature of this news take its hold. The acts of murder, arson and a 'quieting' are spoken without any hint of regret, while an air of satisfaction underlies this deception as common misfortune.

'Brouillard was carrying an object,' says Walsingham. 'This was safeguarded and transported here for our appraisal.'

'May I know the nature of this article?' I enquire.

'You will know soon enough, but not tonight.' He stifles a yawn and presses his body against the back of his chair. 'I would have you accompany me to my house at Barn Elms tomorrow and there you will learn more.' He stands and I am obliged to follow his example. 'There is a truckle bed in the adjoining room which has been prepared for you with other small comforts. Rest now and we will talk again tomorrow.'

I beg his indulgence and request that he sends word to my house in West Cheap that I am detained, and that my time here is no cause for alarm. There is a hint of a smile at the corner of his mouth as he readily agrees to arrange this in the morning.

Encouraged, I mention that I am attending my sick mother and should not wish to be absent from her bedside for more than a day or two. His expression shows a fleeting and genuine concern before he offers a gruff assurance that he does not expect a protracted delay at Barn Elms.

As he turns, two men scurry from their hidden places and usher me towards the door from which I entered. The anteroom has been transformed. A truckle is made and ready with a spray of dried lavender on the pillow. A plate of bread and mutton and a jug of ale are placed on a small table. I have seen terrible sights and heard a strange story this night. I am intrigued that Walsingham should seek my advice, but my overwhelming sense is one of relief that my waking hours will end with no harm and an unexpected show of hospitality.

Two

We arrive at Barn Elms mid-morning under the escort of Captain Askham and twenty horse soldiers. The house is in an expanse of open fields about a mile distant from the south bank of the river. It is in the process of renovation and improvement with extensive wooden scaffolding in evidence on both wings. There is an encampment of soldiers about eighty paces from the house and, together with the various workmen, the scene is one of industry and purpose – not at all what one would expect of a quiet country retreat.

We leave our horses at the stables, Walsingham takes me by the arm and leads me around the back of the house and points to a stone building about thirty feet in height, which has the appearance of a fortified keep. Walsingham explains that it is the old house from the time of the second King Richard, which he has recently restored. I wonder what purpose he has in mind for such a building. Its small windows and crenelated battlements do not lend a homely aspect and it looks more suited to serving as a prison than a place of rest and consultation. Four men are patrolling the perimeter of the building, not uniformed as the soldiers, but well-armed and with an appearance to deter all but the most determined trespassers. One of them, heavily-bearded and with a livid scar slashed down the left side of his face, bows to Walsingham and pounds his fist on a wooden door reinforced with iron straps. The door opens and I follow Sir Francis into the dark interior.

We are ushered into a small room on the ground floor, which has slits in thick walls, throwing narrow shafts of sunlight on to a table and two chairs. A man lights two candles on the table and closes the door as he leaves. Walsingham gestures to one of the chairs and we take our seats.

'I would talk more with you William,' he hesitates and clasps his hands together, 'to prepare you for your task ahead.'

The mystery grows and I confess that I have a sense of nervous anticipation waiting to confront this peculiar entity. I incline my head, inviting him to continue.

He says, 'You know of Doctor John Foxe?'

'I know of him through his *Book of Martyrs*, but I have not met with him.'

'He will be your confederate in the study of the object.'

'I see.' I had not expected this. The prospect of working with another does not appeal to me. 'Doctor Foxe has the reputation of having fixed positions and beliefs. I have not read the fullness of his works, but I understand that he may be described as a Puritan; one with extreme intolerance for opposing views?' I speak too quickly, forgetting that Walsingham is reputed to have Puritan leanings himself, but he does not appear to take offence at my comment.

'You will find him less forbidding than his reputation suggests. His religion is impeccable and his written pronouncements against popery reflect an idealised vision, whereas the man in person you will find pragmatic and kindly.'

His words do little to settle my unease about future confinement with a man who I do not know, but whose reported character I dislike. 'Are there others, in addition to Doctor Foxe and myself, who will labour on this mission?' My words have an air of petulance and Walsingham looks at me sharply.

'Indeed, I expect that two renowned intellects should be sufficient on this matter. Together you will offer a balance of positions on structured thought and free thinking. My hope is that you will arrive at a learned consensus on the nature of this object and its purpose. I suspect that your deliberations will not be without some turbulence and disagreements, but you will come to a collective understanding with my guidance on practical aspects that you will consider.'

My curiosity grows to know what it is that requires such delicate and secretive handling. 'Is my partner in this investigation already at work and will I meet with him soon?'

'Doctor Foxe is in a room above us and you will meet with him in short time, but first a word about the object.' He breathes deeply as if mustering his thoughts. 'You must never divulge to anyone, even to your closest family and associates, the article in particular, or generality, that you are asked to examine in this place. Your task will be to consider all aspects from obscure symbols and script to origin and manufacture. After your tests are complete you will engage in a period of learned discourse with Doctor Foxe and thereafter present your combined opinions and advice to me.'

He hesitates as though considering whether to say more, then rises from his seat and gestures towards the exit. An unseen hand opens the door and Walsingham strides out. I follow him up stone stairs to a heavy oak door at the top, which is guarded by two more of his men. The entrance opens on to a large chamber. It is cold and damp, but better lit than the one we have left and is dominated by a generous rectangular table in the centre covered in green carpeting. At one end of the table, a figure in a plain dark gown and black scholar's hat is hunched over curled papers with a quill in his hand.

'Good morning to you, Doctor Foxe,' announces Walsingham, 'I have Doctor Constable here to assist with your contemplations.'

Foxe lifts his head from the table and regards us with interest. He is a small, elderly man with striking blue eyes and long, grey beard. 'Ah, Mister Secretary, is it still before noon?' His voice is thin and hoarse, suggesting some congestion of the lungs.

I move towards him, bow slightly and extend my hand. 'Good day to you, Doctor. I am William Constable and I understand we will work together these next days.'

Foxe rises from his seat and takes my hand. Hunched shoulders and a stoop add to an impression of frailty.

'It is a pleasure to greet you, William Constable. I have heard tales of your scholarship and quick mind, although our interests are diverse.'

I thank him for his compliment and wait for Walsingham to progress our conversation. I notice that both Walsingham and Foxe are gazing at a linen blanket in the centre of the table. It is dyed in a pattern of deep red and indigo and there is regular shape forming a hump underneath. 'Is the object under that cloth?' I ask.

Walsingham doesn't answer directly, dons a pair of white gloves from the table and carefully folds away the cloth to reveal what lies beneath. I experience a sense of mild disappointment. It's a small chest or large box about three hands square with a depth of no more than one. The colour is very dark; almost black with the top and sides covered in intricate Moorish patterns. I am no expert, but I would hazard that it is made from ebony. It is well-crafted and I can see that markings or symbols have been worked into the design around the side which have the appearance of an ancient script, possibly Aramaic. I peer at the box without touching.

'Do you have an opinion?' ventures Foxe.

His words startle me and I raise my head to see that both men have their eyes fixed on mine.

'No… at least none beyond obvious observation that it is unremarkable from a distance, but a charming article on closer inspection.' I notice that there is a small, circular hole on one side. 'Is there a locking mechanism that can be opened?'

Walsingham produces a small key, inserts it in the hole and turns it slowly. There is a click and he lifts the cover. The interior is lined with red velvet and a square of folded paper fits neatly within its dimensions. He lifts the paper between thumbs and forefingers, unfolds it with some delicacy, smooths it flat with his gloves, then stands back and invites us to inspect. It is an astrological chart. Now the reason for my presence comes clearer.

'Doctor Foxe, do you have any preliminary view on what you see before you?'

'It is far too early to have any reasoning. I am no expert on the stars, so I will have little to say about the paper inside the box. The symbols around the side are a form of Aramaic and I may be able to enlighten in that respect after some study.'

'Good,' says Walsingham with emphasis, 'We do not want instant judgements in this matter. Careful examination, scholarship and an exchange of reasoned arguments are the obligations I place upon you both. I trust that you will not fail me in this regard.' He looks in turn at Foxe and then me. 'I will leave you now to begin your work. You may call one of my men at the door when you require any comfort or supply. Your beds and dining are in the main house, but understand this; while you may come and go, the box and contents must remain in this room.' He removes his gloves, places them with a flourish on the table, nods his head in acknowledgement and departs.

'A dangerous man who should not be crossed,' observes Foxe when the door closes.

'To this point I have found him less severe than common intelligence would suppose.' Although this is true, I have a sense that life would not be comfortable for me if my words and actions in this assignment do not accord with Walsingham's wishes. Foxe smiles and bows his head in acknowledgement of my observation in a way that suggests he has already seen a less amicable side to Mister Secretary. Foxe himself is a challenge to my preconception. He is friendly and welcoming, seeming more likely to chuckle at a coarse jest than to argue the meaning of a passage from the gospels. I must take care not to assume that this face shows the real John Foxe.

'How long have you studied the object?' I ask.

'Your first view was mine also. I met with Sir Francis two days before and was escorted here yesterday evening. I was taken to this chamber earlier and instructed not to lift the cloth until he arrived. I was passing the time by improving some of my writings.'

'In that case, let us examine it together in some detail.'

He inclines his head to indicate his assent, but appears curiously detached as though he may have more pressing and interesting tasks than the one before us. I am struck by our odd situation. Why have we been chosen? Surely, he has men within his coterie that would be competent to undertake this examination.

'Do you not find our recruitment to this current task and location odd, Doctor Foxe?'

'I can understand your concerns, but you must call me John, or our conversations will become overlong.'

'Very well, John. I am puzzled that you appear to have only a mild interest in our task.'

'Forgive me, I am intent on our examination, but there will be time enough and a weakness in my breathing leaves me less alert than I would wish.' He coughs and places his right hand on his chest. I briefly consider whether I should offer to rub his back to help release his congestion, but that would be too familiar. I notice that he is eying a bowl of fruit on the table. 'I have heard it said… that an orange fruit is good… for the relief of chest pain,' he utters with some difficulty in his breathing.

'I believe several fruits help general wellbeing, but I have heard nothing specific about an orange.' I lean over and pull the bowl nearer. 'Would you like to eat this orange, John?'

He hesitates and focusses closely on the orange, but does not touch it. 'I have never before tasted an orange. I have seen them at my Duke of Norfolk's table, but have not eaten one. I eat simply, following the example of our Lord, but I am tempted by this orange.'

'Would you like me to prepare it for you? It may have a positive effect on the congestion in your chest.'

'That would be kind, William.' He sits in a chair and hunches forward to stop another painful cough. 'How is it taken?' he asks.

'I understand that the fashionable way is to dip portions into hot, liquid sugar and then let it cool so that it presents with a sweet crust. For my own part, I have found them to be succulent and tasty in their natural state.'

I take a small knife to tear the skin of the orange and finish the peeling with my hand. I lay my hat on the table, spread my kerchief on top of that and place the segments of the orange on this arrangement. He looks unsure what he should do, so I pass him a segment and take one myself to show how it is eaten. Its taste is delicious; both sweet and sharp. He puts the juicy flesh to his mouth and with a small hesitation bites the orange. He beams with delight at the result and I feel myself smile at his innocent enjoyment.

'It is a wonder to me why our deliberations and the chest are matters of such secrecy,' I say as I lick the juice from my fingers.

He takes another segment and bites it in half. 'We live in an age of mistrust, William. Who is my friend? Why should I believe what I see before my eyes? In a world that changes so quickly there are many questions to ask and secrets to guard.

Mister Secretary appears to me as one who values certainty and will tread carefully in his quest for this elusive quality.'

I know John Foxe for an educated man, but the philosophical nature of his discourse surprises me. 'Forgive my ignorance, John, but by repute you are an unchangeable Puritan with fixed and damning views on those who do not follow your lead. Here, in person, I find you are much gentler and more thoughtful than I would gather from the common assessment.'

He looks questioningly at another slice of orange before slipping it whole inside his mouth with a smile. He finishes this treat in silence with an expression that suggests he is giving some thought to his reply. 'I am of the Puritan persuasion, but was not born so. I became convinced of the righteous way to God through study, reasoned argument and divine inspiration. I desire that others follow this path, but I will not injure or take the life of those who choose a different route so long as they do not endanger our faith, Her Majesty or our state. To my mind, there is nothing so fulfilling as a forceful and logical argument on matters of divinity between opposing views. Through these arguments, we will find a way to contentment and a true knowledge of Christ. Besides… I am not too old to learn new truths. This orange fruit is a reminder of the value of new experiences.'

We exchange smiles and I find I have a fondness for this old man, as well as respect for his intellect. It is time for us to examine the box more closely. I take it in both hands and lift it slowly. It is heavier than it looks.

'Shall we begin by considering this script on the sides,' I suggest.

I look at Foxe for confirmation, but he puts his hand up as if to beg my indulgence. He coughs loudly and struggles to bring up phlegm with a rasping and wheezing that is painful to my ears. He deposits twice in a spittoon and waves his hand by way of an apology. He breathes deeply and composes himself before replying. 'I am sorry for my disruption. The colder weather brings an infirmity in breathing upon me. I will repair to the house for a little refreshment and a seat in the library. Mister Secretary has a fine collection of books and I will study there for a time before returning.'

He shuffles to the door and talks briefly to the guards, before one takes him by the arm and accompanies him down the stairs. His fit of expectoration appears to have aged him and he exits as a less sprightly figure than the one I found on entry. I am alone. The box and chart sit unmoved on the table tempting me to uncover their secrets. I am no expert on Aramaic, but I know a little and will endeavour to uncover their significance before I examine the chart.

Three

I have stood in one place staring at the object for too long and I am jolted from my lethargy by a large spider crawling across the table. The carvings on the chest are accomplished, but above all it is the locking mechanism that fascinates with its small and intricate scale. The symbols on the side are familiar and many resemble the Aramaic I tackled briefly as a diversion some years earlier. I know that there are variations in this ancient language and, although I have deciphered a sequence of symbols as *Malikh* or *Malikah*, which I understand to signify a ruler, lord or king, I can make nothing of the symbols on the other three sides. I must hope that John has a deeper knowledge of Aramaic. It's time for me to visit the main house and examine Walsingham's library. I should also enquire into John's health and perhaps offer my services in the preparation of a curative.

The house is a busy contrast to the stillness and cold of the garden keep. Workmen are plying their trade. Their voices and the working of hammer, chisel and saw bring a warm and cheery feel to the place. I am guided through to the back of the house and the door opens on to a handsome, wood-panelled room with two sides given over to shelving for books and manuscripts. There must be over three hundred volumes – an impressive number for a private collection – and I have a sense of eagerness to examine their nature and quality. John is asleep in a chair by a small fire covered with a blanket of sheepskin. I will not disturb him as he looks rested and at peace.

I spend a pleasant two or three hours looking through the books and manuscripts in the library. I am not surprised to find some of John's works in the collection, including his *Actes and Monuments* or *Book of Martyrs* as it is popularly known. I will not open this book as I know that some of the illustrations will recall the scene of Godfrey's mutilated body. The notable manuscripts of Luther are here as is the popular tome by Calvin, *Institutes of the Christian Religion*. The coverage of subjects is broad with a large section on matters of law and governance; a number of books relating to mathematics; medicine; nautical charts; and, unsuspected, a small selection of poetry and other entertainments such as Lyly's *Euphues: Anatomy of Wit* and Dante's *Commedia*. I can find no reference to the Hebrew or Aramaic language to help with our task.

John is stirring from his sleep and his chest crackles as he takes in deeper breaths. His eyes open and meet mine.

'William, have you been here for some time?'

'I have browsed the books and manuscripts for a few hours. I hope that I did not disturb you?'

'No, I have dozed for too long. I must be about…'

Something falls from his hand as he moves and I stop to pick it from the floor. It is a small round piece of glass, smooth at the edges and concave in shape.

'Is this a glass of magnification?' I ask, as I return to him.

'Yes, it is useful for small and indistinct scripts. My eyes worsen with age.'

'It could assist our investigation, John. Before we discuss that matter further, I wonder if you would like me to prepare you a potion to relieve your mucus and soothe your chest.'

He lowers his head in assent. I leave the library and easily find my way to the kitchens by following the rich odours of roasting meat. The large kitchens hum and clatter with activity. There are about twenty hands scurrying, cutting, pouring and basting. I guess they are preparing food for the workmen and soldiers. A maid approaches and curtsies. I explain that I have need of certain ingredients, together with pots, cups and a hook for heating on the fire. She understands well enough and says that my requests will be taken to the library within the half hour.

I return to find John sat at a table, poring over a book with the glass to his eye.

'What are you reading, John?'

'Ah, you have caught me deep in an act of conceit. I am examining my own writings. Not because of any self-indulgent pride, but to lament the printing errors that it contains. I must be more diligent in my inspection before printing the next edition.'

I move a chair and sit next to him. 'I have examined the box and the Aramaic script was a mystery to me for the most part.

Do you have a good knowledge of these ancient Hebrew symbols, John?'

'I have studied them, but my understanding is far from perfect.'

'I will wager that yours is on a higher level than mine, but let us hope that together we may determine the meaning of those symbols.'

He nods his head slowly and then returns to his book. Again, I am somewhat surprised at his apparent lack of urgent curiosity. Perhaps his age and sagacity lend him this disposition. With no more conversation to be had on this topic, I wander the room and decide to examine some of Mercator's charts. I have always had a fascination for maps and charts and I am lost in admiration of a chart of the New Lands when the door is knocked and two servants enter with my requisition from the kitchens. I clear my throat to gain John's attention, point to the newly arrived items and inform him that I intend to manufacture a natural potion to soothe his chest.

I place more logs on the fire, then grind an onion and dried nettles to make a paste. I squeeze in the juice of two lemons, add a little honey, a pint of water and transfer the mixture to a hooked pot over the fire. When I am satisfied that the mixture is properly infused, I pour through a clean gauze into another pot. I see that John is watching me with an amused interest.

'I am relieved to note that you have not included the dung of a pregnant ewe in your concoction, William.'

'Ha. There is nothing magical or noxious in this potion, John. It will not effect an instant cure, but I hope that it will relieve some of the soreness around your lungs.' I am pleased that his infirmity does not hold back a dry wit.

I pour a measure into a cup, which takes in both hands, swirls and takes a few gentle sips. He smiles his thanks and continues to drink slowly and carefully. I return to my musings over the chart of the New Lands and I am reminded again of the presentation with Doctor Dee in 'sixty-eight when we offered new methods to assist navigation to those intrepid adventurers of the western seas. My recent observations of the stars have brought to mind some improvements to the mathematics and techniques of sighting, which I will set down in a paper in the New Year.

'That was good, thank you, William; warming and flavoursome.' He interrupts my train of thought as he replaces his cup on the table. 'I do not expect that we will have to stretch our knowledge of Hebrew script overmuch,' he says, licking his lips, 'I have an inkling of its intention.'

I raise my eyebrows at this revelation and ask him to explain further. He suggests that we move back to the garden keep so that we have the object in front of us while he explains. That cold, damp room will not be good for John's health and I open the door to summon a house servant to make up the fire and light the candles there before we transfer. As an afterthought, I request bread, cheese and beer to sustain us both while we wait.

After an hour of rest, feeding and some idle talk we are reluctant, but ready, to leave the comforts of the library. The night has begun early and there is a dankness in the air as we make our way to the keep. The room is well lit and the fire has a welcoming aspect, but it is still cold and I feel John shiver as he enters. I guide him to one of the chairs around the table and put on the white gloves before handling the box. I place it before him and watch as he puts the glass to his eye and peers closely at the engravings. He offers no comment and passes me his glass and invites me to inspect using its assistance. It takes a little time to become accustomed to the positioning of the glass to see a clear enlargement, but once I have its measure I am impressed by the precision of view it presents.

'Do you see?' he asks.

'I see a section of the script and under the glass and it is clear that the engraving is recent. The edges are sharp and unaffected by the passage of time and smoothing of hands.'

He sits back in his chair and replies, simply, 'Yes.'

I understand. He wants me to make my own deductions without taking account of his own. I take up the glass and look closely again. I take my time and study it from all angles and finally place it on top of the box and stand back a few paces to take in a wider perspective.

Finally, I announce my conclusions. 'On first viewing the

container is moderately pleasing as an object and Moorish in design. A detailed examination displays fine craftsmanship and I have rarely seen a more intricate mechanism than the lock. The edges to the carvings are sharp and unworn suggesting recent manufacture, which begs the question, why is there ancient script on a modern box? I believe that the script on one side may be translated as ruler or king, but I am defeated by the other symbols. I have not examined the chart, but at this stage it would be reasonable to assume that the text on the box and the chart are linked in some way.'

I pass the glass to John, he declines the offer of the gloves and moves in to scrutinise the box, turning it slowly in a clockwise motion. He runs his finger along the top, opens it to examine the inner and lifts the whole to examine the base. He fixes the glass to his eye, peers closely back and forth along the top, transfers his attention to the base, then each side in turn. He undertakes the same routine another three times before removing his eyeglass and straightening his back with some difficulty.

'Perhaps if you inspect the astrological chart it may help with our overall appraisal, William.'

I have resisted any attempt to study the chart until now, because to make any proper assessment of its accuracy or interpretations would require access to my books and astronomical references. In these circumstances, however, it is unlikely that I am to be allowed a lengthy postponement before passing an initial judgement. It is in a fair hand, in the English language and well-drawn with all symbols and houses clearly-defined. Notes are inscribed around the outside in a poorer hand. There is no name on the chart, but date, time and place of birth are clearly marked and thus there will be no difficulty in checking its thoroughness and accuracy when I have the tools. The sun is in Virgo, the Moon in Taurus and natal occurred forty-five years in the past, so the present time is somewhat late for analysis of the chart to be useful. Wait… am I missing something? My hidden senses have been pricked, suggesting a significance that escaped my cursory examination. Natal is recorded as mid-afternoon on the seventh day of September in the year of 1533 at Greenwich. I recoil from the table. My mouth is open, breaths coming in shallow gasps. I turn to John who eyes me directly with an expression of mild concern.

'It is our Queen!'

John nods slowly, but does not reply.

'The chart – unless I am mistaken the natal on the chart matches our sovereign.' It is treason to create or read such a thing, and even idle conjecture about our queen's future is an offence.

'Yes,' John replies.

'You are not surprised?'

'I know nothing of your stars and charts, but the inscriptions on the box and the fact that it was seized from a follower of Rome signalled some mischief directed at Her Majesty.'

'What of the inscriptions?'

'There are four around the sides and I can offer you my understanding of three. *Malikah* refers to a queen; *Purqana* deliverance; and there can be no doubt that *Rhum* refers to Rome.'

'And the symbols on the fourth side?'

'That is a more troublesome matter.' He settles in his seat and attempts to suppress a cough, which is only partially successful. 'I believe that the Aramaic is *Niqubta*, but the meaning of this term is obscure.'

'Can you hazard an approximation?' John heaves his chest in an attempt to clear an obstruction. It is painful to observe and I cannot stop myself from gently rubbing his back to aid relief. After a few moments his fit subsides and he waves his hand to indicate that I should stop.

'I believe that the word may refer to a mystery, most particularly of the female kind. It may be necessary to seek confirmation from a learned source.' He pauses, then adds, 'There is more. The Moorish design is an arrangement of much smaller Aramaic symbols that represent a female birth – a daughter, a ruler and a far-away land which may be distant in its span on the earth or time.' He pauses to calm his breath. 'It is in the form of a prophecy and the author is named as Hamuda of Judea. There may be one or more dates, but I cannot be certain.' He leans over to inspect the chart. 'What can we learn

24

from the notations around the edge of this elaborate and decorative representation?'

Puritans are known to frown upon explorations into the influence of stars on our lives and a hint of mockery in the tone of his voice is unmistakeable.

'Do you disapprove of such charts, John?'

'It would be impolite in the extreme to dismiss them outright in your presence, William, but it is true that I distrust reliance on the interpretations from schematics such as these. In my opinion, they touch the edge of magic and associated heresies. Nonetheless, I do not discount them entirely, and I know of good men who have faith in astrological divinations.'

I am thankful for his statement on two counts. First, it confirms that he doesn't have a closed mind. Second, he managed to complete his short oration without interruption from that terrible, rasping cough.

We turn our attention to the writing on the periphery of the chart. There are five notations and to my eyes they are hurried and somewhat crude; certainly, a different hand to the one that drew the chart itself. As we assume the chart was prepared for those ill-disposed to its subject, it is no surprise to see annotations reading *ill-favoured, melancholic* and *promiscuous*. Of more interest is the writing of the word *motherhood* and this would be a common interpretation for a woman of Saturn placed within the sign of Cancer. The final annotation reads *issue hidden* accompanied by a date.

'What does this signify?' John tilts his head to a questioning pose and points to this last pair of words.

'It is written against the fifth house, which is the house of children. The signs there are inconclusive – neither fruitful, nor barren. There is a more positive indication for bearing a child in the eleventh house and some of the markers in the first house can be taken as an indication of a troubled or hidden birth. The placing of Saturn and Cancer at natal may also be taken as a sign of motherhood in the subject, or it could indicate the subject's strong attachment to their birth mother.'

'I understand your reason for not wishing to offer an exact interpretation, William. The writer on the chart had no such misgivings it seems. It declares that our queen is a mother and either that the child was stillborn, or put in a secret place. Is that how you read it?'

'Yes, there can be no other reasoned conclusion of the thought behind the notations, although I should caution that we don't know that the chart itself is accurate, or that the notations offer a fair reflection. The writing is in the English language, so we must also conclude that the chart was prepared by a scholar from our country.' It is a dangerous heresy to suppose that our queen is not a virgin. Of course, there were rumours many years ago, but these were largely forgotten or discredited. 'A date of 1560 on the seventh day of August presumably refers to the birth date of the child.'

John settles back in his seat with a thoughtful expression, but offers no comment. I examine the chart again to try and discern any flaws in the annotations. I know of no way to forecast a date of birth with any accuracy and the date noted must have some other source – or it could be entirely spurious. John is inspecting the box again with his eyeglass. His demeanour in comparison to mine, reveals my naivety in bringing an open mind to this task. I should have suspected a matter of high consequence, daring and danger because of the man who brought me here.

'We must try to make sense of our findings, William.' John's statement lifts me from my musings. I incline my head to suggest that he should begin our analysis. He leans back, clasps his hands together and begins. 'To the common man this is nothing but a decorative box. We agree that it was made recently and the ancient script may be there to confuse or, more likely, add weight to the contents by its fake history and association to the time of Christ. The so-called prophecy touches the claims in the chart and a full reading of the script will no doubt bring them close together.'

'I agree, John. Your translation of the Aramaic is clear in its plan to reflect or complement the analysis of the chart contained in the box.' I pause and look again at the box. 'The thought that our Queen may have a hidden child is disturbing and I understand why enemies of our state would wish to spread such an idea, but it seems…'

'Seems?'

'It appears to be an over-elaborate way to present such a fanciful and scurrilous notion. Surely, this cannot be the entire mischief in this matter.' John is about to comment, but a rasping in his throat progresses to another bout of coughing. 'Come, John, let us depart from this cold room and seek our ease in a corner of Mister Secretary's house where we can discuss these matters further.'

At the house, we are shown into Mister Secretary's parlour by his housekeeper, Mistress Goodrich. We are advised that this is his preferred area for contemplation, reading and dining when there are no guests. I ask her if Sir Francis is in attendance. She replies that he is expected in the morning and that she has been tasked with ensuring our contentment this night. I accept her offer of cold meats and some wine, but John demurs and as an afterthought requests an orange if one can be found without much trouble. He smiles sweetly at Mistress Goodrich and it is plain that she is much taken with his politeness and warmth.

Together, we spend the early night in light conversation. We have both visited Antwerp and exchange stories from that fair city, although I choose my narrative carefully so as not to offend his Puritan sensibilities. John relates his meetings with John Calvin in Geneva and the controversy surrounding reforms to Protestantism. Walsingham's parlour is comfortable, the wine is good and the heat from the fire has a dulling effect on the atmosphere in the room. John's eyes begin to close and he is soon asleep. I find Mistress Goodrich and ask her to prepare the bedrooms while I pay one more visit to the keep before retiring.

The fire is out, but I will not wait for its spark to life as I intend only a short stay in these chill, stone walls. I unlock the box and remove the chart, placing it to one side. I take the chest in my hands and rotate it, admiring the craft and artistry of its maker. I move the box closer to a candle to inspect the locking mechanism. John's glass of magnification would be useful for this and perhaps I should wait for a better light before... ah, no... the box slips from my grasp and hits the stone floor.

My breathing is stilled as I imagine the Walsingham's disapproval for my clumsiness. The sound was harsh, but perhaps the chest is not beyond repair. I pick it up and, to my relief, I see that it is still whole, although the light is too dull to assess any damage. I lift it to the table and bring two candles near. The lid and hinges are intact and the only injury I can identify is a looseness in the bottom section. I pull and push gently in an attempt to see what might be amiss when the entire base of the chest appears to slide out smoothly in one piece. I alarm myself with an unplanned, loud exhalation and quickly look around the room to ensure that I am alone. I lift the chest carefully to the light and observe a small glint of metal, which on closer inspection is a spring. It has a false underside. There must be some hidden mischief behind this manufacture and I am instantly overcome by a sense of bewilderment and menace.

There is a folded paper within the secret compartment. My instinct tells me to replace the base of the chest and examine it in the presence of John Foxe, Walsingham, or perhaps to feign ignorance and let it remain undiscovered. But I am intrigued and a close examination of the paper is surely a part of the obligation placed on me.

Curiosity wins out. I lift the paper and with great caution, unfold it and lay it on the table. I move a candle closer to a page filled with characters written in tabular form, in a square hand and with no flourishes or swirls. I recognise the individual letters, but none of the words. It is code. The lack of spaces on the page and the unusual design of the writings are part of the scheme to confuse. I have some knowledge of ciphers, but only those created as a form of entertainment and diversion from academic studies.

I cannot resist the challenge. I pull up a chair and sit with the paper promising myself that I will stay here no longer than a half hour. A full exploration can wait until the morning when the light is good and two minds can focus their attention on the riddle. I begin with a method to identify the three most frequent letters in the code, translate to those that present similar positions in common prose and identify a pattern of difference. It cannot be that simple, but I will eliminate the possibility…

… There appears to be a regularity in the correspondence of characters and yet, there is no sense to the words… and what is the language: Italian; Latin; French?

There is a mathematical riddle at the heart of this code and if I transpose certain letters then a word in the French language appears… That may be coincidental and more work is needed to identify a pattern in transposition.

… But this not the end of the puzzle. Some characters are present simply to confuse, their regularity has no simple pattern and may be the subject of a more complex formulation.

… I think I may have solved at least a part of this riddle. The transposition of characters may not be subject to a system of mathematics after all, but instead conform to an image on the grid of letters. It is both intriguing and maddening.

I have been too long at this and should be in my bed. The message is in French. I have decoded all I can and translated into English. Some words are unclear or obscure and in some of these cases I have conjectured on words that fit with the general sense of their neighbours. The general intent, however, is evident and speaks of a grand and dreadful scheme to take the throne of England.

my lords and true friends - cabinet - chart disclosing the intimate circumstances of a bastard heir will be joined with -- transit chart foretelling the death of the witch q - our p prepares for the printing -- promulgation --- this diversion to the masses -- movements of m and his unknowing maid are close watched - - will be safe until her time - great burning at d -- gathering planned for the early days of February --- our ships and men wait the call to d comforted by p attestation of the poor state of defence - ready yourselves and your followers --- time draws near g

Four

I did not sleep well. My eyes closed, but my mind was too active to allow an escape from nagging wakefulness. Images of Godfrey's wounds mingled with the cabinet and its secrets. The first grey hints of light appeared some time past and the hesitant shufflings and creaks of early dawn have grown to the bolder sounds of an industrious household. It is time to dress and break my fast. I hope that I will have occasion to confer with John before Walsingham arrives. No doubt he will wish to question us closely on our findings from yesterday.

I enter the parlour to find John seated in a chair by a roaring fire and the table laden with food and drink. The draught of warm air as I enter the room serves as a reminder of a cold, sleepless night, and that I must try to dispel a dullness of spirit and the grainy itch in my eyes. I will need sharp wits for Walsingham's questioning.

'God bestow a good morning on you, William,' says John, clearing his throat. His speech and the grey colour around his eyes tell me that his congestion has not improved overnight.

I return his greeting and enquire after his health. He replies that he feels much the same and he would welcome another dose of the mixture I prepared for him yesterday evening. I make for the kitchens to seek out the same maid who delivered the ingredients yesterday. I encounter Mistress Goodrich on the way and she begs to assist. I explain what I am looking for and she offers to make the soother herself, if I will provide instructions. We return to the parlour where I write a few simple lines on ingredients and method of preparation, then hand it to her. She scans the formula, confirms her understanding and advises that she will ensure we have the result with the hour. Clearly, she is an educated woman with an air of competence. I trust her to make the potion well and there will be no harm if she strays a little from my writings.

'I see you are not eating, John.'

'I find that I am not hungry and generally I do not eat until midday.'

'Would you like a cup of ale to freshen your mouth?'

He nods his assent. I pour his ale, some for myself and move a chair near to his so that we can talk.

'Mistress Goodrich is preparing your potion and I hope that will have a reviving effect on your troublesome ailment. Meantime, are you content to discuss our findings from yesterday before Sir Francis arrives?'

He is about to speak when he splutters and bursts into a bout of coughing. I pass him the spittoon and rub his back gently with circular movement. I feel his bony spine and ribs through his vestments with some alarm. I must urge him to eat more and regain his strength. I move to the table and load two plates with smoked eel, pike and manchet. Fish – I had forgotten that this is a Friday.

'Come, John, let us eat a little while we talk. Good food will aid your recovery and shrewd reasoning is never accomplished on an empty belly.'

He appears reluctant to move from his chair, but I lift under his arm and, in a few moments, feel his body submit to my urgings and we both take a seat at the table. I push his plate in front of him, he stares with little interest and then picks at a piece of eel with his knife. Eventually he speaks.

'I have thought on your views about the intricate presentation of the message in the box and chart. Rumours about Her Majesty's intimate relations have been spread before and without evidence or attribution these were easily dismissed and forgotten. The chart and ancient script are intended to lend weight to the supposition, but on their own will serve to produce only a ripple of discomfort. I must therefore agree with you, William that the extravagance and care taken to construct this mischief must be linked to a deeper Romish plot.'

He takes a piece of eel to his mouth. I follow his lead, hoping this will encourage him to take more food. He points his knife in the air, seeming to give thought to his next statement while he chews. He swallows, then continues. 'I trust that we are both firm on the opinion that the assertion about a royal bastard is absolutely false?'

I hear the sound of raised voices nearby. Someone shouts. I cannot distinguish the words, but the angry tone is unmistakeable. The door opens and Walsingham brushes past the outstretched arm and bowed head of a servant without waiting to be announced. His eyes shine with sharp intensity and the atmosphere in the room is changed. A quiet conversation with a leisurely breakfast has gone; the air crackles with urgency and menace.

'Gentlemen, I beg your pardon for my brusqueness.' He eyes the table and our plates of fish. 'I will join with your refreshment. Good food and drink will improve my humor.' He takes a knife, fills a plate, pours a cup of wine and takes a seat across the table. I watch him as he eats in silence for some minutes, his eyes firmly fixed on the business of easing his hunger. The settlement in his mood is visible and eventually, he lifts his head, smiles at John and me in turn and pushes his plate away.

'I trust that you have both had a comfortable night? I am eager to hear what you have learned from your examinations.' His eyes narrow as he looks at John. 'Doctor Foxe, are you quite well? Your colour suggests that you may require some warmth and rest.'

'Thank you for your consideration, Mister Secretary. I regret that an old infirmity of the lungs has returned to trouble me, as it often does in the winter months. William has been most thoughtful and attentive to my needs and I hope that I shall return to full health shortly.'

Walsingham turns to me. 'So, William, the main burden of this task has fallen on you. Have you made progress?'

'John and I examined the box and chart. The Aramaic script on the box and the natal chart together conspire to suggest harm and disruption to Her Majesty.' Walsingham's face is set hard and it is impossible to determine if he has foreknowledge of the message. 'The insinuation is that Her Majesty had a hidden or stillborn child in August of 1560.' I hesitate, unsure of how much detail to offer and John continues after a brief pause.

'The translation of the Aramaic script is unfinished and somewhat cryptic. It is recently cut, but masquerades as an ancient Judean prophecy referring to deliverance from the queen of a faraway land by Rome through a hidden or bastard daughter. The star chart is plain in its assertion of character flaws in Queen Elizabeth and her delivery of a bastard child. Although the box was captured in France, the chart was prepared in England.' He clears his throat before adding, 'We are of one mind. The implication is manifestly false and we suspect that this is part of a larger conspiracy.'

A silence follows. The effort in making his statement seems to have taken its toll on John and his body sags into his chair. The door opens and Mistress Goodrich enters carrying a tray with a steaming bowl of what must be John's soother. She bobs a curtsey to Walsingham, bows her head to me and sets the tray down in front of John. She asks John if the potion might be to his liking. He cups the bowl in his hands, takes a sip and confirms his deep satisfaction to her. She colours a little at his praise, smiles and departs after another brief curtsey to Walsingham. I remark on Mistress Goodrich's efficiency and John murmurs his agreement.

'She keeps an orderly house and she has a good mind,' says Walsingham. 'She has been in my service for over fifteen years and I have come to rely on her management and shrewd observations.' I assume that last part of his statement refers to her watchfulness and reports to Walsingham on his house guests. I cannot think that I have erred in her presence, but must take care with... the box and the papers; was she spying on me? I feel the heat rise in my neck and must hope that this does not show to excess in my face. Walsingham continues. 'I thank you both for your enquiries. The date and scribblings on the chart suggested a similar mischief to me, but it is satisfying to have your confirmation. You should know that this is a matter of extreme sensitivity to Her Majesty. She takes any intimation of an improper liaison and childbirth to heart. I should be grateful if you would pen me detailed notes on your findings before leaving this house.' Walsingham adjusts his seat and shifts his gaze towards me. 'Meanwhile, I should be interested to learn why you consider that this may be an element in a wider scheme against our state.'

Does he know? Why has he turned his attention to me? I must disclose the unwelcome news of my night discovery, but it is of such great consequence that I find my throat has tightened and a brief mewing sound has already escaped me. I cough and beg their pardon. 'John does not know this as I have not yet had time to inform him. While he was resting last night, I returned to the keep for a further examination of the objects. What I found leaves no room for conjecture; there is indeed a deep and malign plot in progress.' I pause and gather my thoughts. 'There is a false bottom to the box, artfully manufactured and almost invisible to the eye. In there, was a paper with letters written in an unusual fashion. It was code. I confess that curiosity overcame caution and I endeavoured to decipher the note.'

I glance at John and Walsingham in turn. John's expression is neutral while Walsingham's eyes betray intense concentration. He nods, encouraging me to continue.

'I am no expert on ciphers, but I did manage to unravel the message save for a few words which I have approximated on this.' I hand my translated note to Walsingham, which he takes quickly. I add that, 'The deciphered message is in the French language and I have taken the liberty of translating to English.' He scans the note several times making tutting noises and twice banging his fist on the table. Finally, he takes the note, folds it carefully and inserts it into a pocket inside his gown.

'Well William, your talents are even greater than I had suspected. You have the makings of a useful intelligencer. I knew of the hidden drawer in the box and the coded message. I hoped that you might discover the drawer, but the deciphering in short time is beyond my expectation. The intelligencer I would have used in this case cannot be here for some days, so you have done a great service. I will need your advice on the words of approximation, but meanwhile, why don't you summarise the essence of the note for Doctor Foxe.'

'Very well, Mr Secretary.' I take a seat next to John and quickly gather my thoughts about the note. 'John, we were correct in our assumption of a greater plot. It seems there is another chart in unknown hands – a transit chart claiming to foretell the date of death of our sovereign. There is a plan to print and distribute pamphlets detailing the untruths from both charts in order to sow discord. There is mention of an "unknowing maid" and persons of significance are designated only by the single letters, "p" and "m". The climax of the plot appears to be a planned invasion by an enemy fleet. There is mention of a "great burning" at a "gathering" and the meaning of this is unclear to me. The use of the word "diversion" is also confusing and may suggest some greater purpose, but I confess that my decryption and translation to English may be inexact and obscure the finer intentions. The note is signed by a singular, "g".'

Walsingham growls a word which I take to be, 'Guise.'

John purses his lips, nods his head slowly and pats me on the arm in the same way a master might offer congratulation to a student who has succeeded in completing a moderately difficult task. I cannot help a creeping sense of pride in the approbation of these two notable men, but this is mixed with unease at the thought that my role in this affair may not be finished. Is my connection with Godfrey unknown, or is it lying quiet to be used at some later date? Walsingham is bent over the table with his fists balled and knuckles showing white as if in a state of intense, concentrated anger. He lifts his head, surveys us in turn and breathes deeply a few times before speaking.

'You sum it up neatly, William. I have a strong notion that the "g" in question is Henry, Duke of Guise, head of the Catholic League and the evil force behind the infamy on the day of St Bartholomew in France. I was there and witnessed such scenes…' His voice trails away as he gazes past us as if recalling the horror of the massacres of Huguenots in Paris six years past. The room stills and I find that I am holding my breath in case I disturb the moment. Eventually, he shakes his head and returns to the present. 'Come, I am grateful to you both for your diligence. You will have other business requiring your attention and I will detain you here no longer than it takes to write the account of your work. I may wish to call on your advice on this matter at some future time. My business takes me to France on the morrow and I expect a return within the fortnight. You may hear from my assistant, Francis Mylles, in the coming days and if you should have any further intelligence or opinion for me, then please send word to Captain Askham at Whitehall. He will know how to handle your enquiries.' He gestures towards the door with his hand. 'Now, gentlemen, I will arrange for an escort to your lodgings or place of business.'

I offer to help John rise from his chair. He ignores my hand, clears his throat and addresses Walsingham. 'I regret that I no longer have my house in Grub Street. I had planned to visit a friend who has a living at St Mildred, Tenterden, but…' His wheezing descends into a rasping cough and he cups his hands around his face to soften the hurt to our ears.

Walsingham takes me by the arm and leads me to a side of the room away from John. He beckons me close and speaks in a low voice. 'I see that Doctor Foxe is unwell and I am loth to see him undertake a journey to Tenterden in Kent at this time. You should know that he is unworldly and cares nought for his money and comforts. I had heard that his house had been sold to cover debts from his travels. He is too trusting in matters of property and it will take me some weeks to recover his position. I would record it as a great favour if you could arrange for him to lodge at your house in West Cheap until the New Year, or such time as his health recovers.'

'I would be very happy to have John as my guest, Mister Secretary. I share your concern about his ailment and I have grown to admire him in our short time together.'

'Good,' he claps me on the shoulder and smiles his approval, 'I am pleased to note that your early misgivings were unfounded.'

Five

We arrive at West Cheap in the mid-afternoon. John has travelled in a small coach supplied by Walsingham to aid his comfort. It was a thoughtful gesture, but the uneven tracks appeared to make his journey more of a trial than would have been the case on horseback. I find him clinging to wooden rails with both hands and the expression on his face tells of his relief at reaching our destination. Gregory is on hand to take Cassius and I open the door to hail Mistress Hilliard and Hicks, my steward. Hicks appears in short time and informs me that Mistress Hilliard is helping Rose attend to my mother. I explain to him that we have a visitor who will require a room, a fire and a bed as quickly as possible. Back at the coach, I find Captain Askham lending his hand to John and together we support him either side through to the hall where we gently lower him on to a stool. Askham declines an offer of refreshment, saying that he must hasten back to Whitehall. He hands me a note before he departs, informing me that it contains the name and location of a contact who will ensure that any urgent message will reach him in good time. I read the note when he has left. The name of Fincham is not known to me, but the *Bear and Ragged Staff* is a nearby inn that, although I have not visited for many years, holds memories of youthful excesses.

I spend the next hour supervising the accommodation and contentment of John. Hicks is a good man and amiable enough in his way, but he lacks sympathy and understanding when dealing with frailty and illness. I am relieved when Mistress Hilliard appears and busies herself with Hicks to put the finishing touches to John's temporary room. She has spent time with Rose bathing my mother and renewing her bed. I go to mother's room, knock on the door and announce my name. Rose opens the door, bobs her head in acknowledgement and leaves, carrying an armful of wool and linen coverings. The room is light, a fresh fire is taking hold in the hearth and there is a pleasant odour of lavender in the air.

'I am pleased to see that you are awake and somewhat revived, Mother.' I kiss her gently on the forehead and take a stool by the side of her bed. She is sitting up, her bedclothes and cap are crisp and white and there is a faint bloom on her cheeks, which offers hope of improvement.

'Thank you, William, I believe that I am a little restored. You look tired, your hair is uncombed and your shirt hangs loose. You have become too thin and appear lanky as in your youth. Do not disregard the need for nourishment and eat well.' She smooths the blankets with her hands. 'Rose tells me that you have visited Walsingham at Whitehall.'

'Yes, he wished for my opinion on a matter of astrology.'

Her eyes show a look of surprise and an understanding that there is more to my story, but she does not press the matter. 'I understand that we have a visitor.' She closes a book and folds her hands over it.

'Yes… I see that you are reading, Mother.' I peer at the slim volume under her hands. It is a book on herbs and aromatics.

'Is there a reason you do not wish to talk of our guest?'

I hesitate to name him as I am sure she will dislike his reputation. 'I met a gentleman at my encounter with Walsingham. He is a kindly man of sharp wit. He is also elderly and has a congestion of the lungs which has enfeebled him.'

'Does he have a name – this gentleman?'

'He is John Foxe. Do you know of him?'

'John Foxe, the Puritan scholar?'

'Yes, it is him.'

'William, how could you ask such a man to our house? You say he is kindly, but a man of such fixed and morose beliefs will surely darken our lives.'

'I felt much as you before I met him, but he is far removed from the common judgement. He is an intelligent man with little malice for those with opposing views. Although our acquaintance is brief I found him to be good company.' She purses her lips and shakes her head slowly. I understand that her free thinking and dislike of a prescriptive approach to religion will sit unhappily with John, but surmise that they are unlikely to meet if they are both confined to their beds. 'He is ill, without lodgings and my conscience would not allow me to deny him our hospitality.' I pause to consider my true motives. Did I offer a room out of simple goodness, or to gain favour with Walsingham? 'Also, I have a mind to prepare new potions for his ailment.'

'You will need this book, then… I am sorry to have judged hastily, William. I trust your opinion, but now I tire and must rest.'

She hands me the book and lowers herself slowly into her bed. I decide against any mention of Godfrey. She is a woman of strong character, but I have no doubt that this news would bring her much distress.

*

I have time to spare and options to fill the space. I could refine a medicine to help John's condition, create a natal chart to compare with the one at Barn Elms, or resurrect and complete some earlier work on the mathematics of navigation that I had set aside. I sit at my desk with an intention to start with a re-examination of my papers on mathematics, but my thoughts stray to the momentous nature of the conspiracy unearthed. I cannot concentrate. I leave the room and head for the stables hoping that a change of air and simple animal companionship will clear my head.

My restlessness has eased after a pleasant time fussing over the horses. Hicks was at the stables with his young assistant Harry Larkin. Together, they were instructing Gregory on how to hitch a small carriage to Mother's mare. Hicks and Larkin left us after a short time and I had some idle conversation with Gregory as he worked. The lad joined my household only four or five weeks past and we have not talked at length before. His care of the horses is good and it is clear to see that there is a fondness on both sides. He is amiable, diligent and his intelligence warrants a higher future than a stable hand. If he is receptive and eager, I will set some time aside to instruct him in writing and simple logic.

I turn my mind to the natal chart and clear the desk so that I can make notes, sketch and read through my books. I will not draw up a full chart, only calculating those readings that will enable me to evaluate the key points of the one in Walsingham's possession.

I have almost completed my calculations when there is a knock at the door. Mistress Hillard enters, announces Doctor Foxe and bobs a diffident curtsey to him.

'John, are you rested so soon?'

'I am William, and wanted to seek you out to offer thanks for providing a welcoming resting place for this troublesome old man. I have been too concerned with my ailments to thank you in a full and proper manner.'

I am glad that he has felt well enough to rise from his bed, but his speech still betrays the hurt in his chest. His body is hunched in a way that suggests he guards against his next bout of coughing. I see that he has an interest in the work on my desk. I explain its purpose.

'This is a natal chart to compare with our discovery at Barn Elms. I am all but finished and, although I have not had time for detailed examination, it is clear that it has a close correspondence.'

'Do you believe that such calculations can be relied upon to foretell births… and deaths?'

'In an exact way – no, I do not. I would never use star charts in this way. To my mind they offer general indications in disposition, experience and the shape of major events in a life.' I pull up a stool for John. 'As I said at our meeting with Mister Secretary, the chart presents the possibility of a birth linked with some complexity, but this could apply to the subject's mother rather than a child.'

John nods his head slowly. He doesn't speak, but his bearing tells me that he is formulating a response. 'I understand and I am pleased that you regard your science with a balanced humor. Many of my friends label me as unworldly, but I know enough of common thinking to recognise how dangerous astrological evidence, could be. Superstition is like a plague and can spread fiercely without regard for logic or even low reasoning. Do you know any of your fellow scholars in this discipline who would be reckless enough to undertake the task of divining a bastard heir or…' he puts a hand to his mouth as if to soften his words, 'when our sovereign passes her final day on this earth?'

I had not considered identifying an author capable or willing to be a party to this grave intrigue. Of course, I know a dozen or more scholars in my field, but none surely, who would knowingly contemplate this treachery. It is, however, certain that whoever produced the chart at Barn Elms has detailed knowledge of the movement and influence of our stars. 'I can think of no-one…' I hesitate as I recall my association with Doctor Dee. He has provided our queen with extensive charts to determine the most auspicious times for key events. These were at Her Majesty's request and I know that he would never risk her disapproval. Our work together ended unhappily and one of the causes of disruption was his attachment to a man named Edward Kelley. Kelley turned Doctor Dee away from the study of mathematics and astrology to the supernatural. He convinced the Doctor that he could communicate with angels through scrying or crystal gazing. I disliked Kelly from the first and remain convinced that he is a cynical manipulator motivated by financial reward, but he does have a strong intelligence and knows how to cast a star chart.

'Yes William – you were about to say something.'

I shake my head. 'I am sorry, John. I was lost in thought of events some years in the past. I know several scholars who have the knowledge to create the natal chart and perhaps only one who would contemplate the risk of producing it.'

'Will you act on this intelligence?'

I consider the possibilities before replying. 'It is no small thing to enquire about authorship. Although I have no fondness for the man in question, I have no doubt that an investigation by Sir Francis would be an unhappy experience for him, even if he has no part in the treachery.'

'You must weigh this on your conscience, William and I will prick you no more on this matter.'

I am grateful that he ends this topic of conversation, but I already know which way I must lean. The dreadful import of the discovery at Barn Elms leaves no room for noble sentiment. I must find a way to seek out Kelley and determine if he had any part in the making of the chart. If it were known to him,

Walsingham would never forgive me for withholding even the thinnest of suppositions in this case. I gesture with my hand to the door.

'Come, I will show you our household. I have a measure of land at the back where I grow herbs and plants that may be used for medications. It is a pleasant place for contemplation and prayer when the weather allows.'

'You say *our* household, William. Are there others here? I have been thoughtless in not asking if you have a wife, children or other kin at this place.'

'I am not married and aside from our servants and steward there is only my mother. My father died in 'seventy-five and my mother is sick in her bed. I consider it unlikely that you will encounter her, but if you do then I must request your forbearance of her free thinking and willingness to give voice to her views.'

*

John has retired to his room. I have thought more about Kelley; if and how I should attempt to contact him. After a period of indecision, I have written a note to him requesting a meeting on an urgent matter of business. The note has been sent to Doctor Dee's house at Mortlake. I know that Kelley lodged there four or five years past, but he may have moved. He is no friend and even if this note finds him there he is most likely to arch an eyebrow and consign it to a fire. I judge that I should offer him this small chance to converse quietly with me, before resorting to a wider alert and the consequent possibility of a harsher interrogation.

I join Rose who is taking an early supper to my mother's rooms. I am surprised and delighted to find her looking alert with a hint of colour in her cheeks. She offers a welcoming smile as we enter. Together we help to lever her up and lean her against the bolsters at her back. Rose takes her leave and I sit on the bedside stool while Mother eyes the broth and cold chicken on her tray.

'Has the pain eased, Mother? I am pleased that your aspect has more spark today.'

She nods her head slowly. 'The pain persists, but has less of an edge and is easier to bear. My breathing has calmed and I have slept well.' She takes a couple of sips from her bowl. 'Is this a social visit from my son, or a consultation with my Medicus?'

'Your health is a concern to both these persons, but in the main your son simply wishes to pass time in the company of his mother.'

There is a stillness between us as I watch her alternately pick at the meat and spoon the broth. She wipes her fingers on a napkin. 'Something preys on your mind.' It is a statement rather than a question. How should I answer? I realise an intention to seek her counsel without revealing any detail of my time at Barn Elms will be impossible. I begin to form a response, but she has seen through my discomfort. 'The summons by Walsingham. I am no fool William and understand that any connection with that man will likely make you fret and stew. I will not press if you are unwilling or unable to tell, but my wish would be that you share your concerns. You know that you can rely on my discretion and the weakness in my body does not signify a faintness of spirit.'

'I do not doubt the strength of your spirit, Mother. It is my assurance of secrecy that gives me pause.' She passes me her tray, smooths the bed linens around her, then clasps her hands and waits for me to continue. 'It is a matter of astrology.'

'I know that much already, William.'

There is no reason to be soft and indirect any longer, so I relate the story about the capture of the box, the natal chart and the Aramaic script. I must not release any information about the wider plot or the other chart, as this knowledge is too dangerous for others to hold, even those most trusted. She listens in silence and when I am done, tilts her head and questions, 'There is more?'

'Surely, that is enough.'

'Rumours about the queen's personal affairs have circulated for many years. There have been suggestions of a bastard birth, but such rumours soon fade.'

'In this case, there is an intention to provide evidence of a natal chart and supposed ancient prophecy to support the claim.'

She puffs air through her mouth and waves a dismissive hand. 'What nonsense, the heavens cannot foretell a birth, nor can a long-dead Judean mystic.'

'I agree with you, but the common feeling has been aroused by less in the past. An unconsidered spark may light a great fire.' She closes her eyes and shakes her head slowly, but has nothing to add. I pause a little and continue. 'You have spent some time at court, Mother. Would an affair resulting in a child have been possible to conceal eighteen years ago?'

'My interval at court was short and before the time of our queen. Edward was our king when I was one of Frances Grey's ladies. I know that Edward was seldom in the company of just one or two true friends and was never allowed private moments alone, poor boy. I knew ladies who… who had liaisons at court. Some were discovered, while others were quietly moved away from general view. Suspicions lingered, but were never proved.' She purses her lips and breathes deeply. 'For our sovereign, such an event would be very difficult to hide, but not impossible.'

'If there was a mating, it would have been with Dudley at that time?'

'Yes, but then, I doubt even Dudley would have the power, influence or reach to organise the deception and maintain secrecy.'

'Perhaps someone like Burghley?'

'Ha, there is no-one like Burghley, but you are correct that it could not have been done easily without him.' She pushes herself up and pats a bolster back into shape. 'William, this talk is fantastical. If there was a living child, it would have been discovered by this time. Where would it be hidden? So many years to guard against a careless word or a changed allegiance. It is a fabrication to cause mischief and unrest – no more.'

'I'm sure you have it, Mother.'

'Then why is Walsingham so concerned?'

'Because it is not enough to simply deny or ignore such an assertion – it must be proven wrongful and the instigators brought to public account.' Until I spoke these words I had not understood Walsingham's view and I think have it reasoned well enough.

'Hmm, you met him only a few days ago and already you have the mind of one of his agents.'

I laugh at her accusation and tell her that it is my greatest wish to steer a path well away from Mister Secretary and his intrigues. Am I being truthful? Is there a space in me that is stirred by danger and political scheming? I have no time to dwell on my motives now and I turn to an examination of Mother's chest and lower abdomen. Her chest is somewhat relieved; congestion is there, but with less production of phlegm and crackle in the breath. Her lower parts remain swollen and tender to the touch. I fear cause and remedy here are beyond my understanding. I will prepare another infusion of chamomile and cloves to assist with her pain and will visit the apothecary for his advice on a purgative. Before I leave I have one final matter on which to seek her opinion.

'I have thought where a royal bastard may be raised away from general view. It cannot be a family close to the Queen, or at court. In this case, it must be small nobility or wealthy gentlefolk; perhaps a merchant. Do you know of any such family with an adopted daughter of near eighteen years? The letters "p" and "m" might be significant in the naming.'

She waves her hand to dismiss me. 'William, you should put an end to this speculation. You must know there is no hidden heir and at best, this is a shameful squandering of your thoughts and efforts. Besides, since your father died, I have had little conversation and mingling with the character of family you have marked.'

Six

It took only a half day for a note to return from the Doctor's house at Mortlake with the news that Kelley was not there. He had departed some months earlier when Doctor Dee left for the Low Countries. His current lodgings are unknown, but he had previously taken rooms near Aldgate. This unexpected and helpful information was written in a careful and exact hand by Jane Dee. I know nothing of her and the Doctor must have remarried recently as his second wife died only in 'seventy-six. I will ask Mother if she knows of the new mistress at Mortlake. Meanwhile, I write a short note to Captain Askham requesting him to call at his convenience. I give the note to Mistress Hilliard and ask that she seeks out the same boy messenger used yesterday to carry it to Fincham at the Bear and Ragged Staff, promising an extra penny if the note reaches its destination before noon.

I enter John's room to find him sifting through his personal bags. Papers and other effects are scattered over the floor and bed.

'Good morning to you, John. Did you sleep and breakfast well?'

'Ah, William, excuse my disorder, I am attempting to gather my writings into a form of regularity so that I may continue the work.'

'I have brought another bowl of your soother.' I put the bowl on a small table, place a stool there and wait for him to take his first sips. I enquire about his chest and he answers that it is much the same, but is grateful for the warming potion as it brings some relief. 'I will set a place for your work, John. There is a room with two tables and a chair for your ease next to my library. It is not big, but should help with your writing and organisation of papers. When a fire is made and all is ready I will have word sent to you. Also, you are welcome to study my books, although the collection is small and the subjects of the texts will be of little interest to you in most cases.'

'You are kind, William, very kind.' He would say more, but his ailment has the better of him. When the fit subsides, he continues, 'I was about to say that I have some books with me which I intend to study. Nevertheless, I thank you for your offer and I should welcome the opportunity to examine your books in due course, no matter the author's field of learning.' He takes up his spoon and is about to sup again when he stops and adds, 'I have thought about the Aramaic script on the chest and I can bring no person to mind who would have the knowledge or leaning to be party to such terrible trickery.'

I understand immediately, that he is seeking information and is not the provider. Although he will not ask directly, he wishes to know if I have pursued my hunch about the creator of the chart. I reply that I have started to make enquiries on his whereabouts and will advise if he is found. This is the first sign of an eagerness in him to uncover the plot. I must not mistake his slow and easy manner for indifference in our future conversations.

Back in the library, I clear my mind and re-read my work of last year on the mathematics of navigation. I had concentrated on more precise forecasts of the positions of navigational stars, but had put this aside with an understanding that such precision would be more than offset by inaccuracies in the measuring instrument. Perhaps my efforts should be directed towards an improved instrument for calculating the angles of heavenly bodies relative to the horizon on a ship's deck. A knock at the door.

'What is it Rose? Has Mother's health worsened?'

'Please sir, Mistress Amy has less discomfort and has decided to leave her bed. She is seated in the parlour with a book and warming fire. She has asked if you would attend her.'

'Of course, thank you, Rose. Do you have her piss for me to examine?'

She confirms that the specimen has been left in her bedroom. This is good news; the first time she has left her bed in the last fortnight. I hope that this is not a false or transient reprieve.

Mother welcomes me with a smile. I convey the joy in my spirits to see her risen and clothed. She puts down her book and beckons me to sit by her.

'What book are you reading, Mother?'

'It is Calvin's *Institutes of the Christian Religion* in the French language. I had thought to refresh my knowledge of the foundations of anti-papist doctrine in case I become engaged in conversation with our guest.'

'There is no need. I am sure that John will not burden you with his philosophy if the occasion of your meeting arises. He is an intelligent man, well able to converse on many topics with good humor and light touch.'

'I will be happy to see the truth in that, William.' She picks up the book. 'This tract does have some fine points, but it is flawed in its unwavering belief in one dogma and unwillingness to allow any freedom from its confines.'

'I read it a few years ago and recall that I disliked it, so left it unfinished.' I pause. 'Did you… did you ask me here to discuss this book?'

'No, William.' She raises her eyebrows. 'That would make both of us a little uncomfortable.' She hesitates as if seeking a form of words, then is about to speak when she closes her mouth and shakes her head slowly. There is a silence between us. Something troubles her. I must tread slowly or she will retreat further.

'I sent a note to Doctor Dee's house and received a reply from his new wife, Jane. Do you know her?'

'Why would you write to Doctor Dee?'

'I was seeking an opinion from one of his confederates on a matter of astrology.'

She will understand that this concerns the chart at Barn Elms, but allows mention of this to pass and answers my enquiry. 'I know the Doctor's new wife is Jane Fromond, although I have not spoken with her. She was one of the Countess of Lincoln's ladies. Dee is thirty years her senior. There was talk of an unwelcome interest by the Earl of Lincoln, and a swift departure from court. It is a strange match, but I had no interest to discover the full facts of the affair.'

I tell her that I only enquired because Dee's last wife was recently deceased and assure her that I have no intention of renewing my association with the Doctor. She looks relieved. I stand and wander the room stopping at the window with an outlook on to our courtyard. It is cold and cheerless outside with a light rain mingling with wisps of snow.

'I know a name that may interest you,' she says faintly.

I turn and face her, waiting for more,

'Despite myself, I could not help considering the families known to us, the letters "m", "p" and daughters of a certain age.'

I sit next to her and put my hand on hers as reassurance, or encouragement.

'Your father was on good terms with George Morton, now Sir George as the member for Maldon. He and your father had a number of shared ventures that went well. He deals in silks and spices and I hear that he now has a permit for sweet wine. He has considerable wealth and I understand has ownership of more than ten vessels.'

'I know him. I recall meetings with father when I was less than twenty years. A large man with a thoughtful manner.'

'He has estates in Essex and Norfolk with a house of business and residence in Leadenhall.'

'There is a daughter in the family?'

'George is a widower and he has a daughter named Helen.' She pauses. 'She is of an age that matches your concern.'

'Thank you…'

'William, do not thank me. You must promise me that this knowledge will not be passed directly to Walsingham. I have no doubt that the Morton family are innocents in this affair, but even so, Walsingham's methods would be an unhappy experience. Any enquiries to absolve the Morton's you must undertake yourself, and with delicacy.'

'You have my word, Mother.'

I leave with a tangle of thoughts. How should I handle this unexpected intelligence? Could George Morton be a willing party to the conspiracy? Of course, the likelihood is that Mother's information is a coincidental fit to the coded note and there is nothing to discover.

Hicks is waiting as I reach my library. A tenant farmer on our lands in Kent has died without heir and a new lessee has been found. There is a question of lodging for the widow. I know the couple and am sorry for her loss. I instruct Hicks that the new tenant must provide free-for-life accommodation in a house on the land, or the lease cannot be completed. He is content with my answer and before he takes his leave I have a question for him.

'Do you know the location of Sir George Morton's house in Leadenhall?'

'Yes sir, I will write you a note and bring it to you in short time.'

'Thank you, Hicks, very good.'

'There is much talk of his new venture in the quays of the North Bank.'

'New venture?' I query.

'Yes, there are grand plans in the hands of Sir George and other notables for an expedition to the New Lands with Captain Hawkins and Sir Humphrey Gilbert. It is rumoured that Burghley himself has an interest.'

'Yes… thank you again, Hicks.' I have not heard of this venture. I shall make an effort to be more aware of matters of high business in the future in case they impact on our position. I trust Hicks, but I must not let him shoulder the full burden of our financials. A thought has breached my awareness – could I use this intelligence in an approach to the Morton family?

I am settled in my library for a short time when Mistress Hilliard announces the arrival of Captain Askham. I summon Gregory to take his horse and guide him through to our receiving room. He accepts the offer of refreshment and I invite him to warm himself at the fireside. I will be circumspect in my conversation as I do not know if he has been taken into Walsingham's confidence about the capture of the box. I thank him for his promptness in answer to my note and wait for him to take a mouthful of brandywine. He licks his lips in appreciation.

'I seek a man who may be able to assist in solving a mystery about an astrological chart.' He will surely question me on the nature and relevance of this request unless he has been appraised of the plot by his master. In reply he simply asks for the name of the man.

'His name is Edward Kelley and I understand that he may be lodging by Aldgate.'

'I know of this man. He has a reputation for scrying and divination.'

'You are well informed, Captain.'

'I will arrange for a search to be started later this day. When he is found, shall I escort him to Whitehall?'

'No, please bring him here and be gentle. I have no reason to suspect that he may be harmful to Her Majesty, only that he may be able to assist in the work that Doctor Foxe and I undertake for Mister Secretary.'

He confirms his understanding in a way that suggests any elaboration on the findings at Barn Elms was unnecessary. He is not one for idle talk and after an enquiry on John's state of health, he takes his leave. The Captain is an admirable and dependable man and it is clear to see why Walsingham places him in a position of trust.

I turn my thoughts to Morton and how I should seek an introduction. Indeed, should I follow this scant supposition or let it lie? No, my mind will not settle until I have made a brief study to eliminate the Morton family from this intrigue. I cannot simply send a boy with a note to his house and I will not ask Mother to smooth the path to his door. I will write a letter for Hicks to deliver. In it, I will express an interest in investing in the expedition and make reference to my task of improving the navigation of ships.

Seven

Two days have passed since the Captain's call and there is no news of Kelley, or an answer to my letter to Sir George Morton. My labour on navigation mathematics progresses, but slowly. Mother's health continues to improve a little and, although John is still racked with inflamed lungs and much phlegm, he has episodes of relief and calm. I have cautioned that he should seek refuge in his bed, but he passes most of the day on his studies and writing. Yesterday, he was introduced to Mother and they had an afternoon of conversation and light refreshment in the parlour together. I am thankful that all seems to have gone well with this encounter. Mother reported that she found him a man of deep learning and tolerable demeanour. John was more effusive in his assessment, pronouncing her a 'delightful companion' with a 'keen ear and sharp wit'.

Light in the afternoon sky begins to grey when three mounted men arrive. Gregory and Mistress Hilliard are already in attendance when I reach the entrance hall. One of the men steps forward and introduces himself as Darby Wensum, Sir George's man of business. He is a slight man of middle height who walks with a limp. I note that his right foot is turned inward and this leg is shorter than the other. His dress is striking in its quality and cut in comparison with his attendants. He removes a thick cloak and velvet cap to reveal a dark green doublet with silver markings over a ruffed neck, black, breech hose and finely-crafted shoes; an unusually affluent display for a man of business. The attendants are led away by Mistress Hilliard and Master Wensum follows me. Save for his name, he has not spoken a word. He gazes about the house as though taking an inventory, then stands in front of the fire and warms his hands. As I search for the words to comment on his lack of civility, he turns and says, 'Sir George has received your note.'

Nothing follows. Should I prompt him to continue? I wait.

Eventually, he says, 'I know your man, Hicks.'

'A good man. He has been with my family for more than ten

years.' I am about to continue on the subject of Hicks, but his attention has wavered. He scans the extent of our receiving room, taking note of the hangings and portrait of my father. When he is done, he folds his arms in a gesture of finality and faces me.

'The venture to the New Lands is on a grand scale. More than twenty ships will be fitted and crewed. Although rewards are expected to be great, the expense is daunting. Only those nobles and gentlemen with substantial situations have been chosen to join with this great adventure.' It appears that he has dismissed my interest with a cursory inspection of man and property. I was not prepared for this and before I can respond, he continues. 'Your family is known to Sir George and he holds the memory of your father with some fondness. He asked me to pass on his good wishes to your mother. Perhaps you would…'

'Of course. Did Sir George wish to give a message to me, other than he has received my note?'

'In short, Sir George invites you to dine with him at Leadenhall tomorrow eve. He had a liking for your mention of improved navigation for ships. This subject will be of particular appeal to Captain General Hawkins, who will also be dining.'

'Please thank Sir George for his invitation, which I will be pleased to accept. Thanks to you also for taking a great deal of trouble to deliver this message to me in person, and with such grace.'

He tilts his head and stares at me, unsure how to react. He grabs his cloak, doffs his cap, bows stiffly and limps towards the door. Was I unwise to mock him so? I have a feeling that I may have nurtured an enmity in one who could help with my enquiries. I curse inwardly at my intemperance. It is a fault that my mother, father and others have identified in me, and it seems one that the passing of the years have not softened.

*

Mother and John have long retired to their beds when I close my studies for the day and head for the kitchen. I am hungry and Elspeth, our cook, has set aside a plate of cold meats and pickles for me. I am sat holding an unmolested chicken leg and wondering how I should prepare for my visit to Leadenhall tomorrow, when the quiet is disturbed by voices at the front of the house. Captain Askham has arrived and is conversing with Hicks. He begs me to excuse the lateness of the hour and asks if we may talk in private. I thank Hicks and take Askham to my library. He explains that he has found Kelley, who is following at a short distance with an escort, and questions whether at this late hour, our conversations with him should be here, or at a place he has reserved at the Bear and Ragged Staff. We decide on the latter. I quickly gather warm clothing and advise Hicks that I expect to return shortly.

We do not enter the inn, but are taken around to a single-storey, circular building at the rear that is used for the entertainment of fighting dogs and fowl. Tonight it is empty and cheerless. The place of action in the centre has been swept clear and set with a small table and three stools. The location is well-chosen. It has an eerie and forbidding aspect that is more likely to entice free talk in the unwilling than the cosiness of my fireside.

Askham and I are standing in the centre when Kelley arrives with two armed men. His beard has lengthened and his appearance has aged more than our years apart. His bearing is tall, erect and his mouth is set in a show of belligerence. His eyes widen as he recognises me.

'You… William Constable. Why have I been brought to this place?'

'You will discover soon enough,' says Askham offering a stool to Kelley.

He treads warily towards us.

I say, 'A fair night and God's greeting to you Edward. It is a long time since we last met.'

I sit and watch as he pulls his cloak roughly around himself and takes a seat at the other side of the table. Askham takes the remaining stool by my side and waves an arm to dismiss his men.

'Please forgive the forceful arrangements for this meeting, Edward,' I say. 'It has no malign intent, but the words that pass between us must be confidential.'

'What could you possibly want with me that warrants such a

coarse intrusion on my person?' His reply is sharp and he folds his arms in a gesture that offers challenge.

'You should know that we are here under instruction from Mister Secretary Walsingham,' says Askham.

Kelley appears unmoved by this news, but I see from the way he blinks his eyes and the small droop in shoulders that this knowledge has shrunk his spirit. He hesitates before speaking.

'I have great admiration for Sir Francis, but what could the master of our state's security want from a simple philosopher such as me. Why, it is akin to requesting advice from a goldsmith on the quality of fine wines or the roasting of a swan.'

I see his wit has not deserted him. 'We understand your area of expertise well, Edward. We are here to seek your views on the science of astrology.'

'You surprise me, William Constable, I had thought that you were capable in that area. For myself, I have little use for star charts these days and find more profit in communication with angels through scrying.'

I feel a stiffening in Askham to my left at the mention of angels. This is no revelation to me. He had convinced Doctor Dee of his facility for scrying some years before and it was one of the reasons we parted.

I say, 'Nevertheless, I know you have a good understanding of the science of the stars. I ask if you believe that a natal chart can foretell a childbirth and the day of this event?'

A shuffling in his seat suggests discomfort – is it physical or in his mind?

'There is a complexity of alignments that must be accounted for. It is no simple task, but... I know of reputable philosophers who have undertaken commissions into this question.'

'Would you accept work of this kind if the reward was sufficient?

'No. I would offer the names of other competents.' His reply is too definite. From my reading of his person, he would turn his mind to this task if the compensation in coin was worthwhile.

'Not even if it was a royal commission?'

'That would depend upon the royal person and the nature of

the request.'

How much information should I disclose in my questioning? I turn to Askham who meets my eye, then takes up the examination.

'Have you travelled to France in recent months?'

'No, not for ten years or more. My business has kept me active here.'

'Do you know of other experts in the study of the heavens who have crossed the channel in the past year?'

'No, I have but few connections with astrological philosophers. As I have said, my primary interest lies in scrying, but strictly within the confines allowed by our church. I am fixed and ardent in my Protestant belief.'

Askham continues, 'Have you ever had sight or intelligence of a star chart, falsely manufactured, that claims to pronounce on events concerning our monarch? You will swear your answer in the presence of God and the earthly witnesses here.'

Kelley hesitates, looks at Askham and me in turn, places his right hand on his heart and states, 'I swear that I have no hand in, or knowledge of, such a chart… save that drawn by Doctor Dee on Her Majesty's order for the benefit of her coronation.'

Askham stares fixedly at Kelley for a few moments, then rises from his seat, asks Kelley to remain and gestures for me to follow him to the edge of the arena. When we are away from his hearing, Askham begs my opinion of Kelley's answers and demeanour. There is an awkwardness in my report. I cannot let my dislike of the man colour my judgement and the high importance of the affair weighs heavily. I do not believe that Kelley was directly concerned in the manufacture or interpretation of the chart, but I have a doubt that he declares the full truth. I am unsure whether he hides something from the matter in hand, or if he harbours guilt from another activity.

Askham says, 'I am in broad agreement with your summation. His manner is not of one with unblemished conscience… but then, who among us does not have misdeed or sinful thought from our past that may surface under close inspection.' He folds his arms, then strokes his chin as if balancing the circumstances of our options. 'He has influential friends he can call on to press his case and I do not consider that we have sufficient to take him for strong questioning. Do you agree, Doctor Constable?'

I confirm that we are of one mind and with nothing further to keep me, I return to West Cheap with a two-man escort. If my visit to the Morton house is uneventful, as it surely will be, perhaps this will signal an end to my assistance in the work to uncover facts about the conspiracy and identity of the plotters. I should feel a straightforward sense of relief at this prospect, but my mind turns in more complex directions.

Eight

I take a deal of trouble and time to choose my dress for tonight. It rains heavily at midday, but clears in the afternoon, which is cold, but dry. I wear my finest doublet and hose and elect for shoes rather than boots as it is a short ride to Leadenhall. Hicks knows where I am going, but I have not disclosed my visit to Mother or John.

The sun is near down when I arrive at my destination. Sir George's residence is more a mansion than a mere house. The front is neatly kept and the entrance is ornamented with two marble figures. A man takes Cassius to the stables while another takes my cloak and guides me to a grand hallway with wide stairs and gallery around the first floor. He knocks on a door, checks inside and bids me enter with a flourish of his free hand. I recognise Sir George immediately. He is a large man, about my height, but with significant middle girth. He is dressed for his ease in white, loose, silk shirt and green hose. He opens both his arms to greet me.

'Welcome to my house, William Constable. Your father was a fine man and good partner in trade, God rest his soul.' His voice surprises as more of a whisper than the expected boom.

I doff my cap and bow, thanking him for his kind invitation and good wishes for my mother. He introduces me to his two companions; a smaller, robust man with ruddy complexion; and a young woman. The man is Captain General Hawkins and the woman his daughter, Helen. Hawkins is friendly enough in his greeting, although his expression is made fierce by the deep-set wrinkles around his eyes and mouth.

Sir George says, 'I have a weakness for indulging my daughter. She will join us when we dine and we will discuss our business when she withdraws.'

She is pretty – very pretty, with fine features that bear no similarity to her father. I am no authority on the estimation of age, but would hazard she has not yet reached twenty years.

She says, 'We have met before, William Constable.'

'I… I am sorry lady, but I do not recall.'

'No matter, I was at my mother's skirts and you were too full of young men's concerns to notice me. It was at your house in West Cheap.' There is a teasing and lightness in her eyes as she speaks.

Sir George shakes his head and says, 'Forgive my daughter, William. She remembers not, but relies upon my telling for her mischief.'

'I hear that you physik, Doctor,' says Helen. 'I have an interest in the wellbeing bestowed by herbs and other plants. Perhaps Father will allow me a little of your time here to show you my still and drying room.'

Sir George sighs and spreads his hands. 'If you are of a mind, William, please oblige my daughter. She is learned in this field and, as you have witnessed, full of conceit and too forward in her manner.' He waggles a finger at his daughter. 'You may go now before we dine, if Rosamund is with you.'

Helen inclines her head towards a door and I follow.

'Rosamund?' I query.

'She was my mother's lady and now mine, although in truth, her influence is wider and she manages this house.'

I am taken down a corridor to the end of the right wing of the house where she opens a door and bids me to enter. An old woman is bent over a bench with a pestle and mortar. She lifts her head to view us and returns to her work without any further acknowledgement.

'Rosamund, this is William Constable, a doctor of astrology and physik from West Cheap.'

She mutters something in return, which could be my name. Helen asks me to excuse the frailty in her hearing. She explains that Rosamund was her original teacher on herbal preparations and continues to assist with the tending and harvesting of their garden plot. The chamber is a large one and has two fires set. There are bundles of herbs hung from the beams and several rows of jars marked with their contents. It is a more generous display than I have seen in any apothecary, even in the Low Countries. I am about to comment on her handsome collection when she lifts a paper and presents it to me. The writing is small, tight and in a regular arrangement.

She says, 'I am observing the healing properties of various herbs from my own studies and those of goodwives with practice in their application. There is knowledge that lies uncollected, and in my judgement it is because the learned men who write their books have no regard for the female intellect or experience.' She raises her chin and wrinkles her nose, as if challenging me to contradict her opinion.

'I am sure that there is truth in what you say. I have received much of my practical learning from my mother. I know that there is abundant wisdom on the application of herbal medicine in the hands of goodwives and healing women.'

She does not respond, but clasps her hands in front of her skirts and adjusts her stance.

I continue. 'A balancing of the humors and lessons from the stars do not offer a complete answer for a physician. The body and soul form a complex mechanism that can relate to the plant world in ways that are of striking benefit.' I pause and add, 'Or their misuse can be harmful.'

'You appear more open in your views than I had expected.'

'Do you apply potions to the sick, yourself?'

'Rosamund has a reputation and is often asked to aid those whose purse will not allow a physician. My father will not permit me to be the principal in these matters, but I attend, observe and advise.'

'I am at the beginning of a study of herbal potions and no expert. I have two patients at my house who could benefit from your combined experience and plentiful resources.' I wave my hand in admiration at the contents on display. 'My mother has a painful swelling in her belly and an elderly guest has congestion of the lungs. In both cases, I fear that a cure may be beyond my capabilities.'

She lowers her head and speaks quietly. 'Your modesty becomes you, but…'

I am too quick. 'No, it is too much to ask.' My motives are confused and I have spoken before collecting my thoughts. It is true that I hope she and Rosamund may assist in healing. I would also discover more about Helen to confirm the Morton family have no part in the conspiracy. She is pleasant company and comely. More – there is an attraction that goes beyond words and appearance. I must stop these foolish thoughts. I am not a giddy youth and have known her only for a few moments.

She says, 'I would like to help and will think on your request. Meanwhile father will expect our attendance at his table.'

*

It is no surprise that Sir George has a particular liking for his food and he presents an impressive supper table. We start with a pike garnished with apples, a half-barrel of oysters and follow with a half-dozen pheasants and two capons. Sir George has eaten four of the birds and bangs the table with delight when two large hams with a sweet glaze are brought in.

'No meal is complete without a ham. Do you agree, William?'

I answer that all the dishes have been excellent and I look forward to finishing with the sweet ham.

'Finish?' His soft voice becomes louder and urgent. 'I will not be happy until we have tasted the sweetmeats and syllabub.'

Our conversation until now has been largely monopolised by Sir George who recounts tales from his youth and early successes as a trader. He speaks with fondness of his wife, Anne, who died three years ago from the sweating sickness. Captain Hawkins has been quiet, but joins in enthusiastically when the subject of overpopulation in the city is broached. There is a natural fear of disease and general agreement that noxious breath from the masses is a hazard in our crowded streets. The solutions proposed range from forced expulsion beyond the city walls to the idea of a network of small waterways built to carry away the slurry and filth from roads and passageways. The latter suggestion is mine; meets with wholehearted approval from Helen and misgivings from the two men who question the funding for such a project.

There is a lull in our conversation, then Sir George says, 'You know that John has been appointed as Treasurer of the Navy?'

'I had heard. My congratulations on an important recognition,' I say.

'The Captain is not only an unrivalled man of the sea and administrator, but is inventive in the design of ships,' adds Sir

George and I bow my head to the Captain in acknowledgement.

Hawkins turns to me. 'I attended your exposition with Doctor Dee some years ago at Whitehall. I was impressed with your methods and am eager to understand if you have an improvement that we may use on our venture. I would also value your opinion on certain modifications to our ships that I have in mind.'

Hawkins is animated as he describes plans to lengthen the ships and cover the hulls with skins of elm planks coated and sealed with pitch and horsehair. He explains this is intended to guard against worms and other small underwater beasts in the tropics that eat away the wood. Most ingenious of all, he proposes to manufacture detachable topmasts which can be hoisted in fair weather and stowed when heavy seas direct caution. I commend his inventiveness and promise to inspect the work in progress on the quays of the North Bank in due course. I am genuinely surprised and enthused by Hawkins' schemes. His reputation is that of a fearless military commander, but there are clearly wider concerns in an active mind.

Our discourse has stretched beyond the last serving of food and Helen begins to weary of the topic. She excuses herself, bobs a graceful curtsey to each of us and retires. I must not forget that I am here to enquire into the date and nature of her birth.

When she has left the room I say, 'Your daughter is charming, Sir George, with learning and wit seldom found in one so young.'

'Ah, Helen, she is a blessing.' He pauses. 'Would that her mother was here. At my age I am too soft in controlling her high spirit. I dote on her.'

He is misty-eyed and I continue to gently probe. 'But your ages are not too distant and she shows proper respect and love to her father.'

'Hah, you flatter me, William. I am less than two years from my sixtieth and Helen is forty years behind me.' He hesitates and would say more, but rouses himself, sits back in his chair and spreads his hands on the table. 'Come now, we are here to discuss our great adventure and your interest, William.'

The scheme is outlined by Hawkins. There are twelve ships in the quays here and ten in the West Country under the supervision of Sir Humphrey Gilbert. The fleet will assemble at Dartmouth early next year, then half will sail for the Africas to gather slaves and other supplies for trading at Santo Domingo and Venezuela. The remaining ships will sail later laden with supplies of cloth, livestock and other goods useful for settlements in the Indies. After trading for the return journey, the whole fleet will rendezvous off the east shores of Hispaniola and form a blockade for the capture of Spanish treasure ships. This last part of the operation is the one that excites both men. Hawkins recounts his intelligence of the fabulous wealth of gold and silver from Mexico and Peru destined for Castile. He describes the exotic and faraway lands in a way that brings the writing of their names on a map into vivid imagination. It is an extravagant plan and one that will bring riches and fame to the principals, if successful. I find myself sharing their eagerness.

Sir George says, 'Our financial interests are settled, William. The Captain General regards accurate navigation as a major influence in the achievement of our aims. Hence, it is your words on a navigational aid in your letter, rather than the depth of your purse, that concerns us.'

I am relieved that I do not have to face the embarrassment in disclosing the small coinage that I can risk. My work on the measuring instrument is not fully formed, but I suspect it is the object I must offer to stir their curiosity. 'I have updated my almanac with more accurate readings of the heavenly bodies and adjusted the mathematics for a more precise calculation.' I pause to examine their expressions, which show that they hope for more. 'I admit that these improvements are slight. My recent efforts focus on an improved instrument to measure the angle of the celestial bodies above the horizon.'

Hawkins leans forward in anticipation. 'I would be glad of this tool. Our cross-staffs are problematic on a rolling deck.'

'My work is incomplete, but I understand that there will be a difficulty in using a cross-staff. I have only a small experience of its use on a ship, but even in steady seas it is a complex matter to take readings from the top and bottom of the transom at the same moment and in the full glare of the sun.'

'Do you have a remedy?' asks Hawkins.

'I experimented on the roof of my house with a staff that casts a shadow from the rear and a sighting vane that allows this and the horizon to coincide with a single sight. To this date my craftsmanship fails me and there is more to be done to perfect the method.' I give no word that this was an unsatisfactory and rough handling of pieces of wood on a single night, and Hawkins appears to be encouraged.

'Very good,' says Sir George, 'I am sure the Captain General will wish to observe your progress in this development and there are over one hundred days before the ships will sail; time enough.' He presses his body back in his seat and meets my eye. 'If your experiments prove to be of value then I am sure that the Captain will find a berth for you on his ships. You are a young man and this will offer you adventure and a share in its success.'

It is an offer I had not envisaged or sought, but is some way in the future and I must not appear lukewarm, so I thank him for his kind offer and say that I will gladly accept, should my circumstances allow.

It is the hour before midnight when we finish our discourse and Sir George commands two of his men to accompany me on my journey home. The Captain and Sir George are pleased with my words, but I am unsettled by my artifice in embellishing the description of a new navigation instrument. I must set to work on this problem with renewed vigour.

As I retire, my thoughts turn to Helen. Sir George is forty years her senior and, although his wife may have been younger, it would be unusual to sire an only child at that stage in his life. Was his mention of Helen as a 'blessing' an indirect marker on the manner she came to be his daughter? Her features are much finer than her father's. Does she resemble her late mother, or…? No, I must banish more thoughts of Helen now, or I will not sleep.

Nine

I rise early and pass a dark morning in the drawing of schematics for the navigation aid. I come to realise that I have taken on a task that is more suited to one who works with hands rather than their mind. When a grey light comes I adjourn to the kitchen to prepare potions for Mother and John. Elspeth and her girl are surprised to see me at this hour and I am quick in my work as I seem to fluster their activities.

I find John in his room. He is in conversation with Mistress Hilliard, who reddens at my entry, bobs her head and takes her leave.

'Have I disturbed you, John?'

'No William, I have been at my studies for some time and would welcome a diversion.'

'I have brought your soother. Are you still troubled by congestion?'

'It is unwilling to depart this frail host, I fear. I find my condition improves with warmth and I am grateful for Mistress Hilliard for making this fire.'

'In that case I will bid her keep a lively glow in your room. Here…' I hand him the bowl. He sups quickly and is soon finished.

'Is the lady Amy, your mother, quite well this morning?' he enquires.

'I will visit her room when I leave you. If she is able to rise from her bed, then I will send word.'

We spend a while in idle talk, but he is guarded and I feel there is a questioning in him that he is unwilling to voice. Eventually, I relent and recount the tale of Askham's finding of Kelley and our examination at the Bear and Ragged Staff. He shows his disappointment at the outcome and asks if there will be further action in the search for the maker of the chart. I shrug and confess that I have no other trail to follow. I do not know why I am cautious with him. I have a mind to visit Doctor Dee's house and request an audience with his wife, but do not mention this. She may know more of Kelley's movements and activities. It is in the back of my thoughts that John will assess my honesty and vigour in pursuing the conspirators and report any failure to Walsingham.

Yesterday's hopes are confounded when I enter Mother's room. She is awake, but restless and in pain. She waves a listless hand at my offer of the potion, meaning she does not wish to drink. I lift her and insist that she should sip. I am forceful, but with more than half the potion remaining she tires and becomes limp. She dozes and I sit at her bedside for a while, pondering ways to relieve her discomfort. If Helen and Rosamund will not minister to her, then perhaps I should seek their advice on herbs for the relief of pain.

I make for the stables to find Gregory. It will be quicker and a smaller expense to ride west and use the ferry to Mortlake, rather than hire an upstream wherry. I wait as Gregory saddles Cassius and watching the lad, decide that I will ask him to accompany me. He is surprised and excited at my proposal and takes longer than he should to lead out and ready his cob.

It is a two-hour journey to the ferry and a chill headwind restricts any option for conversation as we keep our cowls down for protection. Doctor Dee's house is a short distance from the ferry crossing and the sight of his house brings back memories; some fond and others I would forget. The house is big, but has a ramshackle appearance, even more now than I recall from ten years past. The door opens and a young woman; dressed well, but with head uncovered, stands at the entrance. Is this Mistress Dee or one of her house servants?

'My name is William Constable, please forgive this unannounced call. I would talk with the lady of the house, Mistress Dee. I am an historic associate of her husband, the Doctor.'

She stares at me, as though deficient in her sight, then turns and disappears inside without word. The door remains open. I stand and wait. The same woman returns, but with her hair tucked inside a bonnet. She smooths her skirts with both hands and says, 'I am Jane Fromond, now Jane Dee.'

'My apologies, Mistress Dee, I should have known and I am

humbled by my mindless offence.' I doff my cap, bow and hope that my error has not meant a wasted journey.

'Your offence was slight, William Constable, and easily forgotten. Come inside to my fire. Your boy can take the horses around to the stable and thence to the kitchen for his refreshment.'

I follow to her parlour where she offers me a chair. There is an uncared-for and damp air to the house, which is not dispelled by the warmth of the fire. Mistress Dee is pale and has a matching unkept appearance, with a scuff of dirt on her cheek and a straggle of fair hair escaping her bonnet. She is not a beauty, but would be handsome enough in good health and presentation.

She says, 'Did you not receive my reply to your note?'

'I did, lady. I am thankful for your promptness and the helpful information you gave.'

'Kelley is not here.'

'I know, I have met with him thanks to your guidance on his lodging.' 'The Doctor, my husband, is in the Low Countries.'

'Yes, I had heard.'

'Then, why…'

'I have been charged by Secretary Walsingham to examine a matter of astrology. This does not concern your husband, but I believe that Master Kelley or one of his associates may be able to assist with my enquiries.' It is early to speak of Walsingham and I cannot escape the shame of using his name in a way that may cause fright in a lady without the comfort of a husband. 'Did Master Kelley leave your house when the Doctor departed for the Low Countries?'

'No, he was here for some weeks after my husband left.' She hesitates. 'It was intended that he should stay until he returns…' Something is to follow, but she clamps her mouth.

'Did Master Kelley change his plans?'

'No, he… he was the cause of some distraction.' I tilt my head in an attitude that encourages her to continue. 'He paid me unwanted attention. There… I have no love for Edward Kelley and… has he done some mischief?'

'It seems he has wronged you, lady, but I do not have

sufficient intelligence to give an opinion on other matters.' I shift my seat, unsure how I should progress my questioning. 'Were Kelley's attentions of an intimate nature?'

Her head is bowed, she plays with rings on her fingers, then brushes her skirts. 'He said that the angels had appeared to him. He… he had been instructed that he should lie with me to produce a child. He insisted that he had my husband's agreement, but I did not believe him.'

The poor woman, and Kelley – a hanging turd of a man. I am not surprised at his despicable actions or his duplicity in protesting a holy motive. But has Doctor Dee's mind become so enfeebled that he would assent to this arrangement? I cannot believe it.

'I applaud your actions in removing Kelley from your house. His behaviour was inexcusable and I trust the Doctor will deal with him on his return.' I pause. 'I am sorry Mistress Dee, but I must press you a little more. Did Kelley have any visitors after the Doctor departed?'

'Thank you, sir. I… I did not have the force or help here to remove him. He left of his own accord.' She brushes her skirts again and gazes past me, as if in thought. 'Yes, he had visitors before he left on two occasions to my knowledge.'

'Can you describe these visitors?'

'Two men arrived a few days after my husband was gone. I do not know their names. One man was tall and burly. I did not see his face. The other was smaller, shaven and had an injured leg. I am sorry, but I cannot tell more as I paid little attention.'

'Thank you, Mistress. Can you identify the particular leg that was injured, or any other features of the men?'

She shakes her head. 'Those two men came again on the second occasion with another. The third man is named Christopher Millen. I know him from earlier visits to my husband and the library.'

I know this man, Millen, although we have met only a handful of times and we have not conversed beyond opening pleasantries. I have heard that he is from a wealthy family in the shire of York, is ambitious and has obtained patronage from influential clients for his consultations on astrology.

'Did you, by chance, hear words from their conversation?'

She shakes her head again, then frowns as if to concentrate her mind. 'There… there was some excitement at the second meeting, and… mention of Paris, I think. Yes, Master Millen was destined for France, I believe, but….' She spreads her hands. 'I was present only for fleeting moments and I can recall no more.' She screws her eyes, fixes me, and then bows her head. 'I trust that you will not report any error on my part, or that of my husband, to Sir Francis.'

'You have been most helpful. If our meeting is reported to Mister Secretary, you can be assured that your candour and assistance will receive favourable mention.'

My questioning is done. She offers drink and food, which I accept out of politeness. I take my leave with a feeling of guilt that I have left Jane Dee in a poor state, but with a thought that I will try to mend this in the coming weeks.

Have I learned anything of value? The meetings with Kelley may have been innocent, but the reference to Paris warrants further investigation. There will be many hundreds of men with a damaged leg in this corner of England. I must not let my encounter with Darby Wensum cloud my judgement, but it is a finding that I will store carefully in my memory.

Ten

I am called to Whitehall again. This time the summons comes from Francis Mylles, Walsingham's man who, I was alerted, may wish to confer with me while Mister Secretary is in France. Captain Askham is not my escort and two men I do not know wait for me at the front of my house. I speculate on the purpose of this conference. Has Askham relayed details of our interrogation of Kelley? I hope not as I am not ready to disclose my later enquiries with Jane Dee at Mortlake. I have a sense that there is a delicate balance in the circumstances around Kelley and fierce questioning of those associated may tip the evidence into a dark and hidden place. Also, I would not have Jane Dee hurt or upset by others, however well-intentioned and gentle.

I am taken to Mylles' room. It is a large space with a welcoming fire and with several tables placed around the perimeter. A man stands bent over one of the tables with quill in hand, dabbing and scratching at the paper in front of him. He turns and surveys me from head to foot, before placing his quill on the table with some delicacy. He bows his head briefly, opens his hands and walks towards me.

'William Constable, a warm welcome to you on this grey morning.' He is a man of medium height, with dark hair and small beard. His dress is modest and black, save for a pair of soft, blue slippers.

'It is a pleasure to meet with you, Master Mylles. I thank you for your greeting and a warming fire.'

He claps his hands on my shoulders and begs me to take a chair with him. The door closes and we are cast alone in the centre of the room surrounded by tables laid with papers and the walls hung with maps, sketches and arrays of symbols.

He says, 'I had heard of your scholarship, but was not prepared for your triumphant and timely unfastening of the Brouillard cipher. That was a splendid accomplishment.'

I am unprepared for his hearty and extravagant praise and merely mumble a weak, 'Thank you,' in reply. A man appears with a tray and two cups. It is the same man who provided refreshment at my meeting with Walsingham. Mylles hands me a cup and takes one himself. I watch, fascinated as the server makes a noiseless exit, seeming to float over the floor.

'A fortified wine of the best quality from Portugal,' says Mylles as he raises his cup. 'It is my habit to take this wine thrice before noon. It warms the body and alerts the mind on deep winter days.'

It is good. I murmur my appreciation and take another sip. He sits back and waves his hand with an expansive gesture at his place of business.

'You will have conjectured on this arrangement, no doubt. It is the core of our intelligence network for guardianship of the state and Her Majesty. We continue to develop and refine our work on ciphers and we have not yet encountered an inscrutable mystery. The one in Brouillard's box was an unknown variation on the Atbash cipher, but comfortably within our compass to solve, given time and reason. Nevertheless, for an untrained mind, your efforts were remarkable and saved valuable days.'

Does he wish me to tackle another coded message? This question must display on my face, as he is quick to dismiss my involvement in further cipher work.

He says, 'Sir Francis had a notion that could benefit our discoveries and your purse.' He pauses to add suspense and weight to the words which will come. I am both apprehensive and intrigued. He continues, 'A position has been found for you here. You know of Doctor Robert Huicke?'

'Of course, he is Chief Physician to Her Majesty. Is he well?' I am concerned where this may lead and shift uneasily in my chair.

'He is well, by all accounts, but he is… old. His attention has a tendency to wander and his ministrations have lately been the cause of some disquiet, especially among the ladies of the court.'

'I would not wish…'

'Doctor Huicke is well-liked by Her Majesty and retains his position. However, one of his associates, Doctor Thomas Lyle, has suffered the loss of his father and has left this place for some weeks in order to settle his affairs. Huicke is slow in his work and the attendance of Lyle will be missed.'

'You wish me to…'

'Just so… You would offer welcome assistance to Huicke. A handsome and sturdy young physician would be an attraction to the ladies here in particular. Ladies will gossip and chatter loosely about all manner of topics and you would be in a favourable position to overhear and probe the significance of their words.'

I stumble in my response, despite taking care over a choice of words. 'I… I fear my nature is not suited… and I have only two years behind me as a member of the Physicians' College.'

'Come now, William, you are too modest. Sir Francis has a high opinion of your intellect and your practical disposition. Fresh membership of the college weighs little set against a recommendation from Mister Secretary. There is no peril in this assignment and I cannot believe that the company of fine ladies will bring you discomfort. The appointment has no permanence, but you may find that connections made here may bring you future advantage.'

I see there is no profit in further excuses and I accept his proposal with feigned eagerness. I am requested to pay particular regard for any mention of the Queen's birth, her succession, a bastard child, the Duke of Guise, ciphers, the Hebrew language, a mysterious box and astrology. I am to report any suspicion immediately and to confer with Mylles every fifth day.

*

I am taken to the chambers of Sir John Forester, who has care of the small comforts for Her Majesty's courtiers and attendants. He is a petite, pink-faced, alert man with colourful dress and a ruff that hides much of his chin. He is about my age and friendly enough, but warns me that he will not accept any tomfoolery with 'his' ladies. I have my own, modest chamber and access to the anterooms to Her Majesty's apartments, called the great court, where courtiers and petitioners gather. Doctor Huicke is not present today and I have the names of two ladies from the Privy Chamber who wish to consult a physician.

Apparently I must mingle in the anterooms and seek them out discreetly and make myself known, as it is not the practice for patients to attend my room at an appointed time.

A page guides me through a maze of corridors to the heart of the palace and the royal chambers. He stops at three doorways and announces my name to guards before we are allowed to pass. My spirits fall as I enter a large room which is full of colour and the busy hum of voices. There are over one hundred nobles, ladies and gentlefolk standing in small groups, sitting on window seats and strolling with casual air through the colourful hubbub. I am fronted by enquiring faces, the sound of male laughter and skittish female giggles. I feel drab, rumpled and exposed in my unprepared state, standing alone like a lost child. A man raises his head and peers at me over his nose, while his two female companions follow his examination with expressions of mild curiosity. I offer them a short bow and stride to the far side of the room. I have no purpose in my walk and am further dismayed to find an open door leading to another chamber similarly occupied. My rising panic is interrupted by a voice to my left.

'William. William Constable.'

A face I recognise, although with a loss of hair, since our time together at Cambridge. 'Richard Joynes, well met indeed. It is a delight to find a friend from my youth in this confusion. I trust that you are in good health and that fortune has been kind to you and your family in our divided years?'

'We fare well enough, William. And you? I had heard of your time with Doctor Dee, but your name has been quiet in recent years.'

'I have put aside my mathematics and astrology in favour of physik these few years past. It is my reason to be here, although will admit that I question my choice in these first few moments. How come you here? I had thought you returned to your lands in Norfolk.'

'I have been here since the early spring months. My father sent me to petition in a dispute over boundaries and access to the sea. It was a long and unsuccessful postponement. I met with Sir Thomas Heneage this summer, he took a liking to me and sought permission for me to assist in his duties as Treasurer of the Privy Chamber.' He pauses, scans the faces nearby and confides in a low voice, 'It is not an onerous duty and, in truth, it is a dreary business accounting for each oyster, measure of cloth and glass of iron gall ink.'

'Then why do you remain here?'

'Father wishes me to gain a preferment in the trading of wool. I believe it is unlikely, but will show my face a little longer. Heneage has influence and I must not disappoint him.' He pauses and tilts his head in a questioning pose. 'You say you are here as a physician. What of Huicke?'

'I understand that Huicke retains his position, but is absent today. I stand for Doctor Lyle who has returned home to tidy his family affairs. I am to seek out two ladies who desire my attention: Lady Katherine Brydges; and gentlewoman Mary Reed. I am lost in a sea of unknown faces and know not where to start. I would be obliged if you could introduce me or direct me to their location.'

He claps me on the shoulder and confirms that he knows both ladies in question. Lady Katherine is a comely, young chamberer. Mary Reed is the Queen's Keeper of Linens and a gentlewoman of middle years with a reputation for fixed views and stern disposition. He warns that I should not cross her. He leads me through to another room and raises himself in a search for his targets. He directs my view to a group of three ladies in a corner and identifies one as Mary Reed. We return to the first chamber, to a large group gathered attentively around a finely dressed man who is relating a tale with expressive arm gestures. Richard informs that the man is the Earl of Oxford and he points to a young lady on his perimeter as my other intended. Before I can stop him he approaches the lady and touches her sleeve.

'My Lady Katherine, may I introduce a friend of mine, Doctor William Constable.'

She acknowledges Richard, then turns to me. 'Doctor Constable, I was informed that you would attend for Doctor Huicke and you do not disappoint. You are as handsome as in the telling.' A mischievous smile lights her pale features. She is young; perhaps only fifteen years, and her head barely reaches my breastbone.

I remove my cap and bow. I note that the Earl has stopped talking and looks at me with an air of disapproval as though disliking this interruption.

'Lady Katherine, I am at your disposal whenever you wish to begin our consultation.'

'Then, let it be now.' She offers me her hand, which I place on my arm and we depart for my chamber after bidding thanks to Richard and promising that we will meet again in short time.

She is a dainty thing and appears doll-like when sat in the large patient chair capable of accommodating arses four or five times her span. Her feet do not touch the floor.

'Are you well, lady?' She has volunteered no ailment and there is no visible fault except for the pallor of her skin.

'I am well, thank you. I require bleeding, is all.'

'Bleeding, lady – why?'

'Her Majesty does not allow the use of white lead paste in her ladies under eighteen years. Without regular bleeding, my complexion would be as a peasant girl and the other ladies would have a merry time at my expense.' Her bottom lip bulges and quivers at the thought of this teasing. 'Doctors Huicke and Lyle bleed me thrice each week.'

'Lady, there is no need for bleeding. You are quite white.'

'I am? But will…'

'It would be unwise to take more blood at this time. The humors should be balanced and in one of tender years, the loss of too much blood can lead to an excess of black bile and melancholy. Your paleness is most becoming and from my observation you are as white as the other ladies in your circle.'

Her expression shows that she is not fully convinced.

I say, 'An examination of your stars may allow a better understanding of your wellbeing. Have the doctors prepared an astrological chart for you?'

Her curiosity is pricked. 'No, and how would that…'

'It would reveal an understanding of your nature and the treatments most suitable for temperament, health and beauty.'

There is a light of interest in her eyes, but then she frowns. 'Will the stars reveal the secrets of my future happiness, or hurtful things to come?'

'No, they will not be used in that regard.'

'I am told that some astrologers may have a wicked purpose and I should beware of their promises.'

'Told, by whom?'

'Other ladies.' She waves her hand as if to dismiss the subject.

I disappoint her. She brightens a little when I recommend an infusion of white rose petals to soften her skin and maintain its paleness. Our conversation is done and our return to the royal apartments is more subdued than our outward passage.

My second consultation is a sharp contrast with my first. Mary Reed is a formidable woman with turned-down mouth and the build of a foot soldier. She complains of head pains and bright lights which disturb her vision. I also note that she has many black teeth and her right cheek is swollen. There is an unpleasant smell and signs of decomposition in her mouth.

'I will not let your blood today, lady. You must have the teeth on your lower right side removed tomorrow and that will release sufficient blood. That will also help with your head pains. You must take two days bed rest in a darkened room. I will prepare some oil of cloves to rub on your gums and a potion of lemon balm to assist with your rest.'

She leaves me with contrary assertions of dread at the prospect of the extractions and relief that her suffering may be at an end. I suspect that she has endured for too long until the point where agonies overcame her fear of the cure.

I pass the remaining hours of daylight with Richard who introduces me to his friends and acquaintances at court. Our time together is pleasant enough, save for another face of disdain and disapproval cast my way by Oxford as we pass his group. I keep my head down and hear laughter behind me as we step by. Was that at my expense? I am glad when the afternoon sky greys, I can excuse myself from idle talk and return to West Cheap.

*

I am conscious of neglect of my home patients and make straight for Mother's chamber where I find Rose at her bedside applying a cloth to her brow. I bid Rose follow me to the door and ask how she fares in low voice.

'She cannot shit, sir. I fear there is a monstrous blockage in her belly. She has not shat for several days.'

I look over at Mother and see she struggles with her pains. I had thought that the trouble with her bowels had eased with my treatment of rhubarb root and ginger. Her stools were hard and passed with difficulty, but there was movement, although some days past.

'Have you saved her piss for me, Rose?'

'Yes sir, the pot is by the bed.'

'Thank you, Rose. Please ask Mistress Hilliard to prepare an infusion of chamomile and lemon balm. I will tend to my mother.'

The colour and smell of the piss show no fault. I dampen the cloth and press it lightly on her forehead. She opens her eyes and fixes me with a weak smile that speaks of misery and hopelessness. It is hard to bear and I curse my impotence as her physician. I remain at her bedside for two hours, talking everyday nonsense and soothing her brow. Eventually, the brew from Mistress Hilliard calms her and she sleeps.

I join John for supper, but have no appetite for it. John, to my surprise, eats heartily of a chicken and boiled beef. He confirms that he is improved and his fits of expectoration are less. He is grateful for the soothers prepared by Mistress Hilliard. In reply to my question he says that he has taken this four times today and I wonder if he has acquired a taste for this mixture or the company of its preparer. He has been at his studies and confesses that he is pleased at progress made. He does not enquire directly on my activities, so I relate the news of my summons by Mylles, my consultations and mingling with courtiers.

I say, 'My purpose is to sift court gossip and to identify any loose mention that may have a connection with the conspiracy, but I do not hold great hope that my presence there will bear fruit.'

'It is a keen scheme by Walsingham and Mylles, as a new physician in that place will not be suspected of having a purpose other than cures and self-advancement.'

'You may be correct, but I find myself ill at ease in the company. There are so many faces there; perhaps five hundred or more. I am overwhelmed by numbers and uninspired by the conversation.'

'I sympathise, William. The preening and gaggle there is not to my liking, but you must bear it for a short time. Did you meet any notables today?'

'I am thankful that I encountered an old friend who was able to supply names and offer introductions. He is Sir Thomas Heneage's man and of relatively low standing.' I pause and recollect a particular discomfort. 'I saw, but did not converse with, the Earl of Oxford. I regret that he did not seem to hold me in his favour.'

John emits a low growl. 'Oxford. He is a young man of pretty words and questionable morals, who I have long suspected holds Rome in high regard. Unfortunately, Her Majesty is partial to his charms. You must take care with him, William. He is dangerous and unpredictable.'

It is odd to think of John at court. His demeanour is so far removed from the general triviality of the place that I forget he is known and has a considerable reputation, even amongst the highest in the land. I will heed his advice. There is a knock at the door and Mistress Hilliard enters. She hands me a note.

'I am sorry, Master William, I had forgotten that a note was received while you were away from your house today.'

The note is from Helen Morton. She will call at this house with Rosamund tomorrow noon.

Eleven

I rise before dawn and journey to Whitehall, hoping that the great court will be less populated in the early hours of light. Forester is at his table and I hand over the medicines with written instructions for delivery to the hands of yesterday's patients. I tell him that I have other work today and will depart shortly unless there is a particular requirement for my attention. He answers that there is a person who wishes to see me and that I should wait for their conference. He offers no name and sends notice of my arrival.

I find no trace of Richard Joynes in the apartments and return to the physicians' rooms to wait for my visitor. An hour passes and three ladies appear at my door. Two withdraw and a plump woman of middle years steps forward.

'Doctor Constable, I am Blanche Parry.' I know the name by repute, as a favourite and close companion of the Queen. There is a directness and sureness in her manner.

I bow and offer her a chair. I am about to ask the purpose of her visit when she speaks.

'I am not here to seek your services as a physician, Doctor. I am quite well.'

'Indeed, lady, your good health is plain to see and I am honoured that you have taken the trouble to seek out a newcomer to this place.'

'Do not waste your flattery on me, Doctor Constable, I am not here to gaze upon your handsome face, or exchange pleasantries.'

I take a breath, bob my head in understanding and wait for what is to follow.

'You conferred with Katherine Brydges yesterday. I heard that you declined to let her blood.'

'Yes, lady, I considered that to do so would be harmful and instead suggested a kind salve she may apply to soften her skin.'

She waves a hand and continues, 'That is of no consequence. I am most concerned that there was mention of astrology, in which discipline I understand you are a practitioner of note.'

'Yes, lady, there was, but…'

'There will be no more talk of stars and the coming fortunes of ladies at this court, Doctor Constable. Such matters will excite those of a feverish temperament, touch dangerously close to false magic and they recall the ungodly practices of Catholicism.'

'I agree with much of your sentiment, lady. My purpose in astrology is simply to aid a person's wellbeing by a better understanding of their natural state and inclinations. I had a similar conversation in recent days with my companion. Do you know Doctor Foxe?'

Her manner transforms instantly. 'Doctor John Foxe of the *Book of Martyrs*?'

'Yes, lady, he is a friend and guest at my house in West Cheap. We have worked together these past few days and have conversed on many topics.'

She nods her head slowly as if coming to an enlightenment. 'There is more to you than I had understood, William Constable.'

'May I ask you a question, lady?' I pause briefly so that she shows her consent. 'Has there been any cause for you to suspect the misuse of astrology at this place in recent months, and before my appearance yesterday?' I am too open in my question, but decide that I may as well be even more direct. 'In particular, have you knowledge of loose talk concerning a star chart for a bastard heir?'

Her expression shows shock for a moment, but then a grasp of what may lie behind my question. 'There have been many vile and dishonest assertions of this nature from a time before Her Majesty's succession, but none to my knowledge were connected with astrology.' She hesitates. 'There was… a chamber lady confided that she overheard two gentlemen speak of a clandestine royal birth. It was spoken in jest and I have long since ceased to pay regard to this tattle if it is contained and does not reach Her Majesty's ears.'

'May I know the names of these gentlemen?'

'Both are young and recently adopted to this court. I am sure it was no more than a matter of naivety and foolishness. One was Sir Peter Capton and the other, Arthur Perse.'

*

I hasten back to my house to be sure I am ready to welcome Helen and Rosamund. I have two names from Blanche Parry, with her caution that they are fresh faces at court. It is unlikely that they are at the core of the plot, but I suppose I must report them to Mylles if no redeeming evidence comes to light. Then, there is Jane Dee's mention of Christopher Millen. It is troubling that these names are mere hints with no fixed connection to the conspiracy, but it must be the lot of an intelligencer to examine many false diversions before chancing upon an instance that has some veracity.

I wait impatiently in my study unable to concentrate on the navigational aid. I must clear my mind and reserve time to work on this problem, or I will displease Morton and Hawkins. Shortly after the sounding of midday bells, I hear movement at the front of the house. Helen has arrived on a grey palfrey with Rosamund and two men in attendance. I take the ladies through to our receiving chamber and beg Mistress Hilliard to ask John to join with us at our dining table in a half hour.

'Ladies, welcome to my house and my deepest thanks for attending on a cold day.'

Helen bobs her head in acknowledgement. 'Thank you, William Constable, for your invitation, which allows us to escape our familiar surroundings, explore this town and learn from your practices as a physician.'

'I trust that your father was content for you to journey to this place?'

'He was most insistent that I do so. He enjoyed your company at his table and was disturbed to hear of your mother's ailment.'

Rosamund touches Helen's sleeve and says in a voice that is barely above a whisper, 'We should see our subjects before I tire.'

Helen explains that it is Rosamund's habit to rest in the middle of the day and the short ride has drained her strength. She asks if we could shorten our pleasantries here and begin their examinations. Mother is alone in her room, asleep and with an unopened book on her covers. There is a grimace on her face as I touch her arm and murmur words to wake her gently. Her eyes open and a smile at my presence turns to surprise when she sees my two companions. I am perhaps too full in my account of the ladies attendance at her bedside, as she shows signs of impatience and waves me aside. I step to the back of the room and watch as Helen and Rosamund talk in low voices to my mother. Their conversation continues and I leave quietly to check on the preparations for our dinner. John is seated at the table with cup in hand.

'I hear we have guests, William.'

'I am pleased you are in good spirits and have some colour in your cheeks, John. We have a visit from two ladies who are skilful in the application of herbal cures. It is my hope that they may be able to suggest improvements in the potions for you and my mother.'

'Unaccompanied ladies?'

'They have an escort of two men and they are from a family that is known to mine.'

'I will be loath to surrender my present soother for another, but I hope that they may provide some relief for the lady Amy.'

Almost one hour passes before Helen and Rosamund join us for an adjournment of boiled fowl, smoked trout and pickles with sweet wine. John bows deeply in his greeting and I sense a stiffness in Helen when she learns of his name. She casts a questioning stare in my direction as she takes her seat. I introduce the symptoms of John's congestion and he continues with a fuller description. There is some discussion of the mixture I have prepared and a general agreement that it should offer effective release of phlegm from the lungs. John is pleased at this consensus and claims that the remedy has already improved him markedly.

When we have eaten our fill, I ask John if he would like to accompany us to my room of medicines. He demurs and says he will rest before further study. The chamber is small and compares badly with the drying room at the Morton's.

Helen says, 'As to your mother, we are of one mind; her trouble is a blockage in the belly, which may harden her stools and hinder their passing.'

'You are direct in your assessment. I had thought the same, but her discomfort began more than thirty days past and she has had some relief, although the stools were compacted. Do you discount a malign growth in her middle?'

'The possibility should not be ignored, but we would suggest a curative for a more compliant blockage before further causes are considered. Your mother has not passed stools for seven days and that is too long a delay.'

She has a confidence and frankness that is both appealing and bothersome. My talent as a physician is questioned by a young woman, but I must remember that I have other reasons not to dismiss her advice. Besides, am I too proud to admit she may be correct? The health of my mother is at stake and I should be grateful for another opinion, no matter the source.

I say, 'I have treated her with rhubarb root and ginger, would that not provide relief?'

'In mild cases it may be sufficient. Rosamund is of the opinion that your mother requires a more robust remedy. There is better solution, but we must retrieve this from our drying room. We have a consignment of dried plums from France, which Rosamund swears will offer the quickest relief. A dozen of these should be taken each day, with two pints of small beer.'

I note that Rosamund has fallen asleep in her chair. Her head is slumped at an awkward angle. I suggest we move her to an easier position, but Helen says she often dozes in this fashion. I have not heard of dried plums as the essence of a curative for blockages, but I thank her and make an arrangement to call for them the next day. I have no great hope for Rosamund's advice, but calculate that they could do little harm, and I will continue with the rhubarb and ginger as a companion treatment. I ask Helen if she would like to examine the books on herbs and medicines in my library. She glances at the sleeping figure and hesitates before murmuring her assent.

I leave the door to my library chamber open to avoid any claim of impropriety. She gazes around the tables and shelving, then picks idly at the books and papers as she wanders.

'You are a strange man, William Constable. I would not have

expected a friendship with Doctor Foxe, who is noted for his fierce views on religion.'

'Nor I, lady, but as you will have noted, he is not forceful in his opinions and has a quick mind on more mundane subjects.'

She agrees that he was pleasant company at the table and appears to have a kindly nature. She holds the corner of a chart and wrinkles her nose. 'Do you find these star charts are helpful with your treatments?'

'They are in many cases, but I do not hold fast to the belief that astrological charts show the entire truth about the nature and inclinations of a person. I have a fascination with the skies and study them so that we may also know our place on this earth.'

She says, 'Have you cast a chart for Doctor Foxe?'

'No, that would stray too far from his puritanical beliefs, although he does not dismiss their use out of hand.' I pause then add, 'Would you like me to draw a chart for you? It would be harmless and you could regard it as an entertainment.'

She widens her eyes, then purses her lips. She turns her back on me and walks to the far corners of the chamber, feigning interest in the books and charts. When her thinking is finished she faces me and clasps her hands in front of her skirts.

'I will ask my father. It would be improper to do this work without his blessing.'

'Of course, my lady. I will seek permission from your father when I call at your house for the dried plums.' It seems that her high spirits and directness are joined with practical sense in knowing the bounds in behaviour that should be observed. 'May I know your date and place of birth so that I may prepare an outline of the work?'

Her nose wrinkles again. It could be a sign that she disapproves or that she is considering my request. Whichever, I begin to find this mannerism… appealing.

She says. 'I suppose it would not hurt. It was the seventh day of August in the sixtieth year. The place was Maldon in Essex. I am told that my mother retreated from the plague in the city for her confinement.'

There is a lurch in my middle and my skin prickles. I hope

that this does not signify a reddening in my face. The date matches the one on the captured natal chart, but this cannot be… She talks of her mother's confinement. My intention was to dismiss a small, nagging thought and now I am faced with magnified complexity. Is it coincidence, or could Helen be the 'unknowing maid'?

'Is something amiss, William?'

'No… no, lady.' I stammer and must guard against unnatural behaviour. She has called me by my given name and I wonder if this is a sign of growing trust. 'May I call you Helen in return?' She bobs her head and smiles her agreement. I continue, 'I was contemplating the remedy of dried plums. I have not read of such a cure for blocked innards.'

'It is in no book or paper that I have read. Rosamund had it from a goodwife in Finsbury Fields and it has been tried with some success.' She pauses and eyes me with curiosity. 'You have an open mind, William, and it does you credit. I was anticipating that you would deny an unusual remedy not known to you because of your superior standing as a physician.'

My surprise at the revelation of Helen's birth date is soon forgotten as we exchange stories of our younger days, our education and the loss of a parent. Our discussions flow freely and it is plain that we both find enjoyment in each other's company. She was close to her mother and loved her well, but she was sickly for as long as Helen could remember and often confined to her bed. I sympathise and probe a little until I learn that her mother was two years younger than her father. She would have been aged thirty-eight years at the time of Helen's birth, and while this is not past child-bearing, it would be a rare age for a first child. My conversation with Helen is overlong and Mistress Hilliard comes with a message from her escort to say that she must leave before the light fades. I am resigned to conducting further examinations of Helen's history and a sense of guilt at my subterfuge is mixed with pleasure at the thought of more time in her company.

*

Daylight is almost done as I make to the Bear and Ragged Staff to pass a note to the man named Hincham for another meeting with Captain Askham. I will relate the intelligence from my visit to Mortlake to him and request that he finds Edward Kelley and Christopher Millen for further examination.

Twelve

I am woken in the early hours by heavy rain and it is dark when I tread wearily to my study to work on the sketches of the measuring instrument. I am soon engrossed in the task and believe that I may have a solution which could be manufactured, although by hands that are less clumsy than my own. Mistress Hilliard calls and asks if I will breakfast with Doctor Foxe, who waits in our parlour.

I find John in good spirits. He offers me God's blessing on this morning and announces that he has completed a piece of writing to his satisfaction. It is a critique of Calvin's work; he will make a fair copy and ask Mister Secretary's office to deliver it to one William Wittingham, a correspondent with John and former associate of Calvin. He relishes his response. I congratulate him and before I can ask more, his manner changes to a more serious aspect.

He says, 'Come now, William, let us review progress on our main focus at this time; the popish conspiracy.'

I am taken aback by his sudden change from a man at ease with his studies to alert attention on political intrigue. I am reminded that I should not forget the underlying steel of religious certainty in this man. I had hoped to delay news of my visit to Mortlake, but I must tell Askham, and so there is little reason to withhold from John. He knows of Kelley's first questioning and I recount the circumstances of my visit to Jane Dee and her mention of Kelley's visitors. He expresses his agreement that Kelley and Millen should be questioned further and requests that he attend the interrogation. I can find no reason to object.

'What of your visits to Whitehall, William? Have you learned anything of note?'

'It is early in my employment there and you know that I am not easy in the company of idle talk.' His gaze is unsettling. He expects more. 'I met briefly with Mistress Blanche Parry. She reported that a lady of the chamber had overheard two gentlemen referring to a royal bastard. She cautioned that this was almost certainly an unguarded and frivolous remark by two young men who were new at court.'

'Mistress Parry is a formidable lady with sound opinions. You were fortunate to receive her attention.' He pauses and leans forward with keen interest. 'Their names?'

I disclose the names, saying that I plan to report them to Mylles at our next meeting. He shakes his head slowly and admits that he does not know them or their families. He settles back in his chair and picks at a piece of chicken. There is quiet between us as we eat and drink for a while.

He says, 'It was a pleasing diversion to meet with the lady Helen and Mistress Rosamund yesterday. Were they able to offer any assistance on the treatment of your mother?'

'Yes, they suggested an unusual remedy, which I will apply later this day. I confess that my mother's condition is worrisome and I will gladly accept opinions of others with skill and experience.'

'I will continue to pray that your mother's health improves. You say that the lady Helen's family is known to yours. Was there another purpose in their visit?'

Why does he ask? Does he read my thoughts, or am I watched? Perhaps he interprets Helen's visit as an affair of the heart. That would be excusable and... No, I will tell of my interest in the navigation of ships and Morton's role in their great adventure. That is more convincing.

'I have long since held an interest in mathematics of navigation by the stars. I had heard that Helen's father and Captain General Hawkins are leading an ambitious adventure to the New Lands. They have a curiosity in my scheme for improved navigation of their ships and I learned of Rosamund and Helen's expertise with herbal cures by good chance on my visit.'

He appears content with my explanation and enthuses about the discoveries of the New Lands, saying that he would gladly be party to such an adventure if he was a younger man.

*

I had thought to call on Mother before a journey to

Leadenhall, but my mood is uneven and decide to defer until later when I hope my disposition will improve. I carry my new sketches of the measuring instrument with me to show Sir George, although I realise that it will be for Captain Hawkins to pronounce on its viability. The door is answered by a young maid who scurries inside at mention of my name and is soon replaced by a manservant. He makes an arrangement for the stabling of Cassius, begs me to step inside and takes my cloak. I wait in the hall by the grand stairway until another man appears and ushers me through to a receiving chamber. A man waits for me in the centre with hands clasped behind his back. It is Darby Wensum.

He says, 'Sir George is away from this house, Doctor Constable. May I know the nature of your business?'

'Good day, Master Wensum. I trust that my call here finds you well.'

'Yes… yes, thank you. As I say, Sir George…'

'No matter, I have brought some sketches on the possibility of finding Sir George here, but the main purpose of my visit is to collect an item of medicine from the lady Helen.'

He narrows his eyes and folds his arms across his chest. 'You must know that I cannot allow you to call on the lady when Sir George is absent.'

'I am not here to converse with the lady in question, Master Wensum, but to collect a remedy for my mother as arranged during the lady's visit to my house with Mistress Rosamund.'

I see that yesterday's visit is news to him. He beckons the manservant who remains at the door, takes him aside and talks in low voice, presumably to fetch the dried plums. He shuffles over to a table, seats himself on a chair and gestures to a nearby stool.

'Doctor Constable, I am sorry if I have offended in some way. It is in my nature to guard against unwarranted intrusions on this family and perhaps I may have been overzealous in my dealings with you to this point.'

I bow my head in acknowledgement, but will not take this olive branch easily and without more evidence of its sincerity. We wait in silence for a few moments, then he continues.

'I heard from Sir George of the possibilities for the better positioning and rendezvous of our ships by your invention. I am closely involved with the planning of this venture and would be most appreciative to be given sight of your sketches.'

It would be churlish to deny this request, and so I delve into my bags, retrieve one of the sketches and place it on the table smoothing out the roll of the paper. He stands and peers closely at the drawing.

'Are you familiar with the crosshatch measuring instrument used onboard our ships at present, Master Wensum?'

He studies the sketch a little longer then raises his head. 'I have only a cursory knowledge. My work is primarily in the accounting and management of ships' cargoes before departure and upon arrival. The good handling on the voyage I leave to our ships masters.'

I suspected as much, and he does not ask me to elaborate on the significance of the drawings or the meaning of my annotations. He regains his seat as a man appears at the door carrying two weighty leather bags and announces, 'Plums… if it please, gentlemen,' seemingly mystified by the nature of the consignment. The bags are heavy, but conveniently attached by a rope so that I may sling them over my saddle. I thank both men, take my sketch and request that the bags are carried to my horse. Wensum follows to the front door without further comment on the sketch or the plums. I sense that he would ask more, but does not know how to phrase his question.

The door is open, but before departing, I ask, 'Do you know a man named Christopher Millen?'

I see the surprise in his eyes and he blusters, 'I… I have heard the name. Is your question in relation to trade, or… Astrology? I understand he charts the stars. Do you…'

'Thank you, I simply wished to confer with him about my almanac of the heavenly bodies. I understand that he has some expertise in this matter.'

'No, I am sorry, I cannot help with his location. It was a name… a name I heard some long time past, but we have never met.'

*

The clouds have thinned on my journey home and I arrive in bright sun with the wet streets and houses sparkling their welcome of this change. It is a pretty sight, but the holding mud cakes my boots, cloak and nether hose. I drop the bags in the study, then retire to my chamber to tidy my appearance. Rose knocks at my door and says that Mother has asked that I call on her when I return. I should have visited her chamber before Leadenhall; she will think I have no thought for her distress. I ask Rose to take two pints of small beer to Mother's chamber and tell her I will be there in short time. I return to the study, quickly delve into a leather bag and load a sticky mess of dried plums into a bowl.

Mother is raised in her bed, her complexion is grey and there is gaunt look to her features emphasised by a downturn at the corners of her mouth. She asks where I have been and I tell her that I have travelled to fetch the remedy advised by Rosamund and Helen.

'Plums,' she says, 'It will be a wonder if they hold the key to a recovery.' She closes her eyes and breathes deeply. 'Nevertheless, I enjoyed our conversations and was touched by their concern.'

I pick a dried plum between my thumb and finger. It is wrinkled and has the appearance of a small turd. It smells sweet and I lick my finger to confirm this transfers to the taste. I hesitate then place it in my mouth and chew slowly. The flavour is agreeable.

'Mother, these plums are surprisingly sweet and the taste far surpasses their look. You must take twelve of these each day followed by the small beer. Take care with the stones and spit them back into the bowl.'

She shakes her head, signalling that my attentions are tiresome, but eventually she submits and eats all the plums. I wait patiently as she sips her beer. When she is finished she slumps back on her cushion, drained by the effort.

She says, 'She is pretty – very pretty, with a free spirit and good mind.'

How should I answer? Mother is sparing in her compliments to young women and I know she would see me wed. But Helen

– I must not think of her in this way while there is a small chance that she has royal blood.

'I fear that Rosamund is too old to engage my interest, Mother.'

'Ha, your jest signifies that you avoid mention of Helen because there is an attraction.' I do not respond. 'I trust that you have put aside any thoughts of further enquiries into the Morton family's involvement in Walsingham's plot?'

'Yes, Mother, although I have discovered that I may be able to assist Sir George Morton with his next grand trading venture through my work on mathematics.'

She turns to me with an expression of surprise. 'Good, I am pleased that you return to your work on mathematics and navigation. It is a worthwhile enterprise, and if your efforts find favour with Sir George it may progress your suit for the lady Helen.'

'Mother, you are too quick with your imagining. I have known Helen for only a handful of days.'

'William, you will soon pass into middle years. You have lived for near thirty years and it is time for you to wed and progress your father's name.'

I cannot hide my awkwardness from her and consider making an excuse to depart her bedside. That would be a weak response and besides, I have another question.

'Did you know Helen's mother?'

'We were acquainted, but I did not see her often. She was a frail woman and often confined to her bed. I understand she was taken by the sweating sickness.' She pauses and furrows her brow. 'I remember she was comforted by her young niece who was under their guardianship. I forget her name, but she was a handsome young woman who liked to dress in the latest Italian fashion. There was… a scandal I think and she left them. I do not know what became of her.'

'Oh, and what year did she depart?'

'I cannot recall, too many years have passed. No more questions, William. Please ask Rose to attend. I tire and must rest.'

I retire to my study, but I am unable to dismiss thoughts of

Helen and my work is unproductive. I wonder if the mention of a niece is significant and how could I enquire into her circumstances without arousing suspicion. It is time to dine and I will seek John's company after I remove these bags of plums to my room of medicines.

I am about to heft the bags when I notice a paper lying in the top. I pick it out, wipe away the fruit stains and unfold it. It is a note from Helen.

Dear William

I have thought more on your offer to chart my stars. You say it would be harmless entertainment and I do not doubt your intentions. Still, I have decided to decline your offer and ask that you make no mention of this to my father.

Yours humbly

Helen

Thirteen

Captain Askham arrives alone as we are breakfasting. I ask him to join with John and me at our table and, after a small pause, he accepts with thanks. He has the look of a man with little rest and a large appetite.

'John, you know Captain Askham from our time at Barn Elms.'

'Indeed, God's blessing on you Captain, your call is well-timed.'

I wait until Askham has filled himself with a good quantity of eggs, manchet and pickles before recounting my visit to Jane Dee at Mortlake. He nods his approval and says, 'It was prudent of you to follow our questioning of Kelley with this visit, Doctor Constable, and the sign of a man with a strong attachment to our cause.'

Was my loyalty ever in doubt? I leave this thought unsaid and reply, 'Thank you, Captain. Do you think this warrants further investigation of Kelley and an examination of Millen?'

He replaces a portion of eggs and strokes his chin. 'In other circumstances, there would be no fault or suspicion in those meetings, but the mention of Paris and the demeanour of Kelley at our first meeting is perhaps...' He turns to John. 'What is your opinion, Doctor Foxe?'

'They may be innocents, but knowing the magnitude of this threat and, with little else to progress our enquiries, I believe we must act on these hints.'

'Your advice may be sound, Doctor, but Kelley has strong patronage at court and we must not allow indignation at his arraignment to reveal our purpose to a wider understanding.'

'Who are these patrons,' I ask.

'Warwick for one, although it is his wife, Anne Dudley, who has the keenest interest in astrology.'

'Should we wait for Sir Francis to return for his advice?' I wonder if my suggestion will prick Askham's pride and encourage him to act.

Askham stands and paces the chamber. He returns to the table and plants himself squarely before us. 'No, we must not wait. I will order both men detained and will send word when they are ready for questioning.'

*

Forester is outside his chamber when I arrive at court. He hands me a note with two names of those who would consult me. He clicks his tongue with impatience and peers over my shoulder indicating that I am not the subject of his anxiety. As I fold the note and make to pass him by, he turns and says that Francis Mylles would see me when it is convenient.

Mylles is another with an unsettled air. He is pacing his chamber as I enter and he does not offer a seat. He bids me good day and clasps his hands behind his back.

He says, 'Doctor Huicke is at court today and I would have you seek him out and make yourself known. Her Majesty passed comment on him the last day. She was perturbed by his manner and I would have your opinion. Is he to be trusted, might he have passed intelligence from Her Majesty's private chambers, or does his age overcome normal sensibilities?'

I nod dumbly with the thought that others will surely know this man better than I on a first encounter. Mylles shows none of the cheerful charm from our first meeting and it seems that our very short conference is finished.

I find Richard Joynes in the apartments and I am glad that he has a welcoming smile after my first two encounters here today. He introduces me to three of his associates and we talk of light matters for a half hour, then I ask Richard if he can identify Doctor Huicke for me. He is in the next room, deep in conversation with a group of men in the robes of scholars. I thank Richard and start to walk towards Huicke when a man steps sideways and blocks my path. It is the Earl of Oxford. I doff my cap, bow deeply and wait for what is to come.

'Doctor William Constable, good day to you.'

'My lord, thank you, I hope this day is kind to you also.'

He is a handsome man, smooth-faced, of medium height and clothed in splendid colours. His doublet is decked in gold, blues and reds with an extravagant silk ruff. He is joined by several men, spread behind and at each side.

'I owe you an apology, Doctor Constable. I mistook you for another man these few days past; a man with prattling tongue who injured my family name. I confess that I cast an eye of displeasure at you and I trust that your sensibilities suffered no injury from my error.'

This is unexpected and a welcome relief. His language is too rich for my taste, and he sings his words in a way that is likely to please ladies. I can understand why a Puritan such as John Foxe would dislike his gaudy display and pretty words, but I must not hold this as a fault in him.

'My lord, I thank you for your kindness, but I had taken no offence. On that day I was rapt in admiration of your fine garments and I am sorry if my stare was taken as insolence.'

He is pleased with my response. He takes me by the arm and asks that I should walk with him.

He says, 'I hear you are a scholar of considerable reputation, Doctor Constable. Your knowledge of the stars arcs a dazzling array of philosophies from physik to mathematics.'

I murmur my thanks for his praise, wondering why he has taken the trouble to enquire into my history.

He continues, 'I have a fascination with the heavens and how God shapes their movements to influence our lives. We must talk more on these matters when time allows.'

'Indeed, my lord, I wait at your convenience.'

'In which direction do you aim in your current work, Doctor?'

'My lord I am charged with assisting Doctor Huicke in guarding the wellbeing of gentlemen and ladies at this court.'

'You have no other current affairs or matters of business?'

'No, my lord.' Why does he ask? Is this merely a polite enquiry, or does he delve with some firmer purpose?

He stops, gazes at me for a moment, then turns his back and walks away with his followers in close attendance. Did I disappoint or offend in some way? I am mystified at this sudden ending to our conference. Doctor Huicke has moved and I do not see him. I check the names of those who would consult me and go in search of Richard hoping he will know these people.

*

My two patients both complained of loose bowels and cramps in their stomachs. I prescribed two mouthfuls of ground wood charcoal washed down with fresh cow's milk. The first, a lady chamberer, accepted the remedy without question, but the second, a ward of the Earl of Sussex, insisted that he should be bled. In the end, I relented and let a little blood to satisfy him and clear the atmosphere in my chamber. I am pleased to have discovered two gentlewomen near Forester's rooms who act for Huicke and his associates in the preparation of potions, medicines and salves. This will free some of my time and save on the to-and-fro between West Cheap and Whitehall.

I go in search of Richard Joynes again, as I am in need of a change of air. I see a man who I know.

'Captain General Hawkins, it is a pleasure to meet with you here.'

'Ah, William – William Constable, well met.' He turns to the next man. 'Humphrey, this is the gentleman scholar I talked of. He has a scheme for a mechanism that may aid our grand venture.'

I bow and am introduced to Sir Humphrey Gilbert, a partner in Hawkins' adventures. His fame as soldier and sea adventurer is even greater than Hawkins and I comment on the bravery and daring of his exploits. He bobs his head modestly at my flattery. He is of similar appearance to Hawkins; middle height; well-muscled; weathered complexion; and with an expression that speaks of authority and firmness. He asks what brings me to court.

'I have a temporary position as a physician assisting Doctor Huicke.'

Hawkins raises his eyebrows. 'I trust that this duty is not so onerous as to deflect you from your studies of navigation.'

Gilbert adds, 'You have a well-rounded scholarship to be proficient as both physician and mathematician, Doctor Constable.'

'Thank you, Sir Humphrey, my primary concern is fixed on the navigation instrument and that outcome will not fail from my lack of attention.'

'For our part, we are here to receive the promised license for our exploration and discovery from Her Majesty through the hands of Baron Burghley.' Hawkins exchanges glances with Gilbert and continues, 'We hope for a ten-year license, but will be content with seven.'

I say, 'It would be an odd and contrary decision to deny license for such a splendid adventure.'

Hawkins grunts in agreement, then asks if I have made progress on the instrument. I reply that I have new sketches which I will use to make a model. Their interest is keen, so I provide an outline of the scheme.

'I have designed a mechanism around a staff of four feet in length, and this must be used with the sun or moon at the rear. A shadow is cast by a vertical shaft and this shadow is aligned with the horizon by an eyepiece on a curved vane. The eyepiece slides along the vane which is graduated to measure the angle.' My words are accompanied by movements of my hands, which I think will confuse, but both men seem to like my exposition. 'It is a small improvement and restricts measurements to angles of no more than forty-five degrees, but I am confident that further refinement will release this limitation.'

Hawkins claps me on the shoulder and declares that they look forward to sight of the model. They thank me and advise that their time for an audience with Burghley draws near. As they leave, I spot Richard to my left side and join him.

He says, 'I know of Sir Humphrey Gilbert, but not his companion. They showed much interest in your discussions.'

'He is Captain General Hawkins. I have met Captain Hawkins before through a friend of our family.' I will say no more on this, as I do not wish my connection to Morton and his venture generally known.

'Huicke waits in his chambers for you, William. I chanced upon him as he was leaving and mentioned your name. He is a strange man and not easy to engage in conversation.'

I thank Richard generously for his continued assistance and make my way to Huicke's chambers, which are adjacent to Forester's. There is a tall, stooped man standing in the centre of his chamber, who I recognise as Huicke. His hands are on his side, his elbows stick out and his bottom lip protrudes in an expression of belligerence. He is in bad humor, but it is too late to retire, so I approach and bow.

'Doctor Huicke, good day to you. I am William Constable come to assist you in the absence of Doctor Lyle.'

'He replies, 'Fecund,' without further elaboration.

'I beg your pardon, Doctor.'

'Fecund, fecund, fecund,' he repeats and I am unsure whether he addresses me or an invisible companion.

'Do you have a query about a lady's fecundity?'

His eyes dart to mine as though I have just arrived. 'Exactly, you reach the nub of the matter in quick time.'

'Who is the lady in question?'

'It is the Lady Sheffield.'

'May I enquire why her fecundity is significant?'

He puffs air, shakes his head and spreads his hands as though I have asked a question of special idiocy. 'Who are you?' he demands.

'I am Doctor William Constable. Your associate, Doctor Lyle, is away on family business and I...'

'Lyle is a ruffian and indulges overmuch in modern fashions.'

'You dislike his dress?'

He rolls his eyes. 'His fashions for physik.' He corrects me and I am at a loss to know how I should proceed with this conversation when he says, 'William Constable; strange name that tinkles a bell in my memory. You are no relation to Sir Christopher Norris?'

'No sir, I do not know the gentleman.'

'Good, I disliked him fiercely. He died of the pox.'

'You say there is a question of whether Lady Sheffield is fecund.' This seems a safer topic of conversation.

'Yes, yes, Stafford has sent a man from Paris to enquire into the lady's intentions. He wishes to marry, but must be assured of heirs.'

I know little of Lady Sheffield other than she is the widow of Baron Sheffield. I am wary of putting innocent questions that will be met with derision, but I feel bound to continue this line of discussion.

'Have you consulted the stars?'

'Exactly; the stars. I have laboured to produce a fine chart which tells of the lady's good spirit, obedience and robustness. Instead of admiration, the chart was met with indifference and the question of fecundity.'

'The lady has issue from her first marriage?'

'I believe there is a son and daughter.'

'And she is of child-bearing years?'

'Ah ha, she is comely and near her thirtieth year.'

'Well then, it is a simple matter to annotate the text, "Believed Fecund" to the chart. It is not a deception to interpret the readings in a way that will please your client.'

His eyes widen, his mouth opens and he stares at me in disbelief. I fear I have offended.

'Excellent, you unearth the solution with a display of brilliance and virtuosity. I am indebted to you, Doctor Norris.'

I forego the opportunity to correct my name and ask for his opinion on a curative so that I may know more of his practice as physician. After a half hour of confused talk with Huicke, I return to Francis Mylles to report on my meeting. His mood has improved and he welcomes me with a warm smile. I relate an outline of my meeting and offer my assessment that Huicke's mind is not sufficiently sharp to intentionally pass private intelligence from Her Majesty's apartments. Additionally, I suggest that his age has brought on certain unpredictable behaviours and that it would be a kindness to move him gently from his position to one less heightened in importance. I take care not to be over critical of a man who has achieved much in a long and useful life.

Mylles says that he is not surprised by my conclusions and that he will ponder what action should be taken.

I say, 'There is another matter you should know.' He raises his head with renewed interest. 'I met with Mistress Parry and she made mention of a conversation overheard by one of the chamber ladies.'

'Blanche Parry – you have done well in making yourself known, William. What was the subject of the conversation and who were the contributors?'

I start with the caution that it was an ill-judged, but probably innocent, jest about a royal bastard and provide the names of the two men. He writes the names, finishes with a flourish, throws down his quill and sits back in his seat.

'Thank you, William, it will give me pleasure to investigate this offence further.'

I shiver at his mention of the word 'pleasure' in this regard and feel sympathy for the poor unfortunates who will regret an ill-advised moment of youthful high spirits.

Fourteen

Three days have passed since Askham departed this house to detain Kelly and Millen. He called yesterday to inform John and me of his unsuccessful searches. Kelley was not at his lodgings near Aldgate and enquiries at inns and other places of congregation yielded no sightings of either man. Askham has set men at the quays and gates, but fears that we may be too late and that they have quit the city. John's opinion was that their absence deepens our suspicions, but Kelley may simply have business in another town. I further cautioned that we did not know that Millen was in London some days ago, so there may be nothing sinister in his non-appearance. Whatever the cause, we three were vexed in our different ways. John was quiet and brooding, Askham could not be still, either seated or standing and I had difficulty concentrating on my work for the remainder of that day.

This morning, I have finished my finer drawings for the instrument and have asked Hicks to meet in my library.

'Good morning to you, Hicks. Is the matter of our land in Kent settled?'

'Yes, Master William. The lease is signed and the widow housed to her satisfaction.'

'Very good. Do we have full accounting for our wool traded in Amsterdam?'

'The finances are almost settled and the bankers haggle over their commissions. Our price was fair, but below our good fortune the last year.'

I am reminded again how blessed we are to have Hicks handle our business.

'I would have your advice on a matter of craftsmanship.' I push my drawings across the table towards him. 'I have in mind this new instrument to aid the navigation of ships. It is fashioned from wood and metal, requiring great accuracy in its manufacture. Do you know of a man with good hands and careful temperament who might be able to deliver this?'

He scans the drawing briefly, then peers more closely at the detail. He looks up and says, 'It will be a task of some delicacy. There is a man in Spytalfields who is said to do good work for clockmakers. I will be happy to take this paper to him for an honest opinion.'

'I would be grateful, Hicks. Please enquire on the days needed to complete the instrument. It may be required with some urgency.'

'I will, Master William, but he will ask for fair coin, no doubt.'

'Thank you, Hicks. I trust your fairness and good dealing in all matters of coin and business.'

It would be unfair to keep the wider purpose of the instrument from Hicks and so I offer a brief outline of Morton's great adventure. His eyes widen at the scale of the scheme and shakes his head in wonderment at the mention of capturing Spanish gold. He expresses his pleasure at my involvement and says that my father would be proud and overjoyed. Hicks open the door to exit as Rose rushes in. There is excitement on her face and she is breathless.

'Please sir... your mother... the lady Amy... has shat, sir.'

I bound up the stairs to Mother's chamber. The door is open and she is propped up in her bed with book in hand. I am quick to the bedside to kiss her forehead.

'Please, William, it is unseemly to be so enraptured by a lady's movements. You wish to examine my stools?'

I pick up the pot by her bed. The stools are dark and solid, but there are many. It is promising.

'I will examine these in more detail later, Mother. You must forgive my delight at your movement, but I despaired it would never come. You have more colour and light in your eyes. Are you improved a little?'

'Indeed, a sharp ache in my middle remains, but I am more alert. I confess that the movement was agony for a while, but I feel a good measure of relief now it is passed.'

'I wonder if it was the plums or the rhubarb and ginger that worked an improvement.'

'The plums.' She is quite definite in her assessment. 'I have acquired a taste for them and intend to continue their use. You will pass on my thanks to Mistress Rosamund, the lady Helen and seek a regular supply?'

'Of course, Mother.' I hesitate. 'Perhaps we should wait for a greater improvement before attributing a cure.'

'You are too careful, William. I should have thought you would be glad of an excuse to meet with Helen Morton again.'

The small mischief in her eyes gives more certainty that she recovers her spirits well. I go to John's chamber and bring him the good news about Mother. He is genuinely pleased and expresses the hope that she will soon be well enough to join with conversation in the parlour. He persuades me to stay and give my opinion on the writings he is undertaking. His subject is Calvin and his approach to Protestantism. My attention wanders after an hour of scrupulous and pedantic argument on the finer points of religious observance. I am reprieved when there is a knock at the door and Mistress Hilliard enters with a note. It is from Jane Dee. It is short, but I read three or four times to understand the content.

'Is there a problem, William?'

'It is from Doctor Dee's wife at Mortlake, Jane Dee.'

'Has she more to say about Kelley and Millen?'

'No, it is a simple message with the words, "fire and attack" written. She begs me to attend with haste.'

*

It is late to travel to Mortlake and the sky will be dark for my return journey. I travel alone, ignoring Gregory's plea for his company and John's advice to seek an escort from Askham. The tone of the note is disturbing and I feel obliged to call on Jane Dee as quickly as I am able. I am prepared for fire damage to the house, but what can she can mean by 'attack'.

As soon as I leave the ferry on the south bank of the river, I view wisps of smoke in the air. My mind may play tricks, but these gentle curls of grey do not suggest a cosy hearth, but something more sinister. I see that the house stands. As I draw nearer I note that a chimney is fallen. The bricks on the east wing are blackened and the roof… the roof is gone, save for a few charred timbers. A yeoman or servant carries a bucket of water from the back of the house and throws it through a hole that was once a glazed window. He stops as he sees me. I dismount and ask where I may find Mistress Dee. He nods his head dumbly and points to the house. I ask if the stables are in use. Again, he does not answer, but offers to take my reins and leads Cassius away.

The door is not shut. I knock, enter and raise my voice to call her name. The smell is pungent and catches the back of my throat, causing me to cough and leave my announcement unfinished. The air is thick and the whitewashed walls are greyed. The main damage is to my left, so I turn to my right and try another door. It is blocked. An object behind stops a full opening. I push a little harder and squeeze my way into the chamber. The fire has not reached here, but the windows are broken with bricks and other objects scattered on the floor. A table has been moved to hinder entry and a large wall hanging has come loose and droops at an odd angle.

I call Jane Dee's name again and wait. Minutes pass before there is a scratching sound at the far door, it begins to open and head peers around the gap. It is a woman's uncovered head, hair uncombed and with face disfigured by… It is Mistress Dee.

'My lady, you are hurt.'

She enters slowly, brushing her hair and skirts with her hands. The left side of her face is heavily bruised, her lip is split and dried blood is stuck to her chin and neck.

'Doctor Constable, thank you for answering my note. There was…'

'In good time, Mistress Dee, I will attend to your injuries before you tell me more. Is there water to be had?'

There is a trough and well at the rear. She says she will retreat to her refuge in the parlour and wait for my attentions. I walk from the front of the house around the perimeter looking for the man who took Cassius. There is no sign of him, although I see that Cassius is safely stabled. His head is over a closed stall, but all the other stalls are open and the horses gone. I fill a bucket from the well and return to the parlour to find Jane Dee sitting on a stool with head bowed and hands clasped on her knee. I dampen a square of linen and rub gently at her cuts and bruises.

She has a small gash on her scalp and a worse one on her lower lip, but they are clean now and have started to close. Her head is sore, but there appears to be no lasting hurt.

'The library is gone,' she exclaims. 'My husband will be enraged by the loss of his valued books and papers.'

'Hush now, Mistress, tell the story from the beginning. What happened here?'

'It was some time after dusk. A commotion at the rear of the house. There were men; four or five men with flaming torches.'

'Who were these men?'

'They were armed men, with swords and cudgels. They came into my house, chased away my servants and…'

She is breathless and sobbing. I place my hand on her shoulder.

'Where are your servants and attendants?'

'Gone – all gone under threat not to return.'

'What of the man who took my horse?'

'He is a simple man with no tongue. He is named "Cluck" I think as a jest on his disposition. Perhaps he did not understand the stern nature of the threats.' She catches her breath. 'John, our man of horses, tried to resist and he was… he was killed.'

'Killed – how killed?'

'His throat was slashed by a large, hooded man. I saw the blood spurt from his neck.'

She cups her hands over her face and rocks gently as she heaves and sobs. I hold my question until her distress subsides.

'How were you injured?'

'Part of the house was burning. A torch was thrown through a broken window. I ran inside, took hold and extinguished it in the trough outside. One of the men cursed me and hit me about the head, until… until the large man pulled him away.'

'Did you hear them say anything other than curses or threats?'

She shakes her head. 'Nothing, nothing I can recall.'

'Did they thieve any possessions from your household?'

'I have not moved far from my parlour, but I do not think their purpose was theft. Their work was done in a short time, thank God. They were unhurried and departed in evil good humor.'

'Did others come from the neighbourhood to help you?'

'There was me, Cluck and three or four more came later to help to quench the flames. All seemed lost until the rains came.'

Fortunate is not an appropriate word to utter at this time, but the house would surely be gutted without rain. Why would they wish to terrify Jane Dee, fire the building and frighten away the servants? And a murder. Is it retribution or a warning? A warning for who – Jane Dee, the Doctor… or me?

I say, 'Did you recognise any of the attackers?'

'It was dark, they were hooded and it was… too much of a confusion to recall. The large man… I did not see his face, but he had the shape and character of one who met with Edward Kelley.'

'Has word of this criminal and malevolent act been sent to the local justice, watchman or constable?

She shakes her head. 'I dared not shift from my parlour and I do not know these persons.'

My questions are done and I must see to her comfort. She cannot stay here, but there is no horse for her and it will soon be dusk. I stand and pace the room, gathering my thoughts. She looks to me for encouragement. There is an inn, a few hundred yards from here in the direction of the ferry. I will go there and ask for a man to carry a message to Askham. Gently, I explain my plan to Jane Dee. She has a look of panic as I tell her I must leave for the inn, but she is pacified knowing I will return to her in short time.

The sun is down and the door at the inn is locked. It is a small, mean-looking place and I guess that there will be a cold welcome for a stranger. I knock hard and wait. The door opens a little and someone peers out. This is no time for timidity; I push hard and enter. A short man at the door staggers back and narrows his eyes. There are twenty or more men sitting at benches or leaning against beams. The smell is of animal waste and rotting hay.

'Good day to you all. I require one among you to deliver a message this day. The one that steps forward will be well rewarded.'

The inn is silent. Some men stare at me, while others look into their ale.

I say, 'There is silver in it. The message is to Whitehall.'

The man at the door answers, ''Tis dark and no ferry.'

A few begin to grumble and I hear muttered curses. The room turns against me.

'I am sure the ferryman can be persuaded with coin, and if you fear the journey in the dark I will pay for two to carry the message.'

Three men rise from their benches and one reaches inside his coat. My mention of silver was foolish. They see I have no sword and plan to rob me.

'I am Walsingham's man.' The name slows them. 'It will go hard on you and your families if you choose to ignore my generous offer.'

They are stilled. Two of the men regain their seats; the third gazes around him, then faces me and says, 'I will take your message, for a shilling. I am Michael the smithy and my friend Walt will accompany me.' He nods in the direction of the man who rose and put his hand to a weapon under his coat.

'You can have sixpence now and another sixpence the next morning when I know the message is well-delivered.'

I hand over my note, which is folded over a sixpence coin, and tell him that it must be delivered to Captain Askham before midnight. His look is surly, but mention of Mister Secretary has tamed him. He takes the note and assures me that he will complete the task. I have little choice, but to trust him.

Fifteen

How shall I pass this night with Jane Dee? She will not move from the parlour. Her bedchamber is badly damaged and she will not sleep in another. I cannot leave her and so we must spend the night together in this small place. It would be unseemly in normal circumstances, but my presence would surely be forgiven at this unsettling time.

The larder is untouched by fire and I bring cheese, apples and a jug of claret to the parlour. She sips the wine, but will not touch the food. She breaks the quiet between us by begging forgiveness for sending the note of distress to me. Her mother lives by the town of Lincoln and she knows no other in Mortlake or the City that she could have asked for assistance. She has been married to Doctor Dee for less than one year and has ventured from this house only rarely. I do not speak the words, but this is too mundane a life for a young woman with good family.

'Will the man Cluck, stay here this night?'

'He sleeps in the barns and will guard the body of his friend, John the stableman.'

She pulls a rug around her shoulders to protect from the cold draughts. I lift glowing embers with an iron poker and place two more logs on the fire. Her injured face is softened by the light of candles and the flames of the fire, but it will take some weeks for it to heal and the scar on her mind will remain for longer. I hesitate to question her more about the attack, but we cannot spend these hours in idle talk.

'When those foul men attacked, do you think their purpose was to destroy the entire house?'

'Perhaps, but their attention was fixed on the library at the start. Windows were broken with heavy sticks and three torches flung in there.'

'I wonder how those men knew where the library is situated.'

She shakes her head and says, 'Who would want to ruin my husband's library? Does he have many enemies, Doctor

Constable?'

'I know he has many admirers, Mistress, and a few that envy his intellect and collection of books, but I doubt that they would stoop so low for that reason.'

'My husband will be distraught,' she begins to sob, 'as will Master Millen.'

'Master Millen, why should he be so distressed?'

'I think I told you, Master Millen was here often to work in the library and not only to visit Master Kelley. When my husband left for the Low Countries he came to continue his assistance with the Doctor's work in the library. He was pleasant enough, save that he was quite particular that neither I nor the servants should enter the library while he was away. He warned that the Doctor would be displeased if important writings were disturbed. I disliked his manner when he spoke of these things.'

'Did Kelley work with Millen in the library?'

'I do not think so. Master Kelley was often away visiting his patrons and while he was here he had his own chambers where he…'

She bows her head and leaves her dialogue unfinished. Perhaps she thinks of his scrying, communion with angels, or is that the place he molested her?

I say, 'Did it appear that Millen and Kelly were on good terms?'

'They were polite in their exchanges, but I do not believe they were particular friends.'

I am not sure where this intelligence leads. I had assumed that Kelley and Millen were confederates, but perhaps it is only Millen that warrants further examination. Her eyes are closed and she startles herself awake with an involuntary lurch of her head.

'Come, Mistress, make yourself more comfortable and rest your eyes. I do not believe there will be another attack tonight and I will remain awake here until our escort arrives. As we are sat so close together in these circumstances, may I call you Jane? For my part, I would be glad if you would call me William.'

'Very well, William, and thank you.'

I place a stool under her feet so that she can ease back in her chair. She is soon asleep and I am left to tend the fire and structure my thoughts. Time passes slowly, lethargy takes hold and have to fight so that I may stay awake. I find it is images of Helen that keep my mind most active.

*

At first light I leave the parlour and make to the rear of the house. It is cold, with a hoar frost. Thin layers of ice have formed on the puddles in the back yard. The fresh air is welcome after my overnight confinement. I breathe deeply and flex my shoulders to refresh body and spirit. All is quiet save for my footsteps. Cassius is in his stall, standing with head drooped in the far corner. He turns his head with only small curiosity at my presence.

A trail of blood leads from the yard to the neighbouring stall where the half-door is shut. I look over and see Cluck on a bed of straw. He has heard me and is sat, with a length of wood in a raised hand. A threatening snarl dissolves as he recognises my face from last night. He lies next to a body of a man; presumably this is John. A gaping black wound in the neck is confirmation of Jane's sight of the killing.

I am at the front of the house when Askham and his troop of a dozen mounted men arrive. A pale sun has banished the frost and the road has a regular trade of carts, horses and yeoman passing by. Some stop and stare at the damaged building, while others bow their heads and continue on their way. There will be some among them who harbour shame for failure to assist a neighbour in the commotion two nights past.

'A good morning to you, Captain. I thank you for your prompt answer to my note.'

He dismounts and casts a quick eye at the house. 'What happened here? Your note spoke of an assault on property and occupants.'

I convey my understanding of the events of last night: the fire; chasing away of servants; the killing; and the battering of Mistress Dee. I explain the significance for our enquiries in the targeting of the library and my suspicion that this was to destroy the writings of an astrologer, named Christopher Millen. This is a great leap in understanding and the evidence is thin, but I can bring no other motive to mind.

I say, 'There is work to be done. The local justice and constable should be informed and I must take Mistress Dee to a place of safety.'

'Where will that place be?'

'I will take her to West Cheap, although I hope this will be a short arrangement.'

Askham orders his men to spread around the perimeter and secure the house. I take him to pay his respects to Jane and then show him the body in the stable. Cluck has gone and I suspect he hides somewhere with a view of our activities. I describe Cluck to Askham and tell him that he was not an attacker, but a helper; that he is simple, dumb and will not be able to assist our enquiries.

Our next duty is to inspect the library, or its remains. It is a filthy and hazardous exploration. The roofing has gone and it is open to the elements. Two charred beams cross over our heads as we pick our way through blackened scraps made foul by a dousing of water. My spirits are low as I gaze around the ruins of what was so recently one of the finest collections of books in England. Odd fragments of paper flutter and a few leather bindings have resisted the flames, but their contents are corrupted. Askham says that he will have his men recover what little can be salvaged, but neither of us hold out hope of a serviceable discovery.

Four men are assigned to escort me and Jane to West Cheap, while Askham settles necessary arrangements in Mortlake. He is angry that there has been no contact from the justice or constable and assures me that they will be strongly reminded of their duty to uphold Her Majesty's law.

*

It was a quiet, plodding journey from Mortlake to West Cheap. Jane covered her head in her cloak's hood, which made for difficulties in conversation, but I understood that she did not wish prying eyes to see her injured face. My description of the West Cheap household was met with small, indistinct murmurs of understanding, but no more.

On our arrival I offer a hurried explanation to Mistress Hilliard, who takes Jane to settle in her chamber. Hicks is away, but Harry Larkin is about and I bid him take Jane's baggage. I do not know what clothing or comforts she has packed, but her baggage is light and I suspect that another visit to Mortlake will be required to replenish her stock.

I should call on Mother, but John has appeared with questioning face and we retire to his study chamber so that I can relate the story of last night. He offers God's blessing for the man killed and expresses his sympathy for Jane's hurt, but his main concern is the library and books.

He asks, 'How many volumes were lost?'

'Ten years past, Doctor Dee had almost five hundred books in his library, so now it would be more.'

He shakes his head and clicks his tongue. 'It is a great shame to lose such a compilation through an act of wilful destruction.'

'The library was the target of the attackers; Millen worked there often and gave warning that Mistress Dee and others in the household should not enter and disturb its contents. It is too much of a coincidence to suppose that Askham's search for Millen is not connected.'

He nods his agreement. 'So, you believe that Kelley may not be linked to this act, or may have only a minor role in the plot?'

'Kelley – I do not know. If he can be found then he should be questioned, but it seems that Millen may have more to answer.'

I take my leave of John to visit Mother. She has risen from her bed and sits in a chair, although she still wears her bedclothes of linen smock and bonnet. Rose is attending to her bed covers and has brought more logs for the fire.

'You look well, Mother. I trust your recovery continues.'

'Thank you, William, the plums do their work and I am greatly eased.' She thanks Rose and bids her leave us. 'Rose tells me we have another guest; a young lady.'

'Yes, she is Doctor Dee's wife, who was Jane Fromond. Her person and house were attacked last night. The house was burned and she was injured about the head.'

Her eyes narrow. 'Why… why have you rescued this woman?

You told me that your association with Doctor Dee is at an end and that the note from his wife was in response to your casual enquiry. You have not disclosed the whole truth of your affairs with Walsingham.'

It would be futile to hide the facts of our investigation of Kelley and Millen for their possible involvement in the making of the natal chart from her now. I take pains to describe the events that led to my call from Jane last night and offer our opinion that the search for Millen was the cause of the assault. She breathes deeply, clasps her hands together and there is a silence between us.

'I dislike your close involvement in this matter, William. But I understand that it may not be politic at this moment to withdraw yourself. It would appear… unhelpful. You must introduce me to Mistress Dee. I will take her under my care.'

'Thank you, Mother.'

'I had intended to dine at midday. Perhaps you will arrange for Mistress Dee to join me.'

*

I present Jane Dee to my mother and John at the dining table, but say that I cannot join them as I must meet with Mylles at Whitehall. Jane has a look of alarm at my departure, but Mother consoles her with a few sweet words and a promise that she has some ointment that will soothe her bruising.

Mylles has heard of the outrage at Mortlake, but Askham has not yet returned and there is no further word from him. He listens carefully as I detail the circumstances around the attack and my reasons for presuming a connection with the search for Millen. He leans back in his seat and steeples his fingers.

'Finally, there is an action that informs our investigations. You have done well in your deductions, William.'

I suppose I must excuse his lack of concern for the fate of Jane Dee and her house because of his unwavering focus on uncovering the conspiracy. Yet, it will do no harm to prick his conscience.

'I am sure Her Majesty will be dismayed to hear of the injuries inflicted on the wife of a trusted and valued advisor.'

'Yes… yes, you are right to emphasise this aspect. Her

Majesty will hear of her hurt and Mister Secretary may wish to seek out some recompense for the Doctor's house.'

'Have you learned more about the reported gossip?'

'Ah, Capton and Perse. They are empty-headed young men. Capton was indignant and denies speaking or hearing any words about a royal bastard. Perse was more submissive in answering to the same end. They may be witless, but they are not conspirators.'

'Who do they follow at court?'

'They are recent arrivals in Oxford's entourage. The Earl likes to surround himself with pretty boys.'

I am surprised at his easy acceptance of denials from Capton and Perse. Mylles strikes me as a man who would be eager to scour the last drop of intelligence from questioning. He has said little of Millen and any connections or patronage that he may have at court. Perhaps, despite his praise for my efforts, Mylles does not put his full trust in me and worries that I might disclose too much through loose talk.

Sixteen

I am with Hicks and Harry Larkin in their chambers across the courtyard when Mistress Hilliard calls, announces that my mother has visitors and that a gentleman in the party has asked to see me. Mother's visitors are rare these days and I wonder who this gentleman can be. Hicks accompanies me to the front of the house in case it concerns a matter of business.

It is Helen, with a young maid and Darby Wensum.

'Mistress Morton, this is an unexpected delight, and a good morning to you, Master Wensum.'

'Good morning, Doctor Constable, it is your mother we call on. Master Wensum here, escorted us and is eager to meet with you. Rosamund did not wish to stir from the still and drying room today and I have brought my chambermaid, Lucy.' There is a light in her eyes as she registers the surprise in my welcome. Did my mother send a note of invitation without my knowing?

Helen and her maid follow Mistress Hilliard to Mother's chamber. I must be civil with Wensum so that this meeting does not descend into another bout of verbal sniping.

'Master Wensum, is this a social call mixed with protection of Mistress Morton, or do you wish to discuss business? The great adventure to the New Lands, perhaps?'

'If you will forgive me, I have more than one purpose. First, to ensure the safety of the lady, Helen. Second, I would put right the unfortunate exchange we had on our last meeting here. I have come to realise my words then were too abrupt and I am sorry if they caused offence.'

'Thank you, Master Wensum. If I remember, I may have been overripe in my response, so let us both forgive and forget.' I pause. 'Is there a third reason?'

'Indeed, I have been sent by Sir George to inform you about our newest arrangements on the venture and to enquire if you have made progress with your instrument.'

'Good, then let us adjourn to our receiving chamber. You know Hicks, I think.' They exchange stiff bows. 'I trust that you will not object if Hicks joins us.'

We sit for a half hour, drinking claret and talking of inconsequential things. Wensum reminds Hicks of their meeting when he was in the employ of a wool merchant named Phillips, who is long dead. Hicks takes up the subject of wool and there is a discussion on the prices to be had in London and the Low Countries. Wensum recounts the story of his work for Sir George and the expansion of his trade. Finally, Wensum broaches the topic of the great adventure.

I say, 'I have only outlined the bare bones of the scheme to Hicks. Perhaps you would explain the essence of the adventure in more detail before providing the latest news.'

Wensum bows his head and begins an overlong and finely-detailed account of design and preparations. He finishes with itemising the necessities that I would need to bring on board, should I decide to sail with the fleet. For my part, I simply explain that a craftsman has my drawings and will attempt to manufacture an exemplar. We have sat over an hour and I am impatient to seek out Helen and learn the reason for her visit. I say that it is time for me to administer a curative for my mother and excuse myself. I promise that I will return shortly and beg them to continue the discussion.

Helen and my mother are seated together by the fire in her chamber, while Lucy is absorbed with needle and thread by the light of the window.

'Ah, William, at last. Please help me to my bed and I will rest for a while. I sent an invitation to Mistress Morton so that I may offer my deeply felt thanks for her treatment. We have enjoyed a conversation on herbal and other natural medications, but I am unused to such excitement of the mind and I tire easily.'

I take my mother's hand, lead her to the bed and smooth the covers when she is settled. Her colour is good, her eyes are alert and the disposition of her body does not speak of lethargy.

She says, 'It is restful to watch Lucy at her needlework. William, please take Helen to our room of medicines so that she may suggest improvements.'

This is a badly-disguised deception to allow me some time with Helen, alone. Nevertheless, I am grateful for her plan.

We stand awkwardly in the drying room, each waiting for the other's first word.

I say, 'I received your note in the bag of plums.'

'I hope that you did not find my sentiments ungrateful.'

'Not at all. I understand your caution and readings from the stars are not to everyone's taste.'

'It was not a concern about astrology that led me to write the note.' I tilt my head, waiting for more. 'My father would have interpreted the request as a closeness between us.' Disappointment must show in my eyes as she is quick to continue. 'I would not be dismayed at such a situation, given more time. I know my father; he loves me jealously and is likely to act with intemperance at the prospect of a liaison with someone known only for a few days. I considered it best to…'

Her voice trails away and she does not finish. She bows her head as if shamed that she has shown her feelings too openly. I take a step towards her and hold her hand in mine.

'My lady – Helen. You should know that I too, would wish for an intimacy between us in due course. I applaud your prudence in correcting my lack of thought, which may have spoiled this prospect.'

She lifts her head, looks into my eyes, takes her hand from mine, turns and steps two paces away. Now is not the time to continue with this subject. There is quiet, but the air between us is tranquil and our spoken words have seeded a glow of contentment on my spirits.

I say, 'I regret that I must return to Master Wensum to continue our discussions on your father's venture.'

'Ah, yes, Master Wensum.'

'By his own telling, he has been a successful man of business for your father.'

'Yes… yes, he has.'

'There is a trace of doubt in your voice.'

'I know he is diligent and skilful in his trades. My father has come to rely on his judgement and I believe he is well-rewarded.'

'Let me be frank. I am not at ease in his company and I sense that he dislikes my connection with your father.'

Her nose twitches, she murmurs her agreement at my sentiments and adds that she can find no plain reason to mistrust him.

Helen returns to Mother's chamber while I re-join Hicks and Wensum. I apologise for my absence, but it appears that they have both continued their discussion at a lively pace. The topic has moved on to the reliability and honesty of bankers and this is an area where I have little to contribute. After a few moments I advise that our conversation should close as Helen is ready to depart. Wensum rises stiffly and adjusts his damaged leg with his hands. He clasps Hicks by the hand, bows to me and declares his satisfaction at our meeting. He takes his leave in good humor. I wonder if I have judged him too harshly.

Seventeen

It is a few minutes past noon and I am dining with Mother and John. They continue their conversations from the parlour where I found them jousting with words about the history of faith and the relative merits of Jewry and the followers of Muhammad. It is a dry topic and not one I would choose, but they find opportunities for merriment and teasing. It is clear that they are comfortable with each other and I am pleased that they are both much improved in their wellbeing. Mother, in particular, has transformed from a fading old woman to lively middle years. Perhaps I overstate the change, but I am filled with gratitude and wonder at the beneficial effect of a bagful of dried plums.

At the end of a pleasant dinner Mother retires to her chamber and John bids me to stay at our table. I infer from his changed demeanour that he wishes to consolidate our intelligence on the conspiracy.

'What news from Mylles, William? Did his interrogation yield anything of value?'

'He reported that the two young fellows were mindless innocents, and no more.'

He grunts his dissatisfaction. 'I think it is time for me to take a firmer hand in our enquiries. Thanks to you and your household, my body is much recovered and my mind is more active.'

'I am heartened to hear you say that, John. You are certainly sprightlier than when you arrived at this place.'

'Ha, do not overstate my condition, William. I am not ready to hunt wild boar or sail in an open ship. I remain an old man, but I would travel with you to Whitehall on your next visit. I am known at court and my ancient shufflings and bumblings may pick up on loose talk or other intelligence.'

*

I have scratched a few marks on a good quality paper. I have stared at them for too long. It is my intention to write to Helen and put right the clumsy words I spoke in response to her declaration of interest. I struggle. I must convey my serious intentions and I would have them expressed in pretty language. Poetry? I think not; my natural way of thinking turns to mathematics, not flowers and embroidered lace. Helen would see through my feeble attempts to clutch at handsome phrases that sit oddly with my character. I screw up the paper and place my quill in its holder. This was not a good idea. I will endeavour to voice my feelings well when we next meet.

I remember my shock at the telling of her birth date and it is a discomfiting thought that I must delve deeper into her history. If she has royal blood then what will become of her? Our sovereign is unlikely to own up to such a long and devious deception. Worse, if she is recognised as a false pretender, then a grisly and dreadful end beckon her and her father. If I am to have any chance of a future with Helen, then I must gather evidence that she is an innocent in this conspiracy. How? My torment is interrupted by voices I do not recognise.

Two armed men stand in my hall with Mistress Hilliard and the Larkin boy. I know one of their faces from Askham's escort.

'Do you bring word from your Captain?'

'Yes, Doctor Constable. We are ordered to take you to him.'

'Where is he?'

'In Southwark, at a dead-house.'

Southwark; at night; and at a dead-house. That is not a pleasant prospect. It will mean a crossing of the bridge and that is a place I shun, whenever possible.

'It is dark and wet. Would it not be better to wait until morning?'

'We will go now.'

His tone is gruff and will bear no argument. I see that John is standing in the shadow of the door and I reveal the nature of my summons to him. He strokes his beard before offering his assessment that a corpse of some significance has been found and that would be a pity as the dead cannot answer questions. It is a callous remark and one that is not entirely true. The nature of a death may imply motive and provide other intelligence.

It is a short ride to the bridge through narrow streets, but the rain has managed to seep through my cloak and lower my spirits further. The bridge warden bows his head and lets us pass without payment after short word from one of Askham's men. We dismount and lead our horses through the narrow passage. It is another world on the bridge; more hell than heaven, but at least we are covered from the elements. Doxies wave their hand linen in our faces and sellers push their codlings and other pies under our noses. It is a teeming mass of the laughing, shrieking, drunk, happy and miserable. Above all, the confined space highlights the stench of foul and rotting waste. Finally, we are the other side and the gates are opened to the Borough of Southwark, It is a relief to breathe the air and feel the rain, even in this place; the haunt of cutpurses, bawds and other low life.

We head west along a series of mean passages to the brooding, dark shape of Clink Manor. We stop at a small, turreted building at the edge of the manor. We dismount and one of the soldiers points to a doorway set down a flight of stone stairs. A guard opens the door and I follow him into an anteroom where a man sits at a table lit by a single candle that splutters and sparks. He opens the next door and gestures that I should enter. This chamber is larger and lit by several candles. Askham is seated at a chair with a beaker in his hand. Another man sits by a table with his feet raised on a stool.

'Ah, Doctor Constable, please forgive the hour and the place of our meeting. The gentleman here is Warden Oakes, who is the keeper of this mortuary.'

Oakes eyes me with curiosity, but does not move from his seat. A short man with heavy legs and large belly, he waves his hand at a stool and asks if I would take a cup of wine. I take the stool, but refuse the wine.

Askham says, 'Come, William Constable, take wine with us. You will need some fortification for the task ahead.'

That has an ominous chime. 'In that case, I will accept your offer, Warden Oakes.'

He pours into a wooden cup and passes it to me without disturbing his relaxed posture. I wait for an explanation of my visit. Will this be from Askham or Oakes? Both men drink from their cups and I follow. It is sour and unpleasant.

Askham says, 'Word reached me some hours ago of a find on

the mud flats by the bridge. A body was discovered and brought here.' He points his cup at Oakes who continues the story.

'The corpse was corrupted by the river. The corruption was partial and indicated a death some two or three days before its discovery. It was a man in scholar's clothing and his throat had been slit hard so that the head was hanging loose.'

'Has the body been named?'

'It was found near to the chained felons on this side of the river, close to the bridge.' He pauses to take another sup of the rank draught. 'One of the felons, a petty thief of foodstuffs, swore that he knew the man. He named him as Millen, a frequent caller at the stews on the bridge.'

'Is this name confirmed?'

Oakes moves his feet from his stool and shifts in his chair. 'The man, the felon, pleaded to be free for his naming, but he is known to be unreliable and was not believed.'

Askham says, 'I arrived here to question this felon, but was informed that he had died in his chains.'

'The tide was higher than expected and his neck could not stretch for air,' explains Oakes with a shrug.

'Cannot the whores on the bridge verify the name?'

'Ha, the word of those poxy whores is worth less than a wet fart,' says Oakes.

Askham leans forward. 'This is not a matter to warrant triviality or uncertainty, Warden.' He pauses to let Oakes' discomfort take hold, then turns to me. 'I would have your word on the identification, William Constable. You told me you had met with him.'

'Yes, though some years past.'

'Then let us examine the body. The warden assures me that his women have washed the cadaver and laid it with sprigs of rosemary.'

Askham rises from his seat and I follow. Oakes heaves himself from his chair with some difficulty, takes a bunch of keys from the table and meanders unsteadily across to a doorway. He fumbles with his keys and opens the door on to an arched undercroft. It is dark, save for four candles placed at the corners of a table by the far end of the space. We walk through the arches past a dozen or more dark shapes of draped corpses until we approach the candlelit area. A linen cloth is laid over the body on the table leaving the head and shoulders uncovered. The naked body has been cleansed and herbs are spread around the head. The flesh is mottled and bruised, but putrefaction has not set in. My eyes are drawn to the gash in the neck, which is a gaping disorder of pink, white and black. An eye bulges in a purpled socket. It is an altogether ugly sight. But is it Millen? I take one of the candlesticks and hold it close to the head. The look of a dead man will change markedly from the living state, through rigour and then a relaxation of muscle and skin. This mouth is drawn back, a blue tongue protrudes rudely and, with bared teeth. It is formed into a fierce snarl that would never be a natural expression. I place my hand before my eyes, so that it hides the jaw, and squint at the top of the face. There is a familiarity, but can I be sure?

I say, 'Can I see this man's clothes?'

Oakes stands behind me. He screws his faces and spreads his hands. 'The women must be paid for their duties and…'

'Warden,' Askham's voice is harsh, 'I grow tired of your indifference and my belly aches with your serving of foul wine. You say this man had the clothes of a scholar. You would not gift a velvet cap, gown and boots to your women. Bring the garb of this man to us – and with haste.'

Oakes is startled at these words, stares at Askham with open mouth, then turns and scuttles back to his chamber.

'You are unsure?'

'Yes, it is difficult to match the features of this dead man with a living and breathing person I knew, but not well.'

We wait in silence for some minutes until Oakes returns with his hands carrying a dark bundle of clothing. He has a cloak, cap, doublet and boots. All have been cleaned and will, no doubt, fetch a tidy profit for him. I pick the cap and with care, place it on the head of the corpse. I should not be surprised, but the icy touch of the scalp causes me to shiver. I gather up the cloak and drape it around his shoulders. When all is in place I hand a candlestick to Askham, bid him put it by the head, then I step back and peer at the lifeless face, again hiding his mouth with the shade of my hand.

'It is him. It is Christopher Millen.'

'You are sure?'

'Yes.'

We leave without words of thanks to Oakes. Askham orders his men to convey the body to Whitehall and says he will accompany me back to my house.

*

It is near midnight when we reach West Cheap. I offer Askham a bed for the night and he is wise to accept as the rain has turned to a stinging sleet. The house is quiet and I take Askham to the parlour where Mistress Hilliard is asleep in a chair. She wakes with a start at our entry, informs us that John waits in his chamber for our return, then hurries to find Gregory and arrange refreshment.

I say, 'Let us save our talk of Millen until Doctor Foxe joins us.'

The Captain's manner does not lend itself to light conversation and I do not press him. We settle in silence for some minutes until Elspeth brings claret, cold meats and pickles for a late supper. We drink, pick at the food and warm ourselves by the fire while we wait for John.

'Your wine is an improvement to our cups at the dead-house, William Constable.'

'Faint praise, indeed. I note that you were insistent that I should share with your sour tasting.'

He smiles his apology with a tilt of his head as John enters. He looks at us both in turn and mutters a quick welcome.

'What news from the dead-house, gentlemen?'

Askham answers. 'A corpse was found in the mud flats of the river. The cause was murder by a deep cut to the neck and William has identified the body as Christopher Millen.'

'So,' John clicks his tongue and rubs his hands as though anticipating this news, 'how does this inform us about the astrological chart and conspiracy?'

Askham looks to me to provide an answer. 'We must suppose that it is no coincidence and that the prime movers in the conspiracy heard about our search for Kelley and Millen. There was a danger to their scheme if Millen was found and questioned by us, so he was murdered.'

'You have it William, and you summarise the position like a practised intelligencer.'

Eighteen

Three of us are taking breakfast when Mother appears with Jane Dee and joins us. Mother guides Jane gently to a place at the table and takes a seat by her. Jane has her head bowed and is reserved in her manner. The bruising on her face has not diminished and her hand brushes the side of her face with a nervous regularity. She is encouraged by Mother and in a short time appears more at ease and enters into polite conversation. I am pleased that my mother has taken her care in hand and I am relieved of this burden. I would also see her recent unhappiness put to the back of her mind and Mother will be more adept at moving her attention to lighter things. When asked about the presence of Captain Askham, I explain that we supped together last night and that he was offered shelter from the icy weather.

I say, 'We will both accompany the Captain to Whitehall this morning. I will attend Doctor Huicke's patients and John wishes to renew friendships at court.'

John dabs his mouth with a cloth. 'I am sure that the lady Amy and Mistress Hilliard will be pleased to be free of a fussing old man in this household. I have no great love of the court, but I must show my face there from time to time so that I am not forgotten.'

'False modesty does not sit well with you, John,' answers my mother. 'Mistress Hilliard, likes nothing better than to serve you and receive your compliments.'

Jane looks up from her bowl and says, 'Doctor Foxe, did you know of my mother, Elizabeth Fromond, who was one of the ladies for the Countess of Lincoln? She was at court before my birth. I followed my mother to wait on the Countess for a short time before I wed the Doctor.'

'Indeed lady, I remember your mother. I trust that she is well.'

Jane mutters thanks in a low voice and Mother places a hand on hers by way of comfort. Does she miss the company of her mother? I understand that John's short reply will be because he disapproves of the reputed loose morals of the Countess.

Mother rescues an awkward silence.

'I hope that you will hurry back to this house, William. I have invited Mistress Morton to meet with Jane here as she was confined to her chamber on her last visit. She may wish to discuss an adjustment to my remedy.'

Is this another attempt to engineer an encounter between me and Helen? I fear that in this case it will not succeed as our stay in Whitehall is unlikely to be short. Nevertheless it may benefit Jane to enjoy the company of one who more closely matches her age.

*

I regret that I may have been too rushed in an assessment of John's recovery. The cold and dampness in the air causes a recurrence of his hacking cough and our travel to Whitehall is slow. The three of us make our way to Mylles' chamber to report on the events of last night. He is keenly interested in the killing, but disappointed that Millen cannot be questioned. He requests that Askham widens his search for associates of Millen and Kelley.

John says, 'Is it known if either of these men has patronage or contacts at court?'

'I understand that the earls of Warwick, Oxford and Southampton have used Kelley's services,' answers Mylles. 'I know nothing about Millen, but Sir Francis may have some insight when he returns.'

I wait for others to put the question, but when it seems that others will not, I say, 'Would there be profit in disclosing the news about Millen's killing, or should we guard this information?'

'An interesting point, William. What are your opinions Doctor Foxe and Captain Askham?'

Askham is undecided, but John is firmly in favour of holding back the information of our discovery, as disclosure may lead to increased caution among the conspirators. After brief discussion we resolve to follow John's lead. I make arrangements to meet with John in the physicians' quarters three hours after noon and we make our separate ways to the royal apartments.

I meet with Richard Joynes and, together with a group of his companions, we dine together in a large chamber set aside for those of lower consequence. There is a general chatter about Her Majesty's appearance early this morning and the tour of her courtiers with her close ladies. It seems that she was in poor temper and had sharp words for some on her promenade, including two of her ladies dismissed to their chambers in tears and a serving boy who she ordered whipped for his clumsiness.

'What was the cause of her ill disposition?' I ask Richard.

'I believe she had words with Oxford.'

'Oh, do you know the cause?'

'No doubt, coin was at the heart of it. He is known to spend beyond his means. Her Majesty is often displeased with him, but always relents as she values his handsome face and pretty clothes.'

'Have you had any dealings with Oxford or his entourage?'

'I have learned to keep my distance to avoid the risk of scorn for my low station.'

I sympathise with Richard, then excuse myself from the table to attend to my duties.

Forester is away from his chambers and has left me a note of two gentlemen who wish to consult me. I find Sir Peter Layton seated on his own by a fire. He is a large elderly gentleman who complains of gout in his right foot and asks that I consult with him in his chair as it pains him to walk. I confirm his diagnosis and say that I will have an infusion of root ginger prepared and delivered. He greets my remedy with surprise and confesses that he would prefer his usual salve of boar's grease. My last patient is the young ward of the Earl of Sussex who I bled the other day. He is in good health and as I do not have the inclination to argue, bleed him a little again.

I am done a good hour before John arrives at the physicians' quarters. We retire to my chamber with a glass of sweet wine before our homeward journey. His face is a little flushed, which he blames on his liking for the warmth of roaring fires and he appears in good spirits. I mention my understanding of Her Majesty's displeasure with Oxford and her general ill temper.

He says, 'I met with Mistress Parry and my intention was to

enquire about any particular interest in astrology here, but she was full of talk about Oxford. The Queen had discovered that he had sold land recently granted to him and failed to show remorse when rebuked. He was also admonished for neglecting his young wife, who is Burghley's daughter.'

'Was there no mention of Kelly or Millen attending court?'

'I regret not. Mistress Parry regards astrology in much the same way as me, and showed no interest. You will pardon my rudeness, William.'

'Of course, so we learn nothing from our visit, except for the misbehaviour of a young earl.'

*

It is dark, and Helen has departed when we arrive back at West Cheap. John retires to his chamber and I find Mother reading in the parlour.

'You are late, William. Helen was disappointed at your absence.'

I kiss her, take a seat by her and enquire after her health, although the continuation in her improvement is apparent through her appearance and time out of bed.

'How is Jane? Did she enjoy her time with Helen?'

'They are well matched. Jane has a sharp mind beneath her timid disposition. Their conversation was lively and prolonged. Helen promised a salve for her face bruising and has taken Jane to the Morton household in Leadenhall, where she will stay for a few days.'

Nineteen

It is Sunday and seven of our household have accompanied John to St Giles at Cripplegate. John's presence causes a stir and the deacon begs him to take the pulpit. He needs no second invitation and preaches with great feeling and at length about the closeness of the common man to God. He deplores the wicked obstacles placed between man and God by Rome and warns of everlasting pain for those who lapse to the false promises of Catholicism. Mistress Hilliard is clearly enraptured by his sermon and her attention to his words is unwavering. Mother sits composed and thoughtful, but begins to sigh quietly as John repeats his message to vocal expressions of approval in the congregation. His ending is met with great shouts of approbation and I wonder how many of these are genuine.

The air is cold, but fine and it is a short distance back to West Cheap from St Giles. I walk at the head of our group with Hicks and he is eager to inform me that the small dispute with bankers has been settled and we have the funds from our wool trade. Harry Larkin is waiting at the front of our house for Hicks and they head around the house to their chambers in the courtyard. I am in my library when Hicks knocks and enters.

'Some news from Spytalfields, sir. I fear it is not good.'

'What news? Ah, is it the instrument maker?'

'Yes, sir.'

'Does he have trouble with its fabrication?'

'It is worse than that. I sent Harry to enquire about its progress. He has returned with information that the workshop is burned and the master craftsman is dead.'

'Dead, how?'

'I do not know, sir. Harry did not stay to discover the details.'

Another fire and a man killed. I cannot think that there is a connection; houses burn every day and the instrument has no significance in the conspiracy. And yet...

'Hicks, you will accompany me to Spytalfields. I wish to learn more of this poor unfortunate who we entrusted with our work.'

It is another hour before we are ready to begin our journey. We are obliged through courtesy to accept Mother's invitation for light refreshment to mark John's preaching. The conversation is animated; John relishes the attention and reason to expound on his convictions. My excuse to depart with Hicks on a matter of business raises no query and the discussion continue as we exit. Although it is a short distance to travel, it is many years since I visited Spytalfields and am surprised to find a great number of new buildings on the path through Bishopsgate to our destination. I remember it as a place of open fields and scattered dwellings, but now it is more like a small town with close-set houses forming streets.

Hicks leads me towards the ruined priory where there is much building work and plundering of the priory stones. Hicks points to a small group of buildings, some two hundred yards beyond the priory.

'What is the family name of the late craftsman,' I ask Hicks.

'Hutchison; a man of middle years with wife and children.'

A yeoman and goodwife watch us from the front of a house and usher children inside as we approach. I bid them good day and enquire where we may find Goodwife Hutchison. The woman is about to answer, but the man stops her and asks the nature of our business. When he learns of our commission his caution eases a little. He shakes his head.

'She is dead, along with her husband. They were friends to us and we will miss their good cheer and companionship.'

'I am distressed to hear this news. I had heard of Master Hutchison's fate, but not his goodwife. Were they taken in the fire?'

'Do you not know? They were both killed, most horribly by the evil scum that set the blaze.'

We are told a tale that has a terrifying familiarity. After dusk and three days past, a group of mounted and armed men arrived with flaming torches. They broke the door and shutters setting the house aflame in short time. Master Hutchison was grabbed by three men and had his throat slit with a short sword. The goodwife protested, tried to save her husband and when she persisted was run through by the same sword. The two children escaped and are sheltered in the yeoman's house. The constable and justice attended, but the attackers were not identified by the gathered witnesses.

Hicks says, 'Did Master Hutchison have enemies or jealous competitors for his trade?'

'No, he was a quiet and kindly man who could calm a wild dog.'

'Was there no help from neighbours or a hue and cry?'

'It would have been our end if we had got too near. They were hard men, practised at giving injury and death.' The quiver in his voice betrays shame at not doing more to save his friend.

I reach inside my purse and hand two silver crowns to the yeoman.

'It is a most distressing story. Our commission for Master Hutchison is of small account set against this tragedy. Let us hope that the evil murderers are caught and punished with due severity. Please take these coins for the comfort of the poor children deprived of their parents.'

The yeoman mutters his thanks while his goodwife gapes at the coins, the like of which she may never have seen. Before we turn to go, I have one more question.

'Did you see the man who did the killing?'

'He was not known to me and it was dark.' He pauses and adds, 'He had the way of a soldier; a large man with dark cowl over his head. He had no beard; that much I could see.'

Our return journey is quiet as we both consider the dreadful fate of the Hutchison family. I see that Hicks is much affected. I am loth to break the silence, but there is a nagging thought I must put to rest.

'Hicks, who knew that Master Hutchison was charged with the manufacture of my instrument for navigation?'

He stares at me as though I have taken leave of my senses. 'Why, Doctor Constable, you do not think your instrument may be the cause of such calamity?'

'It is most unlikely, Hicks, but Sir George Morton will seek reason for the delay in delivering the instrument.'

'Well, Harry knew and I think Mistress Hilliard may have heard the name Hutchison mentioned.'

'What of your associates in trade for other families?'

'There would have been no cause to discuss this, as it has no concern for our normal business.'

'Did you disclose the name to Master Wensum when he called?'

'Yes, I believe I did, but he is in the employ of Sir George and would have a keen interest in the instrument's safe delivery.'

Gregory takes our horses and I accompany Hicks to his business chamber. I say that I would have him seek another craftsman to manufacture the instrument. It must be done quickly and I will pay the extra coin for haste.

I add, 'Be discreet in your enquiries, Hicks, and tell no-one when a man is chosen. His name must be known only to you and me.'

'Very well, Doctor Constable, I will begin my search this afternoon.'

'Please also find two reliable watchmen to guard our new craftsman's property. They will bear arms, but I do not want drunk or ill-tempered men who will use them too quickly. Do not tell them the purpose of their watch and this also must be done discreetly without the craftsman's knowledge.'

He takes my instructions without comment, but his expression suggests I am too cautious with these arrangements and too extravagant with my coin.

*

Mother and John are both reading in the parlour. The atmosphere is one of quiet contemplation and I presume that they are resting from their lively exchanges earlier in the day. I do not mention the awful events at Spytalfields. Instead, I inform them that we had much to discuss about the wool trade and that we made enquiries about the possible construction of a navigation aid for ships. Half-truths will have to suffice at this time.

My mind is full of thoughts of intrigue and I itch to retire to my library and create a new set of fine drawings from my drafts. But it is clear that Mother wishes me to remain and converse for a while. She tells me that Mistress Hilliard has gone to the Morton household, under escort of Gregory and Harry, to deliver certain small comforts for Jane that were left in her chamber. There is a knock at the door and Mistress Hilliard enters. She begs my indulgence as she has a message. In truth, I am happy for an excuse to leave the parlour and I take Mistress Hilliard to the library.

'Did you find Mistress Dee in good spirits?'

She is unusually talkative and says that the two young ladies were in good health, and happy in each other's company. She apologises for her delayed return and explains that Rosamund took her aside and introduced her to the still and drying room. She is full of eagerness to talk about the wide array of herbs and medicinal plants at Leadenhall and wishes that we could learn from their experience and expand our herbal preparations.

She says, 'I was offered a dried plum that effected such an improvement on the lady Amy. Despite its foul appearance it had a very pleasing taste. Rosamund also gave me a salve of beeswax and cloves to aid my sore hips.'

'I am very happy you have a liking for Rosamund and that your visit afforded fascination and benefit. I agree that we should strive to improve our medicines by learning from the ladies at Leadenhall. You said that you had a message…'

'My pardon, sir, I had forgotten. Master Wensum requested that I invite you for supper at six o'clock this next Wednesday. He apologises for the lateness of the hour of invitation. Sir George, Master Wensum and others wish to discuss, what he called, their "great adventure".'

Twenty

Hicks has found a candidate for the manufacture of the instrument. He is a Frenchman by the name of Chap who has a small house and workshop on Long Lane by the Fleet. I have completed my fine drawings and ride with Hicks to meet this man. When I ask Hicks more about him he is somewhat apologetic at describing his trade as a toymaker. He answers my raised eyes by saying that he has a strong reputation for well-crafted wooden and mechanical toys. He is also known to manufacture small items of furniture, such as gaming tables.

Long Lane becomes narrower and more noxious as we near the Fleet. The buildings overhang so that they almost touch and we dismount to have a safer passage. The mud and filth on the lane sucks in our boots and it is an unpleasant last few steps to the door of the Chap house. The building is small, but well-tended compared to its neighbours with a fresh coat of whitewash and tar on the frontage. Our knock is answered by a neat woman of middle years dressed in black, save for white apron and bonnet. I assume this will be Goodwife Chap. We are led through two dark, small, low-beamed rooms where I am forced to bow my head, through to a workshop at the rear. Thankfully, the workshop is more spacious and has good light. Two men are standing at a table peering at a paper laid flat by stones in each corner. Both are dressed in rough woollen shirts with leather aprons. One has almost no head hair and thick beard, while the other is a youth of no more than thirteen years. Hicks makes our introductions.

The older man says, 'Good day and God's peace to you gentlemen. I am Chap and this is my son Peter.' His voice has an unmistakeable French lilt, but his English is good.

I say, 'Thank you Master Chap. I understand that you are from France. Chap is an unusual name for a Frenchman, is it not?'

'Yes, sir, our French name is Chappuzeau and it is shortened to make our family trade more acceptable in England.'

'You are Huguenot?'

'Yes, we escaped persecution and murder by the Catholic League seven years past. I had another son who did not elude the killing and fire of the mob. To my eternal shame he lies unburied, while his spirit roams the streets of Lyon.'

'I am sorry for your family distress, Master Chap. You have settled well in England?'

'We are grateful for safe harbour in this Christian land, sir. I cannot deny that we have suffered through suspicion of our foreign origin, but there has been improvement in trade and our general tolerance over the years.'

'Good, you know that your trade as a craftsman is the reason for our visit?'

'Yes, I am intrigued. I was told only that it is for a measuring instrument fashioned from wood and metal.'

I take out my drawings and hand them to Chap. He unrolls the first carefully and places it on top of the existing one, replacing the corner stones. Father and son peer closely at the sketch, then Chap begs his son to fetch paper and quill and to write a series of numbers. He does the same with my second drawing. He takes the paper from his son and, with scratching of head and pursing of lips, writes more before he places quill on the table and folds his arms.

'It can be done. I see it is for a ship's master to take readings from the stars.'

'Yes, it is, Master Chap. It must be well-crafted to allow for precision in measurement.'

'I will not allow inferior creations to leave my workshop, Doctor Constable.' It is an effort for him to hold the indignation in his voice. 'Would it be your pleasure to inspect examples of our work?'

We are led over to a corner where he shows a wooden figure of a man-at-arms made for the young son of a wine merchant. It is ingeniously fitted with small metal joints at neck, elbows, waist and knees; all move smoothly and without minor obstruction. Chap tells me with pride that his son is responsible for the painted decoration. A wooden sword slides from its side and clicks into place in a small holder in the right hand containing sprung metal. Next, he shows me a miniature set of drawers made for a lady's jewels and other valuables. There is a locking mechanism which serves to remind me of the ebony box at Barn Elms. It is subtle and finely-worked with a smooth key turn and satisfying click. I have seen enough.

'This is very good work, Master Chap. If you are content that you can manufacture my instrument in quick time, then the commission is yours.'

Hicks nudges me and mutters that we must consider the price before making a commitment.

Chap says, 'My fee will depend upon the urgency of your need. I have other work here that is promised.'

'I would have it after four days, on the Monday of next week.'

He shakes his head, reaches for his paper and scrawls more figures and calculations. 'In that case my fee will be one pound and six shillings.' Hicks breathes deeply and shuffles his feet. Chap adds, 'If you can wait for two weeks then my fee will be sixteen shillings and four pence.'

Prudence demands that I leave these negotiations to Hicks, but I need the instrument quickly and I am confident that Chap will make a piece to impress Sir George and Captain Hawkins.

'I will accept your price for delivery next Monday. Will two crowns be sufficient for a first payment?' He bows his head in agreement and I hand over the coins. 'There is a strict condition to this commission, Master Chap. You must not disclose the nature of the object or my name in connection this work to anyone outside this room. The business of sea trade contains many jealousies for obtaining advantage in the speed and accurate navigation of ships.'

*

A steady drizzle has set in when I reach the Morton house and am pleased to release damp cloak and hat into the arms of a servant for drying by a fire. I am ushered into a receiving room where Darby Wensum stands waiting. He bids me welcome and offers a cup of claret, which I accept. We stand talking of inconsequential things for a few minutes, then he apologises for the absence of Captain General Hawkins who has been detained and will not meet with us this night.

I say, 'Is Sir George in good health?'

'Yes, he is well, but has endured an eventful day and dozes before our supper. I trust that he will be with us in short time.'

Our polite conversation is extended for too many minutes and the silence between our exchanges lengthens, creating an uncomfortable air. Finally, Wensum leaves to investigate whether Sir George is ready to join us. He is gone for over half an hour. I begin to feel there is a strangeness about my presence here, when a servant enters and announces that supper is ready to be served.

Wensum is seated next to Sir George who is sat with his chin resting heavily on his chest and is clearly asleep. We are being served oysters and a bowl is set for Sir George who does not stir save for a bubbling of his lips and low whistling as he breathes. We are done with the oysters and started on an eel pie before Wensum begs forgiveness on behalf of Sir George as he fears that his business has been more tiring than he had thought.

He says, 'Nevertheless, we should discuss your progress with the navigation instrument and I will forward your news to our principals.'

'Perhaps we should wait for Sir George to wake. I believe his favourite dish is gammon and he may rouse at the odour of this food.'

'We could wait too long and if he does not stir shortly I should arrange for transport to the comfort of his bed.'

This is indeed a strange supper, first with the absence of Hawkins and now the deep sleep of Sir George who does not hear our talk, or the rattling of pewter plates and silver serving dishes. It crosses my mind that Rosamund or Helen may have prescribed a sleeping draught.

Wensum says, 'I am surprised that you have not brought your instrument this night. Does it take so long to fashion an exemplar?'

'A rough model may be made in a day or two, but exact and dainty work takes more time. I would have a well-crafted piece to present to Sir George and Captain Hawkins.'

'Do you have an estimate of when it will be ready? You will know that Sir George will be disappointed by an undue delay.'

I mumble an apology and say that I cannot give a date, but

will make every effort to submit it for examination as quickly as possible. Wensum bows his head in understanding and puts aside the subject in order to arrange for Sir George's retirement to his bedchamber. I am in favour of curtailing our supper, but Wensum is determined that we finish the dishes prepared. I pick my way through a pigeon pie, broiled chicken, a gammon and sweet jellies, enduring Wensum's detailed telling of the preparations for the venture, which I have heard before.

At last, our supper is over and I beg for my outer clothes and horse to return home. Wensum returns to our room with my cloak and hat. He apologises that he has no men available to escort my journey home as they have been called for work at one of Sir George's storehouses on the North Quay.

It is a short ride home and the streets are quiet for the most part, with the cold air keeping souls cozied in their houses or huddled over their cups in the inns. I am passing the dark form of St Gabriel in Fen Church when I spy two figures about one hundred yards ahead run quickly into a side alley. I put a hand on my dagger, pull my cloak back and 'click' at Cassius to walk on. I peer closely at the alley as we draw closer, but there is no further movement. There is a shuffling noise to my other side and before I can turn hands grab at my thigh and arm… I am unhorsed… My head… a booming sound as my head hits something solid. Hands… grab my hair, my coat. I kick my feet. I hit something soft. There is a yelp of pain. My arm… twisted… my dagger… I must free my dagger. I smell the sweat and foul breath of a man near my face. He curses and… I am hit… my neck… a clash of steel. My world dissolves and I am lost… falling…falling.

Twenty-One

The silence is grey. I hear a faint drumming or swishing; a peculiar noise, which is within me. Am I dead? I feel pain. My head throbs and my neck… my arm… hand. I am broken – but alive. The sound inside me is my breathing. How alive? I lift my right hand and touch my cheek; my throat; my forehead. A whisper; a croak; a humming from my throat. It is me, trying to speak. Where am I? Alone, in an enclosed grey space, laid flat. My head and body ache as I try to rise. No… I sink back and… I must sleep.

There is light and… a voice. I am dreaming. My shoulder moves, roughly. A man calls my name. I know this man. It is… My eyes open and I flinch as Captain Askham's face is close to mine.

'Where am I?'

'You were attacked, but you are saved.'

That much I know, but how was I saved and how did I get here? Where is this place? I do not recognise the chamber. Askham grabs my arm and helps me to sit. I shake my head, then stop quickly as a pain punches sharply in a space behind my eyes. I am on a hard wooden bed with no bolsters or linens, clothed only in hose and shirt. My other clothes and shoes are on a rough stone floor. My legs are uninjured and my right arm moves with freedom. My left arm will not move… Ah, my breath catches. It is my left wrist that is swollen and hangs oddly. There is dried blood on the sleeve of my shirt and I see that this has spread to my chest. I repeat my last question.

'You are in Sir Francis's house in Seething Lane. I am ordered to take you to him.'

'Sir Francis is returned from France?'

'Yes, two nights past.'

He takes my arm and I stand. My legs bear me, if a little unsteadily. My vision is blurred and I close my eyes. I open them and stagger as the room swims. Askham clutches me and I breathe deeply to regain my balance. I step gently, then with

141

more purpose and we walk slowly towards the door. The door opens and two guards stiffen as we exit. We tread down a narrow passage, up a flight of stairs and then to a lighter area with a wider passage and polished wooden floor. Askham knocks on a door, opens it and gestures for me to enter. Walsingham is slouched in a chair behind a table with a thin dagger in his hand. He appears to be trimming his fingernails.

'Doctor Constable, you are in a poor state.'

'Ah, yes, forgive my appearance, Miser Secretary. I was attacked.'

'Indeed. Your wounds have not been dressed, but you have been examined. Your wrist is damaged and your head will be sore, but I am told that you have no mortal injury.'

My senses are not fully recovered, but I detect a coldness in his manner. Why have I not been treated with more care and comfort? A bare room; hard bed; wounds undressed; no refreshment offered. Something is amiss; a wrongness in the air.

'How was I saved?'

'You were followed. It is fortunate for you that the Captain was close by with another man.'

'Why was I followed?'

He ignores my question and asks one in return. 'Why have you visited the house of Sir George Morton?'

'I… I heard of his great venture with Captain General Hawkins and… it stirred my interest in the art of ship navigation again.'

'It is somewhat coincidental that your interest was revived a day or two after your consideration of the chart and coded message at Barn Elms.'

'That is all it is; a coincidence.'

'Is it also a matter of accident that Doctor Dee's library was burned shortly after your first visit for many years?'

'I do not think that was ill-fortune. I believe it was planned because word had reached the conspirators about the search for Millen. Doctor Foxe and Captain Askham agree with me on this.'

He is silent for a while and continues to trim his fingernails.

He says, 'Why do you think you were brought to me at

Whitehall that night? Was it because I suspected some hidden talent in you for solving ciphers? Your expertise in astrology, perhaps? Or was it a chance plucking of a name out of thin air?'

'You stated that it was my association with Doctor Dee.'

'Ah, yes, I remember. When you arrived that night you will have seen the corrupted bodies of three men freshly killed for their treason. One of those men cried out your name through the agony of cracking limbs.'

'Godfrey Baskin. I knew him a little, but many years past. Why would he utter my name?'

'Why indeed, Doctor Constable?'

'I… I can only think that he was being questioned about his knowledge of astrologers. Then… then you connected him with the natal chart in the box and suspected me.'

'Very good, Doctor Constable. You have clear insights despite your sore head.'

'But you must know that I am not one of the conspirators. I solved the cipher. I gave the names of Kelley and Millen…'

'Ah, the cipher; a quick solution for an amateur. And both of those men known to you.'

'Knowing is not conspiring. There will be many innocents who have acquaintances with those convicted of crimes.'

'Some of what you say rings true and you are fortunate that Doctor Foxe has a liking for you. Also, the Captain speaks in your favour. Yet, I am troubled by this connection with Sir George Morton. It is untimely and too sudden.'

'Does Master Mylles suspect me?'

'He is… undecided, as am I.'

'My interest in Sir George's great venture to the New Lands is genuine and true. I was reminded of my work on the mathematics of navigation at my summons to Whitehall that night. I quickly became absorbed in study to find a practical instrument that will improve navigation and assist in the rendezvous of the fleet.'

He listens carefully and bows his head bidding me to continue. I outline the difficulty of taking accurate readings looking to the top of a crosshatch, then the underside, and the coordination of the two. I detail my solution and he offers paper and quill so that I can sketch my design. He takes the finished sketch, tilts his head this way and that to mimic its use and replaces it on the table.

'Very well, Doctor Constable, I believe you. The story you tell is too real and complex for it to be a screen for some other purpose. Please forgive our hard treatment of your injured body, but perhaps there will be compensation in the thought that our suspicions helped to save your life.'

I had not realised that my body was so tightly coiled until it eases on the utterance of those words. I do not have to mention my attachment to Helen as a further reason for connection to Morton and the probing into her background. Despite his acceptance of my story, I do not have a sense that my position is fully secured with Walsingham. Nevertheless, I must ask a question that nags my thoughts.

'It was a great surprise to see Master Baskin tortured and killed. From my earlier knowledge he had no leanings towards Rome and possessed a balanced temperament. How were you convinced that he had turned to wicked Catholic treason?'

He puts down his dagger and raises his eyes. 'Ha, it is a wonder you return to the subject of Baskin and his Jesuit associates. His mind was distracted by a woman. His wife was secretly devoted to the Catholic cause. There was no doubt of his guilt, which was established before his torture.'

'Why would he mention my name?'

'Men will drag many hidden thoughts and words to the surface under pressure of the rack. Some will have significance to the matter in hand, while others will not, but all must be investigated.' He pauses and clasps his hands together on the table. 'Come, let us talk no further of this unfortunate connection in your past. It pleases me that your loyalty to our cause is unblemished. Your sharp mind may help to save us from this latest plot, and perhaps others.'

He waves his hand and a man appears to lead me from this chamber to another where my clothes and light refreshment are waiting. A servant brings in a bowl of water, sponge and white soap. I try to wash the grime and blood from my injured parts, but it is a slow and cumbersome process and I finish before it is done well. Askham enters as I am dressing, helps me heave doublet and coat over my swollen arm and waits as I drink a cup of small beer.

'I should thank you for saving my life, Captain. I did not know I was followed under suspicion for my loyalty.'

'You were not suspected by me, Doctor Constable.'

I bow my head. 'Then, my sincere gratitude to you for your actions and words. How many attacked me?'

'There were four men. One I killed, and the others were driven off by me and my sergeant.'

It is news to me that an attacker was killed. He tells me that his body is laid in the chamber next to where I was kept and I ask to inspect it.

The trail back to the floor below is slow and it take concentration of the mind to control my limbs. The body is of a young, thickset man with untamed beard. His middle glistens in the candlelight with a spread of sticky, blackening blood, although the wound is small. I do not recognise him.

I say, 'Did he talk before dying?'

'No, it was quick; more the shame.'

'How was your sight of the others?'

He shrugs. 'It was dark. They bore arms like fighting men. Two were of my height or a little shorter, but the third was a large man; taller than you and broader.'

'Was his face hooded with a cowl?'

'Ah, yes I believe it was. Do you know this man?'

'The description is too general to be sure, but it fits the description of the lead attacker at Doctor Dee's house at Mortlake.' I do not refer to the murders in Spytalfields, as this connection is not yet resolved in my own mind. Besides, it would likely lead to awkward questioning about the Morton family and danger for Helen.

We have few more words before Askham takes me to my horse and helps me mount. He insists on an escort of two men although the day is bright and the street is busy. We ride at a slow plod, but within minutes my body complains and I am relieved to arrive at West Cheap and dismount. Gregory stares at me with open mouth and stands, undecided whether to take the horse or help me. I tell him that I fell from Cassius when risking a canter at night and that I am sore, but sound. He takes the horse while I make my way to my bedchamber and lie with some care on top of the sheets. Tiredness soon overcomes my aches and my eyes close.

*

Someone is near. There is a rustling of clothes and a familiar scent. I open my eyes and Mother is sat beside my bed. I try to rise, but there is a fierce pain; in my neck; my head; my arm; my back. My whole body shouts at me to lie still. She strokes my good hand and makes soothing noises, as to a child.

'Mother, I…'

'I hear you fell from your horse.'

'Yes, I was clumsy.'

'It was last night?'

'Yes.'

'Then you were fortunate to find shelter and a place to recover.'

'I was with… Captain Askham and he saw to my overnight care.'

'You were not tended well. Your wound is unclean and your wrist may be fractured and in need of support. I have cleaned the gash on the back of your head and will seek advice on your wrist. You have an ugly weal on the back of your neck and much bruising. It was a bad fall, and Cassius is such a steady horse.'

'He… he must have stumbled. I cannot remember all.'

'Here, you must drink this brandywine and rest. Your body is badly shaken and needs sleep to recover.'

I wince as I lift my head and take the cup. The wine is good and I swallow greedily. I lie back and only then do I notice that I am under the bedclothes and my shirt has been replaced by a linen smock. It is a wonder that I did not wake with this handling, but I will not consider it now. My eyes are heavy.

*

It is dark when I wake again. The embers of a small fire still glow and another cup of brandywine waits on the bedside table. I swivel my legs, stand and relieve myself in the piss pot. I light a candle, sit in a chair and sup the wine. Suddenly, I snatch at fragments of a dream. Helen is with me and we are gazing at the figure of a naked man, horribly corrupt and disembowelled, hanging on a gallows. It is her father, Sir George. I close my eyes tight to dispel the nightmare. I am not a believer in dreams that foretell the future, but the ghastly image makes mischief with my thoughts. I retire again to my bed hoping sleep will come quickly.

*

I am disturbed by the sounds of rustling and grating of metal. It is Mistress Hilliard come to make a new fire. She says the hour is past nine. I ask her to fetch Hicks to help me dress, but I am told that he has business at a storehouse and will not return until mid-afternoon. She will ask my mother if Harry or Gregory can be spared to assist.

It is no surprise when Mother appears to help me dress. She tuts and coos over my bruises and other marks, but the task is soon done. I say that my hurt has eased a little and I am hungry.

'Breakfast is set in your library where your chair offers most comfort. Do not linger over your food and drink as you will have visitors within the hour.'

'Who would that be?'

'I have sent a note to Helen and Rosamund describing your injuries and the return note advises they will attend with ointments, salves and other soothers at ten bells.'

I did not anticipate this. I will be pleased to see Helen, but I am not sure how I feel about her prodding and poking at my body parts. I am sure that Sir George would not approve, if he knows of it.

My belly tells me I should eat, but the eggs lack flavour and the biscuits taste of sawdust. I drink enough to rinse my mouth and cool my throat, leaving most of the food untouched. Our visitors arrive early and are ushered into the library by Mistress Hilliard who fusses around my table and takes away the breakfast tray. I offer them more comfort in the parlour, but Helen says they will stay. Her face has an expression of puzzlement.

'How was it done?'

'It was a fall from my horse. I was inattentive when he

147

stumbled on a stone.'

She takes my injured arm and beckons her maid to come close. She lifts it gently and pulls back the sleeve. They both peer at the wrist and Helen takes my middle finger between her finger and thumb and…My breath is sharp with the pain as it moves. Rosamund prods at the swelling, then turns to Helen and exchanges some form of silent understanding.

Helen says, 'A bone in your wrist is cracked. We will apply a salve for the swelling, then it must be tightly bound so that it cannot move. You will need to rest this arm in a sling for some weeks until it is mended.'

She stands behind me and lifts my hair to examine my cut and softly brushes her fingers over the weal on my neck making me shiver – with pleasure. She returns to my sight and takes her maid by the arm.

'Rosamund, we will need the ointment of honey, charcoal and comfrey for the wound and your cooling salve for the swollen arm. Please ask Mistress Hilliard to bring two large sheets of clean linen for the binding.'

We are alone. Helen sets her stool by my chair, fixes me with a steady gaze and says, 'Where was it done, this fall?'

'It was not far from here; by Cripplegate.'

She tilts her head in a way that signals some confusion.

'I learned that you were at my father's house last night. Cripplegate is not between this place and Leadenhall.'

'No… forgive me, it was not Cripplegate.' I curse inwardly at my folly. 'I did not wish to alarm you and I would keep the true facts from my mother. I was set upon by thieves near Fen Church. I was pulled from my horse and fell awkwardly, but it was a short commotion and they were driven off.'

She stares at me. I cannot read her expression. Is she angry; concerned? She rises from her seat and… kisses me on the mouth. Her arms are around me; her lips soft and moist. I put my right arm around her waist and pull her closer. She does not resist and the kiss becomes… more than a kiss. She pulls away quickly, lowers her head and brushes her skirts. There are no words between us. She sits, raises her head and gazes at me directly.

'Why were you at my father's house?'

'Will you reward my answer with another kiss?'

She wrinkles her nose and repeats her question.

'An invitation was sent via Master Wensum. It was intended that we would discuss the great venture and my invention of a navigation instrument.'

'I had heard of your instrument from my father, but I did not know there was to be a supper last night.'

'Would it be usual for you to know of such an arrangement?'

'Yes.'

'Captain Hawkins could not attend and your father... your father was tired and slept through the supper.'

'My father slept...' She shakes her head slowly. 'That is strange.' She pauses to gather her thoughts. 'Can you describe your escort last night? I will question them about your attack.'

'I had no escort. Master Wensum said that all your father's men were engaged elsewhere.'

She purses her lips and blinks her eyes. 'That would be... uncommon. My father has six men at Leadenhall who could... Did you have words with Master Wensum? Did you quarrel?'

'No, it was a somewhat perplexing supper, but there were no angry exchanges between us.'

She folds her arms and takes a deep breath. I would have another kiss. I rise from my seat as the door opens and Rosamund appears with Mistress Hilliard. The moment has gone.

There is a great fuss as Mother joins Rosamund and Mistress Hilliard to apply the salves to my head wound, neck and other bruises on my body. Helen stands back with an expression of amusement, then steps forward to supervise the tight wrapping of my wrist and making of a sling. At last it is complete and the ladies admire their handiwork. I am cosseted and stared at like a child. I stand to relieve my embarrassment and thank them for their trouble. I admit that my wrist feels more secure and my aches have some relief from their soothing ointments.

Twenty-Two

The arm is troublesome and I cannot settle to my work. For two days I have fidgeted and flitted from one task to another without completing any. I fear that I have exasperated Mother and the servants with my uneven temper and interference in their daily routine. I am poor company for John. My contributions to our conversations are without merit and brief to the point of rudeness. I have many strands of thought, but it is Helen that pushes all others to the background. The taste of her lips and the eagerness in her body is a memory that I would keep above all others. I must complete my search into her history and banish all suspicion of her parentage. But how? I cannot simply demand this knowledge from her or her father. She may not know the full facts, and such a question to her father would surely ruin any chance of my preferment in his eyes. Besides, I must also confirm that Sir George is not a party to the conspiracy. His position as one of the principals in the great venture states his innocence clearly to me, but proof should be presented in a way that will satisfy Walsingham. Even now, Mister Secretary's network of intelligencers may be watching the Morton household and strong questioning or torture may offer conclusions that are misunderstood or in error. I must be quick.

I meet Hicks on the way to my library and ask him to join me.

'How is the watch on Master Chap's workshop?'

'There is nothing to report.'

'And no word of delay from Chap?'

No, sir.'

Good.'

'There is a small matter that I would mention.'

'What is it?'

'It is Gregory's sixteenth birthday today. He was promised a new set of clothes when he reaches this age.'

'Yes, I remember.'

'Then I shall arrange it. Also…'

'Yes?'

'He has a toothache; one that causes him much discomfort. I know you would normally remove the offending tooth, but your injured arm may cause some difficulty with this operation.'

I flex my right arm, which would be up to the pulling, but Hicks is right; my other arm is too cumbersome to manage an extraction.

'Where would you purchase Gregory's clothes?'

'There is a wool shirt, breeches and leather jerkin set aside at Goodwife Croft's shop by Newgate.'

'Good, there is a barber near there who is clean and gentler than most with bad teeth. I will take Gregory for his clothes and tooth pulling. I would welcome the ride and a change of air.'

It is a half hour before we are ready to ride. Gregory's discomfort is clear from a swollen cheek and he is eager for relief. It is unlikely that I am still followed by Askham's men in broad daylight and I detect no obvious trail behind as we depart.

The tooth pulling is painful, but brief and Gregory emerges with a smile on his face. I hand him a tincture of cloves to apply to the gums around the tender area. I am surprised when he tells me that he has been using this same preparation for several days and it was supplied by Mistress Hilliard.

He says, 'She has discovered a keen interest in herbal medicines through her new friendship.'

'A new friendship?'

'Yes, it is the woman called Ros. She talks of her often.'

I did not know that Mistress Hilliard had formed an alliance with Rosamund. I am pleased for both women. Is there a way I could use this connection between our two households?

Gregory has trouble containing his excitement at the clothes shop and claims that he is having a birthday fit for a prince. Goodwife Croft is much taken with his innocent delight and presents him with a woollen neck scarf to ward off the cold. He is a likeable young man and I remember my intention to give him some basic instruction, but that must wait until I am free of my association with Mister Secretary.

*

After supper Mother retires to her chamber and I am left with

John who is eager to discuss the conspiracy. He has received a note from Mylles about the discovery of a pamphlet by St Paul's. This was a short and scurrilous tract which claimed that Her Majesty had given birth to a child and the father was named as Dudley. There was no reference to an astrological chart.

I say, 'Was there specific mention of the child, gender or birth date?'

'No, Mylles noted that it was a text from an uneducated hand with little detail and a poorly-argued exhortation to follow the teachings of Rome.'

'In that case, it may be unconnected to the conspiracy.'

'You may be right, William. Wrong-headed printings of this sort appear from time-to-time. The murder of Millen and the attack on your person suggest that the plotters are alarmed at our searches.'

'It is too much to suppose that they will abandon their plans.'

'Yes, we may know more if they find the printer.'

Our conversation continues for some time and we speculate, but have no firm answers. Eventually, I say that I must change my dressings and go in search of Mistress Hilliard. I find her in the linen room with Rose and ask her to join me in my bedchamber with ointments and clean wrappings.

My arm is purple with bruising and feels strangely vulnerable freed from the many folds of tight cloth. The rest of my body improves with only an aching stiffness in the neck as the other reminder of my closeness to death that night. The winding of linen is a long process and Mistress Hilliard takes care to place and stiffen each circle of the arm.

I say, 'I hear that you are on good terms with Rosamund from the Morton household.'

'Yes sir, we are comfortable together.'

'I know you are eager to learn more of the gathering and preparation of herbal cures from her.'

'Yes sir.'

'In that case we will arrange meetings for your education and companionship.' She smiles and bows her head in thankful acknowledgement. 'You could offer me a great service through your conversations with Rosamund, Mistress Hilliard.' Her head is low, but I detect an air of suspicion in her manner.

'What would that be, sir?'

'Rosamund's Mistress, the lady Helen is… someone I hold in high regard.'

'That is plain from the way you gaze at each other.'

'Oh.'

'Yes, Ros and I have talked on it and we are glad that you share a… fondness.'

'It is a delicate matter and…'

'Sir, I have known you for more than twenty years and you should not be timid on my account. Do you wish me to pass a message to the lady Helen?'

'It is information that I seek, not the exchange of messages, at least not at present.'

She leans forward, eager to learn more. I hesitate, undecided how best to express my wishes.

'There may come a time when I… we would wish for a closeness and the approach must be managed with care. I have heard rumours about Helen's birth and that… that Sir George's late wife may not be her natural mother.' Her eyes widen and she clasps her hands primly. I know she would not wish to be a party to intrusive probing into private matters, so I must soften my request. 'Helen's parentage is no concern to me. She could be born from the lowest circumstance for all that I care. But I would not wish to give offence by enquiring directly, or be the cause of discomfort in Sir George who may feel obliged to reveal certain facts before confirmation of our… more intimate connection.'

She relaxes a little and replies, 'Such rumours are often unfounded and spread by unknowing mischief makers. If it is true then Helen, herself may not know.'

'In that case I would not disclose the intelligence to her, but, as you say, there is likely nothing to this rumour.'

'Well sir, then I will be happy to help if I can.'

'Thank you, Mistress Hilliard. Please do not share the nature of this delicate mission with anyone. It must be our secret.'

I am relieved when our discussion ends. My subtle use of Mistress Hilliard's willing disposition should weigh on my conscience, but the importance of the enterprise frees me of feelings of guilt.

Twenty-Three

It is Monday and the day I had planned to take receipt of my instrument from Master Chap. My intention is spoiled by another summons from Mister Secretary who has sent two men for my escort. I will not ask Hicks to visit Master Chap in my place as I wish to examine the piece before parting with payment. I can only hope that my meeting at Whitehall is a brief one.

I arrive at the Palace of Whitehall as the bells signal ten o'clock and am ushered directly to Sir Francis's quarters. I am kept waiting in the anteroom I remember from my earlier summons on that dark night. It is a wait of over one hour before Padget enters and bids me follow him. Sir Francis is seated at his table and Mylles is in attendance, standing at his shoulder. They continue to converse in low voices until Mylles bows to Walsingham and takes his leave with only a cursory acknowledgement of my presence. This is not a warm welcome and the air of both men suggests that this will not be an easy meeting. Perhaps I imagine hostility where there is none, but I cannot rid myself of a feeling that my loyalty will be called into question yet again. I doff my cap and bow as graciously as my sling will allow.

'Good day, Mister Secretary, it is a privilege to be invited to your chambers again.'

'Doctor Constable, you are improved in your appearance since our last meeting. Do your injuries heal well?'

'Quite well, thank you, Sir Francis.'

He drums his fingers on the table and pauses as if choosing his next words with care.

I take the initiative and say, 'I have heard from Doctor Foxe of the discovery of a pamphlet. Has the printer or author been found?'

He ignores my question and says, 'Do you have a view on whether that pamphlet has a connection with the astrological conspiracy?'

So, the conspiracy has a term now, which links it to all who study the stars.

'I understand there was no mention of the stars or the gender of the supposed royal bastard and it would appear to be unrelated. Doctor Foxe tells me that there have been several similar tracts printed over the years, which insult Her Majesty in this way.'

'Yes, exactly so. I have a leaning towards your opinion, nevertheless we will continue our search for those involved in the distribution and printing of this pamphlet. It will be hard for them when they are found.' He steeples his fingers and stares at me directly as though he is examining my unspoken thoughts. 'You are on good terms with a gentleman named Joynes, I understand.'

'Yes, Richard Joynes, who I know from my time at Cambridge.'

'What is your judgement of him?'

'My judgement? He is sound man of good faith and balanced humors. He is good company and has helped me with introductions at court.'

'He has been accused of speaking in a way that insults Her Majesty. In particular, that he talked about a secret bastard child.'

'I… I find that difficult to believe. Who accuses him?'

'He is named by two men: Sir Peter Capton and Arthur Perse.'

'Why, that is absurd. Those are the two names I gave to your man, Mylles, as those who had spoken of such a thing.'

'Yes, and they denied it strongly when questioned by Mylles. It seems that now they have remembered hearing those vile words spoken by Joynes and have reported back to Mylles. Also, the Earl of Oxford has vouched for the character and truthfulness of these men.'

Oxford – why would he become involved in these petty accusations and counter-arguments? Is it vindictiveness or some other motive that drives these men to denounce Joynes?

I say, 'How does Richard Joynes answer this charge?'

'He waits for questioning. I would have your view on the matter first.' He pauses. 'There is more. You were named as the man in discussion with Joynes.'

'Me. No, this is too much. You cannot believe such a charge, Sir Francis. But why... why would they seek to lay these false allegations, unless...'

'Unless?'

'It may simply be spite and a dislike for me and Joynes.'

'Why would they harbour a grudge against you and Joynes?'

'I can only think that Capton and Perse knew that it was me who mentioned their names to Mylles. Perhaps they seek some form of petty revenge by this counter-accusation.'

'How would they know?'

'I suppose it must have been learned from Mylles.'

Walsingham narrows his eyes. 'You believe my man would have been so careless?'

'Perhaps it was a reason other than lack of care. Mylles may harbour a jealousy of me for the quick solving of the coded message. I considered his praise for that when we first met was too extravagant, and his subsequent manner to me has been less than friendly. Also, I was surprised that his questioning of Capton and Perse was so gentle and brief.'

I have a feeling that I must not be submissive in my answers and will be better served by a willingness to surprise Sir Francis with the force of my responses. But, have I been too direct in mistrusting the motives of a trusted servant? He continues to fix me with a disconcerting and piercing gaze, but remains silent.

Eventually, he says, 'I sense that you consider these men may have another reason for naming you and Joynes. Please, continue to speak your mind.'

'Well, it may be that... that they wish to muddy the waters and distract our search for the conspirators. The attack failed to kill me and so they looked for another way to put me aside.'

Will he regard this as a fanciful and vain statement? I must hope that he sees some merit in the suggestion or it may go badly for me – and Richard Joynes.

He considers for a moment, then says, 'Your speech is unguarded and dangerous in other places, but it is said in the way of an intelligencer, and is welcome in this chamber.' He pauses again. 'But I do not believe that Capton and Perse have the strength of character to be knowing parties to the conspiracy.'

Walsingham leaves something left unsaid about Oxford and I do not dare mention his name without any logic to support a connection. A dislike of the Earl by John and myself will not serve as an excuse to bring his name within the boundaries of the conspiracy.

His manner towards me begins to ease. He changes our topic of conversation and enquires after John's health. I suspect that this is Mister Secretary's way of reminding me that he has a trusted associate who is able to report on my comings and goings, as well as any lapses in behaviour or speech that may suggest disloyalty. I ask what will become of Richard Joynes and he replies that he will be released, assuming that his answers complement mine. I leave his presence, surviving his suspicions and questioning for a third time. I am indeed a fortunate man, as I am sure many innocents in similar positions have fared much worse.

I feel obliged to call on Forester before I depart Whitehall. He tells me that he had heard of my incapacity and did not expect to see me, but that he would be grateful for my quick return. Doctor Huicke has been taken ill with a severe chill and a bed has been set for him in his chamber here. Despite my eagerness to be gone I offer to consult with Huicke. Forester shrugs and says that he doubts I can assist in a quick recovery. Another physician has seen him, but that visit ended in a calamity as, when Huicke was bled he snatched the bleeding knife and attacked the doctor before turning the knife on himself and scoring many deep marks on his arms.

Forester says, 'The room was a bloody mess; Huicke was raving and threatening all who came near. Guards had to be called and no other doctor will attend him in his present state.'

'Is he watched?'

'He has been strapped to his cot as his fevered mind cannot be trusted. His chill was caught through wandering outside at night in his bed shirt in the sleeting rain. I fear there will have to be a new principal physician as he is surely not long for this world.'

I am taken to his chamber and he is indeed a pitiable sight. His heavily-bandaged arms are stained with blood and his head jerks from side to side. When he notices our entry, he sobs like a babe and begs to be freed. His straps are too severe and I ask Forester's help in easing them a little. He gives an expression of distaste, but obliges by easing a strap one notch before leaving to attend his urgent duties. I am alone with Huicke. He stares at me with pleading eyes and utters a strange mewing sound. There is heavy secretion of mucus and snot around his mouth. I take a linen cloth and wipe it as clean as I can. His breathing is laboured and it is clear that his body suffers with a bad chill, but if he is strong enough, kept warm and dry with regular feeding of meat broth and fortified wine, he should survive. It is his mind that poses a greater hazard and I know of no remedy for one as tortured as his. It is the general view of physicians that those with illnesses of the brain should have their heads shaved and be regularly bled from cuts around the temples. I will have no part in a treatment like this; not because it is cruel or demeaning, but I hold no prospect of its success.

He gestures with his head and bids me draw near. He whispers something I cannot hear clearly. I move a little closer.

'Beware young man. There is danger in this place.'

I take a step back. 'Why do you say this?'

'Your head is too full of invention. They will have it. They will lop it from your shoulders.'

He starts to laugh; a soft low chuckle which grows too loud and uncontrolled laughter mingled with coughs, dribbling and other unpleasant emissions. It is not a pretty state that he presents, but I can do no more and exit with some relief.

*

It is too late in the day when I return home to visit Master Chap, so I meet with Hicks and request that all is ready for us to make the journey early the next morning. I write a note to Sir George advising that I will have a model of the instrument tomorrow and offer to bring it to him at a time of his convenience. It is perhaps, tempting providence to pen this note before an inspection of Chap's workmanship, but I am impatient for another visit to Leadenhall. Mistress Hilliard called upon Rosamund there yesterday afternoon and I have not had the opportunity to speak to her alone since then. I must not appear too eager, or press her too quickly for any news about Helen, so I will wait for her approach to me on this matter.

Twenty-Four

We arrive at Master Chap's early in the morning, which is fine, but cold with frozen puddles on the streets and daggers of ice hanging from the houses. Chap's son, Peter, greets us at the door and leads us through to the workshop, where his father is busy fashioning a block of wood with chisel and hammer.

'Good day Master Chap, I am sorry we are late to receive my commission. I trust that it is ready?'

'Good day to you in return, gentlemen. Yes, the article was ready for you on the appointed day.'

He moves to a wooden box in the corner and gently lifts the instrument in both hands from the safety of a bed of sawdust. It is everything I had hoped; a finely polished and slender architecture of dark wood with gleaming brass reinforcements and joints. I take it with my right hand and rock it softly to-and-fro to feel its balance and sturdiness. My left arm will not allow me to test its use between outstretched arm and eye, so I pass it to Hicks and ask him to hold it as would a ship's navigator. All the fittings are attached to the shaft securely and the rotation of the eye slit along the arc is smooth. I enquire if the manufacture is exact and the angle graduation measurements are as designed. Chap replies gruffly that he will stake his life on it. I believe him, but will check this when I return home.

Chap says, 'I see you have trouble with your arm, Doctor Constable. I understand the nature of your invention from your detailed notations, so allow me to demonstrate the use of the instrument.'

He shows its use to good effect and handles it in a way that displays its robustness. It is apparent that he is proud of his achievement and I congratulate him warmly.

'It is well-done, Master Chap, and I am pleased with your work. Of course, it must prove its effectiveness on board ship before full satisfaction can be claimed, but if it fails then blame must lie with my design and not your craftsmanship.'

Chap beams with delight, pats his son on the shoulder and

thanks me for my kind words. I do not mention, but he must know, that if it is successful in practice, more commissions for this design will surely come his way. Hicks hands over final payment and the instrument is wrapped in sacks for transporting back to West Cheap.

*

I have been back scarcely an hour when Rose comes breathless and excited to the library and tells of the arrival of a large party of visitors. It is Sir George and Captain Hawkins, accompanied by Helen, Rosamund and their escorts. I bid them welcome and ask Rose to fetch Mother and Mistress Hilliard. Sir George removes his cloak to reveal a striking crimson doublet decorated with a patterning of ochre around the collar and cuffs. Hawkins is dressed in sober brown and grey.

Sir George removes a tall hat and says, 'Doctor Constable – William – please forgive our hasty and unannounced call on your household. The Captain General and I wish to view your invention and could not contain our eagerness.' He waves his hand at Helen. 'You will see that my daughter insisted on joining us and I could not refuse her. I am told that Helen and Rosamund have business with your Mother and Mistress Hilliard.' He spreads his hands in a gesture of mock apology.

'You are all very welcome and the unexpected nature of your visit adds to my pleasure.'

'Thank you, William. I see that your arm is injured. I trust it is a trivial matter and will not hinder your work?'

'It was my own fault. I fell from my horse and have cracked a bone in my wrist. The pain has eased and I believe it mends well.' I note that Helen has fixed me with a stare. I cannot read her expression, but I refrain from mentioning her role in my treatment in case Sir George is unaware of her last visit.

Mothers enters the hall followed by Mistress Hilliard. Sir George bows deeply to Mother and they exchange words on the joys of renewing a family connection and sorrows for departed spouses. After much fussing and politeness, Mother leads the ladies to the parlour and I take the gentlemen into the receiving room. I call for Rose and ask her to assist Elspeth in preparing refreshment for both parties. When both my guests are seated, I beg to be excused so that I can fetch the instrument from my library.

I carry the instrument in my good hand and both men rise from their seats as I enter. Hawkins' eyes are bright with anticipation and I offer it to him.

I say, 'I regret that my injury prevents me from providing an exposition of its operation.'

Hawkins mutters that it is no matter. He peers closely at the various parts, strokes the main spar with his forefinger and tests the movement of the eye slit along the arc. He refrains from comment and passes it to Sir George who mimics those actions before passing to back to Hawkins.

Sir George says, 'It is a handsome piece, William.' He turns to Hawkins. 'Will it do, John?'

'Of course, it must be tested. I understand the concept, which is a fine one. The avoidance of direct sight into the glare of the sun is a major improvement. The geometry of the invention uses mathematics beyond my capabilities and I look forward to proving its merit through practice.'

I explain in some detail how it should be used, although this is mainly for Morton's benefit as it is plain from his handling that Hawkins already has some understanding.

I say, 'I have a small observatory on the roof of my house. We do not have a horizon, but the sun is out and it may serve to give a taste of its handling.'

Three of us make our way to my observatory. The winter sun is strong enough to cast a shadow and allows Hawkins to manipulate the instrument in the correct manner. Both my guests express themselves pleased with the demonstration and we return to the receiving room in good spirits. There is a discussion about when the first proving of the instrument is to be undertaken, and it is decided that Hawkins will take his ship out for two days this week with several of his captains.

Sir George says, 'We have twenty-two ships, William. If the trial is satisfactory we will require that number of instruments for the start of the expedition. It is planned that all our ships will muster at Dartmouth in the middle days of February, so they will sail from here the week before. Will that allow sufficient time for their manufacture?'

A quick mental calculation produces a figure of little more than three days for each instrument, which will provide Master Chap with a stern task, but not an impossible one. There is a half-formed thought at the back of my mind about the timing and place of assembly, but I cannot unravel its significance now. 'It is a demanding schedule and I will make enquiries tomorrow on its feasibility. There is also the cost to consider.'

Morton waves a hand and dismisses the financial consideration as insignificant weighed against the potential enhancement to the prospects for the venture. As our discussion continues, I find myself carried along with growing enthusiasm for the venture. The prospect of sailing with the fleet is no longer an invitation to decline with polite regret, but one that offers excitement and challenge that may be difficult to resist. The midday bells ring and I interrupt our conversation to invite them to dinner. Sir George accepts readily, saying that our discussions have provided the foundation for good food and drink.

We are joined by Mother, Helen and John, making our number the largest party at our dining table since father died. Although it is unplanned, I note that my mother has the situation under control and the table is laid with our best tableware and glasses. She clearly takes pleasure in the gentle hum and activity generated by our company. I am overcome by a sense of how quiet and empty our house has become in normal times and I should make an effort to rectify this in future, for Mother's sake.

John's introduction has a diverse effect on our other guests. It seems that he and Hawkins have met before and their exchange is cordial, but reserved. Sir George expresses delight at the company of a scholar with such a lofty reputation, while Helen merely offers him a modest curtsey. Most of the conversation is monopolised by Sir George who has trouble in containing his eagerness to inform about the great adventure to the New Lands and his praise for my invention.

'Its effectiveness is yet to be tested,' I remind him.

'Ah, I have no doubt that the Captain General will return from his proving with positive news, William. The recently renewed acquaintance of our families was indeed a stroke of good fortune.' He turns to Mother. 'I am delighted to note that you are recovered from your illness, Mistress Amy.'

'I have your daughter and Rosamund to thank for my wellbeing, Sir George, and to your generous spirit in allowing Helen to attend here. My son had the good sense to seek their advice when his ministrations failed to effect a cure.'

Morton acknowledges the compliment with raised knife while working on a mouthful of roast tongue, then says, 'I understand that you also suffered an ailment, Doctor Foxe.'

'Indeed, I have much to be thankful for, as I am recovered from the worst effects of congestion. This is a house that warms with kindness and good company.'

Mother bows her head to John in appreciation of his comment. She asks Hawkins if he will tell more about his experiences of the New Lands and in particular the character of the natives to be found there. Hawkins describes them as docile creatures with little fighting spirit, prone to sickness and malaise. He portrays them as akin to cattle and this raises protests from Mother and Helen. John joins the argument and asks if they are amenable to conversion from their heathen state to our Christian faith. Hawkins asserts that they are not men and women like us, but a subspecies that have little understanding of the nature of God. John stiffens, but does not respond and there is an uncomfortable quiet. I wonder if this has been a source of disagreement between Hawkins and John in their previous meetings.

It is mid-afternoon when our guests depart taking the instrument with them. I should be cheered by the enthusiastic reception accorded my invention, but my spirits are dampened by the lack of opportunity to engage with Helen in private. It was tantalising and frustrating to have her so close, unable to exchange any word or sign of affection.

I retire to my library and am deep in thought about possible improvements to the instrument when Mistress Hilliard knocks and enters. My mind has wandered, I realise that the fire has died and I have been sitting in a chill room for some time. I ask Mistress Hilliard to make up the fire and I gather my cloak from a hook on the door to wrap around my shoulders.

'Let me help you, sir. You are shivering and 'tis no wonder; this room is no warmer than the courtyard.'

She lifts my cloak over my left shoulder and I pull it around me. She makes to leave, then hesitates and turns to face me. I tilt my head as an invitation to speak her mind. She swallows and casts her head down. I invite her to sit and pull up a stool next to mine.

'I have talked to Rosamund, sir.'

'Yes.'

'Begging your pardon, but you were discussed. You and the lady, Helen.'

'Did you discover anything of note about her birth?' I am too anxious and have broached the subject too soon. She hunches her shoulders and bows her head as if unwilling to continue. I lean over and touch her hand in, what I hope will be interpreted as, reassurance.

Eventually she says, 'I was sworn to secrecy. I made a holy oath that I would tell no-one of the circumstances she described.' She sighs deeply and shakes her head. 'I am in a bad place. I know that you are an honourable man and your intentions are pure, but… but it would be a sin to break my word given freely to Rosamund.'

Ah, this is a pickle. Is there a way around this conundrum? I cannot beg her to break her oath; she is a woman of firm convictions and would do nothing that would bring disfavour in the eyes of her God.

'You gave word that you would "tell" no-one.'

'Yes, sir.'

'Perhaps, you could write a few words that would serve to satisfy my enquiries. I know that you can write a little and you made no mention that your oath concerned writing.'

She lifts her head. Her eyes water with the beginning of tears and she has an expression of hope. 'Would that be a sin? Surely, God would regard it as a measure of trickery?'

'To my mind, God will look for an exactness in the words you swore and there will be no sin in writing.'

She is undecided. She shakes her head and purses her lips as

166

though the proposition is distasteful. How can I persuade her? I think of John. She holds him in high regard and his word on a matter of religion would sway her. But John must not know of my reasons for searching into the history of the Morton family. Will he judge in my favour and will he be happy to pronounce without knowing the full details? It seems I will have to take that chance.

I say, 'Would you take account of Doctor Foxe's opinion on this matter? He is close to God and would surely offer sound and holy advice.'

She nods her head dumbly and I go in search of John. He is in his study at his books. He looks up with surprise at my entrance and welcomes me warmly.

'I have a favour to ask of you, John.'

'I will be glad to oblige, William, unless you wish me to take your place on a ship to the new Lands. I fear I am too old for adventures on the high seas.'

I smile at his little jest and pull up a stool. 'I… or rather Mistress Hilliard, would have your advice. She has information she wishes to convey to me, but has had to swear not to speak of this material.'

'What is the nature of this information?'

'That I cannot say.'

'Cannot or will not?'

'It concerns a matter of the heart and it would not be proper to mention the character of the enquiry or a name at this stage.'

He nods his head slowly as if this brings a measure of understanding. 'I see. How will I be expected to advise?'

'She wishes to avoid sin in the eyes of God. Her oath concerns not speaking of the information and is eager to know if writing of certain words for my eyes only would break this holy oath.'

'I think I understand. I will speak with her, but cannot promise you the outcome you desire.'

'That is all I ask for, John. You will find her in my library. I will remain here and await your return.'

The waiting is hard to bear. I pace the room trying to avert my thinking to other matters, but without success. I flick through pages of John's books, but the text does not register any comprehension. I sit and close my eyes. The tension in my body will not ease and I pace the room again. How long will he take to express a short opinion? It has been more than a half hour… The door opens. He has returned alone. He will not relay any detail of his counselling and bids me to go directly to Mistress Hilliard.

A fire has been made in the library and she is tending it as I enter. Her face is flushed. Is it from the heat of the fire or an embarrassment at the denial she must give to me?

'Well, Mistress Hilliard, I hope you have had a fruitful consultation with Doctor Foxe?'

'Indeed, sir, I thank you for the thought and it was most comforting. I am satisfied that I may write a few words without breaking my oath. The Doctor advises it would be best if the writings were burned before we leave this room.'

My breath has been held and I exhale loudly at these words. I must take care not to be overeager and make her wary.

She says, 'I am sorry that my writing is not good and some of the words I must use are unfamiliar. Those that I know are mundane and concerned with the household.'

I present her with a sheet of paper, dip a quill in the ink well and hand it to her. I am wondering whether to prompt her when she begins to write. Her handle trembles and the scrawling is painfully slow. I move away from her and turn my back in case I inhibit her attempts.

After a few minutes she announces it is done. I turn around and she hands me the paper. There are seven words written. It reads: "Nees dead"; "babe Helen"; "dopded"; "father tewter." I scan the text trying to unravel the meaning behind the scrawl.

I say, 'Does this signify that Helen was adopted?'

She bows her head in agreement.

'The father's name – no not a name; he was a tutor.'

Another assent. Who is dead? Helen was adopted and her father was a tutor – to who? I read the words again, imagining Mistress Hilliard speaking them.

'Ah, I think I have it. A niece of the Morton family died, in childbirth perhaps, and the babe was adopted by Sir George and his wife. The father was a tutor… a tutor to the niece.'

She remains silent, but nods her head, more vigorously this time.

'Do you have the name of the tutor?' She bows her head and clasps her hands. 'Please, Mistress Hilliard, this is my last request. If the name is known to you, please write it.'

She hesitates then takes the paper quickly and writes two words – "Tomas Gore".

Twenty-Five

I have spent the greater part of this morning with Master Chap. It was a satisfactory meeting. Naturally, Chap was delighted at the possibility of a large commission for the manufacture of instruments and he offered to accompany Hawkins and his captains on their proving passage later this week. I endorsed this suggestion and it relieved my feeling of guilt that I have not volunteered my own attendance. In other circumstances I would be glad of the diversion, but now I have other pressing matters which require my attention. The knowledge that Helen was an adopted child of a niece in the Morton family is a great relief, but I cannot rely on the scribbled words from the gossip of two housekeepers. I must find this man Gore and extract documented proof. My prime motive is selfish and personal, but the exclusion of Helen as a candidate for the hidden royal bastard will also contribute in a small way to the task of uncovering the astrology plot. I sit uneasily on the periphery of Walsingham's investigation, not knowing how his work progresses and if the Morton family is under suspicion. I must work quickly in case events overtake my singular efforts.

I am with Mother and John in the parlour when Askham calls. It is another summons by Walsingham for John and me. This time we are to be taken to his house at Barn Elms and this is unwelcome news as it will entail at least one overnight stay there. I had intended to travel to Leadenhall with news from Master Chap and now I will have to rely on Hicks to undertake this task. There is another reason to be wary of this call. I cannot rid myself of a cloud of anxiety about Walsingham and the thought that one day an encounter with him might end with great upset.

Barn Elms is quieter than our last visit. The scaffolding remains and workmen ply their trade in restoration of the buildings, but the band of armed men that was gathered here has disappeared. There is a small pond at the side of the house. It is frozen and a group of small children are playing on the ice. This small touch of normality lifts my spirits as we enter the house. Perhaps this will not be a meeting with a sharp edge of fear after all.

Askham accompanies us to Walsingham's chamber of business and stands by the door as we enter. Walsingham is sat at a large table with Mylles by his side and Mistress Goodrich standing in attendance. She says something to Walsingham then turns to leave, bobbing her head and smiling at John as she passes. Introductions are exchanged and we take seats at the table. Askham is invited to join us and takes a stool to one side. We are offered wine and no sooner have we replied than the silent, floating servant has appeared with a tray of bottles and glasses.

Walsingham says, 'Doctor Foxe, I have taken the liberty of accepting Mistress Goodrich's offer to prepare your hot soother.'

'That is very thoughtful and it will be most welcome after the chill wind encountered on our journey.' John clears his throat and adjusts his seat. 'Thanks to William my health has improved, but I have acquired a taste for his soother and will continue to take it in the winter months.'

'I am glad and that is well done, William.' Walsingham shuffles papers on his table, then steeples his fingers before he continues. 'The Captain's men have discovered the lodgings of Christopher Millen; a place near St Giles. Others had been there before and it appeared that many items had been removed or destroyed.' He pauses to give more weight to what is to come. 'Nevertheless, our searchers were diligent and scraps of paper were found, which in themselves showed nothing.' He stops there and waves a hand at Mylles to take up the story.

'There were many torn pieces of paper of irregular size and I tried to place these together to make a whole. It was apparent after some hours that there was a belonging when letters and lines began to match. It was a long and tedious process, but eventually I was able to assemble this.'

He moves to a side table and takes hold of a flat plank of wood, about two feet square and carefully brings it over and places it before us. Scraps of paper are arrayed on the board, fixed loosely by a form of glue. There are missing pieces, but it is immediately apparent that it is a star chart, or the preparatory working for a chart. Walsingham and Mylles are looking to me to take a lead in its examination and I stand to get a closer view.

It is clear that this is not a finished chart. There are calculations, roughly made and marks to correct errors. A date is writ large in the top left corner – the twenty-fourth day of February, 1579. Lines are drawn from this date to the eighth, fourth and third houses, although most of the detail on the fourth house is missing. The natal is recorded as the seventh day of September in 1533; so this is a transit chart for Queen Elizabeth and perhaps that was inevitable. The intention seems to be… I stand back to appraise the chart as a whole. The placement of the stars was accurate for the natal chart, but I cannot be sure the same applies to this chart. I lean in and scan the paper again to ensure my first thoughts have foundation. I stand back again and consider for a few moments how I should express my thoughts.

I say, 'This is a chart which purports to represent a crisis in the life of Her Majesty. It is a rough draft and the working seems to be an attempt to fit transits of heavenly bodies to a predetermined event at a future date.' I pause to gather my thoughts. 'In the eighth house the moon is shown in transit with Neptune, the Sun, Pluto, Mars and Uranus. This may be interpreted as a major crisis, perhaps one that threatens life itself. However, there is sufficient evidence in the notations to doubt the accuracy of the observations.'

Walsingham glances around the table to determine if others wish to comment, then says, 'If I understand you correctly then, this is the transit chart referred to in the coded message.'

'It is a working model for the chart. The astrologer, Millen, has faced some difficulties in its preparation. Knowing the content of the coded message and the natal chart, there can be little doubt that this was an attempt to create a transit chart which foretells a deep crisis…' Perhaps I am too cautious in present company, but I leave the rest unsaid.

John says, 'It did not take long for you to question the observations. Will you need to consult your almanac to confirm this inaccuracy?'

'No, it is clear to me that it is a deviant and clumsy attempt to create an event to match a date in February of next year. It may be that Millen was under instruction to conjure a complex fabrication to fit a timetable of the conspirators' choosing.'

'So,' joins Mylles, 'There can be no doubt that Millen was recruited to the conspiracy and was murdered to halt further discovery when our search for him was known. More,' he points to the date on the chart, 'this date is of great significance to the conspiracy.'

Walsingham folds his arms, sits back in his chair and murmurs through closed mouth as though remembering a favourite tune. We wait for his pronouncement. 'Yes, it is as you say, we have a critical date.' He sits forward. 'Thank you Francis, and you Captain Askham. You have done well. Please leave us now.'

Mylles and Askham leave the room and Mistress Goodrich arrives with the soother for John. He accepts it eagerly and thanks her for the kindness. Walsingham gently moves the board and chart fragments aside, then picks a paper from the pile by his hand.

'Gentlemen, I have something here which may interest you.' He turns the note towards us. 'It is a letter from Doctor Dee written from Antwerp. He has been joined in that town by Edward Kelley.'

'Does the note throw any further light on the conspiracy,' asks John.

'It is primarily a plea on behalf of Kelley. The questioning by William and the Captain led Kelley to seek refuge from false allegations according to the Doctor. He has some unkind words to say about you, William, but does not accuse you of any particular mischief against our state. He has a concern that you may have violated his wife, but we will put that aside. He protests the innocence of any wrongdoing by Kelley who was propositioned by two men unknown to him. He rebuffed their advances, but mentions Millen as someone who may have been tempted by the offer of coin. The remainder of the letter begs Her Majesty to consider compensation for the injury to his property.'

He holds the letter between two fingers and lets it drop on the table.

'What are we to make of that?' asks John.

'Nothing. It is of no consequence. We already know the astrologer involved in the conspiracy and a future date of significance. This takes us no further.'

'I am offended by the assertion that I behaved improperly with Jane Dee.' I halt my indignation there as it will be of no interest to Walsingham. 'It would have been helpful to have received a description of the two unknown men and I wonder why he would have mentioned Millen? It is a bold and dangerous statement to place a man under suspicion of treason. Perhaps he felt safe in the knowledge that Millen was already killed and unable to deny this accusation.'

Our meeting is adjourned and we are invited to supper. Chambers have been prepared for our stay this night and I retire to mine to contemplate the letter and recent events. I suppose that Kelley cannot be damned for his flight to Antwerp. I may be tempted to this action in similar circumstances. The finding at Millen's lodgings provides confirmation of his involvement, but this was already strongly suspected and it brings us no further forward, except... the date... in February. But, my main concern is Tomas Gore and how to locate him – if he still lives. I am ill-prepared in character and resource for the finding and interrogation of this man.

Twenty-Six

Walsingham has left early this morning and I am greeted by John and Mylles at the breakfast table. Mylles is in a bright mood and keen to discuss the finding of Millen's draft chart and the significance of the February date. I compliment him on his thoroughness and foresight in piecing the scraps of paper and he responds with an apology for doubting my loyalty to the Crown. I ask him for the cause of his misgiving.

'It was your connection to the man Baskin and the ease with which you solved the coded message in the box. To my mind it would have taken an exceptional knowledge of cryptography to reach an understanding in so short a time. The alternative explanation of this brilliance was someone who knew of the message and was prepared to divulge its contents for a malign and mysterious purpose.'

'You are convinced of my allegiance now?'

'Yes, I am – also of your strong and useful intellect.'

'What of Richard Joynes? Is he freed of suspicion?'

'I am satisfied of his innocence and his accusers, Capton and Perse, are watched closely, along with others.'

We depart Barn Elms shortly after eight o'clock. John will return to West Cheap, while I will accompany Mylles to Whitehall. I am conscious that Forester will be anxious for my attendance and I wish to seek out Richard Joynes to learn the nature of his questioning.

*

Forester has five patients who require my attention and it is mid-afternoon before I am freed of my responsibilities and can go in search of Richard Joynes. I encounter one of his associates and he advises that Richard is in the chambers of Sir Thomas Heneage today, occupied with his bookkeeping. I find him in a small, cold and cheerless room hunched over a jumble of papers. He glances at my entry and returns to his work without acknowledgement.

'Good day to you, Richard, and I believe that I owe you an

explanation for your recent experience with Walsingham's men.'

'It is not a good day, but a marked improvement on two days locked in the grime and damp of a traitor's cell.' He sits upright and throws down his quill. 'I have you to thank for this harsh and unwarranted treatment.'

'Was it so very bad? Did they… harm you in any way?'

'It was worse than bad. My body was not harmed, save for exposure to icy cold and the stench and filth left by previous occupants. I was shown the rack, other instruments of pain and told that I would suffer horribly if I did not admit my complicity in a matter which I knew nought.'

'I am sorry for that, Richard. It was an error; a misreading of certain signs and events.'

'I was told that your guilt was certain and that you had named me as a conspirator.'

'That is untrue. Did those words come from a man called Mylles?'

'Yes, that was his name. He was my chief interrogator and a mightily unpleasant man he is.'

'Mylles is…over-zealous in his search for dangers to the state.' How much should I tell him? I cannot give the whole story, but enough to give hope that we can regain our friendship. 'I was approached by Walsingham under cover of a requirement for enlightenment over a matter of astrology. I was under suspicion for my long-past association with a person who assisted two others in a plot against our queen. My innocence is proven beyond question and I have recently parted from Mylles who begged forgiveness for his actions. I did not name you. Our two names were given to Mylles by others at court and in my way of thinking, they did this to deflect attention from their own misdeeds.'

'Who are these others?'

'I… I cannot say. I am sworn to divulge nothing from my questioning.'

He sighs and says, 'Well, then I suppose I cannot blame you for our joint misfortune. I will forget my confinement and threat of torture in time, but I fear that news of my treatment has reached Sir Thomas and caused him to doubt my value as his assistant.'

'In that case I will beg Mister Secretary to assure Sir Thomas of the error and vouch for your unblemished character.'

'You could do that?'

I express more confidence than I feel about Richard receiving an apology from Walsingham, but will try. I return to the physicians' quarters, pen a note with the intention of seeking Captain Askham. I would rather he give the note to Sir Francis as a more reliable conduit than Mylles. I hear someone clearing their throat and look up to see a man I do not know standing in the doorway. He is a young, foppish man clothed in yellows and pinks. His head seems to be straining to escape an extravagant silk ruff around his neck.

He says, 'I am Robert Courtney. Do I address William Constable?'

'I am Doctor Constable.'

'I have a note from the Earl of Oxford.'

He steps forward and hands the note with outstretched hand as though he is fearful of touching a leper. The note is a short one requesting my attendance at his house on The Strand at three bells tomorrow on a matter of some urgency. My spirits sink. This is an unwelcome distraction and a strange bidding from a man with whom I have met only briefly and whose temperament invites caution and mistrust. Nevertheless, I would be unwise to refuse this invitation from a person of his standing.

'Thank the Earl for his kindness and I will attend at the appointed hour.'

Courtney offers a brief, but silent, acknowledgement, turns abruptly and makes his exit.

Askham is in the stables berating a poor stable boy who has not paid sufficient attention to his instructions. The lad casts me a grateful glance then scurries away as Askham turns his attention to me. I explain the purpose of my note and he confirms that he will make sure it reaches Walsingham's hands. He pockets the note and shrugs, saying he cannot be certain that my plea will receive the desired action.

He says, 'Do you return to West Cheap now?'

'Yes, I am finished here and there is business at my house that requires attention.'

'I will accompany you. It is near dark and you would do well to avoid travelling alone under present circumstances.'

The journey to West Cheap is uneventful. I invite Askham to take some refreshment with me before he returns. He demurs initially, but accepts when I am more insistent. We go to my library, I pour two glasses of claret and we warm ourselves by the fire. After a few minutes of light conversation, I broach my intended subject.

'You know of my connection to the great adventure led by Captain General Hawkins and Sir Humphrey Gilbert?'

He bows his head to confirm understanding.

'I have formed an attachment – a personal and unexpected attachment through my meetings with those involved in the expedition.'

His expression suggests puzzlement at first, then a dawning of my meaning. He smiles and says, 'It is good that you seek the company of a woman. It calms the heat in a man to have an understanding wife and children who look to him for comfort and protection.'

'Are you married, Captain?'

'Yes, these twelve years past, with four children. I thank God every day for his grace in aiding my successful suit.'

'I envy your contentment.' I pause before continuing so that he can enjoy reflections on his happy disposition. 'There is a problem that I must overcome before I can progress this attachment.'

He inclines his head inviting me to say more.

'I would talk with a man named Tomas Gore. It is not a matter that concerns the security of our state and my questioning would be gentle and circumspect on a subject of some delicacy, which I am loth to disclose.'

'Am I to understand that you wish me to find this man, Tomas Gore?'

'I am reluctant to ask for a triviality when you have important matters of state in hand, but I am at a loss to know how to locate him. Of course, I would be willing to compensate for …'

'Please do not mention coin. I would be happy to undertake this service for a respected acquaintance, Doctor Constable.' He drains his cup, which I replenish. 'What manner of man is Tomas Gore?'

'He is a scholar who was known for his tutelage of wealthy patrons. I confess that I do not know if he still lives, but if he does I would hazard his age at between forty and fifty years.'

'I will see what can be done. If he still lives in London then the chances are good, but if not…' He spreads his arms to emphasise this constraint.

'I am in your debt, Captain, whether or not your search is successful, and I will not forget this kindness.'

I am reluctant to impose further on his good offices, but feel I must. I am thankful when he agrees to arrange an escort tomorrow for my visit to the Earl of Oxford.

Twenty-Seven

Today should be the final day of the proving passage. I have some confidence that my theoretical calculations will pass the test in practice, as there has been sufficient sun and the wind only moderate. Nevertheless, I have re-checked my calculations several times and, in the process, have thought of a slight improvement. If I replace the vertical shadow shaft with another graduated vane, this should remove a limitation in the angles measured. I draft a revised set of drawings to incorporate the change, but decide to wait before making a workable final set. I should consult with Master Chap as the extra vane may add to the time and cost required to manufacture each piece.

Waiting for my escort to The Strand, I have spent a fruitless period writing a note to Helen. It may be some days before we meet again and the longing for her closeness weighs heavily on my spirits. Remembering the sweetness of her lips and the firm pressing of her body befuddles my thinking and words will not flow. I consign my unfinished work to the fire.

It is Askham himself who arrives as my escort with another man. When I protest that I did not wish to deflect him from other duties, he replies that he has an interest to visit the Earl's household.

We arrive at Oxford's place in town a few minutes before our appointed time. It is an imposing building of three storeys, with the perimeter of land at the rear stretching to the River Thames. A manservant opens the door and is immediately joined by Courtney. He turns an enquiring head at Askham and I introduce him as my friend and escort. He bids us both enter a spacious hall with finely carved staircase and gallery. We wait for some minutes while Courtney goes to inform the Earl of our arrival. He returns with another man who takes Askham through a door to our left and I am led in the opposite direction by Courtney. We pass three doors to a large chamber draped with brightly-coloured tapestries. Here stands the Earl, who I will admit, cuts a handsome figure in white silk hose and red doublet. He stands with his back to the fire, which has the effect of edging his frame in flickering gold. I remove my cap, bow and thank him for the honour of his invitation to this fine house.

'You are welcome, Doctor Constable, and your friend… he is here because?'

'We had business together and he offered to escort me here, my lord. I have some difficulties on horse with my recent incapacity.' I flex my shoulder as a redundant indication of my wrapped and injured arm.

'Oh well, 'tis no matter. I will not take this as a planned impoliteness on your part.'

It is a curious statement. There is no questioning of my injury, yet he takes the company of an attendant to his door as an affront. He must know of Askham as a trusted aide to Walsingham. The tilt of his head and quizzical expression suggests that he waits for an apology, but I choose to ignore this inducement.

'I am intrigued by your invitation, which declares there is an urgency to the issue.'

'Yes… yes…' He adjusts his stance and brings his hands from behind his back, then swings both arms loosely. It seems I have discomfited him in some way. 'The planned great adventure of Gilbert and Hawkins is well known. It fires the imagination and zeal of those who would seek to enlarge the splendour and dominion of Her Majesty. It uplifts and adds the colour of heroism to the dreams of all true Englishmen.'

A return to his normal prettiness of speech is something of a relief.

'I agree, my lord, it is a worthy and magnificent project.'

'I have it in mind to invest in the adventure, but to this point my advisors have argued against, declaring the hazards at the edge of our world may be too great to bear.'

'Indeed, the risks of such voyages are well known.'

'Yet, there may be ways in which the ingenuity hidden in men's souls may surface and offer blessed release from some of these dangers.'

I murmur in a way that may be taken as understanding, but I have an inkling at the way this conversation turns, and I am wary.

He says, 'There is news that you may have designed an implement which could assist our brave pioneers in their explorations.'

'I… I am not certain that I understand.'

He purses his lips and stamps his foot in a show of petulance one might expect of a boy less than half his age. He breathes deeply to aid composure, then claps his hands.

'Come now, Doctor Constable, let us take a glass of sweet wine together so that our talk may flow more freely.'

A servant appears with a silver tray. Oxford hands me a glass of wine and raises his to indicate we should drink together. He moves towards a table and runs his fingers along the polished wood while his mouth works to savour the wine.

'I understand you have a facility with mathematics which extends to examining the exactness of heavenly bodies. Further, you have prepared a schematic which will enable a ship's navigator to translate these readings to a more secure position on the seas.'

'You are well-informed. I have begun work on the design of a mechanism that may be used for this purpose.'

'Begun? Is it not complete?'

'No, my lord. It is a complex apparatus that stretches my intellect.'

He drains his glass, then refills without offering the same to me. There is an uncomfortable quiet while he sips from his glass and wanders back and forth along the side of the table.

'Doctor Constable, I am eager to assist these adventures in discovery and daring. I am impatient for your finished invention and will offer my services to hasten your endeavours. I know of a fine craftsman who I will employ to produce your mechanism.' He pauses and moves a paper, quill and ink on the table in my direction. 'Meanwhile, if you will sketch your working pattern here, it will aid in the preparation for its manufacture.'

His intention is clear; the attempt clumsy and strangely inept for a man with a reputation for cleverness and silver tongue. I finish my wine and place the glass firmly on the table.

'It is a generous thought, which I will bear in mind. I regret that my current obligations will not allow me to exhibit an outline of the design, even for you, my lord. I thank you for this interesting exchange, but I have urgent matters at hand and must depart now.'

I bow stiffly, turn and make my way to the door. Courtney is close by the other side of the door and he starts back with surprise at my exit. I hear angry muttering and the sound of breaking glass behind me, but continue on my way. Courtney hurries after me to the entrance hall. I ask for Captain Askham to join me and that our horses are readied. I am abrupt and hot in my request, but care not. There is much scurrying and shouting as servants are called. Askham appears shortly, followed by three men who peer through the door and then retreat back into their chamber. Long minutes pass until all is ready and we exit from an empty hallway.

It is a short journey back to West Cheap. Askham looks to me for an explanation for the hurried departure and what may have gone before. I remain silent, wrapped in thoughts about the strangeness of the meeting and what, if anything, it may signify. When we arrive home I ask the Captain to sit with me for a while before he leaves. We settle in the library with a glass of claret.

I say, 'It was a peculiar meeting and confess that I find the company of the Earl something of a trial.'

'I am pleased your engagement was short. I was in the company of several of the Earl's companions who regarded me as a curiosity to be stared at. I was offered no refreshment or conversation.'

Askham does not question me on the subject of our meeting and I feel obliged to enlighten him. 'It seems that he was informed about my connection with Hawkins' expedition and sought to discover the workings of the new mechanism of navigation I have proposed.' I pause to ponder again on who may have been the source of his intelligence. Could it be Hawkins or Gilbert; Mylles perhaps; Morton; or Darby Wensum? 'There was mention of a potential financial investment as the source of his interest, but I have heard that the

Earl has vexed Her Majesty because of his difficulties with money.'

'It may be that he wishes his position to rise in her eyes through a reflection of the glory from a successful expedition.'

That may be true, but I suspect that he may have considered there is financial gain through the manufacture and trade of the instrument.

'Well, Captain, I thank you again for your consideration of my security and I am sorry that you did not have an enjoyable visit to Oxford's house.'

Twenty-Eight

I am sitting with John after our breakfast. He has received a note from Mylles which informs that he has seen Capton and Perse again, but their questioning did not yield any new information. I suspect that this interrogation was gentler than that suffered by Richard Joynes due to their connection with Oxford. I turn the conversation to the Earl and enquire about John's knowledge of his temperament and leanings. He confirms his previous statements about his immaturity and excessive liking for the shallow aspects of life. In common with a good number of nobles, he mistrusts his religion and suspects the harbouring of a devotion to Catholicism. Unfortunately, this leads John to offer a long and somewhat tedious retelling of the history of the Protestant cause and our relief from the profanities of the old religion. I am relieved when Hicks arrives with a note to interrupt our discourse. It is from Hawkins who declares that the sea trials of the instrument have exceeded his expectations. He is mightily pleased and he begs me to arrange for its manufacture for all ships in the fleet. John is understanding that I must leave his company to consult with Hicks on this matter.

I say, 'Hicks, we must send a note to Master Chap to attend here without delay.' The memory of Oxford's probing is fresh and I should be wary in case my movements from this house are observed by his men. 'You may think me over-cautious, but I should like you and Harry to ride at the same time in separate directions away from Master Chap. Gregory will then depart a short time later and deliver the message to him.'

I see from his expression that Hicks is not fully convinced that my caution is warranted, but he agrees to do as I ask. He may be right, and the attack on Hutchison's person and property was coincidental, but I will not take that risk with another good family. I will ask Sir George and Hawkins to arrange protection for Master Chap once his work is underway.

*

Master Chap and his son arrive as the bells ring for the hour of three after noon and we adjourn to Hicks' chamber of business in the courtyard. I confess that I am excited at the prospect of the wide use of my instrument of navigation. There will be financial reward, but I am not without vanity and it is the imagining of the enhancement of my reputation as a scholar that is foremost in my mind.

The details of the proving passage are described in some detail by Master Chap and it is plain that he shares my enthusiasm for the project. Many measurements were taken over the course of a day and a half at sea. The results from my instrument were compared with those obtained from cross-staffs, and in all cases the accuracy of latitude was improved.

Chap says, 'You are to be congratulated, Doctor. This may be a momentous time for the safer navigation of ships in the seas away from sight of land. I am fortunate to have a small association with its beginnings. You should put a name to your design.'

'A name?'

Hicks agrees and suggests that my own name is the clear choice. Does my conceit stretch to this? No, it is too grandiose for a thing barely born and not yet subject to the rigours of open and heavy seas. Chap suggests, '*un baton d'ombre*'.

'Shadow staff; an excellent notion, Master Chap. Let us use that term in future.' I take my draft drawings of the improved version and lay them flat on a table. 'Please take a look at this proposal for a renewed design and offer your opinion.'

Chap, his son and Hicks examine the sketches closely while I explain the potential improvement offered by the replacement of a fixed shadow transom for a graduated vane. It is not a simple matter and there is much discussion about the pros and cons of a release on the angle limitation versus the danger of incorporating an untested variation. Further, Chap considers that the changed design will increase the labour required for manufacture bringing us close to, or surpassing, the planned date for the fleet's departure. Our conversation stretches into late evening and I send word for a light supper to be brought to our room in the courtyard.

Harry enters with our refreshment and we move from the table of sketches to a smaller one prepared for our meal. I notice that Chap's son, Peter, is uncommonly quiet. When I pass him a plate of boiled eggs he refuses, complaining of a belly ache. His face is flushed and when I place the back of my hand to his forehead there is too much heat. I say that I will go to my still and prepare an infusion of mint and meadowsweet to cool his fever and aid digestion.

There is an icy edge to the air in the courtyard and I pull my cloak tight to ward against a freshening wind. Wisps of straw from the stables swirl and skitter over the cobbles and some are caught against a small mound, which I take to be a pile of rags. Who would leave this jumble here? It is too dark to see, so I kick the bundle with my foot. What? There is something within; heavy, but soft. I bend to examine further. I stretch my hand and touch... woollen cloth, then hair. I bend and press further. I feel a warm stickiness on my fingers. It is on my shoes. I am standing in... blood. A man's blood. But who? And how? I see a flicker of light to my left side. The shape of a man... A quick movement and then another... a torch is lit in the far corner of the courtyard. I am fixed, unable to force movement into my limbs. What to do? I turn my head sharply. There is no-one behind. Should I shout for help, or try and retreat to Hicks' chamber? I rise slowly. My thoughts are set. Twenty paces to Hicks' doorway. I creep back to where I came, thankful that my outer clothing is black. I open the door, knowing this movement will be seen from the light inside. I close the door behind me and set the latch.

'We are attacked. Be quick. Do we have swords; other weapons?' My voice is hoarse; words whispered, but too loud.

They stare at me as though I have lost my senses. The stillness among us is broken by a shout from outside. Chap is the first to react and uncovers his dagger. Hicks has two swords in the chamber and a large wood axe. I take the axe in my good hand, Hicks and Chap take the two swords. Peter and Harry are each handed a dagger.

'I have a musket, but it will take time to load; an old matchlock,' says Hicks.

'Then do it. We will bar the door if they come. They plan to fire the house, so we must confront them or the lives of those inside are in peril.' My thoughts are fevered, running too fast. 'We will create havoc, a commotion that will halt their determination; as much noise as we can muster.' It is a flimsy plan. What will follow our initial surprise? We five will be no match for trained soldiers. I must hope that Askham's men are close by or that others will join our defence.

The musket is taking an age to prime. I hear voices draw near. I speak in a whisper to Harry telling him to open the door on my command, then ask Hicks to stand by the door and open fire if a figure threatens. I will lead a charge into the courtyard, followed by the others. Chap shakes his head and shoulders me out of the way, protesting that the injury will hinder my effectiveness. There is no time to argue.

I signal to Harry. He opens the door. Two dark figures stand there, motionless for a second as our light surprises. One raises his arm and makes to enter. A crack from the musket splits the air and hits the senses as a physical shock. Chap roars, points his sword and rushes through the doorway, followed by Hicks. Another sound; screaming; is it me? I stumble over a body and I'm in the open whirling my axe and shouting. Three torches flutter in the wind – men; standing; watching us. My legs take me towards them. Chap is at them waving his sword… and Hicks. One turns, drops his torch and runs. I hurl my axe at his back. It misses and clatters into a wall. Peter brushes past me and lunges at a hooded figure who steps aside. Peter trips and falls. The man's eyes meet mine, then dart to one side as Chap screams at him and flails his sword. He backs away, then turns and runs. My ears sing. A door opens in the house; it is Mother. I yell that she must go back inside. But, what if the house burns? Is an assailant inside?

I take hold of my dagger and edge towards the door, with my weapon held out and my eyes staring around for danger. All is confusion. How many of the shadows flitting in the torchlight are ours? I open the rear door to the house. No-one is in there. Through to the parlour, I find Mother, John, Mistress Hilliard and the cooks huddled in a corner. I instruct them to stay where they are. My words startle them. I have shouted too loud. I exit the room and go to my library – all is clear. I check the other rooms on the ground floor and find nothing amiss. I visit the kitchens last. There is a stink of tar and burnt wood. Shutters are broken and there are broken shards of pots on the floor by a bucket and a torch which has been extinguished, but still smoulders. I pick it up, walk through the rooms and throw it in the courtyard. I stop. My head hums with the musket discharge, but there are no other sounds. The feeling is strange; like standing in a large church, alone save for the company of a busy beehive. Four figures are outlined against a flickering torch on the ground. Are they my men? One of them approaches. I tighten my grip, but the dagger is not there, then remember I dropped it in the kitchens. It is Hicks who closes and my breath escapes noisily as my stiffness eases.

'They are gone, sir. We are all unharmed.'

I clasp Hicks on the shoulder and mutter, 'Thank God,' several times.

We are joined by the others and I give profound credit for their courage. I close my eyes and offer a silent prayer of thanks to God that able and willing men were here to repel the attack. I dare not think too hard of the consequences if they were not in attendance.

Chap says, 'We have one of them in the doorway. He was caught by the fire of the musket and I used my sword on him.'

Harry and Peter pick up lighted torches and we move to the doorway of Hick's chamber. A man lies there on his back. He lives. There are gasping noises in his throat. His eyes are wide, he lifts an arm, points and stares into the blackness. His body twitches, his mouth opens to release a long, slow breath, his arm falls and he subsides. There is a wound at the base of his throat and the pink corruption of his innards show through a tear in his belly. I kneel to feel for a throb in his neck. There is none.

'He is dead.' Someone mutters a curse in French. It will be Chap. Then, I remember… 'There is another body over there.' I point towards my still and drying room.

I lead the way and ask for the torches to draw near to the dark mound I encountered some time earlier. When was it? Only minutes, but it seems an age has passed. The body lies face down and I know before I turn it over who I will find. It is Gregory with his throat slit. Oh, poor Gregory, undeserving of such an ugly death. His teeth are bared in a terrible fixed smile and empty eyes stare at the heavens. I close his eyelids as gently as I am able with trembling fingers and say a silent prayer for the peace of his young soul.

A hand rests on my shoulder. I have been kneeling here too long. My bones feel old and I get to my feet with some difficulty. I run the back of my hand across my face to wipe away the dampness of tears.

Chap says, 'Master Hicks has gone to meet with men from this neighbourhood who have gathered here for our assistance.'

I straighten my back and shake my head to rouse my senses. I must see to Mother and others in the house. There is much to arrange. I will send word to Captain Askham and ask for protection. What of Chap and his son?

Hicks has organised notice to be sent to the local justice and constable. Two of Askham's men are with the dozen or so collected in the courtyard and inform that another of their band has gone to Whitehall to send news to the Captain. None of the other attackers were apprehended and I guess they will have melted into the streets and alleys towards Cripplegate. A man in the crowd asks if any were recognised or if descriptions can be given. The dead man is a stranger to me and the rest… it was all chaos and black splintered by flashes of yellow light from the torches. I recall the eyes of the hooded man, but nothing else.

'There were four or five who came with evil intent.' It is Chap speaking. 'They were clothed in black with their heads covered. One was a large man, almost a foot taller than the others. More than that I cannot say.'

The assembly moves to the body of the slain attacker, while I state that I will attend to my mother and servants in the house, and go in the opposite direction.

Mother and John are seated in the parlour. There is a heavy quiet with John's face set grim and Mother bearing a frown of deep perplexity. She tells me that the servants are making good in the kitchens.

'What happened here, William? Why have we been marked for this outrageous assault?' There is a hint of accusation in her tone.

'I do not know Mother. Walsingham has many enemies and it may have been an attempt to remove John and me from his corps of advisors. Or, it may be…' My voice trails away and I shrug my shoulders.

'Indeed, you have it right, William,' John declares. 'It will be the evil of Rome. In particular, they recognise the value of your intellect and skills in the struggle to retain our true religion.' He leans over and pats my mother's lap by way of reassurance and apology.

She says, 'Is there another possibility, William? You appear uncertain.'

'We were discussing my invention for the navigation of ships and I had thought… No, it would be too extreme a measure for such a thing.' I breathe deeply to prepare for my next statement. 'I fear that Gregory is killed. His young life has been taken in most cowardly and horrible fashion.'

Mother opens her mouth, but words are caught in her throat. She buries her head in her hands and rocks gently to and fro in the chair. John murmurs something, which I cannot understand. When all is quiet, I say that I must check the house again and attend to our security for this night.

Outside, our number has grown and formed a circle in the middle of the courtyard. I find Chap and pull him to one side.

'Master Chap, you will be eager to return to your house.'

'Yes, Doctor, I would go now if you are content.'

'You must have an escort. I do not know if our association over the shadow staff is the cause of our hurt, but we must not take this hazard lightly. I will request that two soldiers from Walsingham's guard accompany you this night, and I will seek protection for your family and house from Sir George Morton thereafter.'

'Walsingham? Do you have influence with Mister Secretary?'

'A little, although my association has nought to do with the shadow staff.' I see from the set of his eyes that Chap suspects there is a deeper meaning to my words, but I can say no more.

Twenty-Nine

I slept, but fitfully. My waking moments were filled with images of mortal wounds, staring eyes and the grimace on Gregory's face. I rose before dawn and broke my fast by taking bread, eggs and ale from the kitchens to my library. I have brought my sword down from my bedchamber and idle away time by flexing my sword arm undertaking the exercises taught by my weapons tutor in my youth. The stiffness in my moves ease after a while. Although it is many years since I unsheathed my sword, it seems the lessons are not easily forgotten. Despite my injury, I feel a sense of shame that I did not lead our charge into the courtyard. I should not have allowed Chap and Hicks to bear the brunt of our encounter with the attackers. I will wear my sword and protect those dear to me while this peril remains. Does danger lie in the conspiracy uncovered at Barn Elms, or from my association with Morton and Hawkins? My mind sways in both directions. I must settle this puzzle – and quickly.

Sounds of activity build outside my library. It is time to find Hicks and consult on our priorities for today. The constable came last night to take away the corpse of the attacker. There was nothing on his person to aid identification and we must hope that further enquiries will yield some intelligence. Hicks is in his chamber with Harry. Gregory's body is laid on a table covered with a linen cloth. The air has a strange quality of hollowness and we speak in hushed voices, not wishing to disturb the sadness around his mortal remains. Mother will arrange for Gregory's removal to St Giles for his funeral and Hicks will inform his family when this date is set.

I ask, 'Do you know when the Justice will come?'

'I have a note stating he will attend before noon. No doubt he will wish to question Master Chap as well as our household.'

'I must leave shortly to inform Sir George and seek his help in guarding the Chap workshop. If the Justice departs before my return, please inform that I will be available at his convenience. Do not divulge the whereabouts of Master Chap to the Justice.

I will organise for their testimony to be given here or some other place.'

'Do you wish to speak Harry?' I see the lad fidget as though struggling with shyness.

'Sir, it is… do you consider that we will have to face further assaults?'

'It is unlikely, as we will have four of the Captain's soldiers here for our protection and after last night, I think we can be assured of their vigilance. Although I cannot imagine that anyone wishes your person harm, for the next weeks you must travel only in daylight and never alone.' I pause. 'That reminds me, Hicks. We must see that the soldiers are lodged in our house, both for their comfort and our security. Open streets and doorways will not do. Please consult with Mistress Hilliard and ask her to prepare a chamber.'

Our household is temporarily expanded and I should check if Mother has a mind to employ extra help for our servants. Reluctantly, I must also ask Harry to help with the horses until a replacement for Gregory is found.

*

I am received at Sir George's house and ushered to a receiving room. It is Wensum who appears after a wait of some minutes.

'Doctor… Constable, your visit was not expected.'

'No, Master Wensum, I have urgent business with Sir George.'

'He is not here. He is at our warehouses on the North Quay and will not return until after noon. Pray, give me your message and I will ensure Sir George receives it in timely and accurate fashion.'

'I do not doubt your good offices, Master Wensum, but I must speak with Sir George in person. I will wait.'

He adjusts his stance, gazes at me from top to bottom and says, 'You wear a sword.'

I notice he does not mention my injured arm in its sling. 'It is a simple matter of caution in these troubled times.'

He appears discomfited by my appearance, makes to respond, but changes his mind, bows stiffly and leaves without further word. I am discouraged at the thought of passing idle hours in my wait while others are industrious at West Cheap, but must bear it. Should I seek out Helen, or will this be regarded as improper? I will stay, for the present.

My patience is rewarded in short time as the door opens and Helen appears.

'William, why… I heard of a visitor, but did not know it was you.'

'My dear, I am here to talk with your father on a pressing matter.' She will hear of the episode last night, so there is little to be gained by circumspection. 'Our house was attacked this night gone by a group of men with foul intent. They planned to fire the buildings, but we were able to deflect their purpose.' I hesitate to share the worst of the news. 'Our stable boy was murdered horribly and we killed one of their number.'

Her mouth gapes, then she runs to me, claps her arms around my waist and lays her head on my breast. My wrist is caught in her embrace and there is some pain, but I will not free myself.

'Why… why was it done? A scholar and his family; what could be the cause?'

'It is not known for certain. It may have a connection with the instrument of navigation for your father's venture.'

She raises her head and looks into my eyes. 'I do not understand. Why would such an apparatus be the focus of extreme jealousy?'

It is a question I have considered at length. Before I can answer, the door opens and Wensum enters with reddened and accusing face.

'This… this is unseemly. Sir George will hear of it. You… Constable will break your grip on the lady.' His breathing is heavy and excited. 'Mistress Helen, you should accompany me now, away from that man.'

Helen releases her arms and steps back. 'I will remain here, Master Wensum. I was merely comforting a friend on his misfortune. You may instruct Rosamund to attend us here if you consider that would render our conversation proper.'

He grits his teeth, shakes his head, then turns and shuts the door with unnecessary force.

'Are you harmed; your mother; Doctor Foxe?'

'We are unhurt and recovering from our shock.'

She folds her arms, closes her eyes and shakes her head as though this will help her to comprehend the news.

I say, 'What is your opinion of Master Wensum?'

'I think I have said before that he does well for my father's business. Why do you ask?'

'Do you know if he has an association with other gentlemen not connected to your father's trade?'

'It is strange question.' She wrinkles her nose and tilts her head. 'He has visitors while my father is absent, certainly; men of business and merchants.' There is another pause while she considers. 'Latterly, there was a visit from a party of nobles. Their brightly-coloured dress and bearing marked their quality. I had only a glimpse. Rosamund told me later that the Earl of Oxford was in their number and he had been here once before.'

'Do you remember if your father was away on business when this party called?'

'Yes, he was… William, why do you persist with this line of enquiry?'

'It is no matter. I wonder what I might have done to offend Master Wensum and how I may rectify this condition.' I see that she is not fully convinced. 'Come now, my dear, I will not let this opportunity of our closeness pass without another kiss.'

I put my good arm around her to pull her close. She pushes at me, then surrenders to my urging and kisses me sweetly, but briefly. I want more and eventually, her body melts into a slow and tender kiss. Our bodies press together and I sense a shared hunger for fulfilment of our excitement. Abruptly, she pushes me away and brushes hands over her bodice.

'Someone approaches.'

It is Rosamund who enters. She smiles, bobs a brief curtsey to me, goes to Helen and links her arm.

'Are you here for more plums, Doctor Constable?' There is a twinkle in Rosamund's eye as she speaks. 'You have upset Master Wensum most severely. You must have had the best in your conversation with him.'

I have not seen this mischievous aspect of Rosamund's nature before; she has been quiet and withdrawn in my company.

Helen changes the subject quickly and says that we were discussing an alternative remedy for Doctor Foxe's congestion. We adjourn to the still and drying room to consider this refinement, where I am delighted to find Jane Dee waiting for the return of her two companions. Her bruising has faded and there is a spark to her bearing that speaks well for her recent improvement. The conversation is immediately lively and engaging. There are poorer ways to pass the time while I wait for Sir George to return.

Morton arrives home barely an hour after noon and a manservant begs me to follow him to his private chamber. It is a fine room, draped in tapestries of quality, with cushioned chairs and a roaring fire. Sir George sits in a large seat, with feet on a stool and glass in hand. He offers me sweet wine and begs me to sit.

'I am told you have urgent business, William. I trust nothing obstructs the manufacture of the instruments.'

'It is the safeguarding of that process that I come to discuss, Sir George.'

I continue with an account of the assault on our house while plans for the instrument were laid in Hick's chamber. His eyes widen as I recount the murder of Gregory and the killing of an assailant. I emphasise the heroic nature of Chap's charge and praise the others for stout defence.

'Although there can be no certainty that the instrument, which we will call the shadow staff, is at the heart of this malevolence, I can think of no other issue. I therefore beg your consideration in the employ of guards at the workshop of Master Chap during the period of his labour for us.'

'It will be done, and this is a most terrible episode, William. My sympathies to you and your mother for this disruption to your household. I understand there may be substantial monetary reward from your… shadow staff, but this… this is wickedness beyond all expectation.' He drains his glass and clears his throat. 'It will explain why you wear a sword on your visit. Wensum was vexed at your soldierly appearance.'

'I apologise for that, Sir George. I thought it a prudent measure so soon after our disturbance.'

'Yes, yes, I applaud your caution.' He fills his glass and offers the bottle. 'There is another subject of concern that I would raise with you.' He pauses and fixes me with his eyes. 'I have been informed that you took advantage of my absence and touched my daughter in a most lewd and inappropriate manner. Is this true?'

'No, it is not, Sir George. Mistress Helen showed great alarm at the news of our attack and Master Wensum misinterpreted a brief moment of comfort for her distress.'

'I wonder you felt obliged to trouble her with a story that is sure to bring fright and anguish to a lady. Was it necessary?'

'Your daughter has a strong and perceptive mind, Sir George. I am sorry that I could not withstand the force of her questioning.'

He nods his head in understanding and appears satisfied with my explanation. But now would not be a choice moment to declare a fondness for Helen. I must be patient and wait until the Morton family is clear of all suspicion in Walsingham's investigation.

Thirty

I hurry a breakfast of eggs, honey and milk, then retire to my library. I am impatient to gather the snatched thoughts of half-waking and set them down on paper. There are so many strands to the events to the past weeks, that they confound my attempts to unravel their meaning. I would be better served by transfer to a more permanent record so that patterns and structure emerge from my scratchings.

First, there are the assaults at Mortlake, Master Hutchison's house, on my person by St Gabriel in Fen Church and here, at my house in West Cheap. The attacks at the houses were of the same design; an intention to fire property, innocents killed by slit throats and the assailants commanded by an uncommonly large, hooded man. I cannot attribute a cause to my personal attack, nor can I be sure that this was made by the same villains as the other three. For those others it would seem near-certain that the same body of men and their commander were responsible. Yet, the incident at Mortlake was doubtless linked to Millen and his part in the astrological conspiracy, whereas the murder of Hutchison and the destruction of his house can have no other goal than a disruption in the making of the shadow staff. I must conclude that the two actions have a connection and that those who conspire against Her Majesty also aim to interfere with my efforts for the great adventure. But why?

I have scribbled words, lines and other markings; perhaps there are too many and their order too careless, as the result is more confusion. I take another roll of paper and start to reconstruct the schematic. After an effort of close attention, I pin it to a cupboard and stand back to survey the whole. I have drawn a line inking the phrase in the coded note about the 'great burning at d' in February with Hawkins' assertion that the venture fleet will sail from Dartmouth in the same month; February. There is an itch in my thoughts of another occurrence where this month was writ. It was… the scraps of Millen's transit chart pieced together by Mylles, where the twenty-fourth of that month was marked for the demise of our Queen; further confirmation that the two plots are connected. Yet, I must delve deeper into these markings to discover a reason for their association and clues for players in this web of scheming and trickery.

I am fastened on the death of Millen and the destruction of the library at Mortlake. I cannot unpick anything from my paper that will enlighten. It requires an effort of deep concentration to review events of past weeks. A cracked head in the fall from Cassius may have caused a disconnection in my brain. Did I mention Millen to Darby Wensum on his visit to West Cheap and before the Mortlake incident? It was an unplanned enquiry, but does my memory speak true, or does my dislike of the man create a false recollection? I pick up my quill and mark key moments in my meetings with Wensum. There was a conversation with him about the shadow staff at West Cheap. Hicks stated that he may have revealed Hutchison's name as the maker while I was absent from their company. Then, there was the peculiar supper at Leadenhall with Wensum and the dozing Morton. That was the night of my rescue from an assured death by Askham. Why did I have no escort? Do I recall my departure? Yes, I think Wensum offered an excuse for the absence of men to guard my journey. My recollections from that night are no more than fragmented disorder, yet... I see the marks of Wensum on my paper and there is another name that should be bonded – Oxford. Helen stated that the Earl visited while Sir George was absent. Why? There is no logic to one of Her Majesty's favourites as a conspirator. Perhaps it is lack of coin to feed his extravagance, or John's suspicion that he harbours an attachment to the old religion. Somehow, I fail to see the Earl with a strong devotion to any cause, save his own amusement.

I pause from my reflections and seek my mother so that she may renew the tight wrappings on my arm. My wrist is sore, but the swelling has subsided and I can free myself of the encumbrance of a sling. She calls for Mistress Hilliard to bring fresh linen and we retire to the parlour to tend the injury. The stripping and winding takes some time and my mind returns to the mysteries of the coded note. If the letter 'm' is Morton and 'd' designates Dartmouth, what can 'p' signify?

'Your thoughts are far away from here, William,' says Mother. 'Do you daydream of a particular person?'

'There are several person never far from my thinking, Mother, and one of them is you.'

She raises her eyes and offers a faint smile, then turns to a heavier subject. 'The funeral for poor Gregory is fixed for Saturday next. I have sent word to his family in Essex. I know their living is meagre and it would be a kindness to offer something as a mark of our respect.'

'I had thought to make them a gift of Gregory's horse, saddle and trappings.'

She murmurs her approval and Mistress Hilliard touches my arm gently as a sign of her regard for my offer.

The tending and wrapping are done. I swing my arm a little to savour the small progression towards a mended body. I thank them for their attention and return to my library musing on the singular letters. Does a 'p' denote Arthur Perse? No, he is too insignificant a figure. The 'm' may represent a class of men such as merchants, not the family name Morton; a letter 'd' could indicate any number of places or people. In that case 'p' may signify: prince; principal; palace; or… My mind races in too many directions of chance. I must collect my notions and sift them with care, so that only those suppositions that bear the closest inspection remain.

One of Askham's men knocks at the door and informs me that the Captain waits for me in the receiving room. First, I must take down my schematic and secure it in a private place to prevent prying eyes reading my incomplete perceptions.

'Good day, Captain, will you take a cup of wine?'

'Thank you, Doctor. I believe Mistress Hilliard has the supply of our refreshment in hand.'

He has a pensive look about him. He is a diligent man who bears his responsibilities well, but Walsingham cannot be an easy master.

'Has the slain attacker been identified?'

'The man is unknown, but certain qualities from his person

and weapon suggest that he was not an English man.'

'Oh?'

'His skin is darker than would be common in our climes and his dagger was not forged in this country. It is an uncommonly fine weapon for a rough man and bears the marks of a maker in Seville.'

'A Hispanic, then?'

'Yes.'

Mistress Hilliard appears with our wine. She hesitates before leaving us, begs to be excused, but wants to know if she should prepare another soother for John. He has already had three and she worries that an excess may be harmful. I cannot help but smile at John's attachment. I assure her that a fourth would benefit, but that she should ration him to no more than six in one day.

'Your mother runs a fine household, Doctor. I do not wonder that Doctor Foxe has settled here in cosiness and contentment.'

'Thank you, Captain.' I raise my cup and we both take a mouthful of claret. 'Are you here to consult with your men, or do you have a wider purpose?'

'A man has been found who answers to the name, Tomas Gore.'

I sense my heart quicken at this news, but should not appear too eager.

'My thanks again, Captain. I held no great hopes for his discovery, though it seems your network of watchers was a match for my test.'

'He lodges at an inn in Southwark. I know the inn, the Silver Bell. It is a mean place, frequented by pox-ridden whores, cutpurses and other malefactors.'

'Nevertheless, I should like to question him.'

'Then I will accompany you.'

'Your men…'

'They will stay here to guard your house. Besides, it is my understanding that you would not wish your meeting to be more widely known.' He senses my uncertainty and adds, 'We will be safe in daylight hours. There will be few who care to hazard their destiny against my sword.'

I am grateful for the security of Askham's company on my journey, but discomfited by the thought that he may hear words from Gore that uncover the connection of Helen's birth date to the conspiracy. Well, this knowledge will out eventually and I must find a way to manage it.

*

Our journey to Southwark is uneventful. The air has warmed a little so that our way is over slops of mud rather than iron-hard ground. Our passage over the bridge is unhindered. Askham's authority and bearing is noted and helps to clear the way through the usual confused mingling of people, carts, stalls and other clutter.

The Silver Bell is in a narrow lane and its exterior is not inviting. An overhang from the first storey has collapsed leaving rough chambers fully exposed, while other areas are patched and mended by careless hands. It is a wonder that the whole does not crumble. Askham beckons a man selling codlings from a cart and gives him a coin to hold our horses. There are two doors and we choose to enter by the one that has the appearance of more security and height, although even this one requires both of us to stoop low. Inside, it takes a short time for my eyes to adjust to the gloom. We are in a crude space of low beams, filthy straw and primitive furnishings. The stench is high, but perhaps not as harsh as I anticipated. Five men gathered around a barrel stare at us. Two women with uncovered hair rest full-length on benches and an old man lies on the floor, his mouth gaping wide and head resting at an odd angle against a wooden pillar. He may be dead or merely sleeping. Another woman appears from the gloom and breaks the quiet by enquiring how she may serve us. She is young and sways her hips invitingly at Askham. If she was cleaned and taken out of her rags she might be considered pretty. Now, her attempt at enticement is ludicrous and revolting.

Askham puts his hand on her shoulder, draws her to one side and says in low voice, 'We would meet with Master Tomas Gore who lodges here.' He slips a small coin into her hand.

'There is no-one of that name here.' She glances quickly at the group of five men.

'Do not obstruct me, Mistress, or it will go badly for you and others in this place.'

She opens her hand. A half-penny sits there. Askham places a penny beside it. She turns again to the men seated at the barrel, her eyes begging forgiveness for the hopelessness of her position. He strides towards the men.

'I am the Queen's man under orders of Mister Secretary. Should any of you dare to hamper my enquiries, this place will be torn down and all in here will twitch at the end of a rope.'

The muttering ceases and the air is stilled. He returns to the woman who answers with head bowed. 'Master Gore lies in a room above. I will lead you there, but must caution that he is fevered and his body wracked with illness.'

The stairs are broken and we follow up a ladder to a dark corridor on the next storey. We are taken to an opening at the end that is framed by a torn curtain of grubby linen. She draws this aside and Askham gestures that I should enter, saying that he will wait for me below.

The chamber is small, cold and bare, save for a cot in one corner with a jumble of rags and a leather bag laid by its side. The straw bedding is scattered and soiled. The stench of waste, piss and decay causes me to gasp and cover my mouth. A man's head pokes above grey linen sheets, eyes sunk deep into mottled, greying skin.

'Are you Tomas Gore?'

His mouth moves; a hoarse whisper brushes past his dry, cracked lips. I leave the chamber, go to the top of the ladder and beg for a jug of ale and a cup to be brought. I return to the bedside and place the back of my hand against his forehead. It is too hot. His throat crackles and there are dribbled stains of saliva and blood on his chin. He has consumption and by the look, does not have long to live. I lift the covers with care and place my ear to his chest. The noise of congestion and laboured breath is unmistakeable.

The young woman is at the door with a jug and cup. I pour ale and offer the cup to his lips. He sups greedily, spilling most, and then jerks his head in a request for more.

'I am Doctor William Constable, here to seek information

from Tomas Gore. You are that man?'

He nods his head in confirmation and says, 'Lift… my head.'

I grab his shoulder, raise him as best I can with my good arm and stuff some of the rags between his head and the wall. I hand him another cup of ale.

'You recall a time in the employ of the Morton family?'

His eyes flicker with a show of surprise, but he does not answer.

'You will be rewarded for information on the matter of my enquiry. There is coin, or I can arrange for your comfort.'

He waves his hand. 'What use do I have for coin?'

'This is a poor place to rest your illness. You could be moved.'

His chest heaves as he tries to suppress a cough, but his body is feeble and he lifts the sheets to cover his discomfort. When his sheet falls back the deposit is shown to be mostly blood.

'You were a tutor to George Morton's niece?'

He purses his lips and appears to consider before replying. 'You must wonder how a scholar is fallen to this.' I do not answer and he continues. 'I understand the matter of your enquiry. It was a different age; so many years past; the happiest of times; an ending in despair; and the start of my descent to this foul house for an unremarked death.'

'What can I do for your comfort?'

'Nothing in this world, Doctor Constable. I have heard your name spoke before. You have the reputation of familiarity with the stars and mathematics, I understand.'

I mutter some words about my learning, then, 'I intend no harm. Nothing you tell me will be used against you.'

He scoffs at my offer, then descends into another bout of hawking and expectoration. He subsides.

'What injury could you offer to this frail body that would not bring a swift and welcome death?' He hesitates. 'I will tell you my story and time with the Morton family on a condition.'

'What might that be?'

'I would be cleared of my torment and at peace when I leave this body.'

What can he mean? 'You wish to confess your sins… to a priest?'

'Ha, I have no liking for Rome. I would speak with a holy man who follows the true religion, so that I may know more of how God will greet a sinner. I expect no absolution; simply guidance for my journey and an understanding of His grace.'

I am confounded, but only for a moment. I see a way through this.

'Do you lean towards Her Majesty's high church, or perhaps a spare and more direct position of the Puritan view?'

He waves a weak hand. 'I care not. The man must be near God and not corrupted by earthly distractions.'

'I shall endeavour to meet your demands. It will not be easy.'

'And it must be quick. My life spirit drains. I feel the coming of a darkness.'

'Shall I arrange for your transport to a better place?'

'I cannot be moved. This body will not bear it.'

'Then I will instruct your greater comfort here, with some food and drink.'

'That… would be a kindness.'

His eyes close and he sinks down into his meagre bedding. My company has tired him and I am sure he is right. He has only days or hours to live.

I retrace my steps down the ladder to an uneasy quiet. Askham stands with arms folded, leaning against a barrel. I beckon the young woman to draw near, delve into my purse withdraw a florin and hold it between finger and thumb before her eyes.

'We will return tomorrow. Meanwhile, you will take this coin to provide Master Gore with wholesome food and clear ale. Do not light a fire in his chamber, but renew his covers with clean linen and warm covers. You will see that he lives until our return. If he should die, you will all answer for his neglect and be subject to harsh punishment.'

My threat does not have the force of Askham's, but the Captain stands square and tall by my shoulder to add his intimidating presence to my warning.

There is no conversation between us until we cross to the north side of the river. He enquires if my questioning yielded anything of benefit and why I had talked of a return.

'He is near to death and will not talk openly unless I can bring some comfort to his dying spirit.'

'How can that be done?'

'I must beg Doctor Foxe's understanding and cooperation in the matter.'

*

There is no other way. I must take John and Captain Askham into my confidence, or at least some of the way down the path of my discoveries and suppositions. John is with Mother in the parlour taking a light supper, although it is barely dark. There is some surprise to see the Captain at my side, quickly hidden in a warm welcome and offer to join with refreshment. We are both of the same mind; politely declining food and accepting wine. I briefly consider begging Mother to excuse us so that we may adjourn to another chamber, before a realisation that there will be benefit in her attendance. She will understand my interest in Helen's history and offer a reason to be circumspect about other, wider matters. We pass some minutes in light conversation about the merits of sweet wine, the steadfast nature of the soldiers lodging here and enquiries into the health of Askham's wife and children. Finally, it is time to broach my request to John, but he speaks before me.

'Is there any news of our attackers? We gather nothing from your men here, Captain.'

'It is a regret that none have been taken and our search continues.'

'And is the one killed so bravely by Master Chap identified?'

'His person is unknown, but there are indications…' Askham hesitates, no doubt for fear of disclosing too much to my mother.

John glances at Mother, then says, 'You should know that I have informed the lady Amy of our assistance to Sir Francis on a matter of Her Majesty's security. I trust her discretion and it is fitting that she should know something of the likely cause of the evil assault on her household.'

Mother pats John's arm in thanks for his trust and adds, 'It would be unusual, would it not, for an attack on a private house to attract the interest and protection of Mister Secretary's men. I am not completely unaware of the dangers to our state, although I understand that you would not wish to trouble a lady with the fine details of this threat.'

Askham bows his head and explains the reasons for suspecting the killed assailant was of Hispanic origin. John utters a low growl and asserts that this would confirm his thoughts that papists were behind the attack. Mother turns to me and asks whether I still harbour a notion that my work on the mathematics of ship navigation could be at the heart of it.

'No, I am sure John has it right. The attack here is bound up in the plot upon which Mister Secretary sought our counsel. But of the particular cause on that night, we cannot be sure.'

There is a lull in the conversation as we take food and drink and consider what has been said. I drain my glass and breathe deeply to steady my nerve.

'There is a lighter matter that troubles me and on which I would seek your assistance, John.'

He raises his head, meets my eyes, then leans back in his chair and strokes his beard. 'I would be delighted to aid my friend and colleague, if I can. Does it concern the merits of apple tart or nettle soup, perhaps?'

I ignore his small jest. 'It is connected to a consideration of religion and the easing of a troubled soul before a meeting with God.'

He tilts his head in an expression of surprise. 'We do not talk of your faith, surely?'

'No, it is not me.' I hesitate before choosing my next words with care. 'I have begun in the wrong place, forgive me. I have formed an attachment of the heart to a lady. It is Helen Morton. I believe there is a mutual liking, but there is something unspoken between us.'

I see Mother and John exchange glances, then she smiles and praises Helen for her steady humor, intellect and beauty. John nods his head in agreement.

I continue, 'There is something in her history that troubles me. It is nothing that would alter my respect and affection, but I cannot settle until it is resolved.'

'Oh, William, what can it be?' I have shocked Mother with this statement.

'Some twenty years past a niece lived with the Morton family. The niece was fair and much loved, but her character was not strong enough to resist improper advances. She died in childbirth and the living child was adopted by Sir George and his wife. The event was hushed to avoid disgrace to the family name.' I pause and see the faces of Mother and John hold expressions of concern from this unexpected disclosure. 'The wrong-doer in this unfortunate circumstance was likely the niece's tutor, one Tomas Gore. This man has been found through the good offices of the Captain. His fortune has fallen exceedingly low in the years since the birth of the child and he is lodged at an inn in Southwark with heavy and mortal illness.'

John says, 'This is indeed, news for disquiet, William. But I do not see… how I can help.'

'I would have his confirmed and clear account of the events around Helen's birth. He will only give this on condition that he can consult with a holy man; an incorruptible man who is close to God.'

'You do not expect me to hear his confession and absolve his sins.' John is quick in his indignation.

'No, John, he is no lover of the old religion. He is a Protestant with an inclination towards your way of thinking. He has no wish to be forgiven his sins, merely to understand how he can best prepare for his encounter with God.'

There is a moment of quiet and Askham joins, 'Indeed, we would all wish for such enlightenment.'

'His end is near. He suffers from consumption and has only days or hours left on this earth. I have said that I would return to his bedside on the morrow, God willing.'

John clasps his hands together and bows his head, perhaps in silent prayer or simply to consider how easily this request sits with his beliefs. We wait in silence for his response.

'Very well, William, I will accompany you to this man in Southwark. I will do my best to meet his condition and ease your troubles. We will require guards on our journey in view of recent events.'

Askham confirms that he will escort us with two of his men.

Thirty-One

We depart early in the morning – me, John, Askham and two soldiers. The sky is low and heavy with cloud; dark, grey and purpled. It has a threatening air and I must hope this is not an omen for an unfortunate end to our journey. We may be too late to catch the promised words from Gore; his senses may be addled; or John may be too direct and unforgiving in his questioning. My depressed humor appears to be shared and we exchange few words on our progress to the ungodly borough of Southwark.

It is a relief to find the Silver Bell stands with no further loss of its fabric. Askham's men take the horses through a crooked arch to the courtyard at the rear, while the Captain and I guide John through the door. The young woman stands two paces before us as we enter and bobs a brief curtsey. She will have been warned of our coming. Her hair is covered with a white bonnet and her appearance altogether more becoming than our first encounter. Two men sit at a table, but there are no others to be seen.

She says that her name is Della and asks if we will take refreshment. Askham declines her offer and says we will go directly to Master Gore's chamber.

She turns to me and exclaims, 'He lives. He has had the best of our care and wants for nothing save a relief from the foulness in his lungs.'

I thank her, but will not offer more coin until we see the proof of her telling. Askham is first up the ladder followed by John who climbs with some difficulty. I wait for a misstep while the Captain offers a hand to help him to the passageway on the next floor. They stand aside for me to enter Gore's chamber. It has been cleaned and his bedding arranged as instructed with a sprig of lavender on a small table by the cot. His eyes meet mine as I pull back the curtain.

'So, Doctor Constable, your word is sincere and… I must thank you for the kindness you have… forced upon my hosts.'

His words are faint and spoken with some difficulty through the mucus in his breath.

'I am relieved to find your situation improved and your health no poorer than the last day.'

'Indeed, you may have bought me an extra hour or two in this world.'

His eyes move to those behind and I introduce Captain Askham as my friend and guide.

'This is Doctor John Foxe. I think you will know of his name.'

Breath escapes his open mouth. 'I could not have expected such eminence. I... I have read your *Book of Martyrs*. Who, that truly believes, has not?' He turns to me and narrows his eyes. 'Do you speak truth, or... or is this trickery played on the feeble mind of a dying man?'

'You will discover, soon enough,' claims John who moves to his bedside and sits on the only stool in the chamber. 'You have read my account of the martyrdom of Anne Askew?' Gore bows his head in confirmation and John proceeds to give a detailed report of his research into the infamous torturing of this brave woman and his reading of her account in the book of *Examinations*. It is plain that John's display of scholarship satisfies Gore.

'We will talk of your death and how you may be received into His grace soon, but first you must give a narrative of the circumstances around your departure from employment with the Morton family. Doctor Constable here will write as you speak and then you will add your name to signify a true account.'

I take out paper and writing material from my leather bag and clear a space on the table to prepare.

John says, 'I understand you were tutor to a niece of Sir George and his wife.'

'Sheldon – her name was Sheldon.' He closes his eyes and pauses as if guiding his thoughts to younger days. 'She was the fairest of face and spirit. Her father had land in Essex; broke his neck falling from his horse and the mother died of the sweats when she was a babe. We were bonded from the start; knowing each other's thoughts; delighting in the other's happiness and sharing the burden of each sadness. The movement of her hands and the soft hairs on her neck made my heart tremble. I…' His eyes dart quickly to each of us. 'I know I cannot expect forgiveness. The error was mine, all mine. I was too fevered; not thinking or caring for my… my… beautiful Sheldon.'

'You coupled with her. How did Sir George manage the discovery when she was found with child?'

'I owned it was mine. There was commotion, anger, tears and some talk that we should wed. The learning of her state was late and before indecision could be overcome, Sheldon began…' He tries to raise a hand to his face, but fails through weakness. John takes his handkerchief and dabs at the corners of his eyes. Even tears are too insubstantial to flow freely from his frail body.

John breaks the quiet. 'She – Sheldon died from the birthing complications?'

'Yes.'

'What was the nature of your departure from the Morton household?'

'I was told that the babe was born and breathed, but was before its term and likely to die. I was dismissed and my promise never to speak of the matter rewarded with coin. I stayed close and some weeks later heard that the babe still lived, but Morton had men of arms send me away under mortal threat.' He closes his eyes tight. 'To this day I do not know where… Sheldon lies, or if the babe survives.'

John says, 'Your sin was grievous; this premature and coarse ending to your life a just reward. Nevertheless, no man has met God without stain on his soul. There are many wicked diversions on this earth sent to confound our attempts to remain pure.' John clasps his hand on his chest and is silent for a moment. 'How was your living in the after years?'

'I journeyed to the Low Countries and was tutor to a family of some wealth in Delft. I… I was full of self-hate and easily swayed by earthly pleasures. I was sent away when I was found insensible through an over-indulgence of wine and returned here. My story will be familiar. I was dissolute and as time passed I came to realise… to understand that my mind was set on a fall that would lead to this foul end. I revelled in my misfortune at the card tables, delighted when I was spurned by friends and savoured my aching belly when no scraps of food could be found. It was just punishment for my greatest sin.' His breath catches and the bubbling in his throat causes him moments of panic. It is not pretty to watch him struggle to hold a fast-fading grip on life. He recovers. 'It is a relief to share my shame with a man of such godliness, Doctor Foxe. Please do not stint on your damning because of my pitiable state.'

'I will not, you can be assured. I will ask my friends to leave us alone while we speak of your soul and His grace. Before this, you will provide the date of your leaving the Morton house. Doctor Constable will write this down and you will add your name to mark the end of this part of your arrangement.'

'It was the month of August in the sixtieth year and perhaps the tenth or twelfth day.'

I hand the paper and quill to Gore. With John's help, I lever his body upright and he makes his mark with trembling hand. The effort exhausts, he sinks back and is wracked by a heaving and gurgling in his chest. I wonder if this is his end, but the fit subsides. Askham takes his leave, I start to follow then turn back to Gore and say, 'You have a daughter; a fair maid with fine sensibilities. It is my attachment to her that brought us here.'

My conscience will not let me leave him without this information, which will likely ease his last moments more than any words from John.

We wait for John below. Three more patrons have entered the inn, but they do little to disturb the hushed anxiety that attends our presence. Della busies herself with serving, cleaning and tidying while others mutter with heads bowed, fearful of catching Askham's gaze. We wait and watch in silence. It is a half hour before John descends the ladder with great care. I hand Della a sixpence and we depart, thankful to put this place behind us.

We speak little of our time at the Silver Bell on our return. When we have crossed the bridge John asserts that he would welcome conversation over a cup of wine, and that we should seek a place of comfort away from my house at West Cheap.

Askham suggest that we should make for the Bear and Ragged Staff, which he knows to be a reputable inn.

Askham orders that meats and pickles with a jug of claret be brought to our table. The change in our situation could not be more different from the hovel we have left. The straw is clean, the fire warming and the laughter of good company lifts my spirits. I ask John if Gore still breathed when he left.

'He did not reply to my last questions. His eyes were open and there was faint movement in his chest, but his end was near and he will pass before the day is out.'

'A weak man and a wasted life,' says Askham.

'Indeed,' replies John. 'At the last he was able to muster his senses, admit his errors and open his weakness to His grace.' He pauses while our refreshment is placed on the table. 'The date, William. You will know that its significance does not escape me.'

I am prepared for John's insight, although it is clear from Askham's expression that he does not share John's understanding. 'I must beg your forgiveness for not sharing this intelligence sooner, John. I have concerns…'

'This was too great a matter to keep hidden, William. It is apparent that the young Mistress Morton is the "unknowing maid" in the coded message. Her birth date closely matches that on the false chart of stars.'

'I confess that my growing regard for Helen may have clouded my judgement. I cannot dispel thoughts that her innocence may be no protection against strong questioning.'

John folds his arms and sits back in his seat, while I see that Askham has grasped the substance of our words.

'Do you have further perceptions from this intelligence?'

I see John will not leave this and it will like to ruffle him further if I do not flesh out some of my thinking for him. 'There is a connection with the great adventure led by Sir George Morton and Captain General Hawkins. Quite how that connection is forged I am unsure.'

Askham says, 'The adventure is planned with a large number of ships and fighting men, as I understand.'

'Quite so,' joins John, 'And are we confirmed in our belief

214

that this undertaking has no secret and malign purpose?'

'I cannot countenance Sir George's involvement in the conspiracy,' I answer. 'Surely there can be no question of his loyalty when he seeks to bring glory to Her Majesty's name and enlargement to her treasury?'

'Only if we are firm in our conviction of the true purpose of the venture.'

Askham says, 'Captain General Hawkins was rewarded for his part in the uncovering of the plot of Roberto Ridolfi. Does that not vouch for his loyalty?'

'He posed as a follower of Rome to gain the trust of the Spanish. I had some part in our defence against this danger to Her Majesty and had dealings with Captain Hawkins. I was not easy with his deception. His enactment as a zealot for the old religion was too deep and convincing to be without foundation. He was paid handsomely for his trouble and I have difficulty in trusting a man with such mercenary leanings.'

So that is why the meeting between John and Hawkins was somewhat strained. The root of mistrust goes back to the plot named after the Florentine banker. The Duke of Norfolk lost his head for his part, for all he protested that he was not a Catholic and followed the example of his former teacher – one Doctor John Foxe. If John's love for a former student colours his view of Hawkins then it may be problematic to transform his view to my way of thinking. But is my mind set? It is three-quarters there and I must strive for some time to reach near certainty.

I say, 'I must beg your indulgence and ask for your consideration of friendship by delaying a report of our findings and conversation today to Mister Secretary or Master Mylles. This would be a short adjournment of three or four days, during which I will contrive to arrange a meeting at my house with Sir George and Captain Hawkins. There, you John, with Captain Askham in attendance, can put firm questioning to these men about the venture. From their answers you may be satisfied of their loyalty, find sufficient doubt to warrant further interrogation or damning evidence of their involvement in the conspiracy. Whatever the outcome, I will then be ready to meet with Mister Secretary and present what I believe will be a feasible strategy for revealing the true nature of the plot and arraignment of the prime conspirators.'

They stare at me in silence. Have I overestimated their regard for my abilities and steadfastness? Do they dare risk displeasure from Walsingham by withholding this intelligence? Their faces do not tell me which way their thoughts incline. I see John glance at Askham and receive a faint nod of his head in return.

John says, 'Two days, William. We will allow two days and no more.'

Thirty-Two

I decide that I will deliver the message to Morton and Hawkins in person. A short note requesting an urgent conference would likely arouse concern and result in a return note, asking for elaboration or clarification. I may have awkward questions posed, but I will be there to protest necessity and an assurance that good reason will be provided in time. I have no doubt that my mark will fall when they discover that this is a ploy to lure them to an uncomfortable interrogation, which questions their loyalty to the crown. Well, there it is. I am set in my resolve and must endeavour to find ways to recover my standing in due course.

I hand Cassius to one of Askham's men who accompanies me and pray that I will not have to deal with Wensum as an intermediary on this visit. It is Lucy, Helen's chambermaid, who answers my call. She bobs a greeting and bids me enter.

'Good day to you Lucy, will Sir George be free to answer my call? My words will be brief.'

'Oh, Sir George is away, Doctor Constable. I believe he has business by Aldersgate. Shall I take news of your arrival to Master Wensum?'

'No, that will not be necessary, Lucy. I will wait for his return, or… may I leave a message with your mistress?'

'I fear she is also away, sir. The mistress has been called to the Palace with Mistress Dee. There was much excitement and work to prepare their finest clothing, ribbons and trinkets.'

'Whitehall?'

'Yes sir, they are to be received at court. It is a particular honour, is it not? My mistress… she will turn many heads with her comeliness… if you beg my pardon, sir.'

'Yes, I am sure you have dressed and prettied your mistress well, Lucy.'

'Thank you, sir. They are not long departed and my wits will not calm with fancying and delight at their good fortune.'

'In that case I should like to write a note for Sir George.'

She leads me to a chamber and brings materials so that I may write a hurried note. It is not the method of delivery I had planned, but it must serve as I cannot wait for his return. I congratulate Lucy once more and take my leave. I am filled with dread at imaginings of Helen's questioning by Walsingham, Mylles or other interrogators whose manner may be even more direct than those I know. Surely John and Askham would not have broken their word to afford me two days grace? Could Walsingham's own enquiries have been the reason for her summons? Whatever the source of this unwelcome distraction, I must make haste to Whitehall and hope that my intervention will allow her release. And why has Jane Dee also been summoned? There can be no suspicion of her involvement in the conspiracy.

*

My journey to Whitehall is slowed by a flurry of snow with a wind from the west that bites and clings, so that I am lumbered in a heavy white covering at our destination. I make directly for the physician's quarters and bid a fire be renewed in my chamber. Forester finds me warming hands and feet with steam rising from woollen breeches. He asks me to attend to the urgent needs of two gentlemen and a chamber lady with pained bellies and loose movements. I control my impatience with difficulty, but a refusal would sit oddly with my station here. I answer that I will consult with them shortly. He advises that his assistant will bring them to me as their incapacity will not allow them to circulate freely in the great court.

I am thankful that my consultations are brief. The symptoms are not severe and I suspect in all cases caused by an over-indulgence of poorly-cooked meats. I instruct an abstinence from food for three days, excepting a breakfast of posset fortified with brandywine. The last gentleman is leaving my chamber as Forester appears and says it would be a kindness if I could also call on Doctor Huicke. I submit to his petition, but it is already two hours past midday and the Doctor will have to wait until my primary concern here is resolved.

My aim is to seek an audience directly with Walsingham himself, and I see his scribe Padget emerging from his chamber.

He informs that Mister Secretary is at his house in Seething Lane, but Master Mylles is presently unattended. It seems I will have to settle for my second preference.

'Doctor Constable – William – this is an unexpected pleasure.'

He is reclining in his seat, both feet on a stool and feeding off, what looks like a large chop of meat, held in both hands. He wipes his mouth, throws the chop on the floor and bids me take a stool by his table.

'Good day to you, Master Mylles – Francis. I trust I do not disturb your work.'

'My mind continues in its occupation through greater disturbances than you bring, William. I am happy to see your arm mends.' He drinks greedily from a pewter cup. 'Forgive my coarse way of refreshment; I find business rarely pauses to allow the convenience of an easy dinner.'

'There is nought to forgive. You must nourish your physical being for a perceptive mind.' My mouth is dry and I would be glad of a cup of wine or beer, but he does not offer. 'I have attended patients here and thought to exercise this opportunity to confer with you on our progress.'

He grunts an understanding and shuffles papers on his table. 'No more has come from the attack on your house, save we believe that the killed assailant was from foreign parts. Two men have been questioned on their association with Millen. One is held for further insights as his religion is untrustworthy. The other is innocent and has been freed.'

'Are no more suspects questioned – a woman perhaps?'

'Why a woman? Do you have a particular one in mind?'

'Millen, for example, must have had connections with women, and the frail nature of female kind would render them more compliant to your questioning.'

'Ah, I catch your drift, William. I had taken you to be somewhat squeamish about the interrogation of the fair sex. But no, we have found no woman in that respect. Our searches continue.'

His response appears straightforward and his manner does not suggest that he dances around the subject to extract more from me. He will surely know that Helen is summoned here. And Jane Dee. Millen was often at her house in Mortlake. It is plain that she suffered hurt and could have no malign connection, but even so… No, I must continue to be circumspect and not mention their names.

'I wonder if I could have sight again of your excellent piecing together of the draft transit chart; also the deciphered note from the cabinet. My memory has suffered, perhaps from the crack to my head, and further inspection may help me to untangle threads from the malevolent design.'

His eyes fix me with an expression of mild surprise, then moves his head as a gesture of assent and reaches for papers on his table. He presents the representation of the transit chart first. I examine it carefully and say, 'Has any significance been uncovered about the date in February next year? Does it coincide with any of Her Majesty's planned engagements?'

He answers in the negative and I move the paper to one side. He produces a fair copy of the text of the deciphered note and turns it to my view.

'Here is another reference to the month of February.' I continue to gaze at the note as though memorising the position of each word. I sit back and say, 'Finally, may I have sight of the natal chart contained in the box.'

He takes another paper and places it before me. It is not the original, but a rough copy.

'Here is another date marked. Has any consequence been found in the day written in the sixtieth year?'

'No, we assume it is another contrived date. Do you have greater insight?'

I do not voice my answer, but shake my head and sit back as if in deep thought. This is mystifying. He would surely have mentioned Helen's birth date, if it was known to him. He does not have the air of someone who holds back intelligence and any further probing will surely arouse his suspicions.

'Thank you Francis; that has been most helpful. I will leave you to your important work in unearthing this devilment.'

*

I wander the great court, greeting those few that I know before continuing on my way. I meet with Richard Joynes, who I am pleased to find in fair humor. We converse idly for some time, but my mind is elsewhere and he must notice my inattention as I scan the space around us for any sign of Helen. Eventually, satisfied that she is nowhere in court, I bid him farewell and go to visit Doctor Huicke.

He is the same room I left him in that unhappy state some days past. I knock and enter. The small chamber is poorly lit with only one spluttering candle and the dying embers of a fire serving to illuminate the shapes of a bed and small table. I approach his bedside and am relieved that no straps hold the form beneath the covers. The whites in the eyes of a head turn to me and a voice croaks a word I do not understand.

'Doctor Huicke, this is William Constable, come to visit you.'

There is an unlit candle on his bedside table. I take a light from the other before it dies and replace it. I pour a cup of ale from a jug and offer it to his lips. He raises his head, takes a half dozen sips then lies back with a contented sigh.

I say, 'Are you well fed and cared for?'

'I had a pigeon pie for dinner. The bird was good eating, but the pastry too wet.' His voice is improved, but still faint.

'Do you rise from your bed each day?'

'I am harried and industrious, with many patients who seek my wisdom. They tire me. I must put them to one side so that I may serve Her Majesty.' He turns his head to me quickly. 'Does she ask for me? I will go to her... your arm... give me your arm.'

His hand grabs mine and it is plain that he does not have the strength to rise on his own accord.

'Her Majesty is in good health and does not require your attention this day.'

'Who are you?'

'I am Doctor William Constable, here to assist with your unwanted patients.'

He points his hand accusingly. 'Unwanted... unwanted. You are ill-mannered in the extreme.'

'I beg your pardon, I misspoke. It was the wrong word.'

'I have it. You have been here before seeking relief from your gouty foot.'

'It is much improved, thank you.'

'You have a particular event in mind for the month of February.'

'February. Why do you speak of that month?'

'So many… gentlemen had questions about February.'

'Who, who sought this information?'

'Names… names…' He closes his eyes. I think he sleeps and make to leave, then his eyes open. 'I have it. Capton was a name. There was another…' His voice trails away and his eyes close once more. I push his shoulder. There is no response. I will get no more from Huicke. I stand and wait for a few moments to confirm his slumber, then leave him.

Why would Capton visit Huicke and question him about February? Even if it is true, any testimony from his fevered mind cannot be relied upon. I dismiss any further contemplation on Huicke's ravings and return to the great court.

There is no sign of Helen. Blanche Parry progresses with a group of ladies some yards in front of me. She sees me and tilts her head in acknowledgement. I remove my cap and bow.

'William? William it is you.'

I turn to face Jane Dee. 'Jane. Yes, it is me. You are here. Why did you…'

'We have been here for some time.'

A figure brushes by my elbow and joins Jane. It is Helen. A loud exhalation of breath leaves me. I recover some of my composure and greet both ladies. I bend too low in my respectful salute. They are both in high spirits and Jane puts a hand to her mouth to stifle a laugh. Does she mock my serious face; my reddening cheeks?

I say, 'I was at Leadenhall this morning and heard that you may be here.'

'Do you chase us, William?' Helen's tone is teasing.

'I… no, I was called to attend as a court physician.' There is no indication from their demeanour that their call here had an unhappy outcome. 'I was not told the reason for your summons.'

'It was not a summons, William. It was an invitation by Her

222

Majesty, no less. She wished to sympathise with the misfortune of the wife of a cherished adviser. Jane received much cosseting and coddling from Her Majesty's gentle words about the attack on her person at Mortlake.' Helen smiles and kisses Jane lightly on her cheek.

'Queen Elizabeth had heard that I was lodging at Leadenhall and requested that I should be accompanied by my dear friend, Helen.' Jane returns Helen's kiss.

Their excitement builds and they talk quickly of their audience with the Queen. They go too fast and I am confused. I catch the words, 'jewels,' 'kindness' and 'honour'. All seems to have gone well. Why did I not suspect an innocent motive behind their call here?

'I am happy for you. It is rare honour to be received so kindly into her presence.'

'There is more,' says Jane, 'Her Majesty has offered to lend assistance in the rebuilding of the Doctor's library. It will be a delight to offer this news on his return.'

I take the arms of both ladies and we stroll through the great court speaking of the Queen's gracious manner, dazzling dress and wit. Jane is taken aside by two maids. Helen asks the nature of my business at her father's house. We stand together in the midst of murmured conversations, and the constant flow of courtiers, petitioners and attendants as though we are alone. I see her loveliness as if for the first time. I shiver at the thought of our bodies pressing for greater closeness. But such dreams must be postponed.

'It was an invitation. There is an urgent matter that I must disclose to your father and Captain General Hawkins tomorrow at supper. I should be grateful if you would reinforce my written note by advising on the importance of our meeting at West Cheap.'

No doubt, she thinks my earnestness concerns the great adventure and she does not question me further.

Thirty-Three

I break the news to Mother about tonight's supper over breakfast. I explain that there will be much to discuss about business and she does not hide her displeasure that ladies will not be invited to the table. She complains that Elspeth and Mistress Hilliard are busy in their preparations for Christmastide and will not have time to ready a fine supper for important guests. John comes to my rescue and begs for plain fare that will not disturb our necessary considerations. It is done. I must retreat to my library and fix my formulation for a scheme that will bring the conspiracy to an end. Confidence in my presentation to Walsingham and others will be vital to its acceptance. But certainty is lacking. There are stitches in the tangle of suppositions that can be unpicked. Strong intellects will be there to make the unpicking, and of all those it is John's perception I fear most.

I join Askham and John in the receiving room before the appointed hour. John tells that they have planned their questioning. Askham will examine military issues, then John will follow on the less tangible aspects of loyalty, beliefs and ambitions. I am expected to introduce the subject of their interrogation and write an account, which will be marked by all present. As the time draws near, I am less sure of my plan and the wisdom of subjecting two men of high standing to this ordeal. I am sure that I will be damned by both for impertinence and ingratitude after my offer of inclusion in their great adventure. Will my suit for Helen be lost forever?

It is a mixture of relief and dread I feel when Sir George and Hawkins arrive. Introductions are made and we go directly to the chamber where a table is laid for our supper. I note Sir George's surprised expression as he sees paper, ink and quill at one end of the table. I pour glasses of claret for all, we take our first sips in the name of Her Majesty and then I begin.

'Gentlemen, I have brought you here falsely. I regret this necessity, but the safety of our realm is at stake.' Sir George places his glass on the table and exclaims his indignation loudly, while Hawkins merely narrows his eyes. 'Captain Askham here, is a Queen's soldier serving Secretary Walsingham. Doctor Foxe and I have the honour to advise Sir Francis on the matter in hand.' Walsingham's name has quietened their discontent. 'It is a complex tale, which I cannot relate in full, but your great adventure appears to be tied in some way to a grievous conspiracy against Her Majesty and the survival of our English state.'

'It is absurd. How can this be contemplated by serious men?' Sir George takes his glass and drains it.

'For my part, I have no doubt that you are guiltless parties, but Mister Secretary seeks certainty and the thorough examination of all possibilities. You will be questioned by Captain Askham and Doctor Foxe. I will record the essence of this dialogue. Please understand that you must answer openly and willingly. You cannot refuse to answer or rely on evasion and indirectness.'

There are moments of quiet as both men appear to accept the force of the obligation placed upon them.

Askham says, 'It is known that you are assembling a great many ships and men for your venture. What would be their number?'

Hawkins answers, 'We have twenty-two ships. They are readied and manned here and at Plymouth. A full complement of men numbers two thousand and four hundred, although that is not an exactness.' He glances at me, recognising that I am one of those whose participation is in doubt.

'That is a formidable force collected under private control.'

'They are not all fighting men. Each ship must carry those of a less vigorous nature who attend to the needs of our ships and those who bear arms.'

'I hear that you plan to gather your force in Dartmouth. It is a quiet harbour although one capable of sheltering many ships. It is also one with a geography that would suit a joining fleet from Spain.'

Both Hawkins and Morton huff and snort at this suggestion. Hawkins says, 'You must know that I have no love for Spain.

My efforts in the plot against Her Majesty some seven years past vouch for my loyalty.'

'Yet, you were able to gain the confidence of Ridolfi and were a particular friend to Espes, the Spanish ambassador,' joins John. 'It is known that you correspond still with Espes, and pleaded for the lives of some of those found guilty.'

Hawkins shifts uneasily in his seat. If this is true, Walsingham has been watching Hawkins and intercepting his messages. Is there more to this venture than I have understood?

'Don Guerau de Espes is a fine man who favours peace between our states. He argued against the plot and assisted my part in its confounding. As for Ridolfi… he was easily persuaded of my deceit. A foolish man, ill-suited to politicking, he should have remained fixed to his expertise in money and trade.'

He does not deny his correspondence with Espes. I wonder if the content of those messages reveals any indications of his intent to do harm to our queen.

Sir George spreads his hands to beseech our indulgence. 'The climax of our venture is the arrest and plunder of Spanish treasure ships. You will know this from Doctor Constable. It would defy all logic to suggest we conspire with Spain to harm the sovereign who has provided our license for the expedition.'

Askham replies, 'That could be agreed if your stated scheme is verified and does not hide a malign purpose. You, Sir George, continue to trade in Spanish wines and Sir Humphrey Gilbert, your partner in the venture, trades in slaves with Spanish settlers in Hispaniola and Venezuela.'

'That is trade. We are not at war and there is no consideration of faith or politics in commerce – only profit.'

John will not like this statement, but does not comment.

Askham continues. 'The assembly at Dartmouth is to be in February next. This date holds a significance in our investigations. Why was it chosen for the sailing of your fleet?'

Hawkins answers, 'Our planning and preparations have been over one year in the making. It is the time when all will be readied. Sir Humphrey has a house at Dartmouth and spoke for its convenience and his influence in preparing the location.'

'Also,' says Sir George, 'we consulted on what would be the most propitious date for despatch.'

'Consulted – with who?' It is me who voices this question.

Morton turns to face me with cold expression. 'You must know; it is in your capability. We sought advice on the positioning of the stars.'

'And the name of the astrologer?'

'It was Millen; Christopher Millen.'

There is a pause and then the questioning continues. I do not hear the words as my thoughts are bonded to the name of the proven conspirator. But it was freely given, with no attempt to dissemble, and it would be commonplace to seek guidance from a reading of stars for an event of this magnitude. Does this imply a measure of guilt or innocence? It is John who speaks as my mind returns to the business at hand.

'… spoke of less vigorous men on your ships. Will there be those with you who guard men's souls?'

'We have recruited a number of clerics to our venture and by the time we sail, expect to have a Protestant man of God on each ship.' Hawkins emphasises the religion of the clerics.

'Do you have names of these men of true faith? For example, those that will sail with you and Sir Humphrey?'

'Doctor John Paynes of St Agnes in Godalming sails with me and Doctor Frobisher of Plymouth sails with Sir Humphrey. Be assured that all clerics on our venture have impeccable religion.'

John does not pursue this line of questioning. Does he know these men? He asks Hawkins about his trade in slaves and, while it is plain, he views this operation with distaste, he does not press him on the matter. He probes their motives. Are they fixed on a narrow aim of personal gain; or do they hold some wider considerations for enrichment of our state; Her Majesty; the true faith? In truth, his questioning is somewhat convoluted and both men have a difficulty in providing direct responses.

'What of your investors?'

'Mine is the largest share of material and coin,' answers Sir George. 'There are nine ships in my name and my ready funds are severely depleted by the expense. Many of our investors are bankers who do not wish their names generally known.'

'Are there names you can offer freely that would likely sway our thinking?'

Morton hesitates before replying. 'Commerce and openness are not natural bedfellows. One man – a man of high significance – offered no coin, but we have relied on his valued influence and advice. That man is Lord High Treasurer Burghley.'

Morton sits back and glances at Hawkins. They will surely feel that mention of Burghley will settle this interrogation in their favour. His devotion to Her Majesty, and her regard for him, is beyond doubt, even though he spends much of his time away from court. His focus on affairs of state have become diluted in recent years, with his attention diverted to the building of a great estate.

John is not content to leave it there and continues to question both men about their families, daily devotions and, queerly, their drinking and eating habits. Morton's impatience grows. Finally, John draws our questioning to a close, thanks them and expresses the wish that they will remain at our table for supper. Morton raises his head to disdain this offer and John says they are free to leave once they have signed my papers to indicate a fair record. Sir George examines my writing in detail, signs with a flourish, sets his face in grim fashion and leaves without comment. Hawkins does the same.

It is time for our delayed supper. I go in search of Mistress Hilliard to request its serving and return to find John and Askham deep in conversation. The talking stops as I approach the table.

'Well,' I say, 'Is there a consensus?'

'We wait for your opinion, William.'

How should I answer? They know my mind was set on their innocent part before our questioning, so I cannot be too direct in their cause.

'The mention of Millen surprised, but perhaps it could have been expected and it is another link between the two strands of the conspiracy. To my mind there was no sense of understanding from Sir George of Millen's authorship of the star charts from Brouillard's box and Mylles' compilation.' I pause, but their expressions are neutral. 'I knew nothing of Hawkins's continued attachment to the Spaniard, Espes. That will count against him, but I have known other friendships to break the shackles of general enmity and diverse beliefs. The support of Lord High Treasurer Burghley must weigh heavily in their favour. I know nothing of the significance of the named clerics. In general, I found their protestations convincing and I believe they have no knowing part in the conspiracy.'

Askham looks to John who signals that he should speak. 'I have no doubt of Sir George's virtue in this matter. No guilty man could have played his part with such conviction. As for Captain Hawkins... I wonder if he has used Sir George as a puppet to his devious ends.' He hesitates. 'No that is too fanciful. I conclude that they are both blameless.'

That is two decided, but I hazard that John's view will outweigh both of ours in Walsingham's mind.

John clasps his hands together and sits in silent contemplation. The quiet continues too long, but I must not fuddle his thinking with more words. The door opens; Mistress Hilliard and Elspeth appear with trays for our supper.

We had asked for plain fare, but are presented with oysters, a pike, mutton pie, rabbit in redcurrant sauce and sweet frumenty. Askham takes a large portion of pike and eats heartily. John declines the fish and passes the plate to me. He places a handful of oysters in his bowl and gazes at them thoughtfully before raising the first to his lips.

Askham says to John, 'I was surprised at your questioning of their custom in eating and drinking.'

'You can discover much from a man's daily practise. Irregular and excessive consumption will likely signal erratic behaviour and a wandering mind. Such men are apt to be vain and show weakness when presented with temptation.'

This does not bode well for John's assessment of Sir George's character. He takes more oysters. Askham and I wait in silence for his pronouncement.

'I concur.' He sips his wine before continuing. 'I read Sir George as you both did. Hawkins is not a man I like, but he must also be an innocent. I know both clerics he named. Their religion is flawless and I cannot conceive that Hawkins would have recruited them if he had Catholic mischief in mind. Burghley is final confirmation. He has a sharp mind and would not have granted license to Hawkins unless convinced of his soundness.'

I have been sitting stiffly and sense an easing in my body as he speaks these words. The first obstacle is cleared. Tomorrow, I must convince Walsingham and others of my scheme to bring the conspiracy to an end. My appetite is recovered and we continue with our supper with discussion of the great adventure and the difference in character of the two men cleared of blame.

John says, 'It is a pity that Sir George took such great offence at your little trickery. It is to be desired that your standing with him recovers so that your attachment to his daughter reaches a happy conclusion.'

Askham bows his head in sympathy for my predicament. 'Let us hope that your part in a successful prevention of the conspiracy will take you some way to a mending of his affection for you. I have made enquiries and learned that Sir Francis will be at his house in Seething Lane the next day. I will send word to expect our arrival with news of some importance before midday.'

Thirty-Four

I am waiting in the parlour for John. Mother is fussing. She senses that some intrigue is in progress and resents her exclusion from knowing. The air between us is uncomfortable, but I dare not disclose the events of last night or those to come at Seething Lane. Mistress Hilliard hands me a note and I am thankful of this distraction from Mother's attention. It is from Helen.

William

What have you done? My father is angry. You are blamed for a great hurt and I am not to be informed of its nature. I am not permitted to visit West Cheap and my receiving of notes will be watched.

Helen Morton

I am addressed as plain 'William' and there is no declaration of fondness in her signing. My offence to Sir George may be greater than I had feared. Mother waits expectantly for a sight of the note or its explanation.

I say, 'There is news from Master Chap on a small delay in the manufacture of my instruments.'

My face must show some deeper meaning, for it is clear that she does not believe me. This is not a good preface to an important day.

*

I see Captain Askham enter as we approach Mister Secretary's house. It is a surprisingly modest building, somewhat smaller and less grand than its neighbours, but distinguished by four armed men guarding its frontage. Askham waits for us in the hall and we are led through to a small antechamber where Mylles stands warming by a fire. He utters a vague exclamation at our entry, states he is mystified by his summons here and enquires if we could enlighten him. John begs for his patience and says all will be revealed shortly.

Padget open a door, bows a greeting and leads us into the chamber. Walsingham sits behind a large table. His face has a pinched look and his complexion is sallow. As his physician I would suspect a deep malaise connected to the vital organs, but now is not the time to offer an opinion. Will sickness affect his judgement this day? Four chairs are arranged at the other side of his table. We take our seats and Padget moves to his place at a stool and small table to one side.

'Well, gentlemen, I am eager to learn the reason for this representation,' says Walsingham. 'My time here is short. Her Majesty moves to Greenwich for Christmastide and there are arrangements to be made for her security.'

I would answer, but John is too quick and explains that I will outline a scheme to unravel the conspiracy and identify the offenders. He continues that he and Askham have only a partial understanding of my plan, as its design is complex and my work only just completed. It is generous of him not to mention my two days of grace, which would surely displease Walsingham.

'So, William, you continue to surprise. It may be that your deductions have advanced beyond my practised intelligencers. I will listen with interest.' He turns to Padget and bids him leave us.

'Thank you, Mister Secretary. First, I must acknowledge Doctor Foxe and Captain Askham for their forbearance. I have sketched my reasoning and persuaded them to wait until it is finalised here, at this presentation of a design for unearthing the plotters and securing our state.'

I note that Mylles shuffles uneasily in his seat. He will not like it if his efforts pale in comparison to mine.

'My first discovery was the birth date of a maid who is the daughter of a wealthy merchant, Sir George Morton. That date is an exact match for the one scrawled on the natal chart. This conformity itched at my thoughts and I sought to renew an acquaintance with the Morton family to soothe the nagging. I will admit that I have formed a strong attachment to the maid and it was this that caused me to withhold the intelligence.' Mylles rumbles some word under his breath. 'We were all convinced that the claim of a bastard heir was false and I could not countenance fierce questioning of this "unknowing maid".'

'Even so…' exclaims Mylles.

'Doctor Foxe can vouch for the blameless circumstances of her birth. Together, we took testimony from a dying man who was the father. The mother was a niece who died in childbirth. Helen Morton was adopted by Sir George under conditions of secrecy to hide family disgrace.'

Walsingham put down his dagger. 'What of Sir George Morton? I do not know his character and he must be examined.'

'It is already done, Sir Francis. Doctor Foxe and the Captain here interrogated him at length the last evening. They are firm in their belief that he has no part in the conspiracy.'

'Of course, I place my trust in their judgement, but thus far your telling holds only mild concern. You talk of disqualification from the conspiracy; not its solving.'

He is impatient and in bad humor, perhaps because of his ailment. I must convince without over-elaboration.

'I beg your patience a little longer, Sir Francis. I give word that the end of this story is worthy of your attention, but the tangle of associations is intricate and stretches my abilities in its exposition.'

He waves a hand to indicate I should continue.

'In my introduction to Sir George, I stated a keen interest in his great adventure and the possibility that my knowledge in the mathematics of navigation may help his cause. This was only a partial truth. It was, however, a fortunate deceit and led to a conclusion that the conspiracy had two strands: one to sow unrest and create the circumstances for an invasion by a hostile force; the second to foil Sir George's venture and its design on Spanish treasure ships. The two strands are intimately connected. It was intended to falsely denounce Sir George as a knowing guardian of the bastard heir with a hidden purpose to use his fleet of ships and men to assist a Spanish invasion.'

Mylles is quick to assert that my deductions are reached without logic. He is eager for me to offer names in the conspiracy and firm evidence for my suppositions. John intervenes and restates a plea for their forbearance. Walsingham quiets Mylles with narrowed eyes.

'Sir George and Captain Hawkins were much taken with my idea for an improved instrument of navigation and I set to work to model preliminary thoughts into an object with practical use on the deck of a ship. I confess that my enthusiasm for this project, and the venture itself, grew in my imaginings.'

I pause to gather my thoughts. I must be quick to offer a name or their interest will wane.

'It was two incidents, similar in nature, but diverse in status and location with no apparent connecting thread that steered my thinking. The attack on Doctor Dee's house at Mortlake and the assault on Mistress Dee we now know to be prompted by a desire to hide the role of Christopher Millen in the preparation of the false natal and transit charts. Some days later there was a burning and murders at the house of a craftsman named Hutchison. I employed him to manufacture an exemplar of the navigation instrument to be used on the venture. In both cases a violent attack by four or five armed men bearing torches was led by a large hooded man. Through unguarded talk I named Millen in discussion with a man shortly before the attack on Mortlake. My steward had a conversation with the same man about my instrument and unwittingly disclosed the name Hutchison in the days leading up to his murder and burning of his house. That man is Darby Wensum, Sir George's man of business.'

Walsingham asks Mylles if Wensum is known to him. Mylles shakes his head.

'There is more. The assault on my person was directly after a meeting at Leadenhall, which was arranged by Wensum. It was a curious encounter with little purpose. Sir George appeared to be under the influence of a sleeping draught and Wensum stated that none of Sir George's men were on hand to escort me on my return to West Cheap. The invitation and circumstances of my return journey were planned to assist the assault. I have sufficient vanity to suppose that my instrument was thought to offer an improvement to the positioning of ships and bettering their chances of success in the great adventure. My death was a contingency measure in case their plans to thwart the sailing of the venture fleet failed.'

'What of the incident at your house, William?' enquires John. 'Do you ascribe the same motive behind that?'

'Yes, that and Master Hutchison's fate had the same aim.'

Walsingham raises his hands to halt any further discussion and asks that John, Askham and I leave him while he confers with Mylles. I am not sure whether this signifies that Mister Secretary has dismissed my story. Or, could it be that he wishes to compare my findings with Mylles' own? I am uneasy, but neither John nor Askham can shed any light on the adjournment. We stand in the hallway waiting for our recall; if, indeed, there is to be one. It is a good half hour before Mistress Goodrich opens the door and bids that we return. That is a surprise. Is she to be part of our consultation or merely to provide refreshment? My musing is answered as she takes her place on a stool by Mylles.

Walsingham says, 'I would hear the end of your story, William. But first, a retelling of your account to this point would aid our consideration. Do not stint on the detail of your examinations of Sir George Morton and the natural father of the maid.'

I take this as an encouragement and restate all I have said with added particulars and embellishments about the attacks, the interrogations and reasons for naming Darby Wensum. My eagerness to convince leads to an overlong presentation and I am relieved when wine and sweetmeats are brought to bring a pause in my talking. I caution myself not to stray beyond the extent of the previous telling for there is a name which I will delay until the ending. This name should not be uttered, unless and until my earlier conclusions have been accepted. It is too dangerous. Finally, I bow my head to Walsingham and sit back in my seat to indicate this part is complete. There is a strangeness in the silence that follows. Have I wearied them?

'You have not mentioned the month of February. That date has been the focus of Master Mylles' attention these past weeks.' It is Walsingham who breaks the quiet.

'I agree with Master Mylles. February has significance from the coded note and the date on the transit chart foretelling a calamitous event. It is also the date planned for the departure of Captain Hawkins and Sir Humphrey from Dartmouth. My understanding is that there is a plot to set a fire among the ships in that harbour, postponing or cancelling their sailing, while an invasion fleet heads for Plymouth. I cannot be certain of this landing destination, but it would hold promise for our enemies because of a diversion caused by the "great burning" in nearby Dartmouth. I surmise this invasion will comprise ships and men from Spain and the Catholic League in France.'

Mylles says, 'And what of the date on the torn and mended chart?'

'As it states in the coded note, pamphlets will be printed and distributed claiming a bastard heir. A second wave of pamphlets will assert the date on the chart signifies the demise of Her Majesty on the twenty-fourth day of that month. The intention of both is to seed unrest and alarm in the populous and ease the progress of the invasion.'

Askham straightens in his seat as if recalling something. 'Do not forget the mention of Millen by Sir George.'

I had not forgotten. I did not think this extra detail was needed to strengthen my case, and I did not wish to arouse more suspicion of Sir George by its telling. 'Millen was asked, as an astrologer of repute, to read the stars and advise on the most propitious date for the sailing of the great adventure. February was chosen, but the association with Millen was harmless on the part of Sir George and Captain Hawkins. Whether Millen planned some trickery to be selected as their choice of astrologer, we may never know.'

Walsingham looks in turn at the others. None of them offer to comment. 'Well, William, I trust there is more to your story. The man, Wensum, is surely a lesser figure in the conspiracy. I cannot countenance that Guise or the Spanish crown would hold an arrangement with a man of such low station. You declared a design for the delivery of the plotters into our safekeeping, did you not?'

'Yes, Sir Francis, but it would settle my spirits if others around this table would share their opinions thus far.'

John and Askham declare they are with me. Mylles says that it is 'well done,' but more is needed and he does not have a firm conviction on the significance of Dartmouth and Plymouth. Would a landing site nearer the capital have greater advantage to an attacking force? There is some discussion on this aspect until Walsingham brings it to a close.

'These threads can be tied once we have heard the next part of your unfolding, William. Pray, continue.'

'Some weeks past, I met with Blanche Parry. She told me of a chambermaid's hearing of a conversation in the great court about a hidden, bastard child born to Her Majesty. The courtiers gossiping were named as Sir Peter Capton and Arthur Perse. They are naïve and empty-headed young men and I would have dismissed this as idle tattletale, as did Mistress Parry, were it not for their subsequent actions. After brief questioning by Master Mylles, they returned to him alleging that they could identify the scandalmongers as myself and Richard Joynes. This was false, but was it done out of simple malice for one of those who named them, or was there a deeper intent? At least one of these two men visited Doctor Huicke recently, and while we must accept that his poor mind is addled by age, he stated that Capton had questioned him on the significance of the month of February. Why would Capton call on Huicke? I consider it unlikely that sympathy for an ailing old man was the cause. They will have known that I attended Huicke on more than one occasion. The mention of "Capton" and "February" in the same breath was too great a coincidence. I believe that in both these cases, Capton and Perse were induced by a higher authority to undertake, admittedly clumsy, representation and enquiry.'

I pause to let my words take effect. All eyes are on me and the keenest belong to Mistress Goodrich who stares as though reaching deep into my soul. It is disconcerting. I wait a little longer to gather my thoughts, then continue.

'Through a chance remark by Mistress Helen Morton…' Speaking her name in this company brings a lurch in my stomach. My mouth is dry and I take a sip of wine. '… I learned that Darby Wensum had a surprise visitor at Leadenhall while Sir George was absent, and on at least two occasions. That visitor is also the patron of Capton and Perse. That visitor questioned me closely on my navigation instrument and attempted to take its design from my hands for his examination and use. He is one of the highest in the land and I deduce he is the principal in the conspiracy who corresponds with the Duke of Guise and the Spanish crown. It is the Earl of Oxford.'

A moment of quiet, then a babble of conversation follows. I do not hear the words. Mention of Helen's name has brought her note back to mind. I must mend the affront to Sir George, and quickly. I return to the present matter. John is talking about Oxford and suspicions of his true religious leanings. Askham joins with mention of his recent financial troubles and shaming by Her Majesty. Mylles says that Capton and Perse are watched closely and he shares my view on their involvement on the edge of the conspiracy. Walsingham's eyes dart around his table. His gaze stays with Mistress Goodrich for a time and she nods some form of unspoken correspondence.

'Well gentlemen, it seems there is general agreement that Doctor Constable's deductions have a measure of veracity. You have the mind of a capable intelligencer, William, and in such short time.' He purses his lips and picks up his dagger. 'There is a difficulty. The man, Wensum, can be brought in for questioning. However, we must tread carefully with Oxford. Regardless of Her Majesty's stern words on his profligate nature; he is much favoured in her view. It will take more than suppositions and coincidences to convince her. She loves his pretty figure and tinkling words too much.' He pauses. 'Another reason is his wife, who is a daughter of Baron Burghley. He has some misgivings about the match and it is said there is little affection in the pairing. Nevertheless, he would not wish this connection to be treated roughly.'

John mutters under his breath; Mylles is eager to snatch Wensum and bring him under his care.

I say, 'There may be another way to bring this matter to a climax with the capture of other conspirators.'

Walsingham's play with his dagger stops. 'What do you have in mind, William?'

I take a deep breath and start to outline my scheme. I explain that we have reason to suppose that the conspirators do not know we have Brouillard's cabinet, chart or the cipher. They will assume it was lost in the Paris fire, which was set to conceal the capture of the box. In that case, we may be able to draw in the plotters using the same cipher. Mylles objects and is of the opinion that our search for Millen will have alerted the conspirators to our knowledge of the star charts.

'I think not. It is more likely that my association with Doctor Dee and an earlier visit to Mortlake was the cause of their attack on the Doctor's house and killing of Millen.' I speak with more certainty than I feel. Mylles may be correct.

'How would we use our knowledge of the cipher, William,' enquires John.

'Coded messages would be sent to Oxford and Wensum. We would fabricate these messages using the design of the Brouillard cipher.' I am less sure of my next statement. 'I had thought that these messages would tell of some urgent matter or complication in their scheme that requires consultation in person. A rendezvous will be set. If they answer with their presence we will know, beyond doubt, of their guilt.'

I take two sheets of paper from my doublet and lay them on the table.

'I have drafted two notes using the cipher; one to Oxford and the other to Wensum. Both have the same content. They talk of a dire urgency which must be resolved by a meeting at one of Sir George's storehouses on the North Quay. I confess that this part of my design may be found wanting by those more practised in the art of deception and ensnarement.'

Mylles takes my papers and studies them. Walsingham and Askham discuss how a trap may be best set, how many men would be needed and other possible locations. John turns to me, pats my knee and offers an approving smile. The discussion widens and Mistress Goodrich adds whispered words in Walsingham's ear. He waits a few moments and then brings the chattering to a close by raising his hand.

'The scheme has promise and I confess to a liking for its design. There will be satisfaction from the neatness of its conclusion – if it succeeds. But there are impediments to be overcome. How will the messages be delivered? The manner of delivery as well as the content must convince. The phrasing in the note should be carefully manufactured. Any clumsiness or bungling on our part will alert their senses to our chase.'

I say, 'There is a refinement that may persuade Oxford and Wensum of the authenticity of the message.' Walsingham raises his eyebrows and tilts his head at my hesitation. 'Master Chap, who makes the navigation instrument, is a fine craftsman. I commissioned him to make a box from the wood of ebony. It is smaller than the one taken from Brouillard, but has a similar locking mechanism and hidden drawer. If the box contains a small token from the sender and the coded note is within the drawer, this may offer some assurance of dependability.'

'Yes, indeed,' John exclaims, 'An elegant subtlety that adds lustre to the plan.'

Walsingham and Askham nod their agreement, while Mylles murmurs something which I take to be a form of endorsement. I cannot read the expression on Mistress Goodrich's face.

'We should have two such boxes,' says Mylles.

'Yes, Master Chap already works on the second. It will be ready in two days.'

'Do you have the first for our examination?'

'Yes, John, it is here.' I lift a leather bag from the floor and take out the box. It is no more than a hand in each of its measures and has no decoration. The work on the wood is fine and the mechanisms have a pleasing exactness. I hand it to John, who examines it briefly then passes it to Mylles. He inspects it carefully, opens it, tests the lock and holds it up to the light to catch a sight of the hidden drawer. He plays with it, presses here and there until the drawer slides open. He closes it with a satisfying click. It goes from Walsingham, Askham and, finally, to Mistress Goodrich before it is returned.

'It is well done, William,' says Walsingham. 'I warm to the scheme and the box has settled my resolve on it. Yet, care must be taken in the detail. The next day I will be at Greenwich with the Captain. I would have the rest of you convene here while we are away. William, you will consult with Master Mylles and Mistress Goodrich on the coded note and manner of its delivery. Doctor Foxe, I trust your good sense and godliness to mediate upon any dispute and arrive at a common understanding. Let us convene here at eleven bells this next Friday to complete the preparations.'

Thirty-Five

It is Friday. The bells have rung for the hour of eleven and we wait in Mister Secretary's chamber of business at his house in Seething Lane. The last day, four of us reasoned and argued long into the night over the particulars to the scheme for lure and seizure of the conspirators. It was a tortuous, and at times vexing, passage to the brief we will put to Sir Francis today. We deliberated at length on the text of the message to be sent to both parties. Mylles was all for devising an ornate and protracted message from Oxford to Wensum reflecting the character of the sender. Under the same logic, he proposed Wensum's note to Oxford should be brief and business-like. My opinion was that both notes should be identical and from a third party – the 'g' in the original cipher, which we understood to be Henry, Duke of Guise. I considered it unlikely that Oxford would take well to a summons, however urgent and disguised, from a man such as Wensum. My view prevailed, with strong support from Mistress Goodrich.

It was a relief that Mylles' early tetchiness improved as the day progressed. Words of encouragement and praise from John and me eased his humor and we worked together on the cipher in good spirits. It was a surprise when Mistress Goodrich examined our work and corrected a small error. It became apparent that, not only is she proficient in ciphers, but that she also runs her own network of intelligencers. Her connections are exclusively of the female sex and range from keepers of whorehouses to titled ladies. I had not suspected that the fairer sex would be recruited for employment of this nature. On deeper reflection, this revelation should not have amazed; they are often well-placed to overhear unguarded moments through supposed unworldliness and delicate disposition. I hold Mistress Goodrich in high regard; she has formidable intellect and it is clear that she is well practised in the art of intrigue. Nevertheless, it was her contrivance for the delivery of one of the messages that has caused me great discomfort and unease.

Captain Askham enters the chamber with the news that Walsingham is delayed. Scurrilous tracts have been discovered circulating by St Paul's. He hands a torn copy to me. It is as we feared; the first printing of the claim of a hidden bastard heir and the 'proof' of an astrological chart. I pass it to Mylles. Askham warns that Sir Francis will be in ill-humor when he arrives, so it would be prudent to offer a firm stratagem with one voice. He will not take kindly to argument and uncertainty.

Askham removes his cloak and stands by the fire. He declares the air outside is bitter and expects snow later this day. John has read the tract and offers an opinion on the timing of its circulation. Christmastide is almost upon us and he avers it is no accident it appears now, in good time for the celebrations of our Lord's birth, when labour stops, men mingle and over-indulgence loosens tongues. We are all in agreement.

Askham says that he has diverted his journey from Greenwich with a survey of the North Quay. He has found a storehouse owned by Sir George that offers promise in its location. It lies at the end of a passage only fifty paces from an inn where his men can be positioned. Further, an adjoining storehouse may be leased for a short time and there are ships with an unobscured view of the store frontage, which can be a commandeered as a place of surveillance and control.

We pass the time waiting for Walsingham in our own ways. I join with Mylles to check our ciphers and each detail of our scheme. John reads a book and Mistress Goodrich has left our chamber to attend the organisation of the household. Askham is impatient; comes and goes from this chamber; to the stables; to confer with Mistress Goodrich; to peer over my shoulder; to warm by the fire.

A commotion at the front of the house signals his arrival. He enters the chamber in a flurry of whirling cloak and scurrying servants. My eyes are drawn to the gold chain of office still hung around his shoulders. He strides to the table and takes his seat without word of greeting. His pale face winces with pain as he adjusts his posture and I am reminded of my thoughts about a deep-seated ailment.

'You have heard of the appearance of a foul treatise?' His tone is clipped and sharp. 'Time is short. The matter must be settled.'

Mistress Goodrich enters quietly and dismisses the servants. Walsingham waves his hand to indicate that we should sit. Mylles enquires if any holding the tract have been taken. He is ignored and I take this to imply a negative. He answers John's query about a printer with politeness. More than fifty men are presently searching all known printers' workshops in the City. He unsheathes his dagger and places it flat on the table.

'Come now, please forgive my shortness. I have suffered a troubling start to this day. Is the plan readied? My eyes and ears are eager for the fruit of your labours.'

It is Mylles who sets out the particulars of our plan, although he is somewhat hesitant in his speech. He describes our discussions about the construction of the notes, the final decision to be brief and to mark the summons in the name of the supposed Guise, with the letter '*g*.' The location and timing of the rendezvous await the result of our present deliberations.

'Mistress Goodrich offered solutions for the delivery of the messages. Tuesday next is the day the court will transfer to Greenwich from Whitehall for Christmastide. The Earl has a bedchamber and other rooms near to the Queen's private apartments at Greenwich. The box and the note will be waiting his arrival there on his pillows.'

Walsingham bows his head in approval and says, 'What of the tokens within the boxes? They must be significant and the choice of these articles has taxed my thinking.'

'We are decided on a burnt twig in both boxes, Sir Francis. This would signify a matter connected to the "great burning".'

'Ha, I like it. It is simple and direct,' states Walsingham. 'Your gathering here proved to be rich in invention and good sense.' The improvement in his humor allows an easing in the air and this encourages Mylles to talk with more confidence as he continues.

'The method of delivery of the box to Wensum was an aspect that tested our ingenuity. After much discussion we agreed to adopt the device proposed by Mistress Goodrich. For reasons that are understandable, William had grave misgivings, but in the end acceded to the general view.'

'What is it, William? What concerns you?'

'It is decided that I shall use my attachment to Helen Morton. I will request that she places the box in Wensum's chamber of business while he is away. Sir George has forbidden our meeting and my presence at his house, so I must contrive to meet her in secret. There is a lady known to Mistress Goodrich lodged nearby in Bishopsgate. A note will be sent from this lady to Helen under pretence that a herbal soother is required for childbearing pains. On arrival, her servant will be directed to another matter and Helen will be guided to a chamber where I will wait, in place of the lady.'

'I do not know the Morton maid, but if you have formed an attachment, William, I suspect that she has a strong spirit and will be willing to do your bidding.'

'I thank you for your compliment, Sir Francis. She has a good mind and is of a fiercely independent disposition. Whether she will be compliant… well, I know I must persuade her.'

Attention turns to Askham who is asked to report on his survey of the North Quay. He explains in some detail how his men will be positioned and there is some discussion on how many will be needed.

'The day will be Wednesday next, which is Christmas Eve,' announces Walsingham. 'Does anyone have an opinion of its suitability or otherwise?'

I say, 'It is a date wisely chosen, Sir Francis. The day after receiving the boxes and their messages will shorten the interval in which Oxford and Wensum have to make enquiries about their veracity. No doubt they will question chamber servants and other attendants on the nature of delivery, so their placing must be done discreetly and without their knowledge.'

Askham adds, 'Christmas Eve will be a day of busy preparations and the completion of labours on the quay before the days of celebration. These comings and goings will provide cover for our watching and positioning. A later date, during the work holidays, will leave the quay and its surrounds bereft of normal activity. It will make our quarry wary and the element of surprise more difficult to achieve.'

'Good, we are agreed. The timing during the day is of your

choosing, Captain.'

'Then, let it be midday.'

Walsingham ends with a caution that Oxford must not be harmed. Preference is also for Wensum to be taken alive, with the fate of others left to Askham's discretion. Our meeting closes and we begin to disperse. The Captain takes me to one side and enquires if I intend to be present at the North Quay.

'I had not thought about it, but...'

'It is your scheme.'

'Yes, you are right. I should be there.'

Thirty-Six

This morning the funeral of Gregory was held at St Giles. It was a mournful affair. I spoke of my high regard for his steadfastness in my service, although his time in our household was short. John gave an oration and I was thankful that he did not dwell on matters of high religion and a damning of the Catholic Church. Instead, he was soft and sorrowful at the loss of one so young and blameless. I believe his family were both awed and comforted to hear the renowned Doctor Foxe assure them that the promise of a young and loyal soul would be welcomed into His grace.

Now, I am here, alone in the receiving chamber of a house and family I do not know, waiting for Helen. I have not been told who lives here, nor have I met the master or mistress. I assume the owner is a man of wealth and influence as it is a large house with fine furnishings. The door was answered by a maidservant, who was ushered away by Mistress Goodrich. She has prepared well for this encounter. I have been waiting here for over one hour, undisturbed. The fire is set; wine and a tray of cold meats and pickles await my pleasure on a table; and two chairs are arranged for our conversation. I am impatient for her company, fearful of what I must ask and worried that her affection for me has fallen so low that she will not comply easily, or not at all.

The door opens. It is… Jane Dee who enters, closely followed by Helen. My spirits sink. The speech I have rehearsed will not serve with the two of them present. I bend stiffly and clear my throat.

'Ladies, I bid you God's blessing on this day and beg your forgiveness for this cheap and unworthy deception.'

'Why, William…' exclaims Jane, 'It is a surprise. We are here to…' She glances at Helen, turns to me, smiles and bows her head. 'I understand the meaning of this ploy. I will leave you to request a pot of hot water from the kitchens.'

'No Jane, please stay with us. My father has forbidden me

from meeting with Doctor Constable. He knows this. Some days past it was my dearest wish to be close with him. Now, I must know if my feelings were misplaced by a clever mind and smooth words. I would have him explain away the nature of the hurt inflicted on my father and led to his stern injunction.'

'Helen… my dear… I cannot.'

'Cannot, because you have no pretty words? Cannot, because your behaviour would not be excused? Or, cannot because there is some other impediment?'

'Fine words do not flow easily from me, but it is the third of your reasons that is the cause of my embarrassment.'

'Well, we will be interested to hear of this mysterious force that cast you out of my father's high regard.'

'It is not in my gift to be free in justification. I am bound by a higher authority to guard my words on the matter.' I pause to consider how much I can disclose. 'I will tell as much as I am able to you, Helen. I would spare Jane from a complex and upsetting story.'

They are stilled by my words. Jane touches Helen's arm as though she would go, but Helen holds her back. Jane Dee has played a small, unknowing part in the conspiracy; perhaps she should know. They are undecided. Helen whispers in Jane's ear. They link arms and straighten their posture. Helen has an expression of defiance. Jane is puzzled.

'Very well.' I am careful and deliberate in my speech. 'I found myself in a position where I had to choose between two disagreeable circumstances for your father.' This has not started well. I should enlarge the telling to include the assault on Jane at Mortlake. 'No, I must begin at an earlier place.' I hesitate again. 'I have been assisting in an arrangement to safeguard our Queen. In particular, many of my recent activities have been undertaken in the service of Sir Francis Walsingham.' Their eyes widen and I see a slight trembling in Jane's lip. 'There is a conspiracy in hand to harm our state and Her Majesty's good name. A connection to astrology was suspected and I was consulted on this matter by Mister Secretary.'

'But how does this concern my father?'

'I must outline the initial circumstances first, and beg your forbearance for a short while. A star chart was discovered, with a cipher. Together, these forewarned of a near date for the downfall of the Queen and an invasion by foreign powers.' There is a look of disbelief on Helen's face. Jane has lowered her head and I wonder if she has guessed some of what is to come. 'Christopher Millen was implicated in the creation of the star chart. He has been killed, and we surmise that his murder was done by other conspirators to prevent further intelligence from his questioning.'

'Who is Christopher Millen?' asks Helen.

'He is… was an associate of my husband, practised in astrology,' answers Jane. 'I had no particular love for the man, but would not wish…' She lifts her head. 'So this was the cause of the attack on our house at Mortlake?'

'Yes. Millen is also the man who cast the stars for the most propitious date for the sailing of your father's great adventure, Helen.'

Helen puts her arms around Jane and they embrace. I cannot judge if Jane is weeping, or they simply seek closeness to protect against the images of horror conjured from my telling.

'I suspected that the conspiracy was wider in its scope than planting seeds of unrest about Her Majesty's fate in order to soften the conditions for an invading force. Through my work on the navigation instrument I came to understand that there was a connection to the great adventure.'

Helen breaks from her embrace with a quizzical face. 'I cannot imagine how these two diverse events could be joined? Was there… an intention…?'

'The protection of Spanish interests in the New Lands and the treasure ships that sail from there was the purpose. The conspiracy has two strands: overthrow our monarch; and stop the great venture.'

'In that case my father is an intended victim.'

'Yes, but in a state of heightened alarm and readiness to explore all possibilities, fevered minds guarding our state considered that the ships and men may be gathered to assist an invasion. Your father could have been taken by Mister Secretary's men to a place of inquisition for fierce interrogation.

I pleaded for a gentler alternative for the questioning of your father and Captain Hawkins at my house, by two men I trusted.'

Her mouth is open and she nods her head slowly. 'And he returned home from that questioning in foul humor with intense anger for your actions.'

'I anticipated that he would take great offence at my subterfuge and his questioning, but I hoped that in time…'

She rushes to me, throws her arms around my middle and lays her head on my chest, murmuring my name. I have succeeded in making peace with Helen, but there is more to be done. I am uneasy at the extent and manner of my telling. Was I too generous in detailing the conspiracy? Should I have related the killing of Millen? I loose myself softly from Helen's arms and request they both swear not to reveal what they have heard. Jane agrees willingly. Helen asks if I have told all.

'I have informed more than I should. There are other refinements and intricacies that I cannot disclose and I must ask that you do not press me on these. There will be a time, close to this day, when more can be revealed. Until then, I beg you understand the vital importance of holding secret what you have learned today. You must tell no-one, even those closest and most trustworthy.' I hold their hands and squeeze them gently in reassurance while they quietly affirm their discretion.

'Now, I must speak to Helen alone in this chamber, Jane. Will you excuse us?'

She hugs Helen, bobs a brief curtsey to me and departs. I take Helen in my arms and kiss her. After a little hesitancy, she presses with an eagerness to match mine. The kiss lingers and I feel her tremble as my right hand explores the curve from her neck to the small of her back. Just a little longer… I break from her – too quickly. She is startled.

'I am sorry, my love. My business is not finished. I must beg a favour. I am reluctant to ask, but the exposing of the conspiracy and its ending depends upon your willingness.'

'What – me? What can I do?'

I pick up the box, which lies on the table. 'Tuesday next, I would have you place this box in Darby Wensum's chamber of business. It must be done on that day, without his knowledge, or any other member of the household. Please do not open or tamper with it.'

'Master Wensum, but he…'

'I may not answer your queries, clarify misgivings or confirm suspicions. I simply ask that you trust me and oblige me in this task. Can it be done? Will you?'

I place the box in her hands. She gazes at it then looks me in the eye. 'I will; for you, William, and the Queen.'

The stiffness in my body eases with relief at her compliance. There was no necessity to mention her part in the conspiracy as the 'unknowing maid'. I wonder if an unravelling of the intrigue will bring her knowledge of the true nature of her birth. I must hope not, for it was a deeply unhappy circumstance and the knowing would cause distress. Yet, there is a contrary piece within me that wishes for honesty in something so fundamental.

Thirty-Seven

Sunday. We are in St Giles again and John is preaching. His subject is the relationship of man with scripture and the necessity for each of us to learn directly from its teachings and strive for salvation through obedience and good works. My mind wanders as he is overlong in his oratory. I reflect on the nature of religion in general, and in particular how the proscribed manner of observance changes in our country. There are many, John, included, who consider that the church governed by our Queen does not have sufficient distance from 'popery'. They would remove all colourful icons, gold and silver trinkets from our churches and burn the gaudy vestments of priests. I am struck by the force with which diverse groups attack one another for worshipping the same God in the way they hold to be righteous. I am not a Godly man and mistrust those who proclaim to know the only true faith. Then, why do I tolerate John's certainty? His way is not mine. It occurs to me that we have not had a meaningful or deep discussion on his religion since our first meeting. He finishes, at last.

At West Cheap, I invite John into my library for wine and conversation. I compliment him on his sermon, which was received enthusiastically by most of the congregation. I am direct in my first question and ask if he ever doubts his religion.

'Do you mean, do I doubt the very existence of God, or my understanding of His grace and the nature of our association with the Almighty?'

'My enquiry concerns the connection and your way of worship.'

He toys with his cup of wine and takes a few moments to consider before replying. 'Truthfully, I have doubted both. Anyone who recoils at the wickedness in this world will wonder why a benign God does not intervene. Meditation on the glory of His creation will soon dispel this uncertainty. As to my belief in the true faith... well, I have told you that I was not always of a Puritan leaning. The light came through logic, reasoned argument, a better understanding of the scriptures and how Our Lord wishes to commune with each of his subjects.'

'So, you are set now. Could further enlightenment change your view?'

'I am sure, that if I live long enough there will be refinements to my thinking, but I am content that I follow the true path to salvation.'

'You have never questioned my faith.'

'You are a man of science, William. You study the stars. Your mind turns to logic rather than faith. I understand that every man has his place on this earth and not all can have certainty in their union with God. That is why men such as me are here; to bring the light. You are a good man, William, and I do not doubt that you convene with God in a way that does not cause offence.'

'Then, I have a particular question about the conspirators. Do you consider it is their Catholic religion or their desire to overturn our state that is the greater wrong?'

He sits back and folds his arms. 'It is interesting that you pose this question at this particular time. God willing, the plotters will be arraigned and suffer a most dreadful end for their evil designs. If they were followers of the old religion and went about their business in peace, with no thought of harm to our ruler and state; why then, I would say they are merely foolish and are deserving of guidance for the salvation of their souls, but no physical harm.' He pauses. 'It is the way of the world that violent actions will be met with brutal and corrective force. So, it is their intention to launch a cruel assault on our humanity that must be punished by death.' There is a quiet between us. He takes his cup and sips the wine. 'Does that ease the troubled thoughts that directed your enquiry?'

There is some comfort in his answer. Why? If my design for ending the conspiracy is successful then the guilty will be tortured and killed. Their dreadful end will be the same, whether the cause is belligerence or religion? Yet, there is some reassurance in John's words.

We converse together for some time in relaxed fashion. It is an unspoken pact between us that we leave the subjects of conspiracy and religion behind and talk of travels to other countries, the work of physicians, the art of bookbinding and mathematics. Our dinner is ready. John bids me join him in prayer for a safe and successful outcome to our plans for Christmas Eve. When we are done, we make our way to dinner and John enquires how I will pass the days until Wednesday next. I reply that I will go to Whitehall tomorrow for my last day as a court physician. I intend to resign my position there. As for Tuesday; my mind will be filled with anxious thoughts about Helen and her clandestine delivery of the box to Wensum's chamber.

*

It is a slow plod through a light covering of snow to the Palace of Whitehall. Cassius is no lover of this weather and I share his sense of melancholy. I do not like the place and will be happy to be released from its grip. I go directly to Forester's chamber and find him directing two servants on the arrangement of furnishings and bundling of items into leather satchels. He bids me good day with an air of impatience and harassment.

'May I speak with you, Sir John?'

'Can it be later? I am pressed with our move to Greenwich on the morrow.'

'I will be brief, if I can beg your forbearance.' He shakes his head fussily and dismisses the servants. 'It concerns my tenure as physician here.'

He sighs. 'Doctor Lyle will return here in the New Year and there are others eager to seek the favour of a court appointment. Your attendance has been irregular and, while there have been no grievances, I have also received no commendations on your consultations. Therefore, I regret…'

'You misunderstand. I wish to resign my temporary position here, not prolong it.'

His eyes widen as his chin retreats into his ruff. 'Well then, that is an agreeable end for both parties. You have your reasons, I am sure.'

I do not elaborate. I thank him for his understanding and enquire if there are any patients who require my attention. He huffs and answers that the court is too busy with the impending transfer to Greenwich to concern themselves with trivial ailments this day. He tilts his head and says that if there is no more, he will ensure my bill is paid in the New Year and that he must attend to his urgent business. I make to depart and as an afterthought enquire after Doctor Huicke. He mutters something under his breath and then declares that he has not seen him recently, but assumes he is much the same.

Huicke is propped up against bolsters on his bed and he is reading a book. This is certainly an improvement from my last visit. I bid him good day, go to his bedside and sit on a stool. Closer inspection shows that my hopes for an advancement in his condition were deceived. His complexion is grey, his eyes rheumy and there is an excessive dribble of bubbling saliva from the corners of his mouth.

'Who are you?' he asks with an air of indifference.

'I am Doctor Constable, come to visit you again. I am pleased to see that you are recovered sufficiently to read this book.' I see it is a volume of Aristotle's *Organon*.

'There are words I cannot fathom. It is as though I have a bucket on my head. It is heavy and there are but two peepholes for viewing. They move without reason. It is maddening in the extreme.'

He tries to describe how he sees the world through an addled mind. I do not know what to make of his strange discourse. His way of talking is steady, but the words mystify. I ask if he is provided with food, drink and other small comforts.

'There is a man who brings foodstuffs and beer. I have asserted many times that I do not have the *French Disease*, but he insists on spooning me a curative as though I am a babe.'

'Who is this man?'

'He is familiar, although the bucket obscures his finer features and a name. He is small and pink.'

It sounds like Forester, but why would he administer medicine to Huicke? The new term for the *French Disease* is Syphilis and it is rife among sailors and those that frequent the whorehouses by the quays. I have met with only a few cases and know of no adequate remedy, although many prescribe small doses of mercury. I judge it unlikely that Huicke will suffer from this ailment.

I say, 'Might the man be Sir John Forester?'

'Exactly, if he is sufficiently pink.'

'And does he administer quicksilver?'

'Exactly. You have a shrewd mind. It has a foul taste on the tongue and I will not take any more.'

I know little of the effects of mercury on the human body, but suspect that it will not benefit in the long run. To my mind, the mixing of a metallic with flesh and blood is a recipe more likely to harm than cure. I wonder if his befuddled mind, excessive salivation and sores around the mouth are a result from this 'cure'. I will put a strong request to Forester that he ceases from this practice. He mutters something. I ask him to repeat his words.

'There is danger.'

'Danger – to who?'

'To Her Majesty that is called Elizabeth. I must warn her. They try to stop me.'

'What is the nature of this danger and who stops you?'

'It is foreign and will arrive in ships. The pink man keeps me here; and the other one.'

I try to press him for more, but he jerks his head and complains of the bucket. His eyes stare at me, he points an accusing finger, then shakes his head and subsides. He mumbles more, of which I can make no sense and becomes quiet. I stay at his side for an hour or more, but his lucid period has passed and he is either mute or nonsensical in his ramblings.

I call at Forester's chamber. It is empty and I leave a note instructing that the dispensing of quicksilver to Huicke should cease. I am disturbed by what I have heard. Could there be some coherence in Huicke's assertion that he knows of some malign force that will seek to endanger our Queen? The mention of foreign ships suggests his knowledge coincides with our astrological conspiracy. How would he have come by this intelligence and who tries to confound his warning? The small, pink man may refer to Forester, but as likely some other of the many at court. Or, was it all merely the muddled babbling of a decayed mind?

*

Seven bells have tolled and I break my fast with Mother and John. My appetite is poor and I pick at a couple of eggs on buttered manchet, deciding I have no stomach for the fish. Mother is unusually reserved in her speech and casts furtive glances in my direction. I know what irks her. She has been fractious with me for some days and knows, from my demeanour perhaps, that there is an event of significance in the offing. She has learned of the conspiracy and wishes to share in any intelligence on the progress of our investigations.

She says, 'You have not enquired on our plans for Christmastide, William. Do you not wish to hear how your household will celebrate the coming of Our Lord?'

'I am certain your arrangements are well made, Mother. It is not my usual practice to interfere with your preparations for Christmas.'

John says, 'The lady Amy informs me that we will attend the morning service at St Giles on Christmas Day. We will have dinner with guests and we will serve a supper for the servants.'

It will not be an easy time to have John here, as he will no doubt disapprove of any merrymaking and mummery.

'And what are your plans William? Will you be here, or does important business require your attention elsewhere?'

'I will be with you for Christmas Day, Mother. I will meet with Captain Askham this next day and place the household in your capable hands for this Eve of Christmas.'

John sees my discomfort. He clears his throat and talks gently to my mother. 'My lady, we understand your anxieties and desire to be informed of any advancement in our enquiries into the conspiracy. We respect your discretion, but the matter in hand is of such delicacy that we may not share an account with any person, however virtuous.'

I am grateful for John's intervention and I hope that it has calmed Mother's temper. My own senses are agitated. I am fretful and fidgety in the hallway, assisting Mistress Hilliard with sprays of holly and other greens, when Master Chap calls. This was not expected. I take him through to the parlour where we are alone.

'What brings you here, Master Chap?'

'I had an early visit this morning. It was a message from Sir George, delivered by Master Wensum.'

'What was the nature of this message?'

'I am instructed to halt work on the shadow staff until such time as Sir George permits its continuation.'

This is a surprising and unwelcome development. 'But why? Was any reason given?'

'Master Wensum would only say that you were the cause. The circumstances were not explained, only that you had offended Sir George in a most shameful manner. He no longer wishes to be partnered in a project with you. This, Master Wensum took great delight in the telling. He is a man who does not encourage warm feelings.'

'Indeed. Thank you Master Chap. I am sorry to be the source of this disruption to your work.'

My initial impulse is to condemn the petty nature of this action. It will harm the great venture more than my pride. Is it a signal of my permanent exclusion from his regard and the hopelessness of my suit for Helen? I sense the influence of Wensum in this act.

'I was requested to hand you this note.' He reaches into his doublet and passes me a paper.

The note is signed by Sir George. The text is in a different hand. It will be Wensum's. It reads much as Chap has reported. Further, he requests my presence at his house, midday on the morrow to negotiate a financial consideration for his full ownership of the shadow staff. My consultation will be with his man of business and not Sir George himself. Christmas Eve. Midday. Is this an accidental correspondence with our rendezvous at the North Quay, or something more sinister? The box should not have been delivered by Helen until this day. Has Wensum already discovered it? Was Jane indiscreet in her gossip? Or Helen? I am perplexed and anxious. Walsingham would not take kindly to any alteration in our strategy, and it will be too late. Oxford's box will be waiting his arrival at Greenwich if it is not already opened. Chap says something, which I miss. I ask him to repeat his words.

'I said, shall I take your reply to Leadenhall?'

'What – are you Wensum's messenger? Did he ask you to bring my answer?'

'It is an issue of vital interest to me, Doctor Constable. I offered to facilitate the communications, so there could be no misunderstanding.'

'I see, then apologies to you for my brusqueness.'

'It is no matter. It is clear that you are upset by this development.'

How should I respond to the note? I cannot accept the time and date of meeting, but a denial of my attendance may be taken as an indication that more important matters have been arranged for that hour. To ignore the note and offer no rely would be taken as a discourtesy, and I must do no more to offend Morton.

I say, 'Please convey my thanks for the invitation to next day's meeting. I only discuss matters of finance with my steward in attendance. Hicks journeys to Kent to convey Christmastide cheer to my tenant farmers there and will not return until Christmas Day. Please therefore, request a deferral and an alternative date for my visit.'

This is the only way, although it intensifies my worries. I must sit tight and hope that Helen has succeeded in her task and that the message delivered by Wensum is an unfortunate coincidence.

Thirty-Eight

This is the day when all the tantalising threads are joined to my imagined design. Or, it may see my reputation trod in muck if I am wide of the mark. And what of Helen? Any triumph in a happy resolution to the conspiracy will be Walsingham's. It will require recognition of an exceptional success to relight my star in Sir George's assessment.

Only Elspeth is up and lighting the fires in her kitchens when I rise. I surprise her, but she soon busies herself making coddled eggs for my breakfast. I tell her I will be on the road for much of this day and she packs cheese and bread into a leather pouch. I also take a flask of warming brandywine, as I reason we will have some time to lie in wait for our quarry. I saddle Cassius myself and make my way to the front of the house. The chill air nibbles at my fingers and toes. I pull my cloak tighter and wonder if a snowfall will hinder our plans. Cassius paws at the ground and snorts warm vapour into the cold morning. I hear a faint clatter of hooves on the stone pathways by St Paul's, mount up and ride to meet, what I assume will be, Askham's posse. He is at the head of a group of about twenty men. Will that number be enough?

We exchange a brief greeting and he bows his head in approval at the sight of my sword. I would have a sense of nakedness without it in present company and, although I am not eager for blood, a part of me senses that my role in this scheme will not be complete unless it is unsheathed this day.

We are unhurried in our progress through the dark streets, into Goodman Fyelds and through the villages of Shadwell and Limehouse. We are a half hour or more from our destination when Askham raises his hand and calls a halt. He dismounts and leads his horse into a large barn. His men follow and I am the last one into an area of bustling activity as attendants take the horses to stabling posts, remove saddles and offer buckets of water.

Askham says to me, 'We will walk from here at intervals and

in small numbers. A company of armed and mounted men will attract too much attention on the quayside.'

I depart with the Captain as the sky in the east begins to show promise of a softening sun. The hour is near seven when we arrive at the North Quay. Darkness has gone, but my optimism for the weather was unfounded, as the light is greyed with heavy cloud. Askham cautions me not to gaze at the storehouses and we stride with purpose towards the moorings. It is an industrious scene, full of activity with the swinging of laden ropes, shouldering of sacks and shouts from carts seeking passage through the movement of men and piled cargo.

I follow the Captain over uneven planks of wood on to a two-masted merchant ship. It is a wide-beamed ship that sits low in the water. There are men working and the deck is scattered with wooden crates and a tangle of ropes. Our boarding is unchecked. A thickset man in a wide-brimmed hat and leather apron approaches. Askham takes him to one side and they exchange words which I cannot hear. I assume this must be the ship's master. Askham hands him a small pouch, he unties his apron, places it on a pile of sacking, and then beckons to three men who gather around him for a few moments before they all disembark.

I say, 'What of these other men?' Four men remain busying themselves with the cargo.

'They are mine. All have worked ships before and will convince in their labour, although their loading and unloading will be without purpose.'

'Do we have sufficient men, all told?'

'There will be more than forty when all arrive. Some have been here since the last night and others are due at ten bells.'

He inclines his head towards a storehouse some twenty paces from the ship's stern. So, that is the place of assignation. The doors here are closed, while the stores either side are open and full of activity. He has placed men in these neighbouring stores, others act as cart men and more are housed at an inn down a narrow passage with its entry thirty paces to our left side. The preparations appear to be well set.

'How will you control the actions of all these men in disparate locations?'

'There is an arrangement of flags on the bowsprit. A white flag is for holding positions, a yellow for armed readiness and the red signifies that all should close to where I will confront our prey.'

I congratulate him on his meticulous planning. We adjust the arrangement of crates so that we are largely hidden, but can view the comings and goings on the quay. Now, there is nothing to do, but wait.

It is too cold to be still for long and we take turns to stamp feet, fist our hands and walk the few clear paces cleared on deck, while the other huddles, heavy-cloaked behind the crates. At ten bells I open my pouch and share bread, cheese and warming brandywine. Askham grunts his thanks, takes a mouthful of cheese, then stops suddenly and turns his back to the storehouse.

'Do you recognise those men?' He holds his hand to my chest and bids me to be cautious in my observation.

I move to one side and peer through a narrow space in the crates. Four men stand in front of Morton's store. They are huddled in conversation; one raises his head to survey the wharf; to his left; then right. He bows his head and mutters something to his associates. One, with his back to me, does the same moments later. They remain there for some minutes, two break away and turn down the passage, then the others leave in the opposite direction.

I say, 'I do not recognise them. They have dispersed, two to my right side and two to my left. Their intentions were unclear. It may be that they were waiting for someone unconnected to our purpose, or...'

'They scout the area to ensure a trap is not laid for the midday assembly. I would do the same in their place.'

'They had no swords.'

'They would not be needed at this hour.'

He beckons to two of his men on deck, they confer briefly, leave the ship and walk quickly in different directions. Askham returns to my side and says that they follow those who gathered there and will report back. One returns in short time and announces two have adjourned to the inn down the passage. It is almost a half hour when the other is back to inform he observed his quarry enter a house by Ropemakers Field; a middling place; neither grand nor poor. He watched for some minutes and there were no others arriving or leaving, but he did see an unusual number of horses assembled in the courtyard. None of this is persuasive either way. Nevertheless, Askham avers it would be prudent to suppose they are connected to the conspiracy in some way and increase our vigilance.

The bustling activity has lessened somewhat, but workers, secondaries and their masters still ply their trade. My bones ache from the chill air and my feet are numbed with cold. I envy those that have completed their toil to seek warmth and Christmas merriment in the inn. The brandywine is finished, we exchange few words and our watch is keener as the time draws near. A wagon, half-covered and laden with barrels, stops outside the storehouse. The driver turns and appears to adjust an object behind him, then moves on. I glance at Askham and he nods his head slowly as if he corresponds with my suspicion. A small, hooded figure walks briskly from the passageway, past the store and continues. There is something familiar about his gait. Some minutes later the small man returns, hesitates briefly at the storehouse and walks with short, quick steps back to the passage where he disappears.

'Yellow flag,' I say, half-whispered, but with some certainty.

'Why now?'

'I am certain that was Sir John Forester who traversed the frontage back and forth. He should be at Greenwich. Why would he be present if not for a devious connection to Oxford? Or Wensum, perhaps,' I add after a short pause.

Askham signals to his man at the bow who pulls on a rope to change the flag. He touches the hilt of his sword and mutters words of prayer. We wait for the time to act. The midday bells toll. Nothing. Was I mistaken about Forester? More minutes pass. My mouth is dry and my breathing loud and shallow. I flex my shoulders and clench my fists to ease the icy stiffness. The same wagon appears and comes to a halt outside the storehouse. Half a dozen armed men emerge from the passage, one is at least a head taller than the others, covered in black cloak with a cowl hiding his face. More follow; perhaps another ten. My eyes catch a splash of colour in the other direction. It is Capton leading yet more men. Askham gestures with sharp movement of his hands for the red flag. The hum of voices quietens, labourers, sailors and others about their business stop and make way for the converging forces.

The Captain straightens, mutters that I should stay until it is near done, signals to his men on deck and they leave the ship. He draws his sword as he crosses to the quay. He seems to unbalance on the wood planks, stumbles and sprawls on the quayside. His men attend him. He is slow to rise. The big, hooded man shouts a command and raises his sword. Askham is clearly injured as he cannot stand. His men appear uncertain what they should do. I cannot stand and watch a calamity unfold. I unhook my cloak and stride quickly to join Askham. I brush past his men, point my sword and shout, 'In the name of our Queen, you will release your weapons and be still!'

I am barely ten paces from over twenty heavily armed men clustered around the wagon. They will surely outmatch my fighting skills, yet I am strangely calm. Askham's soldiers are gathering in a semi-circle around me. Our enemies are trapped and we have the numbers, but our advantage is not great. I see Capton in their line; and Perse. Oxford has stayed away, or is he disguised. And where is Wensum?

The large man in the centre pulls back his cowl and his black cloak crumples on the ground. He is younger than expected. I am struck by a handsome face, whose unblemished features are almost feminine in their delicacy; made more remarkable by a patch over his right eye. He bares his teeth – a smile, or a snarl? He lifts both his arms, throws back his head and screams at the sky. He stretches his right arm and directs his sword at me.

'Constable, I rejoice at the death I will give you.' His speaks English with a thick French accent.

There is a moment of stillness before he rushes at me swinging his sword. He is on me too quick. I raise my sword, lurch to one side and my arm trembles as his steel catches mine near the hilt. I turn, but am slow and his blade comes at my throat. This is it. Helen. I sense a profound sadness at my imminent death. Too much is unfinished. His eyes widen, he moans, his right side bends as though deflated. I swing my sword in a fierce arc at his neck. It cuts; blood spurts; he drops to his knees with an expression of surprise. I hack again and feel his skull shatter under the weight of the blow. Why did he not kill me? Askham is on his knees, with bloodied sword. He must have slashed the man's leg from behind. He points to my side and shouts a warning. A man steps over a body and thrusts his sword. There is a sting in my shoulder, but he is open and I slash, swing and slash again until he falls. There is no method in my fight. I swing, jab and thrust wildly. I hear my voice roaring, cursing, screaming; all curiously disconnected from my body. I close on the next man. My whole body is seized by warmth and fierce energy; my senses filled with exhilaration and joy of the moment. Time has slowed. I see eyes; fearful; shocked; mouths open; silent screams. How long has it been? I am slowing; my body becomes heavy; breathing laboured… My arms are grabbed from behind.

'It is over.'

Two of Askham's soldiers hold me. One slaps my shoulder, then walks away laughing. A harsh sound reaches my ears. It is heavy gasping for air – mine. All was quiet a moment before, but now there are echoes of moaning; cursing; threatening. Time has quickened and regained its clamour. On the ground before me is a man, bent and disfigured; the skull is broken and oozes red and grey; an arm is near severed and hangs loose with shattered bone. Did I do this?

Askham limps by with a foot in the air; his arm draped around another's shoulder. He is directing the disarming and securing of our prisoners. I hang back and survey the scene. There are between a dozen and fifteen bodies, some tended, others ignored. Our captives are ringed by Askham's men. There is no sign of Oxford. Capton I see with his head downcast and a rope fixed around his neck. Where is Wensum? I scan the bodies. I see Perse laid out by the wagon with his middle soaked in blood. His head moves. He lives, still. I walk to him. His eyes stare and there is a gurgling deep in his throat. It will not be long.

'Who do you act for?' I lower myself stiffly on to one knee.

He tries to speak, but his lungs fill with blood and he gasps for breath.

'Is it Oxford?'

He moves his head, struggles for more breath, but blood flows from his mouth and nose. He is still. I sigh and my whole body sags. I am weary; uncommonly so. Askham and his support man come to me. I enquire after his injured leg.

'It is my ankle.'

'Shall I attend…?'

'There will be time for that later. We must get our prisoners to The Tower.'

'Oxford?'

'No.'

'Forester?'

'He is not here. He will be taken and questioned with the others.'

'Wensum?'

'Yes, he was on the wagon and taken as he tried to run.'

*

We are back the barn where our horses were rested. I walked here beside the wagon that I learned is Wensum's. Askham rode in the wagon, which also contained four of our number who were wounded and three who died. A cart led our procession with the bodies of nine killed conspirators and another two near death. We brought up the rear, following the sorry line of our prisoners, who were tied by the neck and arms shackled behind their backs.

I help Askham down from the wagon and take him over to a half-barrel where he can sit while I tend his ankle. A man joins us and Askham introduces me to Surgeon Dexter who will attend the wounded. Dexter asks if he should examine the Captain. He thanks him and says his friend, Doctor Constable, will see to his injury. I remove the boot with some difficulty, roll up his woollen hose and place my hands on his hot and swollen ankle. I play with his toes, then gently rotate his ankle. He takes a sharp breath and grunts.

I say, 'It is badly twisted, but I do not believe it is broken. I will get some linen from your surgeon and wrap it tightly. You will need a crutch for several days, as it should be rested.'

Dexter has an ample supply of linens. I return and begin to wind strips around the ankle. I find the task soothing and helps to blank my thoughts.

'You fought well, William.'

'And you Captain... I owe my life to your persistence, despite your accident. I was certain of my death until you hacked at the legs of the large man.' I hesitate for a moment. 'I too, regard you as a friend, but do not know your given name. I should like it if you would allow me to be familiar in our exchanges.'

'For certain. My given name is Hector. My mother was fond of stories of the ancients.'

I smile at his unusual name. It suits a man of arms and I wonder if his mother imagined a soldier's calling for her babe.

I say, 'Was our action as you expected?'

'I regret the loss of men and their forces were greater in number than I anticipated. Nevertheless, the fighting was done in short time and we have sixteen captives. The outcome is good.'

'We do not have Oxford, but the answer to his message will surely condemn him.'

'Yes, I do not know how Sir Francis will confront the Earl, but questioning of this wretched band will uncover the truth of it all.'

He points a dismissive hand at the roped prisoners lined against a wall. They present a pathetic picture; their bowed heads, no doubt full of dark thoughts of the dreadful and prolonged end that awaits them. Wensum is one of only a handful that show any aspect of defiance. His head is straight and his bearing suggests a measure of belligerence. I finish the binding and make towards him. He sees my approach and meets my gaze.

'Master Wensum, it does not please me to find you in this situation.'

'Ha, I think you delight in it.'

'I understand this sentiment, but I find no joy in the manner of your treatment to come, only that the conspiracy has been arrested.' He sets his face grim and does not respond. 'I would know if your part in this was persuaded by your faith, or merely coin.'

A faint smile shows on his face. 'You would have me ease your conscience, William Constable. I know your intellect is strong, but your spirit is soft to be coddled and caressed like a child. I must disappoint you. I am a devout follower of the true faith and will meet my maker boldly, knowing that my actions will be embraced by His grace. I had no thought of financial gain. Your triumph will be confined to a short and unfulfilled earthly existence with promise of eternal suffering in the next life.'

He reads my troubles too openly. I turn my back and return to the Captain. I tell him I have no stomach to accompany him to The Tower. I will return home and wait there for any news that may follow the interrogations. The next day is Christmas, I must try to be merry for my household and put the thoughts of today behind me. And Helen. When and how will I be able to mend my offence to Sir George and hold his daughter in my arms again?

Thirty-Nine

Our Christmas has been a muted affair until now. Mother continues to chide me for my brooding, but I have been unable to rouse myself from a listless and quiet introspection that has infected the household. I returned home on Christmas Eve unaware that my doublet was soaked in blood from a cut on my shoulder. It is a small thing, easily mended, but serves as a reminder of the action on the North Quay. It was the first time I killed a man – perhaps it was two or three lives I took in my screaming madness. I related the happenings that day to Mother and John in bare detail and unexcited manner. Mother was horrified at first, then thankful, and eventually joined with John's fulsome congratulations and contentment at a glorious conclusion to our work and the ending of this threat to our state. I have no sense of glory. In my mind it was a scruffy and dream-like conflict that failed to knot all the loose threads of the conspiracy. Where was Oxford? What part did Forester play? How does a man like Wensum hold such certainty of faith? I cannot dispel reflections on the strong questioning in The Tower and wonder how I would endure such treatment. All these imaginings are mixed with a longing for Helen.

It is the fourth day of Christmas and I am in the parlour with John, when Mistress Hilliard enters in a breathless rush and announces that a procession has arrived. I had anticipated that Askham may call with some men, but it is odd that she describes this as a procession. I follow her to the front of the house. She is truthful in her account. There are fifty or more horsemen with colourful flags and pennants atop their spears. Two men have dismounted and approach. One is Walsingham and the other… it is Lord Burghley.

'My Lord, Sir Francis, you do my house great honour.'

'William, please excuse our unannounced visit,' says Walsingham, 'My Lord Burghley was insistent that we break from our revels at Greenwich to meet the architect of our recent success.'

I am pleased that he is in good humor and his appearance shows a recovery from whatever ailed him at Seething Lane. I am too surprised to utter an appropriate response and simply bow my head a little lower. I am joined by others.

'Ah, Doctor Foxe,' exclaims Burghley, 'I was told I may find you here with Doctor Constable. My pleasure is doubled at the end of this chill and bracing journey.' He walks stiffly and is bent with age, but his eyes are bright and enquiring.

John greets our notable visitors and introduces my mother as a dear and welcoming companion. I lead them through to our receiving room where Mother and Mistress Hilliard fuss over the arrangements for building the fire and refreshment. Burghley asks if we have met before and I mention my presentation with Doctor Dee at Whitehall. His memory of that time is hazy and he bids Walsingham explain the reason for their visit.

'We have learned much from the questioning of prisoners. The plot was devised by Henry of Guise and some of those captured were of the Catholic League. There were also some Hispanics in their number, and it would seem that Spain funded the conspiracy on condition of the inclusion of plans to foil Hawkins' venture to the New Lands. The printer of the pamphlets has been disclosed under fierce questioning and he has been arraigned.'

Mother enters the chamber and the talking stops. John advises that my mother is aware of the nature of the conspiracy and vouches for her discretion.

Walsingham acknowledges her with a stiff bow and continues, 'The man of extreme build who led their combatants was one Pierre Gaspard, who is a trusted lieutenant of Guise. You are to be commended on your brave killing of a dangerous man, William.'

I say, 'Have the interrogations in The Tower been completed?'

'The prisoners are detained, but will soon be squeezed dry of any further information they can offer.'

'Has the Earl of Oxford been held?'

Walsingham looks to Burghley who answers. 'We have both

talked with the Earl. He admits his grievous error and is contrite.'

John puffs in indignation. 'The man deserves more than a cursory admonishment'

'Rest assured, Doctor Foxe,' answers Walsingham, 'He will suffer for his mischief. He understands his near encounter with the axe and he will be useful to future gathering of intelligence for our security.'

Burghley says, 'Her Majesty has been informed of the conspiracy and its ending. There has been no mention of Oxford in connection with this affair. It would cause too much distress for her to learn of a favourite's treachery, but she will be fed scraps of knowledge about the Earl that will bring him low in her regard.'

No doubt, there is also a reluctance for Burghley to contemplate a sudden and ignominious end to his son-in-law.

Mistress Hilliard enters with hot, spiced wine and plates of sweetmeats. The conversation turns to lighter matters and the festivities enjoyed by the court at Greenwich. Burghley mentions the Queen's amusement at an entertainment created by a man named Thomas Kyd. John dislikes to dwell on frivolous diversions such as this and I recall his Christmas oration at St Giles. In truth, it was dreary stuff, but I feign enthusiasm in order to keep the peace. Walsingham shares John's mistrust of dancing, games and mummery, but I see that Burghley is more open in his enjoyment. There is a period of quiet as we drink and eat.

I say, 'How does Captain Askham fare?'

'He is well and rests his injury in the company of his family,' answers Burghley. 'He was introduced to Her Majesty who was enchanted by his telling of the action on the North Quay.'

'I owe my life to his wounding of Gaspard.'

'Her Majesty was gracious in rewarding the Captain with a small estate in Norfolk for his loyalty and valour.' Burghley pauses and looks at me directly. 'Your name was given by both Captain Askham and Sir Francis as deserving of commendation. Our Queen expressed her admiration for your quick mind and bravery in her service. We are here, primarily to inform you of this, and to enquire if there is a preferred way that your vital assistance in this endeavour can be recognised.'

I am rendered speechless by this offer. How should I answer? A demurral would be impolite, but I have no ambition for an estate and to suggest coin would be mercenary. My silence has been too long.

'There is a benefit you could provide, if I am not over-bold in its asking. Would you accompany me now to Leadenhall?'

*

We arrive at the Morton house in full pomp with our escort of richly-attired yeomen. Sir George will have been alerted of our coming and stands at his door with an expression of bafflement. He narrows his eyes as he sees me, then bows graciously to Burghley and Walsingham. We are led inside through to a chamber, which is lively with musicians, dancing and chatter. The place quietens as the entrance of the two most powerful men in the land is noted. I scan the faces arrayed before us. Hawkins is here, Gilbert... and there is Helen next to Jane. I smile and incline my head to her. She stares at me, switches her attention to Burghley and Walsingham, and then returns to me with an expression of bewilderment.

Burghley takes Morton by the arm and speaks to him in low voice. Morton claps his hands, announces that he must leave for an urgent consultation and begs the merry-making should continue in his absence. He makes to go with Burghley, taking Hawkins and Gilbert. I murmur an aside to Walsingham. He obliges me by taking Helen's arm and follows me in our passage to another chamber.

When we are gathered together, Morton addresses Hawkins and Gilbert. 'I am honoured and somewhat mystified by this unexpected event. Lord High Treasurer Burghley has offered to speak on a matter that concerns all here.' He notes Helen's presence and eyes me with suspicion.

'Thank you for receiving us so warmly Sir George and our apologies for this intrusion on your Christmastide entertainments. We have come from Greenwich by order of Her Majesty to honour a great service performed by Doctor Constable.' Burghley pauses to let the weight of his mission take effect. 'A monstrous conspiracy has been foiled, both to our state and your great adventure. It pains me to disclose, Sir George, that your man of business, Darby Wensum was one of the conspirators, now held in The Tower.'

There are murmurs of disbelief and outrage, stopped suddenly by Helen's loud exclamation of 'Oh, William!' Burghley looks kindly on her and continues to detail the dual strands of the conspiracy and entreats them to forgive my arrangement of the rude, but necessary, interrogation by John and Askham. Morton, Hawkins and Gilbert are all full of questions. I hear only fragments, as my attention focuses on Helen. Her head is bowed, but I can sense a contentment in her pose.

The chatter subsides and Morton says, 'William Constable, I see now that I was hasty in my judgement of your action and you are restored, nay enhanced, in my regard. You have gone to a deal of trouble to plan an eloquent and substantial submission on your behalf. I am sure I speak for Sir Humphrey and the Captain General, when I say we are happy to renew your association with our great adventure to the New Lands.'

'My thanks to you, Sir George. I beg your forgiveness, but I would ask for more.' He must have fair notion of my intention, but he waits for me to give voice to my request. 'I declare my deepest affection and love for your daughter, Helen, and beg that you consider my suit for her hand in marriage.'

There is an unnatural delay as he stands tight-lipped and considers my plea. Helen has moved quietly to my side and takes hold of my hand. He breathes deeply, then responds.

'I do not doubt that your suit is well-meant, but she is all that I hold most precious in this world. I will not deny your suit, but say I will consider it more worthy if you will first join with the sailing of our great adventure and prove the value of your invention.'

He presents me with a troubling choice. My suit is accepted with alternative pathways to fulfilment. Marry now with a threat that Sir George will not be wholehearted in his approval of our future life together. Or, embrace the hazards of a two-year voyage and return from a successful adventure with high reputation as a deserving husband. What of a homecoming marked as a failure – or no return? Helen squeezes my hand. What does that signify? I could request a period to consider my decision, but that may be taken as an indication of weak character.

No, I am decided.

End Notes

This book is a work of fiction. William Constable and Helen Morton are imagined characters, but they do encounter historical figures and the story mentions 'real life' events. A very brief description of some of the relevant people, incidents and practices in sixteenth-century England is outlined below.

In 1578, Elizabeth I (1533 – 1603) was 45 years old and had been on the throne for 20 years. There were many plots to depose her and senior ministers such as Sir Francis Walsingham and Baron Burghley were involved in uncovering conspiracies. Rumours about her love life circulated throughout her reign. Catholic opponents challenged her virtue and far from being the 'Virgin Queen,' hostile observers branded her the 'whore' of Europe.

Speculation about an illegitimate child of Elizabeth persist to the present day with most naming Robert Dudley, Earl of Leicester as the father. Edward de Vere, Earl of Oxford has been referred to as both a lover and son of Elizabeth. Francis Bacon has also been mentioned as a son. None of these claims convince.

Sir Francis Walsingham (1532 – 1590) was Principal Secretary to Queen Elizabeth from 1573 until his death and is popularly referred to as her *spymaster*. A firm believer in the Protestant faith, he sanctioned the use of torture against conspirators.

William Cecil, 1st Baron Burghley (1520 – 1598) was Elizabeth's chief advisor for most of her reign, twice Secretary of State (1550–1553 and 1558–1572) and Lord High Treasurer from 1572.

John Foxe (1516/17 – 1587) was a historian, Puritan and the author of *Actes and Monuments* (popularly known as Foxe's *Book of Martyrs*), an account of Christian martyrs throughout Western history. Widely owned and read, the book helped to mould popular opinion about the Catholic Church for several centuries. He was said to be unworldly and had a hatred for cruelty, which was in advance of the age.

John Dee (1527 – 1608 or 1609) was a mathematician, astronomer, astrologer, occult philosopher and advisor to the Queen. He devoted much of his life to the study of alchemy, divination, and Hermetic philosophy. In 1578 he married Jane Fromond (1555–1604/5). Jane was a lady in waiting to the Countess of Lincoln, a position she gave up when she married Dee. His house in Mortlake was vandalised and his library ruined while he was travelling abroad.

Edward Kelley (1555 – 1597) was an occultist, spirit medium and alchemist. He is best known for working with John Dee in his magical investigations. At some point in their relationship, Kelley declared to Dee that the angels instructed that they should share wives.

Francis Mylles (? – 1618) was one of Walsingham's most important servants.

Sir Thomas Heneage (1532 – 1595) was an English politician and courtier.

John Hawkins (1532 – 1595) was a slave trader, naval commander and administrator, merchant, navigator, shipbuilder and privateer. He was appointed as Treasurer of the Royal Navy on 1 January 1578. He was one of three main commanders of the English fleet against the Spanish Armada in 1588.

Sir Humphrey Gilbert (1539 – 1583) was an adventurer, explorer, member of parliament and soldier who served during the reign of Elizabeth I and was a pioneer of the English colonial empire in North America.

Edward de Vere, 17th Earl of Oxford (1550 – 1604) was a courtier of the Elizabethan era. Oxford was a court favourite for a time, lyric poet and court playwright. He was noted for volatile behaviour, reckless spending and was suspected of Catholic sympathies. He has been suggested as an alternative candidate for the authorship of Shakespeare's works.

Blanche Parry (1507/8 – 1590) held the offices of Chief Gentlewoman of the Queen's Most Honourable Privy Chamber and Keeper of Her Majesty's Jewels.

Robert Huicke (? – 1581) was a chief physician to the Queen.

Henry, Duke of Guise (1550 – 1588), founded the Catholic League, was a key figure in the French Wars of Religion and avowed opponent of Elizabeth. He is suspected of plotting the St. Bartholomew's Day Massacre in Paris, at which Walsingham was present as Elizabeth's French Ambassador.

The Ridolfi Plot, named after an international banker, Roberto Ridolfi, was a conspiracy in 1571 to assassinate Elizabeth and replace her with Mary, Queen of Scots. The Duke of Norfolk (a pupil of John Foxe) was implicated and executed. Ridolfi escaped overseas and Guerau de Espes, the Spanish ambassador, was expelled from the country. Hawkins helped to uncover the plot by pretending to be a Catholic sympathiser.

Astrology had a significant influence as a way of explaining and controlling the life of Elizabethans. Natal astrology was used to examine and predict events based on a birth chart. Medical astrology was used to determine an individual's weakness, diagnose illness, and prescribe cures. It was a prerequisite to healing and taught in every major university. It was not always clearly distinguished from astronomy, which described the motion of the stars and their influence on tides, weather and navigation.

The art of navigation developed rapidly in the sixteenth century in response to explorers who needed to find their positions without landmarks. Instruments were used to determine latitude, but longitude required accurate timepieces and these were not yet available. Instead, navigators used educated guesswork or 'dead reckoning' by measuring the heading and speed of the ship, the speeds of the ocean currents and drift of the ship, and the time spent on each heading.

A cross-staff was in common use in the mid-sixteenth century as an instrument to calculate latitude. This device resembled a Christian cross. The vertical piece, the transom or limb, slides along the staff so that the star can be sighted over the upper edge of the transom while the horizon is aligned with the bottom edge. The major problem with the cross-staff was that the observer had to look in two directions at once – along the bottom of the transom to the horizon and along the top of the transom to the sun or the star.

A more advanced instrument was the Davis Quadrant or backstaff. The observer determined the altitude of the sun by observing its shadow while simultaneously sighting the horizon. Captain John Davis conceived this instrument during his voyage to search for the Northwest Passage and is described in his book *Seaman's Secrets*, 1594. One of the major advantages of the backstaff over the cross-staff was that the navigator had to look in only one direction to take the sight – through the slit in the horizon vane to the horizon while simultaneously aligning the shadow of the shadow vane with the slit in the horizon vane.

The shadow staff in the book is an imagined forerunner of the backstaff.

For those of you who have enjoyed this book, further episodes in the life of William Constable will follow. Look for the next instalment later in 2019.

I can be reached via authorpaulwalker@btinternet.com

*

Printed in Great Britain
by Amazon